THE
BABY
SHOWER

BOOKS BY S.E. LYNES

THE
BABY
SHOWER
S. E. LYNES

bookouture

Published by Bookouture in 2022

An imprint of Storyfire Ltd.
Carmelite House
50 Victoria Embankment
London EC4Y 0DZ

www.bookouture.com

ISBN: 978-1-80314-142-8
eBook ISBN: 978-1-80314-141-1

For my friends, all brilliant and brave in their own ways.

PROLOGUE

Wimbham Times Online: 8 *May* 2019

THREE INJURED IN FAMILY SUBURB HIT AND RUN; ONLOOKERS 'SHOCKED AND APPALLED'

Two women and a man have been admitted to Kingston Hospital after what police are calling a potential hit-and-run incident on Wimbham High Street. The collision occurred at approximately 7.30 yesterday evening. According to a spokesperson at the hospital, all three victims are believed to be in their late twenties/early thirties. As yet, none of the affected parties have been named, but police have confirmed that a black Jaguar I-PACE was witnessed driving dangerously, colliding with two pedestrians, after which it attempted to flee the scene, crashing moments later into local French restaurant L'Auberge.

'The car pulled out from up there, by the café,' said eyewitness Cara Mathers. 'And then it went flying – it was going so fast. We were just going into the Old Bear and my friend started screaming. We heard this horrible thudding sound and then the car just carried on like a racing car, like nothing had happened.

We couldn't believe what we were seeing. It was absolutely terrifying.'

Moments later, the car collided with bollards near the traffic lights at Broadway Road. It spun out of control, breached the central reservation and smashed into one of the windows at L'Auberge.

'We'd ordered drinks and were looking at the menu when the whole glass frontage shattered,' said diner Thomas Weaver, a fund manager. 'It's a miracle no one was killed.'

Police were called to the scene at approximately 7.35. Three emergency response units and two ambulances were sent, followed by an air ambulance. Two of the victims were taken by air ambulance to Kingston Hospital; one by ambulance. A further four people were treated for minor injuries and shock at the scene.

DCI Brian Kirby of the Metropolitan Police described the incident as 'truly shocking'. A police cordon remains in place on Wimbham High Street from Broadway to Church Road.

'These are the leafy suburbs, for goodness' sake,' said another L'Auberge diner, image consultant Valeria Sarti. 'People move here to raise their kids. It's supposed to be a safe place. We came here to feel safe.'

CHAPTER ONE

THE HOSPITAL

May

Voices. My eyelids flicker pink.

Wake up. Wake up.

Blink my eyes. Too bright, too bright. It's too bright in here.

Close your eyes, love.

Mum? Is that you?

It's not Mum. It's no one. There's no one here of course. There never is.

I close my sore pink eyes.

I'm in hospital, I know that much. I'd know that smell anywhere: that cleaner they use in hospitals and prisons. *She'll* be in here too, if she's alive. If she's dead, she'll be in the basement, in the morgue, in a cold metal drawer. I hope she is. Sorry, but there it is. She stole my life after all. I'm a nice person, I wouldn't wish anyone dead, but that's the other thing these people steal: they steal all the nice.

I try to lift my head. Can't. Can't move my legs either. I'm screwed into place. That's how it feels anyway. Like I'm Frankenstein's monster. It hurts. Everything hurts.

I open my eyes, just a crack this time. White light filters

through the grey blur of my eyelashes. Another millimetre, two. My neck eases. I stretch it left, then right. It kills, but it's not screwed down. It's not broken. Still can't move my legs though. How ironic will that be, if after standing on my own two feet all these years, I end up unable to walk?

Opposite, there's a row of beds, all occupied. *She's* not in any of them. If she was, I'd wrench myself from this bed right now. I'd crawl over there on my hands and knees if I had to and I'd finish her myself. Toxic. She is toxic.

I wonder where Frankie is. Please God, let him be alive. If he's badly hurt, I'll never forgive myself. But mostly I want my mum. Funny how, despite everything, I still want her.

But she's not here. No one is. No one is here for me, no change there.

This is not my fault. I'm not a violent person. I hate violence. But when is enough enough? Everyone gets to the end of their tether at some point. Everyone has their limit. And that's what people like her do: they push you to your limit. They rob you of your life and then when you retaliate, what, you're the villain?

That woman turned my world upside down, stole my friends, my life, just... helped herself. Because that's what these people do.

I try to push my tongue between my lips, just the tip. Again and again, gathering up saliva. There's a heaviness in my left leg. Wincing, I lift my head – see fat blue toes, a plaster cast. A broken leg – great, that's just great. I'm in a ward though, not in intensive care. At least I'm not going to die. There's no way I'm going to die. The only one who's going to die today is her.

At the far end, a blue-uniformed nurse is walking like he's going somewhere important, silent on those white foam-soled shoes they wear.

Nurse? Nurse, hello?

I haven't spoken; no wonder he didn't turn or stop. All I've done is make a funny noise through the stupid little cat's arse of my stuck-together mouth. He wouldn't have heard me over the crank of the lift shaft anyway. That and someone somewhere moaning on like a zombie. Shut up. Shut *up*. My eyes feel like they've been squirted with that runny glue you get in primary school; I need to bathe them in clean water. I need to bathe my face. God, that would be such a relief from this horrid stickiness. My *head*. My *throat*. My *back* – down low, by my coccyx. A dull ache in my left leg. The scratchy-soft waffle of hairy blanket under my fingertips.

Her. Just the thought of her makes my heart beat faster. I'm vulnerable here, with my leg in a cast. I'm a sitting target. I need to move.

I look about me. There's no one. There's no one here for me. There never is. My eyes are filling. When I close them, tears run down into my hair. I am not strong, not really. I pretend to be, but I'm not. People never see behind the smile. They never see behind what I show to the world.

This harsh light is blinding. I close my eyes, like a child, so no one can see me. *Don't let anyone see you like that. Don't give anyone the satisfaction.*

The high street.

The spaceship car.

The thud.

The breaking glass.

Oh God. Oh God, oh God, oh God.

Finally, my lips unstick. I stretch them wide enough to call him – *Nurse!* – but a hoarse whisper is all I can manage. And now I'm crying. For Christ's sake. I raise my hands, wiggle my fingers, squeeze them into fists. Nothing broken. But I can't be bothered to wipe away the tears. They soothe me like surprise summer rain, rain you turn your face up to and find it warm. My mouth is so, so... It tastes... like hay, like what hay smells like – prickly and dungy and dry.

Frankie, where are you?

Are you alive?

I'm sorry, babe. I'm so sorry it's come to this.

It's all such a mess. But it's not my fault. None of it is. I'm a nice person. Well, I was. I was until she ruined my life.

Somewhere on the left, water splashes into a glass. His face then, looming. The nurse.

'Here, take these.' Sing-song tones, like we're all happy, all in it together. Like we are loved. 'That better?' he asks me kindly, picking up my chart from the end of the bed.

'Yes,' I croak, cough, drink some more. 'Thank you.'

'I'm Kevin, if you need anything,' he says. 'I'm still Kevin if you don't.' He laughs. I suspect he's made that joke before. 'Now, I need to take a few details from you, all right? You were given a sedative last night, which you might not remember.'

I shake my head, no.

'You were having a panic attack.' He smiles sympathetically. He has nice teeth, even and white.

I try to think. Remember my arms being gripped. The sense of being pushed down, maybe into a chair.

'I can't remember,' I say.

'That's perfectly fine, don't worry. But I just need a few details, OK?'

I nod. 'Sure.'

'OK, cool.' He lifts a chart from the end of my bed and studies it a moment before looking up. He meets my gaze. That smile again. 'OK, so if I could just take your name?'

I stare at him a moment, this Kevin. He is sympathy and kindness. He is jokes and reassurance. He is a nice person, like I used to be.

'I'm Jane,' I whisper. 'Jane Reece.'

CHAPTER TWO

JANE

February

Jane's café, she'd tell you herself, is your typical chichi coffee bar on the high street of a once scruffy South London suburb become smart South London village. Since she moved here with Frankie six or seven years ago now, she has witnessed the transition at first hand: the slow increase of skips in the street; the new branch of M&S Simply Food where the twenty-four-hour Wimbham Stores used to be; Paradigm, the slick men's hairdresser's that has replaced Cedric's scruffy red-and-white pole, the yellowing black-and-white photos in the window. Gentrification: the city sprawling ever outwards like coffee spilt on a paper napkin. She and Frankie couldn't afford to move here now if they didn't live here already. But she's part of it, she knows that. Often jokes that she's raising the house prices one soya latte at a time. Her café is another thing she couldn't afford now; its name, A Roasted Development, an ironic nod to the old-school punny business titles she used to love – The Fish and Chip Plaice, Ace of Spades Gardens, A Cut Above Hairdressers... all gone now.

The new breed of inhabitants come to Jane for their daily coffee fix. They like to support, or be seen to support, the independents, at least while they're waiting for their Amazon deliveries. Gaunt mid-thirties mothers in extortionately priced activewear manoeuvre three-wheeled exercise-compatible strollers (not a moment wasted!) around tables pushed together for weekly yummy-mummy catch-ups. Stay-at-home metrosexual dads sip espresso macchiatos while staring into slimline laptops. Under stools, yoga mats curl in wait, and men whose suits shine in a way they're supposed to – not because they're cheap – take noisy business calls, ears plugged white with wireless headphone buds. Tick, tick, tick – they all come to Jane. Almond milk. Oat milk cappuccinos. Reusable takeaway coffee cups for the eco-conscious on the go. Vegan millionaire's shortbread for actual millionaires. It's all a long way from the northern industrial town she grew up in. It's a long way from home in every sense.

But that, of course, was the point.

Besides, there are clichés everywhere in this life, no matter who you are or where you live. That's what Jane thinks. Every demographic looks impenetrably homogenous from the outside. People are just people and most people are good. Jane tries never to lose sight of that. With a mother like hers, it's a philosophy – more than a philosophy actually; it is survival.

Most people are good, most people are good, most people are good.

And it is *people* who tell Jane she's lucky to have her own successful place, to have customers who have become at the very least affectionate regulars, at most friends, over the years. Especially with Starbucks opening up across the street the other month. It is *people* who tell her she has a stress-free job. Work–life balance. Not to mention *all* the coffee, LOL. Jane keeps her face straight and says *thank you, yes, it's great. Yes, yes, I'm very lucky.* Hashtag blessed. Hashtag loveyourlife. She prepares the orders, serves them with a smile that never lets up.

Only those who know her well know what a slog it's been, how hard she and Frankie have to work to pay the mortgage, the business loan, the bills. Kath, Hils and Sophie, the mates she trains with at Runner Beans on Tuesday nights, know most of it. They knew her back when she jacked in her office job and took out a loan and bought a burnt-out business unit that had been repossessed by the bank. A former dodgy chicken shop, uninsured – the previous owners had cleared out in the middle of the night, that was the rumour. A front for drugs, for a local gang – that was another rumour. Hard to find an adjective for what it looked like, but chichi it most definitely was not. It took her a year to get rid of the smell of charred floorboards and rancid animal fat. A lot of the grunt work she did herself, was glad to.

Because what *people* don't know is *why*. Why trade security for risk? *People* have no idea that the loan and the stress and the back-breaking graft were a kind of therapy. For Frankie too. It was the raft they tied themselves to afterwards, the only thing that stopped them both going under. Frankie did all the plumbing, most of the electrics, fitted the kitchen himself. According to him, Jane 'waltzed in with the arty touches'. She loves it when he teases her, especially because she'd feared that what had happened – or hadn't happened – would rob them of what had brought them together in the first place: their ability to laugh at life. But no, A Roasted Development helped them move on after that last failed round of IVF, the heart-breaking decision to call it, to say: *no more*.

The café door swings open, a blast of cold air ushering in Sophie, who's popped in on her way home, as she always does on a Tuesday, for a quick caffeine boost before Runner Beans, the running club they both go to. For running club, see also under *Recovery*: the slow weaning off the citalopram that numbed the pain but made her drowsy; see also under *Losing Weight*, the spare tyre a bitter coating on an already acrid pill. She, who used to inhale a whole packet of Kettle Chips in under a minute, now only has to glance in the general direction of a salty snack to put on five pounds.

Today Sophie has ordered peppermint tea, which is unusual.

'Bit Gen Z for you, isn't it?' Jane says with no more than a raised eyebrow, and gestures at her best mate to grab a seat. She blasts boiling water onto a fine-mesh bag of leaves hand-picked from a mountainside in the Dordogne – maybe – and runs a glass of tap water for herself.

'You OK manning the bar, chief?' she says to her late-afternoon assistant. Kath's daughter Scarlett works here after school each day, a gig she bagged when she brought in some home-made biscotti a few months ago, announced that she wanted to start a baking business, was looking for a part-time job to finance it, and did Jane wish to invest? Jane suppressed a giggle, but Scarlett was so adorably serious and the biscotti were so delicious that not only did Jane give her a two-hour daily shift, she also agreed to sell the biscuits in the café. You can't do *that* in Starbucks, can you? Now Scarlett provides a weekly order of sixty apricot biscotti – always thinking of the nut-allergic – a lucrative little sideline, Jane imagines, since she suspects the flour, sugar, eggs and apricots come from Kath's weekly supermarket delivery.

By way of acknowledgement, Scarlett pushes her spectacles up her nose before bending to empty the dishwasher. Jane wonders if anyone was ever this diligent at fourteen – at that age, she herself was off her face on cider stolen from her mother, but that's another story altogether and belongs in a box marked *Do Not Open*.

'I should give Scarlett a raise really,' she says as she joins Sophie at the table. 'She could run this place without me.'

Sophie smiles in a way that makes Jane unsure she's heard. She blows on her tea but doesn't sip it.

'You on a health kick or something?' Jane tries, nodding at Sophie's mug. Sophie looks particularly pretty today – not that she doesn't usually; it's just her beauty doesn't take Jane aback like it used to. Yes, today her blue eyes are particularly bright, her dark brown hair especially shiny and pulled back into a tight ponytail. 'What happened to double espresso two sugars?' she adds, with mock suspicion. 'You normally take the mick out of anyone drinking herbal.'

Like Jane, Sophie dates from a time before pubs were prefixed with *gastro* and the minimarkets were full of dusty tins of raspberries, but also like Jane, she is not above enjoying the fact that she can grab a stone-fired pizza or some top-notch meze when the need arises. Her late-afternoon Tuesday espresso is a runner's hack, designed to kick in by the time they start at around half past seven but to wear off by the time she goes to bed. Which brings Jane back to why the peppermint tea?

Sophie's mind is not on tea, however. Or running. Or coffee. Her eyes are all sparkly and her smile so dreamy she looks like she's been smoking dope. Her cheeks are flushed pink. Her cleavage looks deeper than normal.

'I'm not drinking coffee just now,' she says with meaning, replacing the mug carefully on the table and fixing Jane with a deep stare.

And that is the moment Jane puts two and two together, four landing in her gut like a rock.

'You're... Are you... pregnant?' She flushes hot, the need to cry immediate and almost overwhelming. But she succeeds – just – in keeping it together and returning her friend's ecstatic smile. She even manages to meet her eye for the briefest second before dipping her head on the pretext of reaching for her hand. But her eyes have a mind of their own; she is helpless to stop them from filling. But that's OK. Friends well up when they're moved or pleased for one another, don't they? And she *is* pleased, of course she is. It is lovely, lovely news. *Look up, Jane. Look up.*

She blinks hard, pushes her teeth into a grin. And looks up. 'Oh my God!'

'Yep.' Shoulders round her ears, Sophie beams, pinks adorably. Then looks away, as if embarrassed.

Jane knows she should say congratulations – that she needs to do better than last time, that she should have said congratulations five seconds ago, ten, fifteen, twenty. And it isn't that she doesn't want to; she does, she really does. But her throat has closed, and if she opens her mouth now, she fears – no, she *knows* – she will burst into tears, like she did last time. And that cannot happen. It cannot. This is not about her. And yet it is, it cannot help but be.

There's only so much that running and jokes and hard work can do. A life raft is not watertight.

She keeps her teeth clamped together, hopes to God the tears now threatening to roll overboard will remain a sheen that could easily be delight, nothing more complicated than that. But of course, with Sophie it can never be nothing more complicated than that, because Sophie knows; that is why she has come here today to tell Jane separately from the others, which somehow makes it worse.

More seconds pass. Sophie's head falls ever so slightly to one side, and still Jane's throat is blocked and still she can't say congratulations, or anything at all for that matter, and nor can she stop her friend from framing the question she knows she will ask in one, two...

'Are you OK?' Sophie squeezes her hand, her smile soaked in sympathy. That's the trouble with real friends: they see you whether you want them to or not. They see you plain as day. And as well as being funny and generous, Sophie has always been so sympathetic. 'I just wanted to tell you face to face, you know, without the others. I'm not going to tell them for a few weeks yet. I wanted to make sure you didn't hear it from anyone else.'

At this moment more than ever, Jane wishes to God she'd never told Sophie. It happened before she really knew her, before Sophie was pregnant with Kyle, at a time when Jane had no idea how bloody awful being on the receiving end of sympathy would feel, how her every reaction to baby-related news ever after would be scrutinised for traces of pain or, worse, envy. She's just glad she didn't tell anyone else. Kath and Hils have always been lovely, but she'd rather keep those friendships as they are. By which, she knows deep down in the darkest corner of her being, she means *equal*.

She digs a serviette from her apron pocket, *A Roasted Development* printed on the corner, and blows her nose.

'Think I might have hay fever,' she says. *Good one, Jane, it's February.* 'Anyway, congratulations, honey. I'm so, so pleased.' She squeezes her friend's hand tight and waggles it for extra excitement.

'Thank you!'

On the pretence of needing to sip her water, she withdraws her hand. She drinks. Drains the glass.

'Thirstier than I thought,' she says, for no fathomable reason whatsoever. 'Aw, seriously. Congratulations, mate. Amazing news.' Breathes.

'Are you sure you're OK?'

'Of course! Of course I am! Why wouldn't I be? I'm delighted! Absolutely! Absolutely delighted! So! Kyle is getting a kid brother or sister, yay!' She gives the air a little punch. 'Do you know which flavour you're having?' Better. She can feel herself getting a grip.

'Not yet.' Sophie's blue eyes widen briefly and she pulls a silly face. 'Strawberry or vanilla, I should imagine.'

'Can you say that nowadays? I mean, it might be pistachio. So exciting anyway. Have you got a list of names?'

'Not yet. I've only just got through the first scan. Do you want to see it?'

God, no.

For one horrible moment, Jane thinks she's said the words out loud. But Sophie is already rootling through what looks like a new bag. It is absolutely enormous – tan leather collapsing expensively beneath a gold clasp with the initials CD. Sophie is wealthy. Married to Carl, who sold his PR business last year for three million and has only a year and a half of his handover period left to work. She works two days a week at a solicitor's office in Norbiton, 'just to get out of the house'.

'Of course I want to see it!' Sweat prickles at Jane's hairline. 'This is my godchild's sibling, for goodness' sake. That's one down from aristocracy.'

She'd imagined it would get less painful with time, but it hasn't, not in the six years since she was diagnosed. Ironically, she'd believed herself to be pregnant. That was why she went to the doctor's in the first place. She'd always had irregular periods, but when she missed three and found her jeans were too tight for no good reason, she put it together with the nausea and assumed nature had taken its course. She'd been elated, as had Frankie. They'd been trying, in a *let's just lose the contraception and see what happens* kind of a way, for a year.

But to their bemusement, three home tests came up negative.

'Do you know what FSH is?' the GP had asked, after a ton of tests, during a two-minute follow-up phone call.

Two minutes to ruin a life, who knew?

'FSH? No, sorry.'

'It's follicle-stimulating hormone. Your ovaries are failing, basically, and that means you're going into an early menopause.'

Jane's skin shrank, her insides coiled tight. The matter-of-fact delivery felt deliberately mean. '*What?*'

'The great cruelty of early-onset menopause,' the GP had said, more kindly, 'is that it can feel a lot like pregnancy. You can try IVF, but with the paucity of eggs, I'm afraid it'll probably be a waste of time.'

Jane had been twenty-seven. A young woman. She is still a young woman.

Sophie has plonked the world's biggest bag on the table.

'Nice bag,' Jane says.

'Thanks, it's from... It was a gift actually. It's only a fake though.'

'Wow. It looks exactly like a real bag.'

Sophie giggles. 'A fake Dior, you twonk. CD?'

'Compact disc?'

'Oh my God, Christian Dior? What are you like?'

Jane laughs. 'Hopeless, sorry. It's really nice anyway.'

But Sophie has forgotten the bag. From its capacious insides she has pulled a slip of paper and, with a wide grin, is handing it over to Jane, who studies it as if engrossed. A grey blob against a charcoal fan shape, it looks a bit like one of those gnarly pebbles you see sometimes on beaches, one that's been battered about by other, harder stones.

She knows it's not a pebble, of course she does. And she must not mess this up. Can't let things get weird like they did last time.

'Aw,' she says. Adds, 'It looks just like Carl.'

Sophie titters, cocks her head, as if to view the likeness. 'I know. Same massive black eyes and tiny little hands. Scans are weird, aren't they? I think I might be having a king prawn.'

Jane pulls a face. 'Bit shellfish, don't you think?'

Sophie groans. They laugh together now and any remaining tension passes, thank God.

'Hey, I'd better get back to work,' Jane says, standing up. 'Don't want Kath suing me for child labour – you know how litigious she can be. See you later, yeah? You can still run, can't you?'

'Of course! I'm not *ill*.' Sophie stands, her peppermint tea barely touched, and hitches her new fake bag further onto her shoulder. 'Actually, you might meet Lexie tonight. I met her at a gym open day a few weeks ago.' She frowns, meets Jane's eye. 'You were working.'

'We're allowed to see other people, you know.' Jane pulls a psycho face. 'I won't put Kyle's hamster in the microwave or anything.'

Sophie laughs. This warm, easy laugh is one of the reasons they became friends in the first place – their ability to provoke it in one another. 'Lexie's the one who gave me the bag actually – she's really nice. Anyway, she's new to the area and happened to mention she didn't really know anyone, so I told her Runner Beans was really friendly and she should come along.'

'Great,' Jane says, thinking that this is typical Sophie, taking someone under her wing like that, like she did, in fact, with Jane. 'Lexie, did you say her name was?'

'Lexie Lane.'

'Very Superman.'

'You're thinking of Lois.'

'So I am, doh.'

They hug goodbye – it is a long, tight hug through which Jane tries to communicate all her good wishes for her friend, for her baby, and to tell Sophie that she is OK, really she is, and that this time, with this pregnancy, things will be better.

They part. Sophie leaves, ponytail swinging, the ends of her coat belt dangling, her shoes wedges where a heel would usually be. Jane raises a hand in farewell before grabbing the mug and the glass from the table and watching, as if from a distance, as both slide out of her grip and smash on the hard tiled floor.

CHAPTER THREE
JANE

At the sight of Frankie's van parked outside their tiny Victorian terrace, Jane feels her chest expand with relief. He's home. He *is* home – has been since he came to her horrid third-floor flat in Southall to unblock the shower, an absolute negligent-landlord-horror-story-gross-out of a job, after which he'd washed his hands with washing-up liquid at her tatty kitchen sink and told her she could pay him next time, or better still, buy him a pint. She knew right there and then he was a good man, mainly because he was nothing like anyone her mum had ever brought home. They've been together for eleven years, a fact that astonishes her as much as it delights her. All she wants to do now is collapse into his arms and watch something on Netflix, maybe order a takeaway. There is no way, no way in *hell*, she can face Runner Beans; she has known that from the moment Sophie left the café.

She climbs off her pushbike and, on the doorstep, takes out her phone. She hesitates, thinks about forcing herself to go along. She doesn't want Sophie to think she's avoiding her or that she's in a state. She doesn't want to take the edge off her friend's joy. But she really needs to take a moment to process the news. Just a time-out while she puts herself back together.

Hey missus, she writes. *Won't make tonight, soz – whopping headache. Have a good one and congratulations again! Xx*

An instant later, Sophie replies. *Oh poor you! See you for Friday drinks? Xx*

Friendship is not always founded on honesty, Jane thinks, as she unlocks the door and wheels her bike inside. Sometimes it's knowing when to let your friend get away with a blatant lie. She remembers once when Sophie took her clothes shopping in town, made her try on a glitzy top she loved but that was well out of her budget. She had put it back on the rail and said she wasn't sure, she'd think about it, maybe order it online later. And then, on Sophie's insistence, they'd gone for lunch at Selfridges and sat on high stools and eaten sushi. Sophie had ordered a bottle of fizz, and when Jane was in the loo, she'd paid for the whole thing. When Jane protested, Sophie claimed she'd been given a voucher nearly two years earlier and it was about to go out of date, that Jane had done her a favour by coming along. Jane had pretended to believe her just as Sophie had about the clothes, just as she had right now about the headache.

Of course, she shoots back, full of gratitude. *Say hi to the girls. Tell Hils to warm up properly and see you all on Friday. X*

It had been Jane's birthday a week or two after that shopping trip. Sophie had gone back into town and bought the top and given it to her, insisting it had been in the sale, another lie they both pretended to believe. Jane smiles, remembering how she'd been slightly mortified but also tickled pink at Sophie's thoughtfulness.

In the hallway, Des trots towards her, his claws tack-a-tacking on the wrecked laminate floor, his mad tail wagging.

'Hello there, Dezzie boy.' She leans her bike against the wall before squatting to scratch under his chin, smiling at the weird, plaintive sound he makes when he's not seen her all day. 'Hello, boy. Hello there, ya big softie.'

In the kitchen, Frankie is sitting at the island with his back to her, staring into his phone.

'Hey,' he says, a little absently.

She slides her arms around his waist and leans her cheek on the soft brushed cotton of his checked shirt. He smells a little sweaty – of dust, other people's houses. He is always so warm, a comfort after the cold drizzle of the ride home.

'You're back,' she says. 'Hurray!'

'Not for long unfortunately. Bathroom leak over in Balham, coming through the living-room ceiling.'

Jane slumps against him and groans.

He drops his phone on the bar, turns to wrap his arms around her and pushes his face into her chest. She runs her hands over the spiky brush of his hair, closes her eyes against the comfort of his touch, his breath warm against her belly. They stay like that, in the silence.

'Are you all right?' he asks, when the moment lasts a little longer than it would usually.

'Sophie's having another baby,' she half whispers.

'Oh God.' He stands, pulls her to him and rocks her gently from side to side. Kisses her cheek, her hair. 'That's so shit. Well, it's not, but you know what I mean. I'm sorry, babe.'

'Not your fault. No one's fault. And it's lovely news for them. Can't someone else do the emergency? What about Rob?'

'I'm picking him up, but there's no way he could manage it by himself; he's still training.' He folds her tighter into his arms and rests his chin on her head. 'Besides, it's money for the jar, isn't it?'

'The jar' is their world trip savings account, rising at the pace of a glacier travelling uphill. Another thing *people* don't see when they're applying their image of *Friends'* Central Perk to her coffee bar is that it only just keeps its head above water. If she hadn't bought the unit, she would've had to close by now. Spiralling shop rents have sent three of her fellow business owners under. She has to go to Staines now to get Des clipped, and Frankie drives to Hounslow to get his hair cut – there is 'no sodding way' he's paying 'thirty-five notes for a short back and sides'. Thank God for his business. No one can hoick the rent on a van and a great reputation, and Frankie has both, although Frank Reece Plumbing has not even a whisper of a pun – Pipe Up, Pipe Down and Flush Gordon getting the hard thumbs-down.

'I've cancelled running,' she says. 'Can't face it. I'll take Des out for a bit, blow the cobwebs away.'

'Don't forget the ball.'

'Course not.'

'You sure you're going to be OK on your own?'

She nods. 'I'll be fine. Just need to get my head round it.'

'I feel bad leaving you.'

He kisses the top of her head. His arms loosen, fall away. In the hall, she watches him put on his work boots. He's so sorry. He'll be back as soon as he can. She tells him not to worry. Can't let the punters down. Besides, it's overtime, and all overtime goes into the jar. She'll save him some dinner.

After he's gone, she reads the news on the iPad, then checks the jar on the Santander app: £3,058.00. A long way off ten grand, but bit by bit, they're getting there.

After the three rounds of IVF failed at the baseline scan, it was Frankie who held both her hands in his, looked her in the eye and told her what, in retrospect, she needed to hear: 'The doctor's right, babe. This isn't going to work for us. We can't keep doing this to ourselves.'

It was the start of a long conversation, all evening, all night, until, as the sun came up, eyes bright with tears, the decision was made. They weren't going to Croatia for donor eggs. There would be no adoption application. They would carry on as they were before the nightmare started – at least, they would try and get back to who they were back then: make love when they felt like it, try and remember how to enjoy each other once again without the spectre of blood tests and scans and injections and thermometers and schedules and anxiety and the constant, waiting dread. What they took with them, what they couldn't help but take, was a pair of broken hearts.

But there again, it was Frankie who told her to jack in her job and take the loan, Frankie who said he'd work all the hours to make her dream of running her own café work, Frankie who came up with the idea of the jar.

'Something else to focus on, isn't it?' he said. 'And we'll do it together.'

In five years' time, the plan is to rent out the house – if they manage to smarten it up by then – hire a manager for the café and just... take off. Although sometimes she can't help feeling, now the dust has settled, that they never did return to who they were, not quite; that it was always going to be impossible. The deeper conversations they used to have have been covered over, bandaged up like an injury, an injury that will only hurt more for the prodding.

She changes into leggings and trainers and puts Des on the lead. Out on the common, she runs back and forth, tries to incorporate some stretches, a little sprint training. Des lopes after her, head twitching, braced for her to throw the ball. Frankie had been joking about not forgetting it. In reality, the ball doesn't exist; they gave up on real tennis balls after losing more than they could count, and after realising that Dezzie was so daft, literally so stupid, that he would run tens of metres after an imaginary ball provided you faked a decent throw. The thing that really cracks her up is that he doesn't run miles for her like he does for Frankie.

Because he knows she can't throw as far.

At around ten, Jane is soaking in a deep bath when her phone vibrates against the electric-blue Radox bubble bath on the chipped MDF shelf.

SOPHIE RUNNING flashes up on the display. A mental note: change contact deets to simply *SOPHIE*.

She thinks about pretending to miss the call, but after four rings picks up.

'It's me,' Sophie says.

'I know. Your name came up on my special futuristic space phone.'

A breath of a laugh. 'How's your head?'

'Fine. Just needed a microwave curry and a bath, I think.'

'You work such long hours. You work too hard.'

Not all of us are married to millionaires... and even if we were...
'I'm fine,' Jane replies. 'I love the caff – you know I do.'

'I know.'

The pause that follows lasts a microsecond too long. Both of them know Jane is not fine, that she did not have a headache. Sophie will know she won't want to discuss her feelings on the pregnancy news. Talking about stuff wasn't Jane's strong suit even before, a fact she bats away with jokes about being northern and a career in the secret service. *Don't let anyone see you cry* was her mother's mantra. *Hold your head high.* Wise if ironic advice from the very person who made Jane cry so often she had to get away, whose behaviour at times made it difficult to do anything other than stare at the floor. Maybe she should talk to Sophie now, but Sophie has no idea how it feels, how there's a world of conversations she cannot have, a club she can't join; how with each passing year, it's getting harder, the silent questions becoming louder than the spoken ones. Sometimes she can see them in people's eyes: mid-thirties, married, financially solvent... why no kids?

But today is about Sophie's lovely news. It would be totally out of order to rain on her parade.

'Lexie came, anyway,' Sophie says into the silence. 'She ran really well. And the others seemed to like her.'

'Great!' For some reason Jane feels a fleeting unease at the thought of Sophie's new friend meeting the gang without her there. She wonders what Kath and Hils made of this Lexie woman before shaking the thought away. She is being ridiculous. They're not at school, where best friends swear blood oaths and write secrets in pink diaries with the world's flimsiest locks. Even the notion of a best friend is childish when you're in your thirties.

'Oh, by the way,' Sophie adds, the words sounding absolutely nothing like an afterthought, 'I invited Lex to Friday drinks.'

CHAPTER FOUR

FRANKIE

For Frankie, it all starts with the watch.

He's an idiot, no one knows that better than him. He wouldn't mind, but he's not even into stuff, not really. Jane, his business, the café, their life together, that's enough for him – more than. Take-away at the weekend, saving for their big trip – it's enough. A baby would have been the icing on the cake, but it wasn't to be.

But back to the watch.

Maybe it starts with the bath actually, thinking about it. Who pays thirty grand for a bath? Frankie hardly recognises this place anymore. Born and bred around these parts, he feels like the outsider now. When he started out with his dad, it was mostly repairs: blocked drains, dodgy cisterns, leaking shower trays. Now it's less make-do-and-mend, more buy-new-and-spend. Frankie has filled more skips than most people have had hot Deliveroos.

So he fits the bath. Huge place over Norbiton way – round-about drive, hedge like an enchanted forest, white pillars outside the front door. The hallway is the size of his and Jane's living room. The couple are nice enough. The wife makes him proper coffee, doesn't just give him the instant like some of them do. Talks to him like a human being, doesn't act surprised when he tells her he's actually a trained accountant. But thirty grand for a bath!

Wouldn't bother him normally, but that day... who knows? Maybe he's tired or something, maybe the whole baby thing is getting to him more than usual. That day, it just pisses him off.

Then on the way home, it takes him three goes to start the van and he finds himself thinking about Simon's brand-new Range Rover Evoque. Divorced, two houses, both kids at private school, and he buys an Evoque, for Christ's sake.

He stops for diesel at the supermarket off the roundabout. And for all the times he's turned the moment over in his mind since, he still can't figure out why he buys three scratch cards when he pays for the fuel. And the fact that on one of those scratch cards he wins three thousand pounds is... well, it's surreal, even now.

'Crikey,' he mutters in disbelief, staggering out of the little kiosk thing they have by the pumps. 'Holy shit.'

At first he thinks it's a scam. But it's not. It's legit.

And this is where the watch comes in. The link is already open on his browser: the Breitling. He's kept it open on and off for years, since he and Jane decided not to go to Croatia, not to adopt, but to get on with their lives. He just likes to look at it, that's all. Doesn't even know why. Like he says, he's not into status stuff, not really. But the problem is, there is so *much* stuff all around him, all the time. The house refurbs, the cars, the foreign holidays, the clothes, and yes, the watches. Simon has a Tag Heuer, maybe it's that. He's had it for years, way before he bought the motor. Carl has a Sector. Pete has an Armani. But none of them have a Breitling.

So.

Frankie buys the watch. He buys it with the money he wins, thinking, well, it's not really earnings, is it? Jane doesn't need to know. It's not like he's taking anything out of the jar, or his profits for that matter. Not like he's defaulting on the mortgage. And if they'd hired a builder to gut the chicken shop and make it into A Roasted Development, that would have cost way more than three grand. But he did all that himself.

So he buys it: a Breitling Superocean Automatic 44 with an English-mustard-yellow dial and a black silicone strap. The face is cambered sapphire, two words he whispers under his breath. Glare-proof crystal. Two thousand nine hundred and fifty pounds. And when they notify him that it's out for delivery, he takes the morning off to intercept it, the thought of Jane seeing it making the tips of his ears burn.

When he takes it out of its packaging, it's in this amazing presentation box with its own little booklet. And when he opens the presentation box and takes it out and puts it on his wrist, he feels his powerlessness, everything he can't fix, can't give to his brave and brilliant wife, drain away like water through a clear pipe. That watch on his wrist, he feels class. He feels invincible.

He knows he can never show it to Jane. Knows the whole thing makes him a moron. What he doesn't know is that this watch will ruin his life. Because if he hadn't been wearing the watch, he never would have got talking to Natasha.

CHAPTER FIVE

JANE

On Friday evening, Jane is first to arrive at the Old Bear. She orders a bottle of Prosecco and takes it in its silver ice bucket, along with four flutes, to a table at the back. These days, the local pubs are well stocked with ice buckets. And Prosecco, for that matter.

Bugger, she thinks when she reaches the table. Lexie. Jane doesn't know what Lexie drinks, but four glasses might look a bit pass-agg, so she returns to the bar and picks up another one. A nervous feeling takes root in her stomach. Usually she'd be excited; Fridays are always a highlight, passing as they do through hilarity, confession, support, sadness sometimes, gossip, and everything else that these brilliant women share when they get together. She's been meeting up with Kath, Hils and Sophie on Fridays for a few years now, their group developing naturally from Runner Beans and the longer weekend meets with other running clubs, which Jane attends on her rare Saturdays off. It's a lovely, lovely group – funny and kind and, she thinks, really quite special. Kath and Hils are in their forties, a little older, a little more down to earth, a little more sanguine about life, which, Jane thinks, provides a kind of balance. The fact that the four of them came together through a shared interest, that Kath and Hils's kids are older than Sophie's and Jane is childless, somehow places them in their own individual orbits and removes any whiff of the kind of competitive parental conversations she can't help but overhear in the café sometimes.

'Hey.'

She looks up to see Sophie arm in arm with a tall woman with long caramel hair cut in a razor-sharp fringe and glossy as oil. Her make-up, Jane is pretty sure, is of a type that is fashionable at the moment. It's meant to appear as if – from what she has gathered – there is in fact no make-up, a kind of enhanced naturalness, if that isn't a contradiction in terms. Some of Jane's customers have this look: sculpted brows, heavy upper lashes, lips plump and almost wet-looking, skin flawless and lightly tanned, pinked apple cheeks. The woman is wearing a red silky shirt dress and black high-heeled leather boots. Her nails are long and painted a metallic grey. She looks like she's walked out of a magazine. All of this Jane takes in in milliseconds, simultaneously regretting her own choice of once black skinny jeans and some second-hand cowboy boots she picked up in Brick Lane. At least she's wearing a shiny top, having changed from her tatty but soft and much-loved Pretenders T-shirt. Still, she wishes now she'd put on some mascara, or at least a lick of lipstick.

'Lexie, this is Jane,' says Sophie. 'Jane, Lexie.'

Jane stands, almost knocks over the table, steadies it, straightens up.

'Hi,' she says, sticking out her hand and taking awkwardness to heroic levels. *This is not a board meeting, Jane. Calm down.*

Lexie glances at Sophie as if to check something with her, then, with a giggle, takes not Jane's hand but the ends of her fingers.

'Pleased to meet you,' she says, bending her knees in a kind of half-curtsey and performing the kind of handshake you'd do with a precociously polite child. 'Sophie's told me so much about you.'

Jane's hand springs back, flails, ends up on the back of her neck. Embarrassed, confused as to why, she sits, then half stands.

'I got Prosecco,' she offers in a strange, overenthusiastic voice she doesn't recognise and sits down. 'I wasn't sure what you drink, Lexie, but I got you a glass just in case.'

Lexie wrinkles her nose, the effect one of affectionate disgust, if that's even possible. 'Actually, I'm a gin and tonic girl.'

Jane is on her feet again. 'Right. Sorry, I... G&T, then?'

'That's so sweet! I'll have a Sipsmith and slimline Fever-Tree if they've got it.' Lexie's smile is somehow only in her eyes, her mouth more of a grimace now that the humour she obviously found in Jane's professional meet-and-greet is gone.

'Not too much ice,' she adds, the giggle making a return. There is a trace of the north in her vowels, Jane thinks, though she could be wrong. She is about to dash off, but Lexie's forefinger comes up. 'And can you bring the tonic separately, 'cause I like to pour it myself. Thanks so much.'

Sophie bursts into open-mouthed laughter, leans into Lexie and slaps her on the arm. 'Oh my God, what are you like? You are *so* high maintenance.'

It is the kind of affectionate mickey-take you do when you know someone well, the kind Sophie often directs at Jane, who in this moment hates herself for noticing.

Lexie throws her eyes heavenwards and shrugs cutely. 'I know what I want, that's all. And if you don't ask, you don't get. Anyway, not like you were complaining the other week, were you?' She cackles, shifts her gaze to Jane. 'I made her try her first champagne cocktail. She was so wasted, weren't you, hun?'

Sophie's cheeks pink. She glances sideways at her new friend with such adoration, Jane feels her stomach fold. Sophie didn't say they'd been out together – she said they'd met at the gym. She has every right to go out for a drink with this woman, of course she has. But why keep it a secret? Why treat Jane like a jealous lover? That's weird, isn't it?

'Sounds amazing,' Jane says, knowing she should go to the bar but unable to break from the sight of the two of them sitting so close together, as if they've been friends for years. And actually, now she looks closer, she notices that Sophie's eyebrows are darker, thicker than usual, her eyeshadow a shiny bronze Jane's never seen her wear before, her lips glossy. Like Lexie's.

Shaking herself, she turns and makes her way to the bar as if through sand. It occurs to her that if Sophie were with her now, they would share an unsisterly laugh about that ridiculous Mariah Carey-style gin and tonic order. But of course, Sophie is not with her. She is with her new friend.

Jane, stop it. You're being utterly ridiculous.

The queue for the bar is three deep. Between the heads, through the space between the optics and the counter, she can see Sophie and Lexie, huddled together as if admiring something on Sophie's lap. Perhaps Lexie's a bit anxious. Perhaps that's what that whole performance was about. Coming into an established group like this must be hard. God knows, Jane herself would be wary of intruding on a close-knit dynamic. And the whole glamour thing, well, that's armour, isn't it, for some – for *many* women? It's how they face the world – literally paint on a smile. Isn't that what Jane's done these last few years? Not with paint as such, but with an actual smile. There have been days at work when she was dying inside, and yet her friendly service never faltered.

'Jane.' Lexie is standing next to her.

'Hey.' Jane has to look up to talk to her. 'Hi there.'

Lexie does that weird nose-wrinkle thing again. 'I was going to say, if they haven't got Sipsmith, can you get Tanqueray? Don't get Gordon's – it's disgusting.' She giggles. 'And is it OK to get a double? Do you mind? It's just you can't even taste a single.' Her lush eyebrows rise, the expression earnest as a girl scout. 'Actually, do you want me to order for you? I tend to get served quickly, for some reason.' She pulls a matey, conspiratorial face.

Jane isn't sure what the conspiracy is, but she's pretty sure she's not part of it. 'It's fine, I—'

'Oh! And Sofes said to get her a lime and soda? I think she forgot about... you know.' Lexie widens her green eyes and tips her head. A shoulder shrug, a cheeky don't-mind-me smile.

Sofes.

'I...' Jane falters. Lexie's words land. Is she referring to the pregnancy? Sophie said she wasn't telling the girls yet. Surely she won't have told...

'It just came out the other Sunday,' Lexie goes on, as if it's a secret they're sharing. 'We were just laughing and laughing, you know that way when you just click? And I think it just popped out.' Her hand comes to rest on her own belly, as if in sympathy. 'I think she was feeling guilty about drinking a few cocktails but I told her not to worry. It's not like she knew then, is it? Aw, it's such lovely news though, isn't it? Should've seen her face when she came back from the loo. I knew before she said anything.' She sighs. 'She's such a lovely mum. So good with Kylee.'

'I think Kylie's an Australian pop star.' The words are out before Jane can stop them.

Lexie's face falls. 'Pardon?'

'Sorry, I... Joke. It was just a joke. She calls him Kyle, not Kylee, not that it matters.' Jane feels herself blush. It is too hot in the bar. Please God, let it not be a hot flash, that really is the last thing she needs right now.

But Lexie isn't even listening. She has pushed forward, leaving Jane behind a thickset man in a too-tight T-shirt, from where she turns back to her.

'It's just that we were so wasted, I ended up crashing at Sofes',' she says over the man's head.

'Right.' Jane smiles, nods the information in, swallows it down.

'And she's so sweet, you know what she's like, she practically *forced* me to stay on for Sunday lunch.'

'Oh yeah, she's so nice like that.' Jane is almost having to shout. A throbbing has started up in her head, and she has to stop herself from adding that she's been to Sophie's for Sunday lunch many times. She remembers Sophie inviting her and Frankie the first time, a little while after they met; how she'd marvelled at what generous hosts Sophie and Carl were, how stylish yet welcoming their home, with its scented candles and coordinated colours, its wood-burning stove, stunning open-plan kitchen and landscaped garden. How she had felt lucky to have been chosen by a woman like Sophie.

'I told her she should tell the girls tonight,' Lexie shouts above the noise. 'I mean, you guys are so close, why not, eh? And I just feel *so bad* that I know and they don't, do you know what I mean?' She pulls a face, as if she finds this genuinely excruciating, which, instinctively and perhaps ungenerously, Jane doubts she does. 'I know she didn't tell you till Tuesday, and I totally told her off about that, so I think she's going to tell them tonight.' Her hands ball into fists at her chest, her teeth press together in an excited grin. She looks momentarily like Wallace. Or Gromit. Jane can't remember which one is the dog.

'Right,' Jane says, still nodding far too vigorously as confusion laps at the edges of her. 'The girls will be so...'

But Lexie has turned away and is now squeezing to the front of the crush, apologising with winks, one immaculately manicured hand half raised as she goes. A moment later, her voice drifts over the heads to where Jane still finds herself.

'Yeah, hi, sorry, can I get a double Sipsmith on three ice cubes and a slice of lemon, with a slimline Fever-Tree on the side, and a pint of lime and soda with loads of ice?' Lexie's shoulders rise to her ears, then drop. 'Oh, and can you give me some crisps and nuts and stuff... yeah... erm, two salt and black pepper, a couple of Thai chilli and a couple of the mixed spicy nuts in those little jar things? Cheers.' She turns and reaches for Jane, somehow managing to part the crowd with a sweep of her arm to allow her safe passage.

Blushing hot and staring at the scuffed toes of her boots, Jane edges forward.

Lexie lays the flat of her hand briefly on her shoulder and guides her to the front like a vulnerable pensioner. 'You're all right bringing the drinks, yeah? I'm bursting for the loo.'

The barman places the glasses and a mountain of snacks on a tray on the bar. When he tells her the price, Jane has to ask him to repeat it, at which point she pushes her cash back into her pocket and reaches instead for her debit card.

'Your mate,' the barman says, gesturing over towards the Ladies. 'Can you get me her number?'

CHAPTER SIX

JANE

By the time Jane gets back to the table, the others have arrived and the sweat is cooling on the back of her neck. Lexie is apparently still in the loo.

'Cheers for getting a bottle in,' Kath says, raising a glass and smiling at her. 'I'll go and get another in a sec; we've nearly guzzled it already.'

Jane's face is aching from the smile she has put there. It is a work smile, she realises, not a real one. She wants, it occurs to her, to go home. With Lexie here, this is no longer somewhere she wishes to be. How quickly this has happened is quite astonishing – a matter of minutes, perhaps even seconds, and Lexie really is just one person.

Sophie – *Sofes* – is holding up the pint of lime and soda, but before their eyes meet, she turns to the others. 'Cystitis,' she says, frowning comically. 'Antibiotics.'

'Oh mate!' Hils says, mock horrified. 'Too much sex, serves you right.'

The others laugh.

'No chance of me getting cystitis,' Hils continues, in her north-eastern burr, to more laughter. 'More like tumbleweed down there, to be honest with you.'

'Decent Brazilian'd sort that out,' Kath quips, deliberately misunderstanding.

The girls hoot. The talk descends into bikini-line management, to more shrieks of hilarity. Hils launches into an anecdote about a disastrous wax at the beautician's on the high street.

'Honestly' – she can barely finish for laughing at her own story – 'a tiny little square she'd given me. I looked like Adolf Hitler down there.'

Kath laughs so much she snorts Prosecco through her nose. Pandemonium ensues.

'Is your Frankie going tonight?' Hils asks Jane when they've all recovered.

'As far as I know, yeah.'

'He missed it last week, didn't he? Wasn't he working?'

'I think he made last orders.' Jane sips her drink, feels herself settling a little.

'He did,' Kath chimes in. 'Pete said he'd bought a new watch.'

Jane frowns. 'A new watch? No, I don't think so.'

Kath shakes her head. 'No? Typical Pete, wrong end of the stick as usual.' She turns to Hils. 'He said Frankie ended up driving your Simon's car home for him.'

'He's not my Simon! Not anymore!'

'I know, but you know what I mean. Didn't Franks give all the lads a lift home?'

'Pete got that bit right,' says Jane, remembering Frankie getting in super-late and telling her he'd ended up as the taxi service. 'I told him he's a bloody mug.'

What she doesn't add is that Frankie had taken the keys to Simon's Range Rover from him because he was way over the limit. Simon is a fool.

'What did I miss?' Lexie is back. Her hair is shinier, her eyes somehow greener, her teeth as white as porcelain.

'Oh, nothing, just the usual filth.' Kath chuckles and sips her drink.

Lexie sits down next to Sophie, wiggles to the back of the seat.

'Cheers,' she says, holding up her frosted glass.

'Cheers,' the rest of them reply.

They sip their drinks. The conversation lulls. Kath and Hils look self-conscious suddenly, as if who they are together, the whole silly double act of them, no longer knows how to behave in front of this new, glossy audience, and in that moment, Jane feels the preciousness of these women, their deep bond, a bond built over years, so slowly she couldn't have said when precisely they became like family to her – at least like family should be. They have done this simply by being there in a low-key, day-to-day way; no hearts and flowers, no drama, just time spent, quiet loyalty, leaving each other alone sometimes, crying together at other times – and laughing, so much laughing. The four of them have been through Hils's divorce, Kath's son Joe's battle with Crohn's disease, Sophie's baby, Jane's café venture and all its trials and tribulations, and countless other important moments.

She looks over at Sophie, who is chinking her glass with Lexie's with a private and meaningful exchange of glances. Hils and Kath don't know about Sophie's baby. There are no rules, of course, and maybe Jane's making too much of it, but Lexie knowing before them feels a bit... wrong.

Jane sips her Prosecco. Lexie and Sophie talk in whispers, their foreheads almost touching. Hils and Kath begin to discuss Tuesday's times and the 10K next Sunday. Jane finds she can't focus, can't sit straight, can't settle at all. An uncomfortable sense of not belonging hovers. She feels a little like she is floating.

'Just popping to the loo,' she says and heads for the Ladies.

In the cubicle, she dips her head between her knees and breathes deeply, a technique her counsellor taught her during the six NHS sessions after the IVF. Her heart slows.

She is completely overreacting, that's what's happening. Sophie's pregnancy has brought everything to the surface – her own grief, and maybe the memory of how awkward things got with Sophie during her first pregnancy. They never fought, never said anything about it at all, but they both felt it and both knew the other felt it. They should have talked, but what was there to say? It was all too hard, simple as that. Jane was still too raw.

Looking back, Sophie probably felt a little unsupported, though she would have understood why. And Jane has made up for it since. She always makes Kyle his special hot chocolate with whippy cream and little marshmallows when Sophie brings him to the café; she never forgets his birthday. She and Sophie have let time do the work, and it has, but...

No. They're fine. They're completely fine. The stress of acting delighted for Sophie's sake has mentally exhausted her. Lexie is new to the area; it is typically kind of Sophie to invite her to the pub with them and help her make friends, just as she did for Jane years ago. OK, so Lexie left Jane to pay at the bar after adding to the order without asking, but different people have different ideas, and yes, it's a bit annoying, but it's hardly a big deal. Sophie clearly thinks Lexie is great, and so Jane just needs to give her a chance. If the woman's a bit pushy, so what? Perhaps she's had to be forward to survive. If anyone knows about survival, it's Jane – and not everyone can go about it in the same way. And if it slipped out about the pregnancy when Lexie and Sophie were together, well, that's hardly the crime of the century, is it? The Runner Beans gang has always body-swerved the kind of tyranny that reigns in the women's groups Jane has heard about – the extravagant birthday celebrations, the eye-watering joint holidays, the who's on which WhatsApp group. Jane is being childish. Sophie does not *belong* to her; she's a grown woman, with a family of her own, as is Jane. If you count Des.

She breathes deeply three more times, counting four beats in, five out, let it go, let it go, words she sings in her mind, having watched *Frozen* about seventeen times with Scarlett.

As she stands, she notices a heaviness low in her belly. Yes, definitely, she can feel a kind of dull ache. And now she thinks about it, she hasn't had a period since... well, since before Christmas. Plus, her breasts feel quite sore. Her bra was tight this morning – yes, yes it was.

Hope she knows better than to acknowledge flutters in her chest. She has one pregnancy test left at home, if you don't count the dozens of used negative ones she keeps, for reasons lost to her, in a box under the bed. She feels quite grim actually. And the pinching underwear isn't fat, she doesn't think. It's firmer. It's swelling. She feels... swollen.

It's not impossible. Is it? A paucity of eggs is not no eggs at all, is it?

Back at the table, Kath has bought another round. Preoccupied by what might, just might be, Jane wonders if she could sneak away and do that test, just to put it out of her mind and begin the process of overcoming the crushing disappointment, but barely has she sat down when Lexie stands and bangs her glass with the little plastic cocktail stirrer.

A slow, bewildered silence falls.

Kath glances at Jane, mouths *What?* Jane shrugs.

'Sorry.' Lexie blinks rapidly, places a hand flat at her tanned collarbone, her nails dark, shining beads. 'Just wanted to say thanks so, so much for letting me come along tonight, ladies. As you know, I'm new around here.'

'Don't be daft,' Hils says at the same time as Kath shakes her head and puffs air into her fringe – *don't mention it.*

Jane wonders if they're finding this whole Oscar acceptance speech shtick a bit much. She knows she is.

'Seriously though,' Lexie goes on, 'I was telling Steve before I came out, I just think it's so kind and welcoming. Honestly, I've known some real bitches in my time, you would not *believe.*'

Jane suppresses a gasp, hopes Lexie's not going to use that word again. It's not a term any of them would use to describe another woman.

'Anyway,' Lexie continues, seeming to falter slightly, 'that's not all I want to say. *Someone* here has some *very* important news.' Her sculpted eyebrows rise, and a mischievous smile spreads across her face. Again the shoulders come up, up, up, and she glances at Sophie, who blushes and grins.

Sophie eyes them all sheepishly and coughs into her hand. 'Erm... I'm not on antibiotics.'

'Oh my God,' Hils says. 'You're up the duff, aren't you? Bloody hell, woman!' She laughs.

Eyes rounding, Sophie leans forward. 'Shush!'

'Sorry!' Hils continues in a loud whisper. 'I thought your boobs looked bigger – honestly, I should have twigged!' She makes a show of clapping her hands over her mouth, but the women have already dissolved into delighted congratulations and celebratory hugs.

Jane is aware of herself hugging, being hugged. The bubbles rise in her drink. The waistband of her jeans cuts into her stomach. A ghostly craving for a cigarette. If she still smoked, she would go outside right now. But no, she has to stay. She has to rise to the occasion and it has to be now.

When the fuss dies down, she raises her glass.

'To Sophie,' she says. To her horror, her eyes fill.

But interpreting only emotion, the others reach for their glasses and join the happy toast. Above their heads, Jane catches Lexie's eye and is caught off guard. The woman is *glowering* at her; there is no other word for it. She is staring at her as if she has said something awful.

A little flustered, Jane looks at the others, but they haven't noticed. Fury, that was what was burning in those eyes.

But why?

CHAPTER SEVEN

THE HOSPITAL

What's the point of these stupid *call the nurse* buttons? I pressed it ages ago. What if I was actually dying? I could be fighting for breath and no one would care. Having a heart attack. An embolism. Honest to God, if one of them doesn't get over here in the next five seconds...

You'll what?

I won't do anything, will I? I *can't* do anything. I need someone to help me up. I need to find out where she is and get to her before she gets to me, even if I have to fall out of this damn bed and crawl to her on bleeding elbows. Only one of us can leave this hospital on two feet, and I'm going to make sure it's me. It's time I took things into my own hands. I've been pussyfooting about for far too long.

Maybe I can wait until dark. The nurse said they'd be keeping me in another night. Although that seems risky. It's too slow. It needs to be sooner rather than later. I need to find out where she is, but I can't ask here; it'll have to be at reception. If I can just casually walk... Well, no, I can't, can I? Not with a broken leg. If I can casually *limp* into her ward, if I can time it and do it without anyone noticing, I can draw the curtain across, all smiles, and bingo! A pillow over the face should do the trick, quickly, while the nurses are putting their feet up, or gossiping, or eating Quality

Street, which is all they seem to do all day. It's pre-emptive self-defence, that's all. It's not like she wouldn't do the same to me; just a question of who can move faster. If she isn't dead already. Which with any luck she will be.

Then I'll find Frankie. Oh Frankie, you're such a good man, and too soft for your own good. I don't care about any of the other stuff anymore – that's all in the past. My priorities have changed these last twenty-four hours. We don't need a baby to be happy. It can be just you and me, and that's enough.

A doctor visits me. Quite superior in his way of speaking, as if I'm not very bright. Tells me I have a fractured tibia, that that means a broken shin, basically. As I say, quite superior. He tells me I'm lucky.

'I am,' I say and smile like butter wouldn't melt in my dry, cracked mouth. 'So, so lucky. Do you have any news on Frank Reece? He's my husband. He was involved in the same accident. I just want to know if he's OK.'

He gives a non-committal nod, scribbles something on his notes. 'I'll try and find out.'

'Thank you so much.'

I lie back, close my eyes. Wonder if I can swing my legs over, lower myself gently down and hobble out of here. I don't think so. I'll need crutches. I'll ask the nurse for some if anyone ever answers this call button.

Tears come again, out of nowhere. It's all such a mess. And it's not my fault, none of it is. It's not my fault I was doing the grocery shop at thirteen – cooking, cleaning, listening to my mother crying. Just because I don't let people see my tears doesn't mean I don't cry. Doesn't mean I don't hurt. I hurt! I hurt every moment of every single day. Just because I don't shout about it doesn't mean I'm not limping along, weeping silently to myself, alone – alone, alone. But I had everything, I realise that now. I even had friends, for the first time since school, before she turned them against me.

And now I'm alone – again.

Actually, alone is how I need to do this. I need to find out where she is myself. If I ask where she is, I'll draw attention, blow my chances. I need my phone – the Friday Drinks WhatsApp group. They might already know about the accident. I can maybe get her ward number, the floor.

'You OK there?'

Jesus Christ, sneak up on me, why don't you? Typical, don't come when you need them, right there when you don't.

'Yes, thank you.'

'Did you want something?' She's older, this one. I could overpower her, I reckon. Even with one leg.

'I was wondering if you could help me out of bed?' I ask. 'I need to use the loo.'

CHAPTER EIGHT

JANE

Once the excitement dies down, another lull descends. Lexie talks. She talks and talks and talks. Tells them all about her amazing boyfriend, Steve, and how amazing he is and all the amazing things he has done for her and bought for her, how his ex was a real bitch – again Jane winces, wonders whether the others are wincing too, what they're all thinking. Lexie tells them how Steve's mother is an even bigger bitch than his sister, his ex, well, she's the queen of all the... By then, Jane is filling in the blanks. These other women are, apparently, not a patch on Lexie herself. She worries sometimes that Steve puts her on a pedestal, worries she's gonna fall off one day, she really does.

Poor thing.

Two or three times, Hils tries to change the subject from Lexie to something – *anything* – else and liven things up with a funny anecdote, but Lexie talks over her. Eventually she gives up and goes to the loo, possibly to get a break. Kath asks Jane quietly how it's going.

'Yeah,' she whispers. 'Not bad, I—'

'Kath,' Lexie calls out, bringing her back to the group as a primary school teacher might to a child. 'Wait till you hear this!'

Leaving becomes impossible. It feels pointed. Jane's body

stiffens and sets; her forearms tense. The physical longing to *get the hell out* becomes almost unbearable. Sophie appears rapt, but Kath and Hils are uncharacteristically silent, smiling benignly, politely. It. Is. So. Boring. Jane can't read their minds, of course, but they look every bit as stultified as she feels. And whatever they're thinking, what is certain is that the usual Friday-night hilarity has been extinguished like a match pinched between damp fingers.

'... and then he took me to this oyster bar in Covent Garden, and when we got there, the champagne was already on the table and he was like, surprise! He had it all *planned...*'

'That's so sweet,' Sophie coos, clasping her hands at her chest.

'*So* sweet.'

'So, so sweet.'

Dear God. Under cover of the table, Jane slides her phone out of her bag. She brings up her text thread with Frankie and is about to type *Call me now*, thinking she can feign an emergency, but before she can thumb a single letter...

'I have to go.' Lexie has her phone to her chest. 'So sorry, ladies! Steve's missing me. Bless!' Laughing and rolling her eyes at Steve and his puppy-love devotion, she stands and grabs her beige trench coat from the chair.

Jane tries not to notice that no one is begging her to stay, tries not to admit that she has noticed, nor that it has given her a small twinge of pleasure.

'Is everything OK, hun?' Sophie is asking Lexie, face etched with concern.

Lexie's smile is sickly. 'He just needs a cuddle, that's all.'

Jane does not mime a finger down her throat, which, granted, doesn't make her diplomat of the year, but she has had a lot to drink and the impulse is incredibly strong. As Lexie holds 'Sofes' tight and makes that dreadful piggy *wheeeee* noise again, Jane stares into her drink, looking up just in time to see Lexie throw out her arms.

'Bye, Janie-Jane,' she says. 'So great to meet you.'

'Yeah! See you soon.' Jane gives a small wave. She does not

throw out her arms. She does not get up. In that moment, it feels physically impossible.

Lexie's arms retract as if she's burnt her fingertips. She steps back and waves, brightly, before, phone clamped to her ear, she turns and strides out of the pub.

Jane feels instantly shitty, a feeling compounded by the realisation that all she wants is for the others to turn immediately to Sophie and ask: *What the actual hell?*

Because this is not just a drink, this is *Friday-night drinks*, and now that Lexie has been invited once, it's going to be very hard not to invite her every week without causing offence. And anyone who suggests they keep it to just the four of them in future will be the ungenerous, unsisterly one.

But no one is asking *What the hell?* Instead, Hils is wondering if they should get another bottle. Sophie offers, but Kath tells her not to be silly, that she's not even drinking. It was Lexie's round, Jane thinks, but there is no way she can say that without sounding like she's counting, which she isn't, absolutely not... OK, OK, she is, she absolutely is. Oh, how she would love to read Hils and Kath's minds.

'I'm going to head off too actually,' she says, suddenly aware that if her symptoms are anything at all, even though she knows deep down they won't be, she shouldn't really have drunk at all. She has had more than she usually would – not to laugh and wind down, but to survive an evening that has managed to be both stressful and boring.

'I'm working tomorrow,' she adds. 'Don't want to be breathing fumes on the customers.'

'I wouldn't worry, pet,' Hils says. 'Half the town'll be breathing fumes tomorrow. Half the country. Our Great British culture, isn't it?'

'True,' Jane replies, but she's already put on her coat.

'I'll pop in tomorrow if I get a mo,' Hils says, adding as she does every time: 'You're so much cheaper than Starbucks!'

'Ha!' Jane grins. 'Congratulations again, lovey,' she says to her closest friend, before giving her and the others hugs that are tighter than usual – and longer. A wave over her shoulder and she's out of there.

Too soon. Lexie is still outside, hovering by the bus stop. For a second, Jane thinks about darting back into the pub, but that would be utterly ridiculous. Besides, Lexie has seen her. She is doing that eyes smiling, mouth a bit dubious thing again. Isn't it usually the other way around?

'Waiting for my Uber,' she says, holding up her phone.

'Cool. See you later. Night!' One hand raised in farewell, Jane turns and heads for home.

CHAPTER NINE

JANE

The house is cold, and in darkness save for the soft glow from the lamp at the end of the hall. Des's paws tack-a-tack, his tail wags so hard it bangs against the under-stairs cupboard door. Frankie is obviously still out with the lads. Jane knew he would be, but still disappointment trickles through her. She grabs a pint of tap water and sits on the sofa with Des, who lays his curly head on her lap as if to say, *Don't worry, I love you.* It is getting on for eleven – early, really, for a Friday night.

She leans forward for the remote. Her jeans dig into her stomach. She undoes the top button, tunes into her body bit by bit. Her head is aching – *that'll be too much Prosecco, idiot.* Her breasts are sore, her bra definitely tighter than usual – she unfastens it under her T-shirt and pulls it off through the sleeves, a trick that amazed Frankie the first time she did it; amazed her that he'd never seen it before. Relief. She cups both breasts with her hands – do they feel heavier? Maybe. She should never have gone back to drinking after abstaining for so long. But the expansion of her gut can't be from missing one single running club, can it? And it's a long time since she kicked the leftover pastry and sandwiches habit by organising a daily box to be picked up by a homeless charity. Though she says it herself, that was a genius two-birds-with-one-stone move. Her hand comes to rest on her belly. It is firm, not flabby. Distended.

Womb?

Or wind?

'Shift off, Des,' she says, gently moving his head from her lap.

Upstairs, she finds the last pregnancy test hidden at the back of her bedside-table drawer. This is masochistic. She isn't pregnant. She shouldn't do it. They work better in the mornings anyway. And she promised Frankie: no more tests.

But the urge is too strong, and fifteen minutes later, she is still staring at the single line in the world's tiniest, loneliest window, her body a bag of rubber bones. Forty-five minutes after that, Frankie finds her asleep in the foetal position, the test still in her hand – something she only realises when he wakes her.

'Babe,' he whispers, shaking her softly. 'Babe. Hey. Come on, you're freezing.'

She didn't cry at the test, but now, at the sight of him, she does. He sits beside her and throws his dressing gown around her shoulders, pulls her to him.

'I'm so sorry,' she sobs, breaking another promise: to stop apologising. She has had to banish all thought of blame, has had counselling for it, but still, she feels it, she does. It is so hard not to feel like a failure, like she's letting Frankie down when he could, they both know, have children with someone else.

'It felt different, honestly. I was convinced. I'm sorry.'

'Don't be sorry. I just hate seeing you hurt yourself, that's all. How come you even had a test? I thought you'd thrown them out?'

She sniffs hugely. 'I had one left. Thought I'd keep it in case, you know? And maybe it's false – I mean, you're supposed to do them in the morning really.'

For a moment, he says nothing, only strokes her back in slow circles. He is so patient. He would have been such a lovely dad. More tears come.

'You have to stop doing this to yourself,' he says softly, not even taking her on about the false negative, because he knows it's not false, as does she.

'I'm sorry,' she says. 'Sorry for being sorry. I've had a bit too much to drink.'

'Sophie's news has hit you hard, that's all.'

'Did Carl mention it?'

His mouth presses tight, his forehead creases, he shrugs. Yes, then.

'Are you OK?' she says. 'Was it awkward?'

'Why would it be awkward? They don't know about us – well, maybe Carl does through Sophie, but he's never said anything to me, and the others don't know, I don't think. It was fine. We took the piss out of Carl for a bit, then we went back to, you know, just chat.'

'What did you talk about?'

'Oh, you know. Feelings, relationships.'

She smiles. 'Football then? ISAs? Cars? Do you think we should tell them? What if they start asking? It's going to be obvious pretty soon. We're all getting older.'

'It's no one's business, is it? And if they start asking, well, that's just rude. It's private. Lots of people don't want kids, for lots of reasons. It's a valid choice. You said yourself, you wish you hadn't even told Sophie. If you tell everyone, then it won't just be her doing the sympathy thing, will it?'

'She doesn't do it anymore.' She leans into him, remembering Sophie's big, sad cow eyes when Jane first used to visit her and Kyle, asking with too much concern whether or not Jane wanted to hold him, as if not being able to have children meant you couldn't be near a live one, which to be fair wasn't far from the truth. 'Well,' she adds, 'she did do it when she told me, but it's a hard thing to say, isn't it? But yeah, the whole *poor you* thing would be unbearable. I won't buy another test. I promise.'

Her phone buzzes. She ignores it.

'How about marmalade on toast and a cuppa?' Frankie suggests. 'In bed?'

She kisses him. 'You're an actual angel. Decaf for me please. I should sleep, but I'm too wired. I'm going to be so knackered at work tomorrow.'

He leaves her to go down to the kitchen. She picks up her phone and sees that Lexie Lane has been added to the Friday Drinks WhatsApp group.

'*What?*'

From the small ID circle, Lexie pouts, head half turned away, staring into the middle distance like a model. There is a message from her already:

So nice to meet all you lovely ladies and thanks again for tonight! And I was thinking on the way home, we should totally have a baby shower for you, Sofes! We can talk about it next time, yay! Love yaz! L xxx

Baby shower? Love yaz? Oh dear God.

Frankie returns with their snacks and teas on a tray. At the door, he hesitates.

'What's the matter? Has something else happened?'

Hell, she wants to say. *Hell is what's happened. And her name is Lexie Lane.*

But his lovely face is all furrowed and worried. He's working all the hours trying to fund their dream. She suspects busting a gut is how he's dealing with his own hurt: action – don't stop, don't ever stop; if you stop, you think. Sophie and Carl's news will have hit him hard too, and here he is with toast and tea and safety. It's always him piecing her back together and holding her until the glue dries, never the reverse. At least that's how it seems right now.

And in that moment, she decides that if Lexie gets her way, as she seems so very good at doing, and makes them throw a baby shower for Sophie, she will tough it out on her own – for Frankie's sake.

CHAPTER TEN

FRANKIE

He gets to the pub late that Friday. Would have been on time but for a last-minute call-out from a woman with a blocked drain in the flats over Kingston way. Only needed rodding – council should have done it really – but she looked so skint he didn't even charge her.

So he's late. Normally he wouldn't bother after a sixteen-hour day, but if he's honest, he wants to wear the watch.

He drops his kit, has a quick shower, puts on the Ben Sherman shirt and the indigo jeans Jane bought him for Christmas and legs it to the White Lion.

By the time he gets there, Carl has gone home but the others are well on the way to battered. Frankie nods and grins his way through the usual abuse, only this time when Pete taps his wrist and asks what the hell time he calls this, Frankie punches the air before bringing the Breitling to his face and making a great show of answering: 'Personally, I make it time for last orders.'

At which point, the lads crush round, oohing and aahing, pulling his hand this way and that.

'Mate,' Simon says. 'That. Is a thing of beauty. How much that set you back?'

'What d'you do, win the lottery?' Pete adds, no idea how close he is to the truth.

'None of your bloody beeswax,' Frankie says, laughing; they're all laughing, except Frankie's trying to think of a way of asking them not to mention the watch to their wives in case one of them tells Jane, but he can't figure out how to do that without sounding like a dick. So he says nothing. Simon hands him a pint of London Pride, and it's at the sight of Simon's wrist that Frankie goes from feeling like an idiot to feeling like a prize lemon. Because Simon, whose Tag set Frankie off on this whole trip in the first place, is wearing a Swatch. A fucking Swatch, and Frankie realises in that moment, a moment that has come far too late, that the *Swatch* is the pinnacle – not the Tag, not Carl's classic black leather-strap Sector, not Pete's gold-plated Armani, and not his own brand-new Breitling Superocean Automatic 44 with the English-mustard-yellow dial. No, the Swatch blows them all out of the water. The Swatch says, I earn a quinty-squillion a week. The Swatch says, I don't need an expensive watch anymore. The Swatch says, I am beyond watches.

Fuck.

But he doesn't get much further, because that's when Natasha bumps into him and makes him spill his pint all over his shirt. Except he doesn't know she's called Natasha; he sees only a sophisticated woman with sleek long dark hair and blue eyes, who's apologising and trying to dry his shirt with one of those little black paper napkins they put under women's drinks.

'I'm so sorry,' she's saying, her voice smooth and low. 'Please let me buy you another.'

He wants to lift her hand from his chest, but he doesn't feel right touching her wrist, so he takes a step back. 'Don't worry about it – it's fine, honestly.'

'I insist,' she says. 'London Pride, wasn't it?'

'How do you know?'

'It says so on the glass.' She smiles, her eyebrows rising. Her blue eyes under the dark hair make her look a bit exotic, he thinks.

When she turns away to order a pint, the lads pull stupid faces. Pete makes a fist at his chest and mouths, *Get in.*

'Guys,' Frankie says, spreading his fingers at them. 'Get a grip, you bunch of animals.'

'I'm Natasha, by the way,' the woman says, handing him the drink. She's bought herself one too. A small glass of red wine.

'You didn't need to do that,' he says. 'But thanks. I'm Frankie.'

'Pleased to meet you.' She clinks her glass against his. When she glances at the others, he takes his cue and introduces them. She shakes their hands, tells them she's here with her colleagues, Tamsin and Freya, waving over towards the other side of the bar.

They raise their glasses and say cheers, as you do, all of them like overexcited schoolboys trying not to look like they're elbowing each other. Natasha tells Frankie she likes his watch, likes how it picks up the yellow check in his shirt. She's never seen a watch with a yellow face before.

'Well,' Frankie says, knowing she's flirting, that he's flirting a bit too, 'it was worth coming out tonight then, wasn't it?'

She laughs, even though he knows it wasn't that funny; doubts that she finds it funny at all. But like most of the people in here, she's had a few drinks, isn't to know that he's stone-cold sober.

The lights flash, the signal that the pub is closing; they have ten minutes to drink up.

'I'd better get back to my friends,' she says, tipping her head to one side in a kind of courteous little bow. 'But it was nice to meet you, Frankie, and sorry again about spilling your drink.'

'Don't worry about it.'

She locks eyes with him and gives that closed-mouth smile again before taking a step back. But she doesn't walk away. Instead, she hesitates. The pub is as noisy as a football crowd; Frankie notices it then, loud in his ears.

'What do you do, by the way?' she asks.

'Er... I'm a heating engineer.' He feels himself blush.

She cocks her head. Her eyes widen. They really are a startling blue. 'As in bathrooms?'

'I fit bathrooms and kitchens, yeah. Central heating systems, boilers, that sort of thing. I have my own business.'

'Right, right.' She appears to nod the information in. 'I'm actually looking for a new bathroom. Do you work in Wimbham?'

He nods. 'Yeah. And round about. I live here, so...'

'Do you have a card?'

'Er, yeah. I might have.' He digs in his back pocket, pulls out his wallet. He has a couple of cards in there for exactly this sort of thing. 'There you go. Number's on there and everything. Best thing is to drop us a text.'

'Frank Reece Plumbing,' she reads then glances up, meets his gaze without hesitation. 'I'll call you next week, week after, OK? You can come and give me a quote?'

'Sure. No problem. Whenever.'

'Well, thank you. Nice to meet you.' She glances down at his chest and smirks. 'And sorry again about your shirt.'

And that's it. She pushes through the crowd and is gone. He doesn't see her for what's left of the evening, despite them staying in the pub for another half an hour; doesn't see her outside when Simon pulls out the car keys and Frankie tells him not to be a pillock, that he's wasted, that he, Frankie, will drive him home. Doesn't see her when he jumps up into the driving seat of the Evoque and waits for his boozed-up mates to get in. Doesn't see her there, smoothing his card between her finger and thumb, watching.

CHAPTER ELEVEN

JANE

Jane wakes to indigo sky, the buzz of a pre-dawn alarm. Head pounding, mouth dry, eyes sticky, she grabs her phone and kills the grating drill of noise. Not quite ready to haul herself out of bed and into the shower, she lets herself drift a moment. She was dreaming about her mother. The dream was from childhood. She's had it before, but not for a few years now, and she doesn't know if it's a real or fake memory. Maybe, like most memories, some of it's real, some of it not.

She's quite old in this one. They're in the supermarket. They're going up and down the aisles. Mum's putting that cheap, strong cider she used to drink, the one that came in brown two-litre plastic bottles, in the trolley. She has already slipped a smaller bottle of vodka into her handbag – Jane knows this but doesn't know how she knows. She's watching out for security guards, terrified they will get done for shoplifting. If they're caught, like they have been once before, it will be more embarrassing than the time her mother sent her to school without ingredients for food tech, with a note addressed to the teacher saying they didn't have the kind of money for her daughter to be baking Black Forest gateau and why didn't they teach them something useful like how to boil an egg or make a cup of tea?

But if they get out of here without getting caught, it's not much better. *I know where this ends*, child Jane is thinking, fingers curled around the smooth metal grid of the trolley. I know how I will find her later. But most of all, I know not to say anything.

Her mother pushes the larger bottles underneath a bumper pack of cheap loo rolls and eyes her like a wolf: *No one's business but ours.*

This is not their usual supermarket. They must have come to one in another town, or maybe they've moved again. Is this before or after? Jane isn't sure. They don't always buy cider in the supermarket. Most often she is sent to the corner shop, because the man there, Bill, whose name is not really Bill and who wears a turban and is kind and friendly, lets her buy alcohol for her mother. If it is that town, the one where they lived near Bill, it's the one they went to after. Jane knows this because years later, Bill was still letting her buy booze without realising it wasn't all for her mother.

They are watching the tills, making sure they can't see anyone they know before they go and pay. They are watching the tills when a shout cracks the air.

'*Bitch.*'

The word runs through Jane like hot liquid. A woman she doesn't know is shouting this word at her mother.

'How can you even show your face?' she cries. 'You ruined my life.'

Behind her, cowering, is a girl. She is older than Jane and wearing school uniform.

'Me ruined your life?' her mother shouts back, and Jane fills with burning shame. Her mother laughs – it is a callous laugh, a horrible laugh. 'I'm not to blame for the shitty state of your marriage, love. You need to look to yourself for that, I'm afraid.'

She takes Jane's hand and turns her roughly. They leave the trolley in the middle of the aisle. As they go through the exit, Jane sneaks a glance over her shoulder. The woman is crying. Her daughter is trying to hug her. The daughter is crying too.

When they get home, Mum pours half the bottle of vodka into a glass and drinks it like water. Her hands are shaking.

'You'll have to go to Bill's,' she says.

Jane sits up, a little breathless. She makes to get out of bed before any more memories can follow, but too late: the window smashes, the brick lands on the living-room floor. She knows this memory because she has it often, used to have it every night in the last moments before she fell asleep. This one is definitely before they moved that final time. It was possibly the reason, although like so many things, she has never spoken about it with her mother – Victoria, as she began to refer to her around about then. Jane is fourteen, fifteen. She remembers that disgusting green carpet with the yellow swirls. The brick is wrapped in paper, held on with one of the blue elastic bands the paper boys leave round the estate. Her mother pulls off the elastic band, reads the message, screws up the paper.

Later, when her mum has passed out, Jane digs it out of the bin.

BITCH, it reads.

Frankie stirs, rolls over. The soft settling of his breath.

'Gah.' Jane throws her feet over the side of the bed. Last night comes back in flashes. The gin and tonic order. The barman asking for Lexie's number. Lexie putting herself in charge of Sophie's big announcement. Lexie staring at Jane, fury in her eyes.

She should have left the pub after the first bottle, cut her losses. Her early start is always the ideal excuse to bolt, though she knows for a fact that Kyle often wakes Sophie at six, that the others have various kids' athletics clubs to get up for. Still, on days like these, she wonders why she ever decided on a business that involves a 5.30 a.m. alarm call on a Saturday.

She sits on the loo and pees. But when she wipes herself, the paper colours red.

She plunges her head into her hands and groans. The swollen breasts, the tight jeans, even last night's irritability – not a pregnancy at all, but this.

'No baby,' she whispers into her spread fingers. 'There never was.'

An hour later, she's at work. Because that's how this goes. Because what else can she do? She's showered, dressed, has thrown the 'ball' into the yard a few times for Des, cycled to the café and is now steaming a large glass of milk. She adds a double shot of espresso and stirs in three sachets of brown sugar, thinks of this morning, the blood, last night.

Lexie, this is Jane. Jane, Lexie.

That palpable seething animosity from Lexie. It felt almost, well, animal.

But was it real?

Does she have it right?

The craving for a cigarette is always worst at this time of day. It is a craving she suspects will never go, despite giving up over ten years ago. In the prep kitchen, she sips her latte macchiato while she organises the deliveries and briefs Tom, who she found through an organisation over in Feltham specialising in getting homeless people back into work. Tom lost everything to substance addiction – his wife, his kids, his job. In the two years he's worked here making and pre-packing sandwiches, plus doing the weekday platters for local business lunches, he's been one hundred per cent reliable, apart from once when he was mugged on the way to work, the thief getting away with the princely sum of £18.53. He lives on his own – that's as much as Jane has gleaned – and is mad on yoga, which he does at home for an hour and a half a day. He is mostly sinew, incredibly quiet, and something in the way he moves his delicate hands makes sandwich prep look like an art form.

She drags herself from the near-hypnotic sight of Tom layering up a mozzarella, avocado and tomato ciabatta to go and fills the till with change from the safe. Next, she gives the window display a thorough wipe-down: a world of funky crockery from teapots to matching coffee sets, hemp bags of coffee beans, tins of amaretti biscuits, rustic brown sugar lumps, pastel pink and blue sugar cubes, some of Scarlett's biscotti, gift-wrapped in clear cellophane bags with cute little gingham ribbons – in short, the paraphernalia of coffee culture.

Checking that it is clean, even though she cleaned it last night, she lines the pastry basket with fresh cellophane and transfers the pastries one by one with the tongs. After that, she runs two water-only cycles through the shining chrome beast that is the Gaggia D90 Evolution – quite a claim for a coffee machine – before lifting the chairs off the tables and giving them all a brisk once-over, even though she did this last night too. The napkins, sugar, salt and pepper holders on the little table next to the bar were refilled yesterday before close, but still she checks them as well.

Routine is everything; it soothes her.

Tom brings through a selection of sandwiches, along with Jane's favourite, the cheese and ham croissants, one of which she heats up in the press before practically inhaling it with a long drink of water. Better. Her headache is clearing. By eight, when she opens the doors to the awakening street, the café is sparkling and she feels almost human.

Saturday mornings are slow until after nine, so she runs the place alone until her second in command, Jude, arrives and A Roasted Development makes the most of the fact that Starbucks doesn't allow dogs. The dog walkers are friendly – straightforward takeaway orders, easy to get through. Jude and Jane work with and around each other, barely aware of the near-balletic harmony of movements practised over a year working together in a small space.

Frankie calls in with Des to say hello before taking him for his walk. He thanks her for his coffee, kisses her on the cheek and tells her that he's making spicy veggie burgers for dinner. She watches him as he leaves, whistling a tune from the Lianne La Havas album they're listening to a lot at the moment, and thinks about how normal they must seem, how no one would guess at the scene that played out late last night in their cold bedroom, how that whistling man picked her up and put her back together and brought her toast and a hot drink in bed.

More customers arrive, to read the paper or catch up with

friends. It is a cold February day, and only after she's popped outside to sweep the pavement, which she does on the hour, every hour, does she notice how cosy it is back inside, the air infused with vanilla, cinnamon and espresso. She smiles to herself. A Roasted Development is what she dreamt it would be: a haven, somewhere to come and just be – as much for her as for her customers.

She is halfway through a hot chocolate order when she sees Sophie at the door.

'Hey!' she says, smiling, gesturing to the one remaining stool at the bar. 'Not often I see you at the weekend.'

Sophie's smile is a little crisp. She does not meet Jane's eye. A small pit forms in Jane's stomach. A quick check of the shop floor: customers all settled and the coast is clear. Recognising Sophie, Jude nods at Jane – *go chat, I'll hold the fort* – so Jane takes Sophie's cappuccino over to her. Sophie never pays. She never has. She has given up trying.

'I brought you a cappuccino,' Jane says, sliding it across the counter. 'Sorry, I didn't think. Are you allowed?'

Sophie shakes her head. 'Sorry.'

'No, I'm sorry. Herbal? I've got chamomile?'

'It's OK. I'm OK, thanks.' Sophie looks away, at nothing in particular.

It occurs to Jane that she has no idea what to say next. Usually they dive into some chatter or other and don't come up for air until one of them catches sight of a watch and shrieks, *Oh my God, is that the time?*

'Did you want a croissant?' she asks. 'Pain au chocolat? Raisin Danish? I had a ham and cheese croissant earlier I *think* might have saved my life.'

Again Sophie shakes her head. 'Carl did a full English.' Her tone is clipped, her face unsmiling. The pit in Jane's stomach hardens.

'Jealous,' she tries, a little confused. 'I could've done with that. I'm hanging by a thread this morning.' When Sophie doesn't reply, Jane rattles on. 'I bet you're feeling smug though, no-hangover-face.

How come you're here anyway? Did Carl give you the morning off?'

'I said I had to pop to the high street for some pregnancy stuff.' Sophie takes a tentative sip of the coffee, despite having said she didn't want it. 'Actually, he's started taking Kyle to swimming lessons on Saturday mornings, so I had the house to myself.'

'Fifty kids under five in one pool,' Jane says. 'That should sort the pH levels out.'

Sophie doesn't laugh. Funny, Jane thinks, how even in a crowded café with background music she can still hear silence.

'So, you met Lexie,' Sophie says. She still hasn't looked at Jane directly.

'I certainly did.' Jane notices a crusty bit of something on the countertop. She scratches at it with the end of her thumbnail, wipes the loosened crumbs with her cloth.

'And?'

'And what?'

'Did you like her?'

Jane makes herself look at her friend and pushes her bottom lip out. 'I don't really know her yet. But yeah, she's very... lively.' *Lively? What is she, a cocker spaniel?*

Sophie takes another sip of her coffee, the cocoa powder sticking to her upper lip. She must feel it there, because she wipes it with her napkin. Her eyebrows are back to their normal colour, though what that has to do with anything...

'It's just, she called me late last night.' Sophie shrugs, though the effect is not indifference, and continues to stare into her coffee. 'She said you were rude to her.'

'What?'

'At the bar, when she came to help with the drinks, she said you were really quite mean. Hostile, actually, is what she said. I have to say, I noticed you were a bit... frosty when she tried to give you a hug. And then when you left, she said she tried to talk to you in the car park but you ignored her and walked off.'

The words are out but their meaning is still floating down. They are the words of a fourteen-year-old in a she said/she said spat, lines from one of those high-school teen movies Jane watches sometimes with Scarlett. She tries to meet her friend's eye, almost to see if she is serious. She looks serious but is still staring at her drink.

'Oh no,' Jane replies, as calmly as she can, though confusion is running like insects across her skin. 'I wasn't rude to her, honestly I wasn't. I wouldn't be. I mean, I didn't mean to be at all. Why would I be rude?'

Another little shrug. 'She just said you were really sarky. And passive-aggressive.' Still Sophie will not look up. Jane has an almost overwhelming urge to grab her by the chin and ask her who she is and what she's done with her friend. Mostly, though, her head is pounding.

'I made a joke,' she says, leaning in so that Sophie can hear her. 'She called Kyle Kylee and I made some joke about... you know, Kylie Minogue. You know what I'm like; you can imagine me saying something like that, can't you? I didn't mean anything by it; I was just trying to be funny, that's all. It certainly wasn't aggressive and I remember saying I was joking. It fell flat more than anything. I didn't hug her when she left because I don't know her that well yet, and let's see, when I saw her later on, outside, she said she was waiting for a cab and I said *cool* or *goodnight* or *see you* or whatever, I really can't remember, but I definitely didn't ignore her. I just said goodbye and went home.' Is it OK that I went home, she thinks, or did Lexie want me to pull up a sleeping bag until her taxi arrived?

Sophie looks up, but only briefly, before dropping her eyes once again. 'I don't know.'

'You don't know?' Jane's voice trembles a little. *You're my friend*, she wants to say. You *should* know.

Still Sophie doesn't look at her.

'Listen, you like her.' She drags the words out. 'That's what matters. I don't even know her. I suppose I thought... I *suppose* I thought it might have been a bit soon to invite her to Friday drinks, that's all, but it's fine, it's not a prob—'

'You see.' Sophie's eyes flash with something Jane can't name. 'You don't like her! I could so tell.'

'That's not what I'm saying at all.' Jane glances around the coffee bar, conscious of people overhearing. Jude is serving the elderly couple from the flats behind the high street with tea for two, telling them to go and sit down. Jane lowers her voice. 'I'm just saying, it's always been the four of us. We've got a lot of history, that's all.'

'And I'm saying you didn't give her a chance. She's fun. She's a *lot* of fun actually; she really knows how to have a good time. She's a bit... outrageous sometimes, but she's young, isn't she? I mean, you should see her Instagram, it's, like, woah, you know? But only 'cause she's younger than us. I mean they're all like that now, aren't they? But honestly she's really great, she always has time for me, and she's so, so generous.'

Why does Jane feel like she's just heard a list of all the things she herself is not? Like she isn't, suddenly, fun enough, outrageous enough, young enough? And by generous, does Sophie mean rich? In the time they've been friends, Jane has always had a full-on job, particularly when they were building the café. She can't always hang out for hours at a time and doesn't have the money for champagne cocktails or leather bags, by real or fake designers. She has never had cause to examine herself like this, but now she does. Her generosity, she feels, comes in the form of small acts – like free coffee, like funny little texts or stories saved, like babysitting sometimes, stuff like that. This has always been enough. Until now.

'She didn't leave because of me,' she says. 'Did she?'

Sophie meets her gaze, finally, and frowns. 'Steve needed her home. But she called me later. Jane, she was really upset. You can't just invalidate her feelings.'

'I'm not! I'm sorry she was upset, honestly I am. It wasn't my intention to upset her, I promise.'

'I just think...' Sophie begins. She appears to hesitate, then decides to continue. 'I just think this week has been hard for you, that's all.'

Jane is so hot she has started to sweat. She can feel the prickle under her arms, the itch on her neck, the heat in her face. The not-quite-argument they are having feels like a quiet catastrophe. And even though they are keeping their voices down, she is aware of people glancing over. She has, she realises, no idea how to reply.

'Well, anyway,' Sophie goes on, 'Lexie wants to organise a baby shower for me, so hopefully you'll be OK with that.'

Jane frowns. 'Well, yeah, of course, I saw that on the Whats-App, but...'

'But what?'

'Just... well, you didn't have a baby shower for Kyle. Expecting people to bring presents for your unborn baby just because you'd had sex with your husband, you said – I remember you saying it.' She remembers how deep it cut, for different reasons.

Sophie flushes pink. 'So what? Are you *judging* me now?'

'No!' Panic rises. 'Not at all. If you want a shower, you should totally have one. I'm sure they're a lot of fun. I just thought... I don't know what I'm saying really. I've got nothing against baby showers per se, but it... it just doesn't seem very *you*, that's all. But maybe it is and that's totally fine – of course it is. Maybe...'

Maybe what? Maybe she doesn't know Sophie as well as she thought. Maybe this is a side of herself Sophie has kept hidden. Maybe she's changed.

But Sophie has slid from her chair and is standing over her, cheeks and neck blazing, eyes glassy. Her chin tips up, her eyelids lower. 'Maybe I *did* want a baby shower for Kyle.'

'What?' In her gut, Jane feels the shift.

'Maybe I just felt *uncomfortable* having one.'

Jane is dumbstruck. But even if she could speak, it is too late, because, head dipped, ears glowing pink, Sophie is striding out of the café.

Uncomfortable, Jane thinks as she watches her friend cross the high street. *She meant uncomfortable because of me.*

CHAPTER TWELVE

JANE

Three tables need clearing. There is a cake wrapper on the floor and a scattering of crumbs. A queue is forming at the till. In the metal jug, milk screams, purrs, growls. Jane grabs the jug from Jude before the milk boils.

'Shout the orders, mate,' she says. 'Sorry about that.'

Jude takes the payments and calls out the coffees. Jane works through them on autopilot, making three, four, five at a time. One oat milk flat white, one chai latte, two regular lattes and a single espresso macchiato. The jug shakes in her hand. She matches the coffees with their owners, aware of herself doing this and somehow – *somehow* – smiling. Once the rush has died down, Jude takes the huge round non-stick tray and swoops through the tables as if on roller skates. Cups and plates are picked off like targets in one of Frankie's computer games. Fighting dizziness and a strong need to cry, Jane cleans the steamer nozzle with more vigour than is strictly required. She is trembling from head to toe.

She has never fought like that with a friend, not at school, not at work, not ever. In the five-plus years she has known Sophie, Sophie has told her off about things, little things, and has been moody on occasion, a bit bossy sometimes, but she has never pulled anything like that, whatever the hell that was. When they met at Jane's first Runner Beans session, she was kindness itself. She even matched her pace to Jane's, despite being a much faster runner, and Jane is in no doubt, now that she knows her better, that this must have been hard for her, naturally competitive as she is. After that first time, Jane gave her a lift home in Frankie's van.

'Oh my God, a van!' Sophie said, climbing in and patting the bench seat with joy. 'This is so cool. I've always wanted to have a ride in one of these. So is your husband, like, a labourer?'

'Well, he's actually a trained accountant, but he hates office work so he requalified and set himself up as a heating engineer. He used to help his dad out when he was younger, so he already knew the ropes. He likes roaming about, going from place to place. He likes fixing things, helping people, you know?'

'Right. Right. So cool! Carl can't even change a fuse. I mean, he's in IT but he knows literally nothing about computers. That's why he's the CEO, ha.'

Outside Sophie's double-fronted Victorian villa with the sleek black Audi parked on the drive, they fell to chatting until they were both shivering with sweat gone cold. Ironically, Sophie had just lost a baby, a confidence she shared there and then. When she began to cry, Jane put her arm around her, told her not to get upset, that it would come right soon enough. They talked it out and talked some more, and even though Jane had told no one back home – not her best friends from school and certainly not her mother – even though she'd decided to tell no one at the club the real reason why she'd joined, to simply say she was on a fitness drive, for some reason, there in the silent van, she told Sophie, even though they had just met.

'Oh, you poor darling,' Sophie had said, eyes watering up again in sympathy. 'That is so tough.'

'Don't tell anyone. I mean, I haven't told anyone.'

'Of course not.' Looking deep into her eyes, Sophie shook her head. 'Not a soul.'

Jane was already regretting it, already realising she'd only offered this piece of herself as a way of making friends, was beginning to worry she'd taken Sophie's pain and made it all about her.

'Anyway,' she blustered, 'all I wanted to say was, if you've conceived once, then the chances are you will again. There's hope.'

'Of course, of course.'

'Miscarriages are really common, especially with a first child. One of my customers had one and she's got four kids now. She reckons she's got too many, in fact; she's sent her other half for the snip!'

Sophie laughed.

'So yeah,' Jane added, into the silence. 'I joined Runner Beans to help with... all of that.'

Sophie, who by then was holding both Jane's hands, rolled her eyes. 'The only reason I joined is to stop my bloody thighs from ballooning. Honestly, since I've got married, I'm getting a right arse on me. If I'm not careful, Carl'll be off with another woman.'

At the time, Jane believed Sophie was joking. No one really thought like that anymore, did they? Frankie wouldn't care what size her arse was, just as she didn't give a hoot about the beer belly he was getting – they loved each other no matter what. God knows, she'd watched her mother store all hope of keeping a man in her appearance, never seeming to understand that shoplifting and drinking yourself unconscious most nights was the thing that made them leave, not a few extra pounds around the hips.

But now, as she tidies and wipes down the countertops, the memory of that night with Sophie alters its shape. Sophie went on to join a plush gym, is now much thinner than she was then, and very worked out. It is as if her body is something Carl owns, and that if it becomes used or imperfect, he will trade her in. Back then, Jane didn't see it that way of course. She was just glad of a friend at a tough, tough time. They'd swapped numbers, and the very next week, Sophie invited her and Frankie to a little gathering she was having.

'I collect people,' she said with an ironic smile, and again, Jane had always assumed she was joking, but now, in the shaky aftermath of their quarrel, she is not so sure.

When she and Frankie got to the party, they saw straight away that the crowd there were wealthier, with understated designer clothes and better shoes, but they were friendly and good fun. It was there that she got chatting to Kath and Hils, whom she knew a little from Runner Beans, and discovered they were well off, yes, but also grounded and funny and unpretentious. Before she knew it, she was part of the Friday drinks gang and Frankie was going out with the 'other halves'. Sophie did that. For her. Sophie gave her the lovely friendship group she has become so attached to.

Which means, of course, that Sophie could take it away.

Jane doesn't sleep well. The argument comes back in flashes. Do women's magazines cover this stuff, she wonders – how bloody awful it is to fall out with your closest friend? She wouldn't know, having stopped buying them in her early twenties. As far as she is concerned, they are up there with Instagram and Facebook: the devil's work, designed to make you feel inadequate.

The next morning, she texts Sophie:

Hey. Sorry things got a bit fraught yesterday. Am honestly truly sorry I upset Lexie, I didn't mean to at all. I'm just a bit socially awkward sometimes. Of course a baby shower will be fun! Hope you're OK anyway. Xx

She drives with Frankie out to Shere and together they take Des on a long walk, throw the invisible ball countless times, remark as they always do how great it is that they never lose it, how utterly stupid their dog is, how much they love him. But Jane is going through the motions, is preoccupied. Sophie hasn't texted back, which could mean she is busy – except she is always on her phone and always texts back.

An e-sending to Coventry then. A ghosting by 4G.

'Hey,' Frankie says. 'You're quiet. You OK?'

'Fine. Still processing Sophie's news and, y'know, wishing I hadn't done that test.'

It is half true. This is why they stopped the treatment. Each disappointment brings its own grief cycle – no one can live like that. If she's honest, the situation with Lexie is bothering her more, but today she wonders if other people's joyous baby news will lock her and Frankie every time into their quiet, separate worlds of pain. They should be talking about it, she thinks. But neither of them wants to bring the other down.

On the way home, she checks her phone. Still nothing. Unease grows within her by the hour. She was perhaps not her warmest self towards Lexie. She did not stand up to hug her when she left. She did not chat to her while she waited for her cab.

But no, Lexie put her on the back foot from the word go. She monopolised her best friend and has immediately caused tension between them.

But maybe she didn't monopolise her. Maybe Sophie was just looking after her because she was new, a bit nervous. Maybe Jane should have chatted to her a bit more, tried a bit harder.

Before she goes to bed, she checks her phone again: nothing. Nothing from a friend who a week ago always texted back immediately. The change is so stark. It is unsettling how alone it makes her feel.

On Monday, there is still no word from Sophie. Jane's feeling of discomfort grows. It is all so unpleasant. It feels so much bigger than it needs to be. And it has happened so *quickly*. She wonders what Kath and Hils think. They looked bored to death on Friday when Lexie proceeded to suck all the humour out of the evening with her self-aggrandising stories and bad-mouthing of other women.

But then Kath and Hils didn't see how she behaved at the bar, did they, didn't see the way she glowered? They don't know that Lexie complained about Jane to Sophie or that Sophie is, apparently, not speaking to her. And perhaps, in all of this, there is some-thing in what Sophie said during the argument. Last week was hard. It was. Sophie's news *did* upset her. Perhaps she *was* being oversensitive, defensive, sarcastic. Perhaps she should not have gone on Friday. Perhaps she should've taken more time to process things. Perhaps meeting Lexie after Sophie's news was a bit much.

Yes, perhaps she was a bit rude. A bit.

It's quiet in the café, so Jane spring-cleans all the cupboards and the fridges and returns home grimy and exhausted. Frankie is already asleep. She eats a piece of toast standing up in the kitchen, showers and goes to bed at 10 p.m.

On Tuesday morning, when there is still no word, she texts Sophie again. It takes a couple of attempts to find the right tone:

Hey. Did you get my text? Are you swinging by today? Wd be gd to chat before Runner Beans. X

Especially, she thinks, if Lexie is going to be there. Jane doesn't think she can face Lexie and Sophie together without talking to Sophie first.

The reply comes, but it is hours later: *Sure. Will try and pop in.*

She'll *try* and pop in. As if it's an effort, not something she does every single week. Jane hates herself for noticing the absence of a kiss on the text. What is she, twelve?

But late afternoon comes and there is no sign of Sophie, and no text to say she can't make it after all. Jane closes up the café and walks her bike home, brooding, wondering whether to text again. Pride tells her not to. But pride shouldn't come into it, surely? It isn't a competition; they're not scoring points.

Hey, she texts again. This time it takes several attempts to compose a message. *Sorry not to see you at the café. Are you going to RB later?*

To her near-ecstatic relief, the rolling ellipsis starts up instantly. Sophie is responding immediately, like she used to.

But the reply is a punch in the gut.

Yep. Lexie's picking me up at 7.

'Right,' Jane says, to herself, momentarily winded. 'Right.'

There is no doubt – after more than five years of close friendship, Sophie is now giving her the cold shoulder.

'Right,' Jane says again, shaking her head in dismay.

There is no way she's going to running club, that much is obvious. Sophie and Lexie arriving together in force feels too much like an ambush. She's not feeling strong enough to face that. She needs more time to get her head around the pregnancy and Lexie's apparent shit-stirring before she risks making a mess of things like she obviously did on Friday.

She sends a jokey message to the group, so that it doesn't look like she's making some sort of point. She isn't; she just can't, cannot possibly, go through with it.

Hey guys! Guess who pulled a hamstring walking the dog this morning! Clue: me! I'll be back next week. Don't forget to warm up, and have a good one! J xx

Later, as she is heading up to join Frankie in bed, a WhatsApp message pings. It is from Lexie to Friday Drinks.

Hey gang. Great to see you all tonight. Sorry you couldn't make it, J-J, but just to say, Sofes and I have decided on Saturday 13 April for her shower, so put it in your diaries! Woohoo!

Cool, comes the reply from Hils.

In diary, from Kath.

From Sophie, a single heart emoji.

Jane stares at the phone. She cannot go to that baby shower. She cannot. No way in hell. She'd rather stick pins in—

The phone rings, alive in her hand. *Lexie Lane*. Lexie is calling her? What the hell?

'Hello?'

'Janie, babes. Hi, it's Lex.'

Janie. Babes.

'Yes,' Jane replies, closing her eyes, biting her lip. 'I mean, hi, Lexie. Everything OK?'

'Everything's fine, hun. Just thought I should give you a quick ring, because I know Sofes is too sweet to call you herself, but just to say, I really hope you can come to the shower. I know Sofes will be gutted if you don't and I just think *someone* should organise something, 'cause she needs the support of her friends right now, do you know what I mean?'

'Right,' Jane manages, reeling. Lexie has called to tell her how to be a friend to her own friend. Is that what's happening here?

'I know you guys had words,' Lexie adds, 'but she'll calm down, you know she will, and between you, me and the gatepost, I don't think Carl's being as supportive as he could be. I just think we need to be there for her.'

Jane opens her mouth but can think of nothing, not one thing, to say.

'Janie? Are you still there? Can I count you in, hun?'

'I... er, I...' Jane stammers, head spinning. 'Er, yeah. Of course. I just hadn't had time to reply, that's all. I only got the message a few seconds ago.'

'Great. I'll tell Sofes, and I know she'll really appreciate it.' Lexie gives a contented sigh. 'See you on Friday! Take care, hun. Byeee.'

The line dies. A moment later, Jane finds herself sitting halfway up the stairs in the dark, staring at her phone, with no clear idea what just happened. She creeps back downstairs and into the kitchen. Pours herself a glass of water and sits on a stool at the bar, waiting for the confusion to clear, for her adrenaline levels to go down and bring her heart rate with them.

So, she thinks. To recap. Just so she knows she's not losing her mind.

Sophie has moaned to Lexie about their argument.

Lexie has apparently provided a sympathetic ear for a problem she herself caused.

Lexie has just called, in the role of Sophie's best friend, to tell Jane – *Janie* – not to worry about *Sofes* being angry with her, as if she were here to smooth things over.

She has done this without one shred of acknowledgement that she is the source of the trouble.

As Jane runs the short conversation over and over in her mind, layers of revelation accumulate like dust. This woman has been in her life for a matter of days – *days*. And now Jane has been brow-beaten by a stranger into going to a party she – according to Lexie's pass-agg insinuations – should have organised because Sophie *needs the support of her friends right now*.

There is no way out. Lexie has used a kind of emotional black-mail-by-proxy to get her to agree to come to an event she absolutely cannot bear the thought of but which now, she knows, she will have to attend. Because if she kicks up a fuss or says plainly that she cannot go, things will become strained. And if things break down any further with Sophie, the friendship will founder and it will be too awkward to go to Runner Beans, or Friday-night drinks. There will be no more social life, no more fun friendships. Life in the town she lives in will become difficult and stressful. She will find herself crossing the road to avoid awkward, distant greetings with people she used to be close to. Because now her place in the friendship group she loves so much is dependent on her going to that shower.

Wow.

She drinks her glass of water down in one go. Slowly, the confusion she has felt these last days falls away. She's been the victim of a master stroke of manipulation. It is possible that Sophie has been a victim too. The fake Christian Dior bag, the champagne cocktails, and now the baby shower. Isn't that what they call love-bombing? Jane read about it in one of the Sunday supplements the other month. It has happened so quickly it has all but taken her breath away. And now, whatever Lexie's plans are for Sophie, Jane is part of them. And the problem is, much as she hates the word that Lexie seems to bandy about so freely, a word once tied to a brick and thrown through the window of Jane's childhood home, if she doesn't go to this godawful baby shower, the only one who will look like *that word* is her.

CHAPTER THIRTEEN

FRANKIE

Natasha calls him a couple of weeks later, on the Tuesday. He'd almost forgotten about the encounter in the pub but recognises her name when she says it, her low, well-spoken voice, her way of sounding confident and just a little bit flirty.

'Remember me?' she says with a breathy laugh. 'The demon pint spiller of old Wimbham town?'

He laughs. 'Of course. You all right?'

'I'm very well, thank you. Listen, are you still available to come and see my bathroom?'

'Sure, sure. Course.'

He agrees to call in the next day after work and asks her to text the address. When he hears nothing, he begins to think she's changed her mind, but the next morning an address in an expensive part of Barnes lands in his phone, signed off with the initial T, which confuses him until he realises she must go by *Tasha*. At the memory of her, he feels himself blush. He didn't fancy her, it wasn't that, but he let himself get a bit flirty when she did, and in the cold light of day this makes him feel disloyal. He keeps his text businesslike, doesn't want to give her the wrong idea. He'd never, never do anything like that to Jane.

Got it. Should be there after 6. Frank Reece

While he remembers, he texts Jane:

Hi, babe. I'll be back late. Quoting for a bathroom in Barnes. Xx

The house is proper massive. A modern architect job, sectioned into big cubes, with great sheets of glass and horizontal struts that look like oak or cedar or some quality wood like that. At the front, there's a row of round trees and silver orb thing, palm plants, ferns – no roses, nothing pretty. No car on the driveway either, so he parks the van there and jumps out, boots crunching on the gravel.

The doorbell is silent outside but he hears it chime deep in the belly of the house. Dusk has brought the external lights up; he imagines they come on automatically – a soft orangey glow that's there before you're even aware of it. Everything is tasteful in the understated way that comes with confidence as well as money, the know-how his richer clients seem to carry in their genes.

He bets Natasha's other half wears a Swatch. Or no watch at all.

No, that's sexist. Natasha might be the MD of—

The door opens. At the sight of her, he almost apologises. She must have forgotten he was coming, because she isn't dressed, not properly. She's wearing Ugg boots, silky pink shorts edged in white, and a grey top thing that has fallen off her shoulder. No strap. She isn't wearing a bra. She is tanned from head to toe. Or maybe that's just her skin tone, her colouring dark apart from those call-of-the-wild eyes, like a husky or a wolf.

'You said to call round,' he says after a moment. 'I'm a bit late, sorry, I should have phoned first.'

'It's fine,' she says, smiling, stepping back to let him in. 'I'm afraid you'll have to excuse me though – I'm in my loungewear. I was just having a glass of wine actually. Would you like one?'

It's seven o'clock in the evening and he's been on the go for twelve hours; of course he wants a glass of wine. He shouldn't, but one unit won't hurt. And he doesn't want to be rude. The house, her appearance have made him a bit nervous.

By the time he's taken off one work boot, she's gone ahead. As he pulls off the second, she disappears around a corner at the far end of the white hallway.

He closes the door and hobbles after her – feet swelling into the freedom of his sweaty socks. He glances back, horrified to see the fading moisture prints of his toes on the polished concrete floor. He thinks about dashing back, putting the boots back on. But he can't exactly go traipsing through this place in his dusty work boots, can he? He should have gone home and changed, put on a fresh T-shirt, clean trainers, but it's too late now.

He finds her in the state-of-the-art dove-grey gloss kitchen, which gives onto the back garden. The back wall is almost entirely made of glass. Outside, on slabs of stone, pools of light paint the underside of shrubs and trees a creamy white; the same creamy white splashes on cubes that echo the house design, their centres dark with soil, more spiky plants. In the back corner, clad in black, a summer house hunkers behind ferns that look like something off a David Attenborough documentary. The chalet has been dug out of the lawn, steps leading down to it, like a whole separate property – bigger than his parents' bungalow in Sunbury, or about the same size anyway. At the rear is a slim rectangle of impeccable grass, another silver sphere the size of a baby elephant about a third of the way in. It takes him another second to realise its undulating surface is in fact flowing water.

'Nice place,' he understates helplessly as she hands him the glass of white wine he never actually said yes to. It is the size of a balloon – there must be at least half a pint in there. He will sip it, to be polite. He won't finish it.

'Sorry my husband's not here. Gareth works away a lot, so you'll have to make do with me, I'm afraid.' She meets his gaze incredibly directly, though she is more subdued than in the pub.

Sweat pricks at his hairline. The banter the other week was all very well, but it was just that – a bit of harmless chat late on a Friday night in a crowded pub. He'd assumed she was as drunk as everyone else in there, thought she'd be straighter today, more businesslike. Clothed. There's a lot of flesh on display. The heating must be on full blast, because it's really warm in here. Her get-up isn't for him, he doesn't think. She probably just likes to have a hot house and chill out in her PJs. There's no way she's dressed like that for him, no way.

'Come and sit down,' she says, going ahead once again, crossing the hallway.

He takes a large gulp of the chilled wine – it's very dry, he thinks, though he's not a big white wine drinker so he's not exactly primed for top notes of gooseberry or anything. He follows her through to a living room so vast it has different zones – three sofas make a horseshoe around a television screen the size of a pool table in one part, a smallish grand piano stands in another, and a table and twelve upholstered dining chairs in another. Two of the walls are almost entirely made of bookshelves, which meet at the corner. Like the kitchen, the back wall gives onto that enormous garden.

She sits on the far end of the sofa and pats a space next to her. 'Sit!'

He takes another long gulp of wine, worries that his feet probably smell. He wishes he'd left his shoes on, wishes he'd asked her if he could wash his hands, which feel sticky. He wishes he hadn't come. He's not sure he understands what's going on.

'I need to get back,' he says, perching on the edge of the cushion nearest the door. 'I'll just take a look at the bathroom, thanks.'

She cocks her head, eyebrows rising in amusement, and tips her hand to her forehead in a sarcastic salute.

'OK, boss,' she says. 'Very professional.' She gets up.

In his confusion, he almost drains his glass. He gets the impression he's offended her. Which would be a shame. Judging by the house, this will be a well-paid job. He can pay back the stupid watch, maybe even tell Jane about it, have a laugh at his own expense. Or he can sell it on eBay, which in that moment he decides to do anyway. He's starting to hate the damn thing – its yellow face burns on his eyelids and, like the sun, he can see it after he's closed his eyes. He can see it even when it's hiding in the glove compartment of the van or at the back of his bedside drawer. He can see it for what it is: a sad shake of the head for every failure of judgement he's ever made, a reminder of his stupidity, the vain little man inside the one who pretends he's above caring about all that status, all that stuff.

He stands up just as Natasha drifts past, lifting his glass from his hand in one smooth motion. She smells of freshly cut limes, and her hair reminds him of his mum and dad's mahogany dining table.

He follows her, is aware that this is all he's done since he got here, follow her like a dog. She's gone back into the kitchen. He finds her pouring more wine into their glasses, these ridiculous goblets big enough for a goldfish. He raises his hand, *Stop*, but she either doesn't see or doesn't take any notice. He takes the glass from her without a word. He will just hold it. She can't make him drink it, after all.

'Let's go to the bathroom then,' she says, widening her eyes, and again he feels like she's telling him off, reads in the words she doesn't say an affronted *since you're so keen to leave*.

'Sure.'

She laughs; he isn't sure why. A glance over her shoulder, her forefinger curling, she says: 'Follow me.'

CHAPTER FOURTEEN

JANE

On Wednesday, Frankie texts to say he'll be late. He's going to quote for installing a bathroom over in Barnes.

OK, babe, Jane replies with a sinking feeling – another night in alone.

Bored, a bit lonely and aware that she's had her mother on her mind lately, she decides to bite the bullet and call her, a decision she regrets almost the moment she gets through.

'Jane? Is that you? Bloody hell, I thought you'd dropped dead.'

Victoria Preston, ladies and gentlemen. My dear mother.

'No,' she replies evenly. 'I'm just busy. How're things?'

'Oh, you know.'

Down the line, Jane hears her mother drinking. It might be tea, she thinks, then thinks how incredible it is that all these years later, this hope still comes to her.

'So,' she perseveres. 'What've you been up to?'

'I was beginning to think you'd dropped dead.' The words are not only repeated and no kind of answer, but also slurred. Jane closes her eyes momentarily. Not tea. Definitely not tea.

'Still alive I'm afraid,' she says calmly.

'Chris left.'

'Chris?'

'You know. From the hardware shop.'

She has no idea who her mother means. 'Oh no. That's a shame.'

'Judgemental prig. Went off with the Hot Pilates instructor. I wouldn't mind, but it was me who introduced him to Hot Pilates in the first place.'

'Oh well, better off without him.'

'You're not wrong. You are *not* wrong.' Her mother takes a breath, another swig of whatever it is. And launches in.

Jane holds the phone a little away from her ear but near enough that she will hear when her mother stops talking and be ready to add an affirmative *hmm*. The monologue will be the same as it always is: men, can't live with 'em, can't shoot 'em. Another swig, the strange phonics of her mother saying something while her lips are still on the glass. Jane pulls the phone a little further from her ear, for a break, but the rising intonation tells her Victoria is asking a question. She replaces it.

'You remember Donald?' her mother is saying. 'The head teacher?'

A flashing image of her mother pressing the letter into her hand, the funnelling of the paper under the hard press of her thumb. *Make sure you give it to him, into his hands, do you hear? Into his hands.*

The hard wood of his office door against her knuckles.

'Come in.'

'Sorry, sir. My mum said to give you this.'

She would have been what? Fourteen? A mass of raging hormones and near-crippling self-consciousness. End of Year 9, she thinks. Mr Dawes, the head teacher, at his desk. Bushy black eyebrows meeting over his glasses, her vague disgust at what she half knew about him and her mother – the noises they thought she couldn't hear coming from her mother's room. The desk stacked with leaning towers of dog-eared paper. The relief when he told her she could go. The click of his office door behind her as she pulled it shut. The heat in her face in the noisy school corridor.

The foggy yet certain knowledge that she had been used as her mother's messenger for something darker than she could understand.

A week later, a month, she's not sure, Mr Dawes moved into their house.

'Call me Donald now.' The bushy eyebrows meeting, the dried splash on the lens of his spectacles, the mild nausea that would become part of her biological make-up. 'Mr Dawes at school, Donald at home, OK?'

But that summer, they moved. And by the time the new school year started, Jane had been transferred to a different school. It was awkward, her mother had told her, for Donald, being the head and that. There was a worry Jane might get bullied. They were not concerned enough to tell her this until three days before, when her mother laid the new uniform on her bed and told her she must thank Donald later because he'd paid for all of it, even the sports kit. She can remember wondering later if the hasty move was connected to the brick through the window a month or two earlier. Donald's wife, she has always presumed. Though the details are foggy, the last person she's about to ask is her mother. She has never even asked what happened to her own father.

'Mr Dawes,' she says now. She has used his surname on purpose. Not exactly sticking it to her mother, but it makes her feel about half a per cent better.

'Don't call him tha'! He bloody lived withuss for three years.'

To his credit, he lasted longer than the others.

'So, you saw him, you said?' She hears her voice, bright with management, hates herself for it – managing her own mother.

Down the line, the trickle of booze into glass. A short trickle, no shh of bubbles. Vodka, then. 'Saw him in the new wossername, the new Morrison's. Looss old. Hair compledely white now, would y'b'lieve? Said I hadn't changed a day, noddaday.'

She steels herself; her mother is sliding even as they speak. 'Is he on the scene again?'

'God, no! Wouldn' pissh on him if he were on fire... I wouldn'...

No, he was with some young thing fit tobee issown daughter, y'know? Lives in Chester now, la-di-da. Anyway, why you calling? You pregnant or sommink?'

Nice one. A deft ice pick to the solar plexus.

'Mum? Listen, Frankie's on the other line. I'll call you back, OK? Just give me a sec.' She hangs up, relief drawing down her shoulders, guilt landing a second later. She has cut her own mother off. But two things: one, her mother will not remember that she called, and two, Jane cut her off a long time ago, mentally if not physically. It was the only way of hanging on to herself. She is not responsible for what her mother is like. Frankie taught her that. Frankie, oh Frankie, where is he? It's nearly nine o'clock – he said it was a quote; surely a quote doesn't take this long?

She texts him: *Hey, love, you OK?*

No reply.

She watches some Netflix, texts again a little later: *Everything OK?*

Nothing.

She tries to see where he is on the app, but his phone must be off because he is untraceable. Not unusual; his phone is always dying – he forgets to charge it at night. He must have got called somewhere else. There's always someone with a blocked loo, leaking shower tray, you name it. There's always someone who needs him more than her.

Too antsy to sit still, she fires up her Kindle, lies on the sofa and tries to read the latest in the Kim Stone series. Des curls up beside her, his head on her shins. Just as he loves to chase the invisible ball, so he loves to read a good detective novel. With his eyes closed.

The hours pass. She finishes the book, which was gripping – enough to take her mind off her troubles. It is 11 p.m. This is late even for Frankie.

Hey again, she texts. *Assuming you've been called to an emergency but please let me know you're OK. I'm getting worried xxx*

She hasn't told him about the drama with Sophie and Lexie.

She hasn't seen him to tell him. She's not sure if she's even mentioned Lexie to him. She hasn't wanted to burden him, that much is true, but maybe part of her is aware that what's happening to her right now is what they call playground politics. Only nothing like this ever happened to her in actual school, where there was an actual playground. There, she had two best friends, Carla and Penny, and they were both great. She sees both of them only occasionally, because they both still live up north, both with kids now, but all they ever did at school was laugh themselves silly, even when boys came on the scene. She's heard other women talking about their hellish school days, but for Jane it was an escape from the hell at home. So yes, part of her wonders how she would find the words to tell Frankie what's happening. She isn't sure she knows them herself.

She could call Kath or Hils. But what would she say? *Lexie told Sophie I was rude to her and now Sophie won't speak to me?*

No. Just no. She would sound ridiculous. She sounds like a child even in her own mind. If challenged, Sophie would say she's been busy and texted Jane to that effect. Why is Jane causing trouble? Jane is overreacting. Jane is jealous. Jane is petty. And it is petty. Yet she is *floored* by how much distress it has caused her, how trapped she feels, how all her enthusiasm for the things she loved only a week or two ago – Runner Beans and their pant-wettingly funny Friday nights – has all but evaporated.

Is it possible for one person to do this? Surely not?

Her phone beeps. She startles, blinks. Her phone tells her it's 2.03 a.m. There's a text from Frankie.

OMG sorry babe, phone died. Emergency over in Wimbledon. Absolute nightmare. On way back now. Xx

Relief hits her in the chest – so hard she bursts into tears.

CHAPTER FIFTEEN

JANE

Legs under the duvet and she's too hot; legs out and she's too cold. The joys of the thirty-something menopausal woman. At the foot of the bed, Des snores softly, as if to rub it in. Frankie won't be long now.

Restless, she switches on the bedside light, grabs her phone and opens Instagram. She has been lax, hasn't posted any A Roasted Development updates for weeks. She came off personal social media completely at some point during the IVF – it was more than she could handle trying to live the life she had without having a window into the edited highlights of other people's. Knowing it isn't real didn't help, or didn't help enough. These days, she's only on Instagram for her business. Now the café has taken off, it's enough to keep up with the publicity posts and to repost customers lovely enough to take a photo of a perfect flat white and give her a plug.

Since Sophie mentioned Lexie's Instagram profile, Jane has promised herself she wouldn't look at it. But now, in the lonely dark, tired, a little anxious, she cannot help herself. There are a couple of accounts under *lexielane* that turn out to be private; the third, lexielane1991, has a thumbnail that looks like Lexie and the name Alexandra Lane underneath. The 1991 must be for her birth year. Crikey, she's still in her twenties.

Jane goes to the account.

Lexie Lane. Three love hearts followed by: *Girl about town. Traveller. Life lover.* Underneath is written: *Beauty is Truth, Truth is Beauty. That's all you need to know, guys.*

'"Truth beauty",' Jane mutters, GCSE English branded on her brain. Lexie hasn't even attributed it to Keats, just put it there as if it's her own wisdom. Is it supposed to make her look *deep?*

The first five images pummel her – they are all of Lexie and Sophie, one from Friday-night drinks. Neither Jane nor Hils nor Kath were there that night, it would seem. The pub is tagged, Sipsmith is tagged, Fever-Tree is tagged and Sophie is tagged. Good grief, Jane thinks, why not tag the loo roll? The brand of soap, the hand lotion in the Ladies? Hashtags include *#girlsnight #girlsnightout #friendsaregold #friends.* Jane doesn't read the rest.

There is one of the champagne cocktail night: Lexie and Sophie, glasses raised, looking polished smooth and somehow tanned, not to mention younger, with the simple caption: *S losing her champagne cocktail virginity. Oh dear, LOL.* A dozen hashtags follow: *#friends #cocktails #bestfriends #bestfriendsforever...* The list continues long after Jane has glazed over.

She scrolls, cursing herself – how could she have not expected this? Has Sophie seen it? Wouldn't she have found it a bit overkill, being a hashtag best friend on what looks like it must have been their first date? Because yes, a date is what it looks like.

Once she's scrolled past the lovefest of Sophie and Lexie, there are some stylised pictures of Lexie draped in various outfits, coats, swimwear. The images are all smooth, the colours vibrant and warm. In none of the pictures is Lexie's face fully visible. Many are taken from the back, to show that mane of glossy caramel hair, often ringleted at the end, and a perfect peach-shaped bottom. There is no mistaking the fabulous figure – the long legs, the square, athletic shoulders. Lexie has a tattoo of a rose the diameter of a coffee cup on her toned, tanned upper left arm – *#tattoos #newink #roses*, a heartfelt thanks to @davieinks, who is presumably the tattoo artist. On some photos, her hair is blonder, on some reddish, even pink...

One photo does show her whole face, close up. A red mouth, lips fuller than Lexie's real-life ones, blows a kiss. The perfectly made-up eyes are the vibrant green of Kiwi fruit flesh rather than the plain green of, say, an actual eye, the complexion silkier, but it is unmistakably Lexie – staring right at her. Caption: *Here's lookin atcha*. Hashtag... oh, who cares?

There are more half-hidden portraits – some of one side of her face, some of her mouth and chin, some of her intense eyes, sometimes as dark as hazel, sometimes hinting at turquoise or teal. They create a kind of mystery, a kind of tease: I'm looking back at you; I'm spying on you. But you will only see what I want you to see, you will never know me, not really. Jane suspects there is little to know, that a scratch to the surface would reveal yet more surface. But it is very effective. Enticing, even.

There are a *lot* of photos of coffee distributed throughout: iced lattes, cappuccinos, flat whites, all photographed from above and tagged, to Jane's mild irritation, @starbucksuk or @caffenero

No Monday until I've had my coffee, LOL! reads one caption.

I wouldn't say I'd die without coffee, just saying other people might, LOL! reads another. Hashtags abound.

There are cocktails too, so many cocktails, in every colour; fuzzy hints of trendy bar interiors, the occasional shot of a muscular tattooed arm or the side profile of a man Jane assumes is Steve. All have cutesy captions along the lines of *The sun is over the yardarm somewhere, LOL!* or *Cheeky cocktail with the gorgeous Mr!* accompanied by winking emojis, kissing emojis, love-hearts-for-eyes emojis, tags with names of bars, cocktail companies, brands of vodka, gin, whisky, countless hashtags... Really, Jane could learn from this.

What else?

Tropical fish. *On hols in Meheecooooo.*

White clouds through a plane window. *Time to go home* – sad face emoji – *till the next holibobs!* – winking face; *#foreigntravel #holiday #escapetothesun*, etc., etc.

There are poached eggs atop avocado toast, cherry tomatoes wilted on the vine, balls of ice cream piled high in sundae glasses – *#foodporn #foodiesofinstagram* and on and on; rose petals in a hotel bath; bubbles rising in champagne flutes; the silhouette of a muscular man on... is that Brighton Pier? Ah, yes – *Brighton Rocks, LOL, #beachlife*; a private swimming pool, *#outdoorpool, #swim*; toenails with the edge of a fluffy white bathrobe – *thank you @corinthialondon, #spaday #pedicure #luxury*; an enormous living room with a television as big as a table-tennis table, part of an interiors-themed photo slideshow – *#homesweethome #livinginbeauty #livinglifeincolour #beautifulhomes*, a long list of similar; a gleaming gym; another gleaming gym, another fifty hashtags varying from *#fitness* to *#muscles* to *#perfectbodies*; an ornate front garden to rival Hampton Court, all the gardening hashtags; the hint of an amazing house, hashtags a-go-go; a huge black car – *Hello, Lex, gotta new motor? Love my new Beemer, thank you @bmw...* It goes on and on, too many screaming lifestyle signifiers to absorb, every photo tagged and hashtagged to absolute buggery.

Jane scrolls and scrolls, gripped by a kind of morbid fascination she cannot break.

Who lives a life like this? Who defines their life like this? Who finds meaning in all this... stuff?

Lexie Lane obviously.

Sophie never said what Lexie does for a living.

This, Jane suspects. Maybe this is what she does. She is young, younger – young people do this stuff, don't they? It is like breathing to them; they live their lives here, in this augmented reality.

Then what on earth is Lexie doing in this actual reality, hanging out with a bunch of trainer-wearing women, two of whom must be nearly twenty years older and whose idea of a cool jacket is a breathable cagoule? Although, come to think of it, none of them feature here, do they? Perhaps she's hoping to erase them in real life just as she has from her online life. Sophie, the most glamorous of them, the most Instagrammable, is the one Lexie has chosen

And what about Sophie – Sofes, now – who always professed to hate Instagram and *all that bollocks* – actual words she said... what is the attraction? Sophie, whose eyebrows were different on Friday. Sofes, who now loves a champagne cocktail. Sophie/Sofes, who collects people.

No. She can't. She can't start thinking like that. Sophie is her mate, her best mate. They've had a row, that's all, and she has some sort of crush on this woman, but it will blow over. It will.

She checks her notifications. The café has been tagged in three posts: one is an oat milk flat white posted by one of her regulars, with the caption: *Best flat white in South London, end of.* Coffee and lifestyle hashtags run away in a long list. Everyone is so much better at this social media stuff than Jane is. Maybe Scarlett could do some when the café is quiet, teach her the tricks. She types her thanks, checks and thanks the other one – a double espresso macchiato with simply: *Perfection @aroasteddev.* The third tag is a murky beige mess of what might once have been a latte, and instantly Jane's nose wrinkles in disgust. But the caption shocks her to the roots of her hair: *Worst #cafelatte ever. Do not go to @aroasteddev on Wimbham High Street. Rude service too. Disappointing.*

'What?'

The account is someone called Gourmet on the Go. The profile photo is a blueberry muffin, by the looks of it. The photograph is the only one on the account and it is not, absolutely not, a coffee from Jane's café. The crockery is different, for a start, that's not one of her tabletops, and she would never, ever let anyone serve or drink a coffee like that – the milk has clearly been boiled to an insipid foamless mess.

But she has no time to investigate further, because a key rattles in the front door.

Frankie, thank God.

She switches off her phone and waits for the one solid human being in her life to come upstairs and hold her tight.

But fifteen minutes later, Frankie is still clinking about downstairs. Impatient and beyond sleep, Jane goes down to find him at the kitchen bar, head cradled in his hands and a half-empty wine glass in front of him. Odd. He never drinks wine unless he's eating.

When she says his name, he startles. When he looks up at her, she falters. His blue eyes are shot with red.

'Frankie? Oh my God, are you OK?'

He shakes his head. His face crumples. Through all they've faced, she has never seen him cry. Heat kindles in her stomach. She crosses the room to him, but he holds out a hand, keeping her at arm's length.

'I stink,' he says, grimacing. 'I've been up to my elbows in... y'know. I need a shower.'

'OK.' She wants to say she doesn't care, but he does, so she gives him space. But still, something about him isn't right. 'Did something happen?'

He gulps the rest of his wine, grimaces, as if it tastes disgusting. She wonders how much he's drunk in the short time he's been home.

'Is it Sophie's news? If it is, I'm over it, don't worry.'

'That's good. That's good, babe.'

'Franks. You look terrible. You're working way too much. You must have been on the go for what, eighteen hours? You have to start saying no to people, OK? We don't need a world trip. That was just... something to focus on while we got ourselves together. I'd be happy camping in Wales if I was doing it with you. Honestly. I hate seeing you so tired.'

He nods. Sniffs.

They stay like that, in the silence and the dark, for a long while, until Jane shivers with the cold, at which Frankie sniffs again, straightens up and places a hand over his eyes.

'I'm so sorry,' he says. 'I love you – you know that, don't you?'

'There's nothing to be sorry about. Sophie's baby isn't your fault and neither is me doing that stupid test. And I love you too, you idiot. Obvs.'

He grimaces, as if what she's said has caused him physical pain, and for a moment she thinks he's going to cry again.

But instead, he whispers only, 'I love you so much.'

And for some reason, it makes her feel unfathomably sad.

CHAPTER SIXTEEN

JANE

On Friday morning, Sophie finally texts: *Are you coming tonight? X*

No acknowledgement of the argument, of Jane's attempts to talk about it, of the fact that they haven't spoken all week. It seems like the ghosting is over. Jane is out of the doghouse. The relief this causes is almost overwhelming, as is the subsequent disappointment she feels in herself for being so relieved. When did she become so pathetic? She should be telling Sophie and Lexie to fuck off, frankly. Who puts their friends in the doghouse for days on end, for goodness' sake?

But Sophie is asking a question: is she going to drinks?

With Lexie there and without having seen Sophie for a coffee to smooth things over, it is the last thing Jane wants to do, but she supposes she has to, otherwise it's going to look like she's avoiding everyone. And if Sophie and Lexie want to act as if nothing has happened, then so will she.

Of course! she replies. *See you there! X*

Jane arrives late, planning to leave early. She won't drink too much. She cannot afford to lose control.

The pub is packed. Hils and Kath are already there, but there is no sign of Sophie or Lexie. Jane had hoped that by arriving late, she could somehow manage the situation, choose where to sit. But actually, it might be good to see Hils and Kath on their own.

'Jane!' Hils is grinning at her. Kath is already pouring her a glass of fizz. 'Sit down, woman. How the hell are you? We missed you at Runners.'

For the first time in a week, Jane feels something close to happiness. This, *this* is what she can't lose, why she will avoid drama at all costs. She sits down and takes the glass from Kath.

'Up yours,' she says.

'Up yours!' Kath and Hils laugh at the well-worn toast, Kath adding: 'Cheers, lovely. So good to see you.'

Jane looks about her. 'No Sophie?'

'Not unless she's under the chair.' Hils slugs back a good half a glass.

'No Lexie though,' Kath chimes in.

'Every cloud,' Hils mutters – perfectly audibly.

Jane laughs, hope rising. But a squealing sound is coming from behind her head.

'Sorry we're late.' It is Sophie's voice.

And now Sophie is shuffling along the bench. Her coat falls open to reveal a loose blue shirt over her skinny jeans, an indica-tion that her clothes are getting tight already – Sophie always, always tucks her blouse in. The Martin Scorsese eyebrows have made another appearance, and as she passes under the light, her foundation is tan and thick on her skin, the apples of her cheeks coral pink. Her eyes have black licks of fifties-style eyeliner, her lips are wet with gloss. Her hair, usually loose or pulled into a messy bun, has been straightened and curled at the ends.

She looks like a different person.

She looks... a bit like Lexie.

'Sorry, girls.' Lexie appears. She too is wearing a loose blue shirt – the same shirt, in fact, as Sophie, over skinny jeans with a trendy rip at the knee. How bizarre. 'My fault we're late. I was giving this one a makeover.' She thumbs at Sophie and rolls her eyes, as if to say: *The things I do for my friends*.

Jane smiles as best she can. She will not get up and buy a round, she will not. Absolutely no way.

'Shall I get another bottle?' She is on her feet, as if pulled up by invisible strings. 'Lexie, same as last week? You like the Sipsmith, don't you? Double, slimline Fever-Tree on the side, am I right?' She smiles. She can do this. Rise above. Stay classy.

Lexie's face almost falls. She gives a curt nod, her mouth set in a line. 'Thanks, yeah.'

Jane waits. Sophie is chatting to Kath but eventually looks up. Jane manages to catch her eye. 'Lime and soda for you, Sofe? You can always have one glass of the fizz if you fancy. You're allowed one, aren't you?'

'Actually,' Lexie says, 'I'll have a Virgin Mary.'

'A what?' Realising her question might have sounded rude, Jane clamps her mouth shut before trying again. 'I mean, what's a Virgin Mary? Sorry, I've never heard of one, that's all.'

'Tomato juice, hun. Big Tom if they've got it. No vodka. I'm... I'm not drinking tonight.' To Jane's confusion, Lexie is looking at her with open hostility, her eyes blazing coals, her mouth a mean smirk, all totally at odds with her tone of voice.

Jane glances towards the others, for witnesses, but they are chatting and have not seen. Her body fills with something like dread. Whatever is happening is as instant, as unpleasant, as invisible as a gas leak. But if she leaves now, there will be no opportunity to clear the air with Sophie. Besides, these women are her family, at least what has to pass for her family, and she's buggered if she's going to let bloody Lexie bully her out of her own friendship group with this, this *nothing*. There is, for the moment at least, no way to tackle this invisible gas without looking oversensitive – a bit mad, even.

Hils looks up momentarily. 'You OK, Jane? Do you need a hand?'

'I'm on a health kick!' Lexie laughs, touches Jane affectionately on the arm. The transformation is instantaneous. 'A bit of solidarity for Sofes, y'know?'

Jane tries to laugh too, but what escapes is more like a sigh. Her nerve endings feel like they've been exposed to a stiff wind.

'Tomato juice,' she says to Lexie, giving a thumbs up. And to Hils: 'I'm OK, mate, cheers.'

She returns ten minutes later and puts the loaded tray on the table.

'Aw babes,' Lexie says. 'Did you get the Worcester sauce and the Tabasco?' Her nose is wrinkled up, her head cocked to one side in apparent sympathy. 'Sorry.'

'Right. Sorry. One second.'

By the time Jane reaches the bar for the second time, she knows beyond any doubt that she cannot stay. This awful woman has got her running around like a waitress on speed.

When she gets back to the table, armed with the requested condiments for her ladyship, Lexie clears her throat and smiles, one hand to her collarbone in that now-familiar pose, the other hovering over her stomach.

The group falls silent. And in that moment, Jane knows, knows with absolute certainty, what Lexie is going to say next, Lexie, who ordered a tomato juice and who is now giving a coy shrug, looking up shyly through her lashes. But she is not shy. She is not at all shy. She glances now at Sophie, and when she speaks, it is to Sophie alone.

'Just wanted to say one tiny thing. I mean, I suspected it last week but I just thought I was, y'know, a bit late, but then I found out for sure and I wanted to tell you so, so much when we went for coffee on Tuesday, but you were still so excited and I, I dunno, I didn't want to, y'know, make it about me, but the thing is, yeah, the thing is...'

Sophie glances at Lexie's hand over her belly. 'Oh my God,' she almost shrieks. 'You're pregnant too?'

Jane's chest empties. Her hand covers her mouth, the impulse to be sick throwing her forward. But she isn't sick, not quite.

Lexie is squealing. She and Sophie are embracing, rocking each other from side to side, laughing, crying, breaking apart, wiping their eyes, embracing again.

Time slows. Before any of them have time to react, or perhaps sensing that none of them know how to, Lexie lets go of Sophie, turns to the rest of them and raises her glass high. 'And just to let you guys know, I've booked our baby shower, woo!'

Sophie frowns. 'Our?'

'I thought we could have a joint one, yeah? Yeah, babe? So I was thiiinnnkinnng... wait till you hear this: I've booked' – Lexie's eyes moisten; she holds up a forefinger – 'the actual Ritz!' She gives a small, quiet, feminine scream. 'Afternoon tea, champagne, the works. My treat, OK? No arguments! We'll have a proper girlie day, just the five of us.' Eyes shining with tears, she beams, places a hand over Sophie's and lets her gaze play over each of them in turn.

'You've all been so kind to me,' she says, her free hand caressing the base of her neck. 'I just want to say thanks.'

Outside, a thunderstorm is passing overhead. Jane has waited until the fuss has died down so as not to appear like she isn't excited. She isn't excited, of course she isn't.

'Will you be coming, Janie?' Lexie asked her shortly after the announcement, staring directly into her eyes with that almost indefinable hardness.

'Of course,' Jane replied – already lying, already concocting the excuse she would give at the eleventh hour when the time came. 'Why wouldn't I come?'

Lexie smiled in that weird way of hers and said, 'Good. That's great, babe. Just didn't want you to feel like you couldn't, you know?'

Jane's mouth dropped open. But before she could reply, Lexie turned away and laid one hand on her own stomach, the other on Sophie's, the two of them pressing foreheads together and sharing a private, delighted giggle. And at that point, Jane claimed she wasn't feeling very well on account of an out-of-date tiramisu she'd eaten earlier, grabbed her coat and left.

Now she waits in the porch, watches the rain bounce on the York stone paving of the courtyard. Three women under a golfing umbrella shriek and run up the steps to the door. She moves aside to let them through. There is a brief and supremely British exchange about the weather and they're gone, their laughter receding into the body of the pub lounge.

'Jane.'

She turns to see Sophie is standing just inside. 'Oh. Hey.'

'Are you OK?'

'Yeah, I just feel a bit sick and I've got an early start in the morning.' She stares at the patterns in the carpet: a heavy plaid of reds, turquoises, browns.

'So, are you going to come to the baby shower?' Sophie asks.

'Of course, why?'

'Just, you didn't reply to Lexie's WhatsApp message, that's all.'

The follicles on Jane's scalp tingle. 'I... I said I was coming, just now, in the pub. And I spoke to Lexie. About two seconds after the message. In person. I told her I was coming.'

Sophie's dyed eyebrows rise in what looks like genuine surprise. 'You spoke to her? She never mentioned it.'

'Didn't she? Oh. You must've thought I was being so rude.' There is a pointedness in Jane's tone that she hears and tries to curb. 'Well, anyway, I did reply, just verbally, that's all. Lexie said she'd let you know. Maybe she forgot.'

Sophie nods, appears to be taking this in.

'Look,' Jane says into the silence, 'I'm sorry we fell out, OK? If I was unfriendly towards Lexie, I didn't mean to be and I honestly didn't think I had been. She was probably feeling a bit, you know, new girl, and maybe you were right, maybe I was still a bit raw after hearing your news. I just needed some time to process it, that's all.' There is some truth in what she's saying. But only some. She has been through much worse than whatever this is, and if anyone can smile for hours on end while inside they are falling to pieces, it's her. Isn't she still doing that – right now, in fact?

Sophie smiles. 'Apology accepted.'

'Good.' For some reason, Jane feels aggrieved.

'Shall we travel into London together for the shower?'

Won't Lexie mind? are the words Jane manages to bring screeching to a halt.

'Great,' is what she does say. 'That'd be really nice.' Outside, the rain has stopped, the change in the sky brightening the interior of the pub.

'I'll see you Tuesday anyway, yeah?' Sophie turns to go back to the others.

'OK. But Sofe?'

She turns back. 'Yeah?'

'Next time, you know, if you're upset, can you just talk to me? If I've done something bad, it's very unlikely to have been on purpose.' Her legs have started to tremble.

Sophie blushes deep crimson. 'OK, sure.'

Sensing there will be no return apology, Jane turns and leaves. Behind the thin rain, the houses that line the common, the faintest trace of a rainbow emerges in the mottled sky. I've said my piece, she thinks. It was hard but I got the words out. Things should be better now. Sometimes you just have to stick up for yourself.

And it's not as if Lexie's dangerous, is it?

CHAPTER SEVENTEN

JANE

March

The baby shower is postponed twice, for reasons unknown, and is arranged finally for Friday 26 April. Quietly seething, Jane rearranges half a day's cover for the café yet again. But like a true art student, Jude is cool about it, saying only that they could use the extra money for supplies.

Poor Frankie is working longer hours than ever and seems even more exhausted and stressed than Jane. Lately, all conversation between them is in passing, if they exchange words at all; the two of them are only just staying afloat. Like some sort of metaphor, the kitchen is falling apart. The floor looks like a scratching post for a dog. Which, she supposes, it is.

Runner Beans Tuesday comes around. Jane resolves to attend without fail. The afternoon wears on. She wonders if Sophie will be a no-show again. Sure enough, at quarter to four, she texts: *Running late. See you at RB x*

Jane fights with herself not to wonder if Sophie is having coffee with Lexie as she did last week, a fact Lexie no doubt enjoyed slipping into her announcement at the pub. Either that or she's avoiding her. Surely not? They've made up. This horrid, pinched feeling in her chest is silly jealousy – *for God's sake, Jane, get a grip. Sophie's just juggling being pregnant, the demands of looking after little Kyle after a full day at work and a husband who quite often acts like he arrived in a time capsule from the 1950s. There are people starving in this world, women and children being chased from their homes, refugees drowning out at sea. And you, Jane, after all the battles you've fought, for God's sake find wherever your big-girl pants have got to and put them back on before you lose your mind.*

She texts back: *Sure thing. See you there.* X

It's ten to four. No one in the café but too soon to close up. Scarlett is in the back putting biscotti into cellophane sheaths. She's made some chocolate and date ones that Jane almost wishes she hadn't tried – they are the crack cocaine of biscuits. Shame she can't advertise them as such – they'd go a bomb. Especially round here.

The door squeaks open and her heart lifts. It's Angie, her favourite customer. Well into her seventies, she's one of the few who remember this place when it was a greengrocer, before it became a chicken joint.

'Hiya, Angie. Haven't seen you in a while.'

'All right, darlin'.'

'How're you doing?'

She clicks her tongue; the merest tilt of her white head. 'Been over Walthamstow. At my sister's.' Her East End accent sounds strong after a day with the other customers, whose childhood accents have long since faded away or been dropped on purpose. 'Broke her hip, stupid cow.' She titters and sits down in her favourite seat – the one in the corner nearest the window, where the sun shines warm and yellow at this time in the afternoon.

'The special?'

'Please.'

'Keep an eye out for me.'

'Will do, darlin'.'

Jane pops behind the café front to the prep kitchen, flicks on the kettle and pulls the jar of Nescafé red top out of the cupboard.

'I should think that's enough, love,' she says to Scarlett, who is the very image of concentration in her blue hygiene gloves, tongue trapped between her lips. 'Just put the ribbons on and then I'll let you off early.'

From over her glasses, Scarlett gives her a worried look.

Jane grins. 'I'll still pay you till five, don't worry.'

'Thanks, Jane.' Scarlett's cheeks pink and she returns to her task, giving rise to a huge rush of affection in Jane. She has babysat for Hils's football-mad boys and for Kyle many times, but Scarlett is the only kid who ever tapped her watch and announced it was her own bedtime. Kath sometimes jokes that if anything ever happened to her, she'd want Jane to raise Scarlett. Jane always replies that she'd take her in a heartbeat. And she would.

She nicks a biscotti – biscotto? – winks at Scarlett and returns to Angie.

'Here you go.' She places the Nescafé and the biscuit on a saucer on the table. 'Chocolate and date. Scarlett's latest creation.'

'I shouldn't really.' Angie dunks the biscuit into the hot coffee and bites off the end. She closes her eyes momentarily. 'Oh, that's bloody lovely, that is. She's a talent.'

'She is.'

'Here, sit down, for Christ's sake. Take the weight off for five minutes.'

Jane laughs and sits. She is edgy, she realises. Knowing why and knowing it's stupid doesn't help. Neither does having faced bigger things. That trauma makes us stronger is a myth. Cracks repaired are still cracks.

'What's the matter?' Angie is looking at her. No, she is scrutinising her. 'You ain't yourself.' She pulls off her lemon crocheted scarf and wriggles out of her fur coat – Jane is mostly veggie, but still, she loves that coat.

'I'm fine. Just tired.'

'Bollocks to that.'

Jane laughs. 'OK, I'm not. But I will be.'

'Man trouble?'

A woman in activewear rides past on a gleaming bicycle with a bright red carriage at the front bearing two small children. She is shouting into a headset; the sound reaches them, though not the words. Angie watches her pass before returning her inscrutable hooded gaze to Jane.

'I'd say I don't wish to pry,' she continues, the place where her eyebrows once were rising in two deep arcs. 'But I do, frankly. It's got to be more interesting than our Miriam's hip.'

Jane studies Angie a moment: her ancient burgundy cardigan, her greyish skin carved with the grooves of a heavy ex-smoker, the no-nonsense purse of her thin, puckered mouth, today painted a vibrant coral. But she can't tell her what's bothering her; Angie is from a time when this place was more... real, for want of a better word. She will think the whole thing's totally pathetic. But then again, she times her visits for when the place is empty precisely so that Jane will sit with her a while and chat.

'Not man trouble, no,' Jane says, deciding to say a little but to keep it brief. 'Except he's working too hard. Friend trouble actually. Not really had that before. It's just put me off my stride a bit, that's all.'

'Close friend?'

'I thought so, yeah. She's got a new mate, which is fine obviously, but now I can't seem to do anything right. It's all gone a bit who said what to whom and who didn't reply to the WhatsApp quickly enough. I mean, when I think of the state of the world, you know? It's all so petty. I can't think why it's got to me so much.'

'That's pettiness for you though, isn't it?' Through the doorstop-thick lenses of her glasses, Angie blinks her magnified pale grey eyes. 'Think you're close and next thing they're putting you in the freezer without even telling you why or, half the time, that you're even in it.'

Jane had expected Angie to roll her eyes and tell her to take no notice. But she has not.

'That's it,' she says, encouraged. 'That's it exactly.'

'Ain't petty when men fall out, is it? Entire wars are started over who has the biggest willy, and we're encouraged to believe there's no alternative. To my mind, it gets to you precisely because it *is* so bloody small. You think, *Hang on, I thought we were bigger than this*, don't you? Then you wonder why you're so upset, and you can't tell anyone in case they think you've lost your bleeding marbles.'

'Like, if you say it out loud, it'll sound stupid.'

Angie pops the last of the biscuit into her mouth, an act that doesn't deter her from speaking, the bulge roaming around her left cheek like a mouse under a sheet. 'Cheapens everything, don't it? Makes you wonder if you ever had it right in the first place. And yes, there's bigger things in life, but honestly, love, never put up with bad men, bad friends or bad coffee.' She takes a large swig of her Nescafé and smiles in appreciation.

'I love my friends,' Jane says. 'They're like family – well, except I chose them.' She gives a brief laugh. 'I joined this running club and they were just so down to earth and friendly, and until now it's been great, you know? It's just, there's this new one and she's a bit of a... she's a...'

'Bitch?'

Jane shudders. 'I suppose so. But I don't want to think that, especially because she's, like, super-glam, you know? And rich. It's the cliché of it, the whole sisterhood thing. Calling a woman... that word just because she's beautiful or rich or whatever. I know I'm a scruff-bag, but honestly, I've got no problem with nice clothes, make-up and stuff. I even wear it myself sometimes. And I've got nothing against people being rich either. I'm not that into money or buying things; I mean, I have my Vespa, which I love, and my bike. And my house. But it's not what makes me tick, do you know what I mean? I don't put my happiness on stuff. Sorry, I'm rambling, it's just, if I'm honest, she annoys me. I can't help it. Even the way she dresses annoys me. I feel like saying, calm down, love, it's just a drink with the girls, no need to get the tiara out. That makes me a rubbish feminist, doesn't it? I'm a disgrace. But the thing is, she's been really rude to me, but only when no one's looking, and she's told lies about me to my best friend, and now my best friend has really cooled on me, like, we're not even close any more when literally a few weeks ago we were. I mean, I thought we were.' To her mortification, she finds she's welling up.

'Sounds to me like it's the way she's acting, not what she's wearing, darlin', so I wouldn't worry about the sisterhood.'

'Thanks.' Jane sniffs, swipes her fingertips over her eyes. 'I mean, both my mates from school look like the Kardashians and I bloody love them.'

'There you are then. Sounds like this woman's the disgrace, being rude to you like that.' Angie presses her mouth so tight her lips disappear. She looks, instantly, incredibly stern. 'I like to think I know people. I see you with your mate's kid and the bloke who delivers the cakes and all the customers with their screaming toddlers throwing baby-bloody-cinos on their iPads. You look after people all day long.' She gives a dismissive tilt of her head. 'You don't like the word *bitch*? Well, let me tell you something. I was part of an underground feminist newsletter back in the day.' She laughs, points at Jane. 'Didn't see that coming, did you? Oh yes. Consciousness-raising. I've been happily single since I was in my fifties, when I found my Bill in bed with the woman who ran the pet shop. Brenda, her name was. Brenda Gibbons.' She leans forward, one knotty-knuckled finger jabbing at Jane almost aggressively. 'Her goldfish only ever lasted a week; I should've known she was bad news. All I'm saying is, I've been around the block more than most, and if I say this woman's a bitch, she's a bitch. Don't see the point in calling it a digging implement if it's a spade.'

By now Jane is laughing, can feel the muscles in her back loosening. 'I suppose.'

'Whoever she is, if she gives you any more trouble, you send her to me. I'll knock her bloody block off. I mean, I'd've been delighted if someone'd nicked my Bill, but if they'd nicked my Helen, I'd have been after them with a meat cleaver.' Angie allows herself a chuckle. 'And I even had a meat cleaver back then too. My Bill was a butcher.'

Jane wipes her eyes. 'Thanks, Angie. You've made me laugh at least. Are you and Helen still close?'

Angie tips her head back. When she returns her gaze to Jane, her pursed coral lips press together again before loosening to let out a heavy sigh. 'I lost her. Five years ago now. The big C.'

'Oh, I'm so sorry.' Jane lays her hand on Angie's arm.

To her surprise, the old lady covers it with her own and pats it affectionately. 'What's the point in having friends if you don't love each other? Helen and me never fell out, but if we had, it'd have upset me something terrible. Just because it's not your love life don't mean it ain't love. Don't mean it don't hurt like hell when it goes wrong.'

'Yes, that's it, that's it exactly. It *hurts*. It hurts like hell.'

CHAPTER EIGHTEEN

JANE

Down at Sainsbury's car park, where Runner Beans meets due to the free parking after 7 p.m., Hils and Kath are stretching out and chatting nineteen to the dozen amidst the throng. There are about ten of them tonight, fewer than normal, but it's cold, really cold.

Jane locks up her bike and jogs over, chafing her arms, blowing into her fists. They exchange hellos and she begins her warm-up. 'Sophie and Lexie not here yet?'

'The happy couple will be joining us shortly, I'm sure,' says Hils. She and Kath snigger like schoolkids.

Jane has no idea how to respond, isn't even sure if Hils meant it cattily – her humour is always pretty mischievous. She decides to say nothing and they continue to warm up in silence, jumping up and down to keep the blood moving.

After a few minutes, Andrea Frost, the club chairperson, comes over to tell them they're going to go on ahead because some of the members are getting chilly. They can form two groups and still stay safe.

'Sure, yeah,' Jane says. 'No problem. We'll wait for the stragglers.'

The other women run off, slowly at first, in the direction of the park, until their high-vis vests are just acid-yellow blobs bobbing up and down in the distance. There is still no sign of Lexie and Sophie.

'You two definitely going to the baby shower then?' Jane asks.

Hils shrugs. '*Sofes* seems into it, and it might be a laugh.'

Again Jane rides past Hils's subtle dig. 'Do we know who else is going?'

'I think it's just us,' Kath replies. 'She's just moved here, hasn't she?'

Jane lowers herself slowly into a hamstring stretch. 'Do we know where she's from?'

Kath shakes her head. 'No idea. I've not really spoken to her one to one.'

'Can't get a word in,' Hils says then laughs. 'I'm not getting a big expensive present, by the way,' she adds in an irritated tone. 'No offence to Sophie, but can't we wait till it's born? I mean, so you're up the duff, so what? Hardly compares to pushing it out, does it? Yes, then you deserve a bloody medal, never mind a plush Babygro and a finger sandwich. Not to be tight, but how many presents do you need?'

Kath laughs. Jane almost joins in but is still caught in a kind of hovering confusion, unsure how to react. There is no mistaking Hils's feelings for Lexie. And while she is not criticising Sophie directly, this is not something she would say to her face. But that's just Hils – she doesn't mean anything by it, and it's one thing to find a kind of party ridiculous, another to loathe the person hosting it.

'Baby showers are popular with young people now though, aren't they?' Kath says. 'And Lexie's in her twenties. They're all about the Instagram and the filters and the whole *extra* lifestyle thing. I went to my cousin's one and it was really sweet.' She stoops forward and, without bending her legs, presses the palms of her hands to the tarmac. The woman is ninety per cent rubber. Jane is aware that she herself has put on a few pounds around her middle just from missing a couple of weeks' running. Early menopause: the gift that keeps on giving.

'Hopefully it'll be fun,' she offers. 'And I've never even set foot in the Ritz.'

Hils cackles. 'You *almost* sounded like you meant that. Don't come if you don't want to, mate. I think it's pretty over the top and you're not even into kids.'

'I am! I just can't eat a whole one, that's all.' The joke almost protects her from the sickening thump to the chest. 'Besides, Scarlett's going to be mine once I've bumped Kath off.'

'Oh, Scarlett'd *love* that,' Kath says. 'It'd be a dream come true.'

Sophie's black Audi pulls into the car park. For some reason, Jane had assumed Lexie would be giving Sophie a lift in the BMW from Instagram. But no.

'Hi, girls!' Lexie is sashaying – there is no other word for it – towards them in blue camouflage leggings and a matching off-the-shoulder top, with a fluorescent orange sports bra beneath – nowhere near enough layers for the weather. Her white trainers are brand new. They look like fashion trainers rather than actual runners, almost look like they have a wedge heel. She shivers and pouts. 'Oh my God, it's freezing!'

'Let's get going then.' Kath is jumping up and down, slapping at her upper arms.

'Yeah, come on,' Hils says. 'I'm freezing my knockers off here. Well, I would be if I had any.'

'Shall we just let Lexie and Sophie warm up quickly?' Jane says. 'It's super-cold – we don't want any pulled muscles.'

'It's fine, come on.' Lexie is already off, running a little ahead, really quite fast, as if it's a race.

But it's not a race.

The others follow. Jane hangs back for Sophie, who has locked the car and is jogging over. They fall into step, already trailing the others by a few metres.

'How's things?' Jane starts. In front, the others are pulling away; Lexie must be setting a hell of a pace.

'Fine, fine,' says Sophie. 'Busy. Knackered.'

'Don't overdo it, will you? Precious cargo and all that.'

'I'm fine. I might start swimming instead of running though, less impact. Lexie said I should drop Runner Beans, as my gym membership is gold so it includes the pool.'

'Right. I mean, good idea.'

They fall silent. It isn't awkward, not exactly. More like the plug has been pulled out of them. Seeing one another always charged their batteries somehow, brought them to life, made them funnier, more interesting. Not this evening. They carry on; Jane is aware of them both breathing.

Up ahead, a cry of pain rings out.

They share a glance. In front of them, the others have come to a halt. Jane jogs up the lane alongside Sophie to where Lexie is sitting on the ground clutching at her ankle.

'Ow,' she says. 'Oh my God, ow. I think I've sprained it.'

At least you looked trendy in the trainers. Jane clamps her jaw shut, as if she's already given voice to the thought.

'Oh no,' she says instead. 'You poor thing.'

'There's no point running on it,' Hils says, hands on hips. 'You'll risk serious injury if you do that. You need to get home, get it raised, get some ice on it.'

Lexie pushes out a glossy bottom lip. She is in full make-up, Jane realises. And that is her right. That is absolutely her right. *For God's sake, Jane, what kind of shrivelled little shrew this woman has reduced you to.*

'Shall we call an ambulance, or...' Jane finds she can't look directly at either Lexie or Sophie. Nor can she make a joke to ease the tension as she usually would. She doesn't dare. Lexie might take it the wrong way. And then Sophie will ghost her for a week.

'I should've warmed up,' Lexie says, flashing Jane a glare while the others are focused on the doomed ankle.

'I'd give you a lift home, but I'm on my bike, sorry,' are the words that leave Jane's mouth. Kindness on autopilot, kindness under stress. Under fire. Old habits.

'I'll take you,' says Sophie, a hint of annoyance in her tone. Jane's effort not to feel pleased about that is nothing short of

Herculean, the fact that she even has to make that effort sending her further into a fug of frustration at herself. For crying out loud, she thinks. Lexie is like the 'Ten items or less' sign at the supermarket checkout: four little words that make snarky little point-scorers of us all.

Lexie sniffs and looks up through her lashes at Sophie. 'Actually, can we go back to yours, hun? It's just that Steve's out and I don't think I should be on my own tonight. You know, in case it's more serious than we think.'

'I can take you straight to the hospital?' Sophie offers.

'It's not that bad. I'll go later if it swells up or anything.' That hard G. Her accent comes and goes. But then so does Jane's – the result of living in different places, the effort to shed her past not always fully successful. What is Lexie's past? Who *is* she?

Whoever she is, she is being helped up by Kath, who hands her over to Sophie. Goodbyes and hope-you're-all-rights are exchanged, but frankly it is too cold to stand about. Hils, Kath and Jane watch as Sophie and Lexie hobble away down the road, arms around one another like drunks. The sight should, Jane knows, bring relief. Lexie has gone – breathe. But for some reason, she is filled with foreboding, the familiar sense that she has done something wrong, something else wrong, something she doesn't yet know about but for which she will be punished, if not tonight then at some future point. But no, she was nowhere near Lexie when she fell.

There is nothing Lexie could possibly accuse her of, not this time.

CHAPTER NINETEEN

JANE

Frankie's van is parked outside. But as Jane approaches the house, she notices that the living-room windows are smeared with something grim. A little closer and she sees, in the street light, that it is raw egg. Her chest tightens. On the windowsill, on the ground, are broken eggshells.

'What?'

Someone has thrown eggs at her house. Who? Why?

Inside, she switches on the hall light, wheels her bike through the house. Des comes trotting through, panting softly, jumping up at her. Heart still quick, skin alive with tension, she fusses the dog before continuing on and out of the back door to take her bike out to the shed.

Back in the kitchen, she grabs a bucket and fills it with hot soapy water. Twenty minutes later, the mess is cleaned up, but she is still unsettled. Kids, undoubtedly. A meaningless prank. They're not to know that eggs, specifically, would bring back stressful memories.

But still, a horrible thing to happen, put together with all the rest of it.

She fixes herself an elderflower cordial and, one hand pressed against the sink, drinks it down in one go. Des gives a desultory sniff of the kitchen floor before curling up in his basket.

It's half nine. Frankie is obviously in bed. Her heart shrinks with disappointment. How she wishes he was down here, awake. He would have helped her clean up the mess, reassured her that it was just kids, as she has had to reassure herself. Lately, she has felt so alone, she realises. Frankie is so damn tired. All the time. It's got much worse lately. How long? Since around the time of Sophie's news, she thinks. And he's developed a haunted look in his eyes. When he speaks, his voice is smaller somehow, as if only half of him is left inside. Could he be depressed? She has to get him to ease up, maybe see a counsellor. The world trip can wait. It must. She'd rather never leave this island again than see him like this – she must convince him of that.

She is about to go upstairs when her phone buzzes. She finds it on the kitchen table, vibrating almost imperceptibly, but as she reaches it, it stops. She picks it up, sees three missed calls from Sophie. And as is increasingly the case these days, hot dread fills her.

She calls back, her throat thick with something close to fear.

'Sophie? Hi. Is everything all right?'

'No. No, it isn't actually.' Sophie's voice is laced with ice.

Jane's chest tightens. 'Oh no,' she says, with as much sympathy as she can muster, even though her gut tells her it's not sympathy Sophie is looking for.

'I can't believe you made Lexie run without warming up.'

'What? I—'

'You know what I'm talking about, Jane – don't pretend to be all innocent. I was prepared to forget the fact that you pretty much stormed off last Friday, but trying to cause Lexie injury is way beyond the... It's just way out of order.'

'I didn't storm off on Friday – I left early because I wasn't feeling great and I had an early start. And I didn't cause Lexie injury! In fact, it was me who told her to warm up. I told her, but she said she didn't need to and she just ran off at full tilt.'

'That doesn't make sense. Lexie's been to Runners a few times now – there's no way she'd just set off without stretching first.'

'And yet she did.' Jane hears the hardening in her own tone.

'Hmm. I dunno. She didn't get injured any of the other times.'

The subtext chimes clear as a bell. Lexie didn't get injured when Jane wasn't there. Her chest swells, her heart fattening with anger. This is bullshit. *Why call it a digging implement if it's a spade?* 'Look, Sophie, I don't know what to say to you. As if I'd deliberately sabotage someone like that. It's just not something I'd do, no matter how much I hated them.'

'Oh, so you admit you hate her?'

'I don't hate anyone. I just can't stand drama, that's all. I had enough of it growing up – you know that. I moved hundreds of miles to get away from it, but it's starting to seem like ever since you introduced Lexie to the group, things have been... well, terrible.'

Sophie sighs. 'I don't know what's going on between you two.'

'*Going on?* You make it sound like I'm participating in some way! Can you even hear what I'm saying, or is it not audible unless Lexie says it?'

'Oh my God!' Sophie is wailing, actually wailing. 'I can't help it if Lexie and me are both—' She makes herself stop. *I can't help it if we're both pregnant* is the phrase that hangs heavy between them. 'I can't help it if she's so nice to me. She's just looking out for me, that's all. It's not against you.'

Really?

'Look,' Jane says firmly, 'I'm happy you've found a pal to be pregnant with. You'll be good company and support for one another, now and when the babies come. Honestly, I don't have a problem with that, trust me. I know you know my... circumstances, but that's got nothing to do with anything, OK? I don't know what Lexie thought I said, but I told her she should warm up. Hils and Kath heard me, if you want to check. Maybe Lexie heard it wrong. Maybe she thought I said *no* time to warm up or something.' She waits, listens.

After a long moment, Sophie speaks. 'Maybe it was just a misunderstanding.'

'Maybe.' *Misunderstanding, my fat white arse.*

'And I know it's hard for you.'

'It is. It is hard. But I'm happy for you. You know that, don't you?'

'OK,' Sophie says, quieter now, calmer. 'Well, listen, we won't be coming to Runner Beans anymore. We're going to go swimming instead.'

We.

'Fine. Good idea.' Jane waits. When Sophie says nothing more, she adds, 'And I might not make the pub this week, because I haven't seen Frankie for ages and we need some time together. In fact, I think I'm going to lie low for a while. I need to economise a bit; our hall floor is coming up at the edges and the dishwasher's making funny noises.'

'But you're still coming to the baby shower?'

'Of course. We can go on the train together. It'll be fun. We can... catch up.'

'Actually, I have to go earlier. With Lexie. To set up.'

'Set up?'

'I think Lexie's bought some prizes and stuff.'

'Prizes?'

'I think she's going to do a raffle or a quiz or something. She's putting so much effort in. She's booked a suite.'

Momentarily aghast, Jane finds herself searching for what, what on earth, to say. A quiz? A raffle? A *suite*? What fresh hell...

'OK, great,' she makes herself say, hopes Sophie can't hear the tremor in her voice. 'See you there then. But Sophie?'

'Yeah?'

'I know you really like Lexie but you've known me a long time, OK?'

Sophie sighs. 'I think you and Lexie just operate in different ways, that's all.'

Operate? Operate? Jane closes her eyes. Let it go, let it go-oh, tra-la-la-la-la-la-la-la-la. She thinks of Hils and Kath laughing at Lexie behind her back. Perhaps that is the answer: to laugh. Short of killing her and dancing on her broken bones singing *ding dong the witch is dead*, yes, that is what she must do: laugh, laugh her head off. It is hilarious, really, when you think about it.

'I'll maybe see you in the café then,' she says into the silence with the manufactured cheer of a holiday rep. 'And if not, I'll see you all dolled up at the Ritz, OK? Should be great fun!'

By the time she ends the call, she is shaking. Disgust. She is disgusted with herself, with this performance she has given of someone who is not her, who is not feeling what she is feeling. Because she is not excited. She does not want Sophie to come to the café and she does not want to go to the baby shower. And there is no misunderstanding, not anymore, no room for interpretation. Lexie, new to the area and in need of a friend, is deliberately blackening Jane's reputation to somehow insinuate herself into Sophie's affections. Jane has tried not to believe it, but it is too damn obvious. If Jane had Lexie's address, she would ride round there right now and confront her. Well, she wouldn't actually, but she bloody well feels like it. It is systematic. And it's not even subtle – it's like a bad film, Lexie a ham actress, with her evil-queen offence and her borderline comedy shit-stirring and her fake injuries and her lies and her eyelashes and her Victoria Beckham sports kit and her ridiculous extra lifestyle and her stupid fucking swishy hair...

'Argh.'

It is as eloquent as Jane can be, there in the silence of her shitty kitchen, her bruised life. Because this isn't a film. It isn't Instagram. It might not be perfect, but it's hers and she has worked hard to love it and the people in it. It is a life established over years with the man she chose to spend it with, with quiet respect and kindness and solidarity between the women in it. It is a life in which she had finally begun to feel safe after the train wreck of her upbringing.

I collect people. Again Jane finds herself thinking of Sophie's words. Back then, she was a waif for Sophie to pick up and take under her wing. Was that what happened? Was that what Sophie saw, that night in the van? A fragile woman in need of friends, a real live working-class person, something to add a little grit to the mix? Yes, that night, Sophie added Jane to her people collection, Jane sees that now. And that's all she's done with Lexie, isn't it? Taken in another waif, new in town and lonely, in need of Sophie's largesse, Sophie's friends, Sophie's Sunday lunches. Lexie is the new collector's item: young, fun-loving, extravagant. Rich, glamorous, able to pay for her own cocktails.

It is like Sophie has fallen under a spell, been mesmerised. The only comfort is that Hils and Kath appear to be as bemused by Lexie's appeal as Jane is; they are skirting close to properly slagging her off. They are already joking about her. But if they can laugh, it is because they are kind of best friends with each other, in as much as grown women can be. But Jane's best friend, as childish as it is to think it, was Sophie. *Was*, she thinks, acknowledging to herself with a deep, sinking feeling of sadness that yes, that ship has sailed. Whatever exists now is a cardboard cut-out of something she thought was real. It is as Angie said – this is what pettiness does: undermines love, turns what was solid into smoke. If Hils and Kath can laugh, it's because it's not personal. They have not been targeted. Because that's the other thing that's dawning, no matter how much Jane tries to deny it: it *is* personal. Lexie Lane is waging a hate campaign against her in order to have Sophie all to herself.

But what on earth can she do, apart from try her best to rise above it all, keep her head held high and go to the damn baby shower?

CHAPTER TWENTY

THE HOSPITAL

'I can manage without that,' I say. The nurse is being a bit overkill on the whole helping-me-to-the-loo deal. A wheelchair? Is she for real?

'I'm afraid you'll have to use it for the moment. Has the doctor spoken to you about your injuries?' She wrinkles her nose – mouths *ouch*. 'A fractured tibia, lovely.'

Going to have to disagree with you there, Nursey. I might have broken my shin, but I am not lovely, not anymore. Lovely is in the past. The past, as they say, is a different country now, and yes, I'll be doing things differently here. Should have done things differently a long time ago.

'Can't I have a stick?' I ask. 'Like, a walking stick or crutches or something?'

'I'll get you some crutches to help you in and out of the cubicle, but we can't put weight on it for now, so we just need to be a bit patient.'

'I am patient. Patient with broken shin.'

'Good one,' she says, humouring me. 'Hold on to my arm – that's it, lovely – and lower yourself in, easy as she does it. That's it – grand.'

I let her help me into the chair. She disappears and returns after about ten minutes. It's a good job I'm not desperate, I think. I would have wet myself by now. Or worse. She hands me a pair of grey isosceles-triangle crutches, armpit rests like gym horses, extra padding on the handles. Tells me again they're for getting in and out of the cubicle in case, I suppose, I've got brain damage. I thank her. I'm so grateful. You nurses do such a great job. The NHS is amazing. Et cetera.

Two can play at the humouring game, *lovely*.

She lifts my feet onto the supports and pushes me out of the ward towards the loos. I don't protest. Best to play along. I'm not confident she'll leave me to do what she thinks I have to do, let alone what I actually have to do. It's going to be tricky giving her the slip. Maybe I can plead constipation, wait till she's called away or too bored to hang around.

Or, I think, considering the crutches, I can take more direct action.

CHAPTER TWENTY-ONE

JANE

April

The Ritz reminds Jane of Lexie, with its Hollywood dressing room bulb lighting and extravagant awnings, and, let's face it, the sheer in-your-faceness of the place. If Lexie were a building, she would be this one. Yes, the gloves are off in Jane's mind, and down, down, down her thoughts run, along with the sweat from her armpits, as she approaches the glitzy monolith. If only they were just meeting in a nice bar or a pub, or even at Lexie's place. They could still celebrate, couldn't they, still wish the two women a happy, healthy pregnancy without all this pressure? They could have done something cosy, something intimate and supportive, something more *them*.

Outside, she pauses to take out the Bach's Rescue Remedy she bought on the way and, turning away from the crowds on Piccadilly, squeezes a few drops onto her tongue. Not that she thinks it will do anything, but hey ho, it was too late to get a prescription for Valium and the woman in Boots recommended it for the mild but constant feeling of dread that has grown over the last few weeks and which Jane is now experiencing at every moment of every day. This unpleasant, uneasy feeling is one she hasn't had since she was a child. It is a feeling she left home to escape and it saddens her that her closest friend should be the cause of it now. Because since Anklegate, Jane has realised she is managing a two-headed beast: Sophie and Lexie – Solex? Lexsoph? – as she once managed her mother. Having a horror of confrontation, all she has in her armoury is all she had back then: keep smiling, keep your head down, hope it blows over, which right now doesn't feel like enough.

Runner Beans has been a chink of light these last few weeks. Without Lexie and Sophie there, Jane has managed to enjoy the endorphins and the lovely rambling chats with Hils and Kath. All of them have avoided the subject of Lexie, and Jane presumes this is because it brushes too close to Sophie and they are all, it seems, hanging on tight to loyalty.

Perhaps they are *all* smiling, keeping their heads down and hoping it will blow over.

Jane has not, however, been to Friday drinks. She has kept her friendship with Sophie to texts alone lately. If she's honest, the thought of any kind of encounter with Lexie makes her feel a bit sick, and since she can't have Sophie without Lexie, she prefers not to bother. This in turn makes her feel pathetic for letting one person, who is only a person, after all, upset her this much, which puts her on a kind of inert stress loop. But the fact is, she doesn't trust any situation with Lexie in it, doesn't trust herself not to fall into a trap simply by opening her mouth or not opening her mouth, doing something or not doing something, and then being punished by a telling-off from Sophie, who may or may not throw her in the freezer for an indeterminate time. Isn't she in this situation right now? Damned if she doesn't go to this baby shower, damned if she does? All she can hope for is that by going along with it, she, Sophie and the gang can pick up once – *if* – this Lexie thing blows over

And in all of this, there's also the fact that Frankie is a worry, having skipped the last few lads' drinks. Jane has tried to ask if he's OK, but he says only that he's tired, that it's work, and that he's fine. In other words, he has closed up like the rolling shutters of her café at night.

But then she hasn't exactly talked to him either, has she?

She checks her phone for any new incoming messages, glances over the Friday Drinks WhatsApp group, which, instead of being a repository for banter and memes, social arrangements and support, has now become the site of all things baby-shower-related. As if this weren't fresh hell enough, a secondary group has been set up by Lexie, without Sophie in it, entitled GIFT FOR SOFES.

Hey gurrlzz, she had written. *Just thinking we should club together for something really special for Sofes. I suggest £30–£50 each so we can get her something decent like a deluxe baby gift basket. I've seen one for 200 squids and its the absolute bomb so I'll organise it! Yay! Love yaz! Lex xxx*

It's, not its, Jane thought, pedantic irritation prickling over her skull. But regardless of minor punctuation errors, the transition was complete. Lexie was now firmly established as Sophie's closest friend, the one who best understood her needs, her handmaiden. The rest of them were lesser ladies-in-waiting in some weird royal court scenario. And in this new order, anything less than fifty pounds each was mean.

Fortunately – hallelujah – Hils saved them all by replying immediately:

Would have loved to but have already bought so can't afford another thirty squids – soz! X

Followed by Kath: *I've bought something too. Nice thought though! X*

Jane had breathed deep, sweet relief, swiftly followed by a nasty gut-twist of self-doubt. Kath and Hils had responded at face value. Jane, meanwhile, had read all sorts into it, had known or thought she'd known that it was not generosity but a power play. Had she been wrong? Was she seeing things that weren't there? Added to this, Hils and Kath's perfectly pitched refusals had brought her a kind of mean-spirited joy in Lexie's 'defeat', and she wanted no part of being that kind of person. She was back to counting the items in other people's shopping baskets. She was back to becoming the word she never wanted to use.

It took her seven attempts to compose her reply:

Hey there, just catching up. Thanks for this, Lexie. I guess if everyone's getting their own, that's what I'll do too, if you're all agreed. Really nice idea though, cheers! X

Exclamation mark. Kiss.

Typing these, she was reminded of her favourite Smiths' song. Why, she had thought, why exactly was she effectively smiling at people she'd much rather kick in the eye? Lexie, she thinks now as she approaches the main door of the ridiculous hotel, is shrinking her by the day, sucking all the joy out of her. If this carries on, she will be a bitter little raisin.

Outside the Ritz is a doorman, dressed in a black top hat and tails trimmed in gold. Jane stifles a smirk, almost points, tells herself off for being immature, all in the time it takes her to step...

... inside.

She stops dead, the sheer scale of the foyer a stun gun. There are entire fountains of fresh flowers, the most monumental mirrors, frighteningly gargantuan pendulous chandeliers. Antiques everywhere. At the curved oak reception counter – is it a counter? Is it oak? Wood, anyway, yes, definitely wood – there are four men, all in three-piece suits, one of whom eventually condescends far enough to direct her to the Ladies, but only once she has given a valid reason for her presence.

'My heels are rubbing the backs of my ankles,' she adds needlessly and to his obvious distaste; unable to help herself, she continues, 'I just need to put some plasters on.'

This helps no end.

She is wearing the Whistles dress she got married in. It's not that she doesn't have a few dressier glad-rags, but on one of the myriad WhatsApp messages, Lexie stipulated actual dresses. At least, Jane thinks she did, but she couldn't then find the relevant message in the thread, which by then was longer than a Dead Sea Scroll. The dress is, she suspects, a little dated. A cheap thing from

H&M would have been better, but she couldn't justify it, and besides, she hasn't had the time to go clothes shopping.

Still, Frankie liked it.

'Wow,' he said earlier when he saw her all dressed up.

'It's my wedding dress.'

'I know that. You're tall.'

'Heels. Also from our wedding. I can barely walk.'

'Well, you look... lovely.' His blue eyes were at odds with his words – as if he found the sight of her sad. 'And it's just girls, is it?'

'It's just, you know, the Runner Beans and Sophie's new pal Lexie.'

'Lexie?'

'Yeah, remember I mentioned her? It's Kath's birthday – I told you. We just fancied treating ourselves.'

'Where you going again?'

She had not told him – not about Lexie, not what kind of do it was. She had not wanted to tell him the real reason and she couldn't bear to lie, so the less said, the better. And now she *has* lied, twice. He can't remember Lexie because Jane has not mentioned her, and it is not Kath's birthday at all. But how, how the hell, could she tell him she was going to celebrate not one but two pregnancies? She could not. Besides, he would have stopped her from going. He would not have let her put herself through it.

So why was she putting herself through it?

'Some posh place up in town,' she added, using the hall mirror to apply a shade of lipstick so identical to her lips she may as well not have bothered. 'Sophie booked it.' She turned to him and held out her arms, already embarrassed. 'How do I look?'

'You look beautiful.' For a moment he looked like he might cry. It wasn't her beauty that had made him emotional, she knew that. She is not a beautiful woman by anyone's standards. But it *was* love, of that she had no doubt.

She kissed him, stroked his cheek. 'And you, Mr Reece, look exhausted. Promise me you'll switch your phone off and put your feet up?'

'Stop fussing. I'm fine.'

But he didn't look fine. He didn't look fine at all.

She pushes the door of the Ladies and gasps. It is like walking into a bag of marshmallows: all soft creams and pinks, more mirrors, more flowers. A pond scene decorates the walls – Narcissus staring in, entranced. Individual white hand towels are folded in triangles on a stand-alone occasional table. There is an actual sofa. Why, she wonders, why on earth would you need a sofa in a loo?

'Jesus,' she mutters, tottering painfully into a cubicle, where she applies plasters to her heels, which have started to bleed. After taking advantage of the facilities – yes, there are actual toilets in here too, who knew? – she puts her head between her knees and makes herself breathe. She could go. She could just turn on her scabby heels and run, catch the train back home, grab a bottle of red and go to bed with Frankie for the entire afternoon.

But no. She just has to get through the next two or three hours. Keep smiling, keep her head down; it will blow over. Sophie and Lexie will have their babies and time will move forward, and whatever crush Sophie has on this woman will burn itself out. Things may or may not return to normal, but there's nothing Jane can do about that now. She has done nothing wrong, no matter what Lexie has claimed, and frankly, she has bigger things on her mind, namely Frankie's ghost floating about where Frankie used to be. Sitting here now on one of the world's poshest toilet seats, it occurs to her once again that he's been like this since around the time she told him Sophie's news. It's as if he has forgotten his own feelings and put all his focus on her, on supporting her, telling her over and over that she mustn't blame herself, but now, now that she is moving on, the grief has hit him full force.

Her eyes prick. Poor Frankie. She has been so absorbed in this nonsense she has neglected him.

She glances at her watch. It's after 2.30. Bugger. She's running late. A flame of dread rises in her belly as she crosses the soft pink carpet of the opulent foyer. If she's late, Lexie will interpret it as an insult. Sophie – well, who knows what Sophie thinks anymore?

A different man at reception tells her the Green Park Suite is Room 703 on the seventh floor and directs her to the lift. The lift is as glossy as all the rest, a portrait of a Victorian lady with a parasol staring at her from the back wall. It's like being trapped inside an olde-worlde trinket; she is a curio, a moth in amber.

As the floor numbers light up and go out, her stomach heats. She digs in her bag and pulls out the Rescue Remedy, considers it a moment before removing the pipette and downing the entire bottle. She should have brought a hip flask. This stuff is just brandy, isn't it? Is it possible to overdose on Bach's Rescue Remedy? She imagines the headline:

Woman Found Dead in Hotel Lift, Police Suspect Plant-Based Essence Poisoning.

The lift doors part. She scuttles down the thick patterned carpet, counting the room numbers, aware that the doors are so much further apart than in, say, a Travelodge. Finally, there it is, in gold cursive script on the door, and her stomach folds at the sight:

The Green Park Suite

703

CHAPTER TWENTY-TWO

JANE

The high babble of women's voices reaches her out in the corridor. They are all inside, together. She is outside, alone.

She knocks, breath caught in her chest. Inside, the voices hush. Jane thinks she hears her name. Sweat beads her hairline; she presses the back of her hand to it. Senses movement from within, and a second later, the door opens. Please God, let it be Sophie.

'Jane, finally!' It is Lexie. Of course it is. Her eyes travel to Jane's shoes and back up, to her hair, the subsequent expression hard to describe. *Oh dear*, perhaps. *What have you come as?*

'Er, hi,' Jane says, waving minutely. Awkwardly.

'We were beginning to think you weren't coming!' Lexie's tone does not match her face. But then her tone is for the benefit of the others, her face for Jane alone. Distaste, that's it. That's the expression. Like she has noticed some poo on Jane's shoe.

'Only a few minutes late,' Jane says, grinning like an absolute imbecile.

Lexie checks her watch and whispers: 'Erm, nearly forty actually.'

'But... wha... you – you said half two? It's only twenty to three.'

Lexie cocks her head; her tadpole eyebrows rise. 'Two o'clock, hun. I sent you a text?'

'You didn't. Sorry, I mean I... I didn't get a text.'

'Funny. The others all did.' This Lexie says quietly, so very quietly, before releasing a patronising smile across her no-make-up made-up face. 'Well,' she says loudly, cheerily, 'you're here now! Come in, babes. We're just about to start!'

Start.

Jane follows Lexie into a hallway. The hotel room has a hallway? Of course, it is a suite – suites have more than one room, don't they? Past smooth white walls she continues into an enormous... oh my days, it is an *enormous* living room. There's even a dining table and chairs, pink and blue helium balloons tied to their backs on matching shiny twine, bobbing and swaying together in ghoulish welcome. For some reason, she'd imagined them all sitting on a double bed drinking fizz in some re-enactment of the Pink Ladies sleepover scene in *Grease*. But no. No, the girls are sitting on plump candy-striped sofas around a glass coffee table, on which stands an ice bucket with champagne – the bottle the only thing sweating more than she is – bowls of salty snacks and an enormous platter of fruit.

'Hi!' they trill, holding up their glasses and grinning wildly. They are all dressed up and they look lovely, pink-cheeked with excitement. Scanning those faces, just for a few seconds, Jane feels a familiar and fleeting moment of happiness, of belonging.

But the moment passes.

'Hey,' she says, raising her hand to her chest in salute.

Neither Lexie nor Sophie is wearing a dress. Perhaps there was no message to that effect, perhaps Lexie deleted it, perhaps... oh, who knows? Who cares? Whatever the dress code was, both Sophie and Lexie are wearing identical collarless postbox-red silk shirts over black skinny jeans, like grown-up twins. Lexie's bump is clearly in evidence.

The windows catch Jane's attention. Huge clean panes looking out over...

'Is that Green Park?' she asks.

'Doh,' Lexie says, giggling. 'The Green Park Suite, babe. Clue in the title?'

Jane fakes a laugh. It's the kind of jagged humour that tears at the nerves like acrylic nails down a blackboard, the kind that says, *If you can't take it, you're a wimp. Get a grip, Jane.*

'Drop of 'poo, matey?' Hils is on her feet, face manic. 'Ritz Reserve, if you don't mind.' She appears to have changed her tune from her cynicism all those weeks ago. It's no wonder. None of them have ever done anything like this, been anywhere like this before. Few people have, she imagines, and for the first time, she wonders how much a suite like this costs, even for a few hours. Lexie, it seems, has *bought* them all. Hired them anyway.

'Try the chilli nuts,' Kath says, budging up to make room, her vintage frock draping loosely over her long, athletic legs. She is wearing the turquoise-green cowboy ankle boots Jane loves. Kath is by far the coolest chick in their coop. 'They're actual heroin – I can't stop eating them.'

Jane sits, is handed a glass of fizz. All her closest friends are here. And yet she feels something close to fear.

'How come you're late?' Sophie asks, her tone not unpleasant.

'I...' What can she say? *Lexie, your new best friend, didn't tell me the time had changed but is pretending she did.* But what's the point? Sophie won't believe her. 'The train was late coming into Waterloo and then my heels were bleeding and I had to stop and put plasters on them. Classy.' She attempts a laugh, but it dies halfway out.

'Where are they from?' It is Lexie who has asked, who is now sitting in an armchair. The armchair is higher than the sofas, giving the impression that she is raised above them all, about to give a talk or a performance.

'They're just Band-Aids. From Boots.'

Lexie laughs. 'No, I meant the shoes.'

'Oh! Sorry. Erm, Schuh, I think. I can't remember. They're from my wedding actually. I don't really wear heels. More of a trainers or boots girl. Flip-flops sometimes if I'm feeling wild.' Shut up, Jane. Shut. Up.

'Yeah, you're quite tomboyish, aren't you?' Lexie nods like a counsellor, narrows her eyes. 'I've always wanted to try short hair, but you have to be able to carry it off, I think, otherwise you look like a bloke in a dress, like Eddie Izzard or someone.' She laughs, though none of the others do. 'And with heels you have to be so careful. I always go for Russell & Bromley. You pay a bit more, but they don't rub as much.' Having delivered this pearl of wisdom, she flattens her mouth and shakes her head, in apparent sadness. 'It's about quality at the end of the day, isn't it?'

Jane sips her drink. The room has gone quiet. Before she came in, she could hear them chatting happily. It is she who has brought the silence in. She hasn't meant to; it is simply that Lexie has the effect of vacuuming away any conscious thought she might have had about what to say. At a loss, she pretends to admire the room, setting her mouth in a pleasant smile. The curtains look like they're made of duvets. They must weigh the same as a live elephant – two, maybe. And swags – is that the word? Those tie-up things that hold curtains back in an artful bulge. What are the extra bits of fabric at the top called? God knows. Pelmets? Or are they for beds? She gulps down half a glass, stops herself drinking the rest.

'Let's start the games.' Lexie claps her hands before nodding to the spindly occasional table in the corner. 'There's smellies for prizes!'

Jane wonders about feigning illness. A heart attack? A stroke? But no. She's played that card. Even if she had an actual aneurysm, she suspects it would be interpreted as a snub. And much as she can't stand Lexie, she cannot lose the others – after Frankie, they are all she has.

The first game involves the gifts. They each have to hand over their offering, Lexie explains, and once it has been unwrapped, say a few words about why they chose it and what they hope it will mean to the baby.

Oh dear God. Jane isn't entirely sure she can think of an actual *reason*, not one of any depth beyond *I needed a gift idea so I just googled* top ten baby presents *before ordering two matching teddy bears from a reputable department store while bathed in a light sweat of panic.*

She glances at Sophie, realising too late that no look will pass between them, nor will they studiously avoid meeting each other's eye for fear of making the other one giggle. Sure enough, Sophie is smiling at Lexie with no trace of irony whatsoever, as if she loves this sort of thing. A pang of grief like sadness passes through Jane. It is shocking, bewildering. It is actually a bit heartbreaking.

Hils starts, standing to hand a gift each to Lexie and Sophie. 'OK, so I thought I'd go gender neutral because we don't know what we're getting yet, do we?' She is already slurring slightly, and it is only then that Jane notices an empty champagne bottle on the far side of the room on an antique sideboard that looks like it's made entirely out of tortoiseshell.

The tear of paper. Sophie and Lexie are opening their presents. Identical Babygros in soft lemon velour rise like spirits in identically manicured hands. Yes, Sophie now has the same dark nail varnish as Lexie.

'I just thought,' Hils says, 'you can't have too many, can you? And... I hope the babies will be all lovely and cosy in these.'

Hils is improvising, Jane can tell. She will be filing it away for an anecdote, enjoying the champagne, going with it, whatever *it* is, only to rip into it later with her trademark ballsy humour – *I didn't know what the hell to say, I just came out with some bullshit about the babies being cosy.*

As the pregnant women coo and say their ohmygodthankyous, Jane's entire being flushes with relief. She lets out a long, deep exhalation. Hils has spent about the same as her. And she's given the same gift to both. There's a *chance* that Jane hasn't got it wrong. Dimly, it strikes her that relief on this scale is totally out of proportion, that two months ago she would have laughed at herself or found herself pathetic, or both. This change is... it's humiliating.

Kath is summoned to hand over her gifts. From floral wrapping paper appear two pairs of teeny-tiny trainers, both black with white stripes.

'I went gender neutral too,' she says. 'But I just thought, let's start 'em young, eh? They can be the two youngest Runner Beans!'

Bollocks, thinks Jane. That was *good*. Kath has never said anything so twee; Jane wonders what she's really thinking.

'Aw,' Sophie says. 'Little Runner Beans – that's so sweet.'

'That is so sweet,' Lexie echoes. 'So, so sweet.'

'Sweet,' says Hils.

'So sweet,' Jane chimes in, a beat too late, with no idea what she means, but then, as there is no one else here and Lexie is rolling her hand at her, she realises it is her turn. She hands over her parcels, meets Sophie's eye as she does so, tries to communicate kindness, friendship, love – what is left of it. Sophie smiles briefly, inscrutably.

Jane retakes her seat, closes her eyes to the rip of paper.

'Aw,' Sophie says again. 'A teddy! Oh my God, he's so cute!'

Jane coughs into her hand. 'I didn't really know what to... I mean, I just thought it's nice, you know, to feel safe, isn't it? And cuddling something makes you feel...' She feels herself blush.

'So cute,' Lexie parrots. 'And are they checked, you know, for safety standards?'

Jane's cheeks burn hotter. 'Safety standards? Erm, well, I bought them from John Lewis, so I can't imagine they'd be—'

'John Lewis,' Sophie jumps in. 'They'll be super-good quality then. Thanks, Jane, that's so kind.'

'I'll take mine into the Kingston store and check,' Lexie says. 'Just to be safe.' She holds up her teddy bear and wrinkles her nose. 'So sweet!'

'Top-up?' Hils stands, sways slightly, grabs the bottle. 'Ah, no. We're out.'

'I'll order another!' Lexie stands as Hils sits and makes her way towards another occasional table. She picks up a Victorian phone handset. Quietly they sit, smiling inanely like strangers, while

Lexie orders another bottle of Ritz Reserve and tells the staff they can bring the afternoon tea up now.

'Before we play the next game,' she says, returning to her throne, 'I've got something too. For little Freya.' She hunches her shoulders high and throws a sickly smile in Sophie's direction.

'Freya?' Jane says at the same time as Sophie protests:

'But you said we weren't getting each other anything!' Her mouth drops open in pink outrage that may or may not be genuine. 'And you're paying for all of this as well, oh my God!'

Lexie laughs and flaps her hand in dismissal of her own incredible generosity.

Freya, Jane thinks. It is all she can think. Lexie knows Sophie is having a girl. And she knows what she's going to call her.

'I know I said I wouldn't,' Lexie is saying now, 'but you know how much I wanted to say' – she looks round, her eyes glossing – 'thank you, Sofes, for taking me under your wing.' She reaches behind the armchair and pulls a large holdall from the floor. It is brown, with pale tan straps, and has a chequerboard kind of pattern made up of four-leafed things and the initials LV.

Jane knows that pattern. Remembering Sophie teasing her for not knowing what CD stood for the other month, she racks her brain for the name of the designer. If she can say something complimentary but also knowledgeable, Sophie might be impressed. LV. LV, LV, LV. Nothing. All she can think is Luncheon Voucher, which she's pretty sure isn't it. But Sophie is shrieking:

'You said that was your overnight stuff!' Her hands fly to her mouth.

'Overnight stuff?' Jane finds herself looking from Sophie to Lexie, whose smile is all benign mischief, cosy conspiracy.

'It was the same price to book the suite for twenty-four hours,' she explains to the group. 'So we thought we may as well have a girlie sleepover, didn't we, hun?' She gazes lovingly at Sophie before giving another little excited shrug and zipping open the bag. Out comes a very large and very professionally wrapped pink parcel topped with an extravagant pink bow.

Jane realises her mouth is open. She shuts it, tight.

'Sorry not sorry.' Lexie giggles, standing to hand over the preposterously sized gift.

'Oh my God,' Sophie says, her eyes filling. 'I can't believe this!'

'Christ,' Jane mutters into her drink. Out of the corner of her eye, she glimpses Hils raising one eyebrow to Kath and is filled with the desire to go and kiss them both on their foreheads.

Sophie opens the package. It takes an age; she tears off the sticky tape one millimetre at a time, half laughing, half crying.

'I just don't want to spoil the beautiful paper,' she says. 'It's like actual silk.'

Jane finds she has drunk all her champagne. The next bottle cannot come quickly enough.

Meanwhile, glaciers melt, entire continents drift, the temperature of the planet rises by a fraction of a degree. Eventually the gift is unwrapped.

On Sophie's lap, almost obscuring her face, is a baby-pink wicker basket lined with pink satin. Peeking out of the top are roses made from pink, cream and white fabric – little socks, Jane realises, a dozen of them, offset by dark green synthetic leaves. Someone has made roses... from socks. There are bibs, larger flowers made from what look like burp cloths, and a pink cotton hat tied in a topknot. And waving from the top of what it now dawns on Jane is the deluxe baby basket Lexie asked them to chip in on, and which she has bought on her own, is a beautiful old-fashioned teddy bear.

CHAPTER TWENTY-THREE

JANE

Sophie bursts into tears.

'It's too much,' she says. 'Thank you so, so much. And the hotel and everything, you must have spent a fortune. I don't know what to say.'

'Well, you didn't get spoilt rotten last time, did you?' Lexie says, smiling as if she is saying something kind. 'And you deserve a fuss, hun.'

No one says a word. They all bought Sophie presents when Kyle was born, Jane thinks, desperate to know if the others are thinking it too. Not while Sophie was pregnant, OK, but after. They visited the hospital hours after the birth, dropped oven-ready dishes round to the house; Jane took him for long walks in his pram to let Sophie catch up on sleep. She burped him and rocked him and babysat while Carl and Sophie went out, even though she was often exhausted herself, even though the smell of his little baby head made her cry and cry and cry. What constitutes getting spoilt rotten? What Lexie is doing is not a fuss. It is total materialistic insanity.

'Louis Vuitton,' Jane gasps.

'What?' Kath asks.

'What? Nothing.' A blush spreads hot down her neck.

A knock on the door. Thank God.

Lexie jumps up. 'That'll be the afternoon tea!' On her tasteful wedge heels, she strides out, leaving the rest of them once again looking at each other. It is hard to read Hils and Kath's expressions.

'You've definitely been spoilt rotten now.' Hils's eyebrows almost reach the fringe of her silver-grey bob. 'Sorry if we didn't make enough fuss last time.'

It is hard to know if she's being sarcastic. Even harder to fight the hope that she is.

'We're a bit older, I suppose,' says Kath, a hint of apology in her voice. 'We didn't have baby showers for ours, did we? No one did. It wasn't really a thing.'

'Don't be silly,' Sophie says, waving a hand in dismissal. 'I didn't expect anything. I think Lexie just loves this stuff. She wants to do a gender reveal next month!'

'Gender reveal, yeah,' Jane replies. 'Except she mentioned you were having a girl, so...' The passive-aggression clangs. 'Freya. Nice name.'

Sophie adjusts the angle of her head, as if to free a trapped nerve. 'We were just comparing notes, that's all. It was just one of those conversations you have with other—'

'Look! At! This!' Lexie is following behind a man in the now familiar butler's livery pushing a black-and-gold wheeled trolley.

One of those conversations you have with other pregnant women, that was what Sophie was about to say. Conversations that Jane cannot have, as if by being unable to conceive, she has been ruled out of this entire area of womanhood, as if she is not, in fact, a woman at all. She blinks hard. She will not cry. She will not.

On the shining trolley are two three-tier plates piled carefully with assorted savouries, cakes, miniature trifles and artisanal choco-late fancies that look like wedding hats. With a deft sleight of white-gloved hand worthy of an art thief, the butler lifts the sweet tower and hides it below in the body of the trolley, which, he tells them, is refrigerated. Everything has been thought of. Everything is perfect. Everything is like something from Instagram. And sure enough, Lexie is taking photos with her phone. *Cheeky little afternoon tea @theritzlondon, #girlyday #afternoontea #TheRitz #livingmybestlife #friendstealer #bitch.*

The pop of a champagne cork. A squeal from the group.

'I'm going to be legless,' Hils mutters.

'We'll pour.' Lexie dismisses the butler with a flap of her hand, even though he is, as far as Jane is aware, a human being. 'You can leave.'

The man returns the bottle to the ice bucket and departs with a subtle bow, his footsteps silent, the closing of the door behind him the faintest click. Jane imagines him in the corridor, flipping Lexie the V and cussing her under his breath.

'Let's have those glasses,' Lexie says with glee.

Sophie puts her hand flat over hers. 'No more for me.'

'Right you are, babe.' Lexie pauses, bottle in hand. 'Jane, can you pop into the kitchen and grab the fruit juice from the fridge?'

There's a *kitchen*?

'It's back into the hallway,' Lexie continues, 'then go left instead of right? It's just there.'

Jane is in the kitchen before she realises that she has been dispatched, much like the butler, without so much as a please or a would-you-mind? She is never, ever going to socialise with this woman again. She hates her.

The kitchen is a small galley – ultra-modern, white high-gloss units. There is a pod coffee machine, a kettle, both brand new. Against the excited giggling of the girls, Jane opens cupboard after cupboard to find: a full service of crockery, glassware, cookware and, ah, there, the fridge, disguised as a cupboard. Inside is a pint of milk, a bottle of white wine, one sparkling mineral water and one still, and a bottle of freshly squeezed orange juice. She retrieves the sparkling water and the orange juice and grabs a glass from the cupboard; but then, spotting a tray in a special tray-sized cubbyhole, she adds the still water and glasses for all of them. She'd thought getting drunk was the only way through this, but now it feels dangerous. She needs to keep a clear head or frankly there is a risk of violence. And she doesn't mean from Lexie.

On impulse, she opens the white wine and pours the whole lot down the sink, fills the bottle with water and replaces the screw top. She puts it back in the fridge, unsure what she's achieved.

'Found some water too,' she says as she re-enters, feeling now even more like the help. She sets the tray on the coffee table. 'Sparkly, still or orange?' she asks Sophie. 'Actually, you love orange and sparkly, don't you?'

Sophie smiles. 'Thanks.'

Jane turns to Lexie. 'Would you like a soft drink, Lexie?'

'Soft drink?' Lexie blinks. 'Oh, I suppose so. I mean, yeah, I should take it easy, I suppose.' She laughs. 'I'll have a still water, babe, cheers.' She swigs back her fizz like a kid told not to drink Coca-Cola, necking it before anyone can stop her.

'We gave the prize to Kath,' Sophie says. 'For the baby trainers.'

Jane meets her eye, for a second utterly lost. 'Prize? Oh, prize, yes! The trainers. Yeah. Yeah, great.'

'Lavender bath salts,' Kath says, holding up a white tub.

'They're REN,' Lexie shrieks.

Kath's face is pure puzzlement. 'I thought they were lavender.'

Lexie laughs loudly. 'LOL! You're hilarious. REN? It's a brand?'

Kath blushes. 'Oh. Right. Sorry, yeah. I usually just have Epsom salts, so...'

'Epsom,' Hils drawls. 'Because you're worth it.' She sniggers.

'Next game,' Lexie says. 'Best birth story!'

Jane's hairs rise. A burning sensation spreads over her skin. When she looks up, blinking hard to try and hide her mortification, Lexie is staring directly at her, eyes a deep green with flashes of turquoise and brown. Eyes full of challenge.

'Jane,' she says, 'I know you don't have kids yet, but you can maybe tell us about your own birth, yeah? But the rest of you, I want all the gories, OK? Woohoo!' Lexie rubs her hands, shoulders high around her long neck. 'This is gonna be *so* bonding. Come on, Sofes! You first.'

Jane scans the room, scalp tingling with misery and a deep, deep need to leave. Hils and Kath are sipping their drinks – settling in to listen or keeping their opinions to themselves, it is hard to gauge. When Jane looks towards her former best friend, she sees she has gone red. Is Sophie embarrassed on Jane's behalf, or is she simply shy of telling the highly personal story of Kyle's birth?

The fact is, they all know the story. All of them except Lexie, it would appear. It was a planned C-section in a private hospital over in Cobham, paid for by Carl's work insurance, as Jane remembers. But that's not the point. The point is, or seems to be, that Lexie has chosen this game to make Jane feel left out. She doesn't know Jane can't have children, but the fact is, she doesn't have any, so there *is* no story she can tell. Her own birth is not the same; it is a second-hand coat in a store full of this season's stock. It is inferior, like her shoes, her dress, her haircut that is apparently so hard to pull off, meaning she can't pull it off, meaning she looks wrong, mannish, unattractive.

The only shred of comfort is that Kath and Hils think she doesn't want kids – an idea she never gave them but one she plays along with, to spare their feelings as well as her own, and to escape any form of sympathy. Only Sophie knows the truth. Only Sophie is blushing. Jane hopes it is with empathy, and that she will wake up now and see the cruelty in Lexie's game.

But Sophie starts her tale, any embarrassment seemingly overcome. Jane downs her entire glass of champagne. Her head is beginning to ache.

'... and then it was really weird,' Sophie is saying, 'because I was on this trolley thing in the hospital lift and next to me was this plastic cot, like an incubator except it wasn't, it was just a crib, and what was weird was, I was on my back and this crib was next to me and I can remember thinking: that crib is exactly the same shape as me – like, round, you know? And I remember thinking, all I have to do is get this' – she points to her belly – 'into there.' She points at the imaginary crib and laughs.

Jane stares into her lap, heat filling her. Everything around her is insubstantial, hazy, dreamlike.

'And then?' Lexie says. That there's still something she doesn't know about Sophie is a small marvel.

'And then I was on a bed and there was this screen across me, like a... like when a magician chops his assistant in half? And next thing these big fat yellow legs come up in the air and I'm like, whose are those horrible yellow legs? Honestly, they were the colour of cheddar cheese and they were just, like, these massive triangles. And then I realised they were mine! They were my legs!' She laughs hard. The others laugh too.

In the shallows of Jane's lap, the geometric patterns of her old dress warp. Her vision blurs. Her breath vanishes.

'I mean,' Sophie goes on, 'I hadn't seen my own legs for months, had I?' She gives a hoot, and despite herself, somehow Jane smiles at her hands, clasped now to stop them from shaking. This is Sophie. Funny. Able to send herself up. Grounded. Human. This is the woman she used to be friends with, used to laugh so hard with, talk to with barely a pause for breath. The fact of it makes her heart shrink with pain.

Sophie continues, tells them how she felt like a car, mechanics rummaging around under the bonnet, trying to find a hammer they'd dropped there earlier, continuing across peals of laughter.

'And then.' Her voice quietens; the others too fall silent. 'Then... they pulled him out. And out he came and he was all red and a bit blue and his little fists were screwed up so, so tight, you know? And then they put him on my chest, and he was so warm, almost hot, and I thought: he's come from *inside me*. Like he was part of my body, like a heart or a lung, which he was, I suppose, but now he was outside, and his blood was my blood and his heat was my heat and he was alive with my life and his little arm came up and it was...' She starts to cry. 'Sorry. Hormones. But all the backache and the weight gain just... disappeared. Because he was there. And he was a miracle, just... a miracle.'

Like rain, two tears drop onto Jane's clutched white hands. Sophie had told her this very story that day in the hospital, and she had swallowed down her pain in gulps, had sat on the bed and taken Kyle in her arms and wept for her friend, for herself, for how unbearable and complicated life can be, for how impossible it was in that moment to separate her own sadness from her friend's joy, her own joy on behalf of that friend, relief at the two of them having worked through the wedge that had been driven between them.

Sometimes, friendships are injured by kindness – two people trying to spare one another's feelings, ending up distanced by misunderstanding. But it is kindness that will repair them too. And now it seems all that kindness has been replaced by champagne cocktails and hotel suites and expensive gifts – by so much *stuff*.

Hils and Kath are a little flushed, their eyes shiny with emotion and, perhaps, the champagne.

Lexie is smiling, her head cocked to one side. She bites her lip and wiggles her fingers in front of her face.

'Oh my God, that's made me really emotional,' she says. But her eyes are not shining. She is not moved as the others are. She does not, Jane thinks, love Sophie like she and Kath and Hils do. She looks... like she's been told she has to wear cheap shoes.

There is a pause, during which the women tuck into the tea. Jane is desperate for another glass of champagne. Ordinarily she would pour herself one, top up the others. But ordinarily has been replaced by this... this game and she is unsure what the rules are. Waves of sadness are rising around her. She is sinking, she knows. She is a moth trapped, muted by its case of amber. If she cries, she's not sure anyone will hear. If they hear, that will be a disaster. As horrendous as this day is, it's not about her – it's about the friend she used to love, still loves.

'Are you thinking of having kids?'

She looks up to find Lexie gazing directly at her again, that same cold defiance. 'Sorry?'

'I asked if you're thinking you might have kids one day?'

Jane glances at Sophie, whose ear tips are aflame, whose scalp glows red in the parting of her newly caramel hair. Why can't she look up? Surely she hasn't told Lexie? Surely not? No. If she had, Lexie wouldn't have asked.

No one is that monstrous.

'That's a very... direct question,' she says. Breathes in. Breathes out. Rude. It is a rude question.

Lexie throws up her hands; her eyes widen to suggest that Jane has overreacted. 'Sorry, I was just *asking*.'

'I... we... I'm still building up the business and Frankie's... well, he's working all the hours at the moment, he's got his own business too, you see. Maybe in a year or two. When we find our feet financially.'

She takes a bite of her roast beef and horseradish finger sandwich, mostly to shut herself up. The white bread sticks to the roof of her mouth. She dips her head, tries to unstick the bread with the tip of her tongue. Her pulse thuds in her head. The bread comes away in a damp lump. She makes herself look up. She has nothing, nothing to be ashamed of.

Lexie is sitting back in her chair and now clasps her bump with both hands. 'You should go for it sooner rather than later, you know,' she says, as if they know one another well. 'Honestly, it's the best thing that's ever happened to me. I had quite a hard time growing up and I suppose I feel like this is my chance to give someone the childhood I never had.'

Jane looks up, sees something real but fleeting cross Lexie's features before she appears to return to herself, adding: 'And it's really brought Steve and me closer together.'

A mobile rings: 'Halo', by Beyoncé. On the coffee table, what looks like the latest iPhone vibrates. The name *STEVE* flashes.

'Talk of the devil,' Lexie says, standing up. 'Oh my God, the man can't leave me alone for five minutes! Excuse me one sec.' She grabs the phone, gets up and heads towards the hallway, laughing.

'I thought I told you not to call me.' The words come sailing through, the tone an affectionate mock telling-off. Another second, a door opens and closes. Silence.

Jane cannot look, cannot go anywhere near looking at Sophie.

'Actually,' she says, 'I really need the loo.'

It is a half-lie. She does need to pee, but most of all she needs to be alone – five minutes to compose herself, remember who she is. She wishes she'd saved some of the Bach's.

'There's an en suite off the spare bedroom...' Sophie's voice trails after her.

Jane heads for the hallway. On the right there is another door – she must have walked past it on the way in. She pushes it open and is immediately aware of Lexie's voice coming from further inside.

'I told you not to fucking call me,' she is saying – a loud whisper full of menace. 'I can't believe you'd call me in the middle of my special day.' There is a pause. Jane's heart quickens. The king-sized bed suggests this is the master bedroom, not the spare, although it's anyone's guess in this pumped-up reality. Whichever it is, Lexie's voice is coming from the bathroom. Caught between conscience and curiosity, Jane hovers.

Curiosity wins. She moves further into what an estate agent might call an incredibly spacious bedroom, the clean blues and whites making her think briefly of her mother's old Wedgwood collection, the one Jane smashed by dropping it piece by piece from the window of their fourth-floor flat after coming home early from school on the last day of term to find intimate noises coming from her mother's room, a thought she pushes quickly aside because Lexie's voice is amplifying, the pitch rising.

'I'm not being funny,' she says, 'but you agreed to this. And anyway, it's too late, I've paid the balance...'

So... hang on, *what*? Has Steve paid for the baby shower? How much did it cost? Hundreds? Maybe even a grand? Jane has no idea.

'Well, you *can't* have it back,' Lexie hisses. The door to the en suite is open. Jane can see Lexie in the mirror, staring at herself while she talks, angling her face this way and that, admiring her appearance even while arguing, smoothing her hair, plucking a stray eyelash from her cheek. 'I know. I know that. But I wanted to, OK? It was important to me, OK? This is my lived experience, my right. I can't believe you're being so fucking cheap, to be honest.'

Jane edges towards the bathroom door. She is spying, there is no other word for it, but the discrepancy between Lexie's Instagram life – her various allusions to Steve and the perfect relationship they share – and what is playing out now is so shocking it has given her something approaching a thrill.

As Lexie continues to berate her poor boyfriend, she slides her free hand under her red silk blouse. The blouse lifts. At the back of her waist is a beige strap. At first Jane thinks it must be a medical support of some kind – no, a hidden wallet. She dares to look closer. The front of Lexie's blouse has ridden up too. And now, huffing with irritation, Lexie tucks the phone into her shoulder and, with both hands, readjusts a round, flesh-coloured dome.

A flesh-coloured dome. On her perfectly flat, tanned belly.

CHAPTER TWENTY-FOUR

FRANKIE

February

Frankie follows Natasha upstairs, filled with dark apprehension, almost fear.

She is leading the way – again. Again he follows. Up the banister-free concrete stairs, stairs like in an art gallery, and actually, there is enough art on the walls for it to be a gallery. Jesus, the money in this house.

'Through here,' she says. He realises she's been chatting to him while they walked and that he hasn't been listening.

She is sitting on a tall chair in the corner of an enormous bathroom. There is marble everywhere, grey and fawn and white. Like the chalet, the bath is sunken, big enough for four people. Perhaps that's her thing – their thing – getting it on with other couples. He fights the blush he can feel rising in his cheeks, looks about him in the most workmanlike manner he can scrape together, although tiredness is kicking in and his concentration is failing. He sips the wine to hide a rising anxiety that feels close to panic. The shower is a walk-in – no door – and again it is spacious. When he looks closer through the smoked glass, he sees that there are two shower heads, two controls.

'That's our double shower,' she says, reading his mind. 'All rather kinky.'

He drinks again, again in panic, even as he tells himself to stop. The wine is hitting him – hard. He hasn't eaten since a bacon sandwich at eleven this morning from the van outside Wickes.

'So, what is it you want doing?' he asks – the bathroom is perfection. Nothing needs doing, nothing at all.

'I'm thinking jacuzzi,' she says. 'See the bath? Basically, I want to know if I can get a jacuzzi fitted to what's there or if I have to buy a whole new set. I mean, is there a jacuzzi tap fitting or whatever? Sorry, I've literally no idea.' She gives a low giggle. 'I just thought it might be fun to have bubbles, you know? I love bubbles, inside my glass and out.'

'Gotcha,' he says, the word thick in his mouth.

'You don't have to tell me now. You can measure up or whatever you need to do, then text me a quote later?'

'Hmm.' His head is spinning.

'Are you all right?' Her hand is on his forearm. 'Frankie? You look a bit dazed, lovely. I bet you're drinking on an empty stomach, aren't you? You've probably been working hard all day, you poor lamb. I should've offered you some snacks, sorry. Come on – let's get you a glass of water.'

He is aware of her taking his hand, of staggering a little as they walk together down the sloping floor of the hall. He wants to tell her to let go of his hand. She is chatting; the sing-song of her voice reaches him, but it sounds like birds.

They take a turn, another. The insides of his head lurch. They are not in the kitchen. They are in a bedroom. The pressure of her hand on his chest. The bed sinks underneath him.

'Soft,' he says.

'Lie down,' she says. Two hands now on his chest.

He lets himself fall backwards. The duvet is so clean, so...

'I'll get you some water. I think your blood sugar is low.'

'I...'

He tries to sit up, but it feels like the most monumental effort and his arms collapse. 'Natasha?' He closes his eyes. The smell of lavender. The room spins.

'Hey.' Beside him, the bed sinks; he feels himself roll to the right, fears he might roll off.

He opens his eyes a fraction. Natasha is sitting next to him. She is holding out a glass of water.

'Are you OK? You look a bit spaced out.'

'I bought a watch,' he says. 'I've been so stupid. So stupid.'

'Don't say that.' She is stroking his hair. It is so soothing, but it's confusing too, because in his belly, he feels like he's got an exam, like his head and his belly belong to two different people.

'Stupid,' he says, thinks he says.

'You're not stupid. No one thinks you're stupid, Frankie.'

His fists clench, nails sharp against the palms of his hands. 'You don't understand. I only bought the watch because of the bath.'

'The bath?'

'Yes. But it's not the bath. It's the baby. She can't. My wife. Jane can't... we can't have kids. I can't do anything about it.'

'Oh, darling.' She is still stroking his hair, firm but gentle, like his mum used to. 'It's not your fault.'

'I bought a watch,' he says. 'But it was stupid.' He starts to cry, doesn't even care that he's crying in front of her. 'I'm so stupid.'

'It's not stupid to want nice things.' She strokes his face, his neck. 'I like nice things. I like your watch. I liked the shirt you were wearing the other night. Having money and taste isn't a crime, you know, and you work hard for what you have. You're a self-made man.'

Dimly he is aware of her putting the glass somewhere near his head while somehow unbuttoning his shirt. His hands come up – *stop*. Fall away.

'I wish I could make it right.' He thinks that's what he's said. His lips have gone numb, his tongue fat. He's said things he shouldn't, things he's never told a soul. There's a dark patch on his brain. He swats at it – go away, go away. 'I wish... I wish...'

'I know you do, baby. I know.' Her fingers run over his chest, half scratch, half caress. 'Don't get upset. It's all right. It's OK. It's not your fault. It's just not. You're not stupid. I don't think you're stupid. I think you're tired. You're so tired. You work so hard, Frankie, so, so hard. I think you're amazing.'

Air, warm on his stomach. The butterfly kiss of eyelashes on his chest. Lips on his belly.

'No,' he says. Blackness. Something blacker still, hovering.

The clank of metal. A glimpse of her long dark hair. Shiny mahogany hair. Keep your elbows off the table, Frankie. Sit up straight. Close your mouth while you chew. Good manners cost nothing.

The fabric of his trousers is peeling away down his legs, the bounce of one foot, the other, the soft crumple of the trousers hitting the floor. His socks. They're still on. His stinking feet. The ticklish trail of her fingertips up his thighs. A stirring he doesn't want in his boxers.

Blackness.

Later. A flash of white light. She is naked. She is moaning, moving above him, on him. Her head is thrown back. The base of her chin is pale. Her breasts sway about, their shape strange, the nipples large, purplish, her skin tanned. They are not Jane's breasts.

'That's it,' she says. 'Oh yes, Frankie, that's it.' She is getting louder. 'That's it, that's it, oh God.'

Later. The bed is soft. He startles, gasps. Wakes. He is naked. The woman, Natasha, is naked beside him.

He sits up. He is panting, his heart racing. 'What?'

She stirs, throws out her arm, covers his cock with her hand – casually, as if it is hers.

'Hey,' she says. 'Tiger.' She smiles sleepily.

He blinks hard, pushing at his temples. They were in the kitchen. No, the living room. No, the bathroom, her cross-legged on a chair. The wine. He can taste the acid tang of it in his mouth, feel it lodged in his stomach. His stomach, oh God. He lifts her hand and tries to get up. Head spinning, legs almost giving way, he staggers, then crawls to the bathroom. Just about makes it to the loo, groans, hands to his face, his skin slick with sweat.

'Oh God,' he says. 'Oh God, oh God.'

'Frankie?' she calls to him. 'Come back to bed, darling.'

CHAPTER TWENTY-FIVE

JANE

April

Jane jumps back as if electrocuted. Finds herself crouching, cowering in the shadows. Her heart is beating fast. Lexie is wearing a pouch. She is not... Lexie is not pregnant. There is no baby. There never was.

Lexie is still arguing. Oh my God, if she'd looked into the depths of the mirror for one second, one split second, she'd have seen Jane here on the floor: spying, eavesdropping.

Did she?

No, she is still lost in her own reflection, expletives spilling out of her with a fluency born, Jane thinks, of much practice. What a way to talk to someone you love. Jane can't imagine ever talking to Frankie like that, not even in anger.

Nausea rising, still crouching, she manoeuvres herself in clumsy half-steps, edging backwards. Lexie is wearing a fake bump. She is not pregnant. Is that what she has just seen? Is that what this means? Does it? It must. It does. There is no other explanation. She is faking her pregnancy, the fact so utterly unbelievable that for a moment it hangs in the air as two separate possibilities caught in a kind of warring stasis: it cannot be true; it can. It must be something else; it can't be anything else.

But Lexie is winding up to a kind of feverish, hot whispered climax.

'This isn't just my baby, you know,' she hisses. 'You didn't seem to have a problem making it with me.'

Survival instinct kicks in. Jane turns, crawls on her hands and knees into the hallway, where she stands, tiptoes past the living room, finds another door towards the kitchen that leads her to a smaller room with one single bed inside. This – this is the spare room, where she should have come for a pee.

Breath caught in her throat, she closes the door behind her and leans against it. Her chest is heaving. She lays her hand flat against the rise and fall. She is sweating; her legs feel weak. After a moment, sensing she's recovered enough to walk without stumbling, she makes her way to this second en suite, lowers herself onto the hard, cold loo seat, one trembling hand lifting to her open mouth.

'Oh my God,' she whispers to herself. 'Oh my God, oh my God, oh my God.'

Lexie is pretending to be pregnant. No matter how many times the fact loops, still it remains as ungraspable as mist. She appears to be fooling her boyfriend – no, *conning* him – into thinking he's fathered a child, extorting money from him as a kind of punishment, as if she resents him for getting her pregnant. But she isn't pregnant. So that doesn't make any sense. And how is it even possible to fool your boyfriend about something like that?

Maybe they don't actually live together. Maybe they're not as serious as she made out. Or maybe they're living together but sleeping in separate beds. Jane remembers Sophie telling her she slept in the spare room for a few months when she was pregnant with Kyle. She wasn't sleeping well, had been tossing and turning, and Carl was getting cross with her, complaining he was tired for work. But what Jane has just heard sounded much more deep-seated than that. The whole relationship sounded utterly toxic.

Poison can seep into relationships when things get tough. Jane and Frankie went through hell when they were trying to conceive, and there were times when they could both have been kinder.

But they never spoke to each other like that – ever.

Something clicks. During that terrible time, when the constant crushing disappointments were getting on top of them, when Jane's own insecurities at being the one with the problem dripped poison into her thoughts, it did make her defensive, needy, miserable. She was never as mean as Lexie sounded just now, but people are different – they have different boundaries, different ways of expressing themselves. What if Lexie and Steve are struggling to conceive? Perhaps *that's* why Lexie is faking it, to save her relationship. It's madness, but God knows, Jane was half mad back then; she understands how frankly insane infertility can make a person feel, how Lexie might be feeling right now, and despite everything, she feels sorry for her.

But if she's trying to bring her and Steve closer, why speak to him like that? It was like she'd forced him to pay for this ridiculous baby shower out of some misplaced spite.

Unless... this isn't about Steve at all. Unless this is about Sophie. Could Lexie be obsessed with Sophie? In love, even? Not necessarily in a sexual way, but something possessive, jealous, unhealthy. From experience, Jane knows all too well how Sophie can make you feel like she's taking you in – adopting you, almost. She was the first real friend Jane had made in a long, long time; the first person she truly trusted after her school friends – apart from Frankie – once she'd left the north and, of course, her mother. She's had colleagues, yes, pals to go for a beer with, but as the treatment consumed her and she gave up drinking, then gave up socialising, then gave up office work, those pals dropped away. People drift apart. Jane and Frankie were two penguins on a block of ice, floating away in an incredibly cold sea. But Jane never had obsessive feelings for Sophie; she was grateful, that was all, for quite a time after Sophie welcomed her into her world of barbecues and nights out and... well, friends. Sophie helped her *and* Frankie off that block of ice. Maybe that's why it's such a shock to find herself now in the freezing water.

Think, Jane.

Lexie's relationship with Steve doesn't sound kind, that much is definite. So yes, with her extravagant 'generosity' and the makeovers and clothes designed to make them look the same, maybe she has fallen in some sort of love with Sophie – a girl crush, a proprietorial drive to *own* her, as if Sophie is yet one more new possession – *#bestfriend #twins #mineallmine*. Interesting that she only announced her pregnancy after Sophie's, then made it into the same 'event'. Yes, the more Jane thinks about it, the more she thinks this has little or nothing to do with Steve. Perhaps this fake pregnancy, this con, is a way of becoming close to funny, beautiful Sophie, with her successful husband and her double-fronted Victorian house and her posh car and her nice life; a way of becoming closer than anyone else. By inventing a baby, Lexie has created this huge, deep thing to have in common. Yes, yes, this makes the most sense. This is about Jane, yes, but not really. Jane is the target, but only because she has to be eliminated in order for Lexie to 'get' Sophie.

Jane's hands clench into fists. She groans.

She doesn't know. She doesn't know she doesn't know she doesn't know. That she doesn't know is all she knows. It is all guesswork. It is all too weird. She could sit here on this toilet seat breathing in this floral air freshener in this millionaires' hotel trying to figure it out for a week and she wouldn't get any further. Only one thing is certain: she has to get out of here. And it has to be now.

'There you are!' Lexie is positively beaming as Jane returns to the sitting room. 'We were wondering where the hell you'd got to. It's your turn to tell your story!'

Jane forces a brief smile before, eyes down, she grabs her jacket and bag from the back of a chair.

'Guys,' she says, 'I'm really not feeling a hundred per cent. My stomach's been really tricky lately; I think I'm going to have to see a doctor. So, so sorry, I'm going to have to head off.'

'What?' It is Sophie. 'We haven't had the cakes yet!'

Jane cannot look at her, she cannot. Besides, she doesn't need to; knows what her expression will be from her voice: hurt, confused, questioning. Despite their arguments, no part of Jane wants to hurt her friend.

'Enjoy the rest of the shower,' she calls, trying for fragile cheer, a voice that says, *Hey, wish I could stay, really I do, but I'm not well at all.* She raises her hand in a wave. 'Don't get too drunk, ladies. Really sorry.'

It is all she can do not to run, but once in the corridor, there is nothing stopping her and she lets her legs carry her as fast as they can to the lift. She waits, panicking, shaking her hands in front of her as if to dry them. The lift numbers light up: 3... 4... At 5, she hears her name.

'Jane? Jane? Wait!'

Sophie. Sophie has followed her out. All Jane can do is pretend she hasn't heard, even though that won't fool anyone, not for a second.

... 6... 7. The lift announces itself with a soft ding. The doors open. Jane steps in.

'*Jane!*'

The lone Victorian woman with the parasol stares impassively from the glossy back panel of the lift. Jane makes herself turn. She is a trinket in a box. She is a moth in amber. She opens her mouth, but before she has managed to form any words, the lift doors glide shut. She closes her eyes, but the expression of hurt and confusion on Sophie's face is exactly as she imagined it. And it burns into her mind's eye like a hot coal.

CHAPTER TWENTY-SIX

THE HOSPITAL

The nurse is waiting outside the cubicle, for crying out loud.

'You don't need to wait for me,' I call out. 'I can manage on the crutches – I'll see myself back.'

'It's fine.'

'I might be a while,' I try. 'I think I'm a bit constipated.'

'Take your time. There's no rush.'

Constipation as alibi – how has my life come to this? I thought the NHS was under-resourced? Just my luck I end up in the world's most over-staffed ward.

I groan, to keep it authentic. I've done some pretty humiliating things in my time, but this takes the cake. Why can't she go and drain an abscess or something? Empty a catheter? Bandage a limb?

A crackle comes from outside. Sounds like it's coming from the corridor. I hear her shift on her foam soles then walk in the direction of the door. Voices then. I can't hear the words, but from the intonation, it sounds like a question.

'Yes,' I hear my nurse say. And, 'One.' And, 'Jane Reece.'

I close my eyes, wonder how long I'm going to have to sit here.

The foam soles squeak back. 'How're we doing in there?'

'Who was that?' I ask. 'I heard voices.'

'The police,' she says.

'What did they want?'

'Oh, they're looking for... someone.'

'Who?'

No answer. I don't need one. I know who they're looking for.

'Jane?' Nursey's voice is close. 'I'm just going to pop out a second, OK? I'll be back in five minutes.'

Brilliant.

CHAPTER TWENTY-SEVEN

JANE

'Frankie?' It is only a little after six, but the house is dim and silent – no lights on, no radio, no football commentary.

Des whimpers at her, his tail wagging madly. 'Franks?' She crouches to tickle the dog behind his ears, pushes her face to the top of his head while he makes his strange throttled sea-lion sound. 'Hey, Dezzie, hey, boy. Where's your daddy, eh? Where's Franks?'

In the silent stillness, the fridge hums. Frankie promised her he would rest, but she knows that if he got a call, he will have answered it. He hates to let anyone down.

Suddenly incredibly tired, she plods up the stairs. More than anything, she needs to lie down, get the thumping in her head to die away. Hopefully she can grab a nap, anything to get a break from thinking about that nightmare baby shower: the over-the-top extravagance, Lexie's defiant stare, the way she spoke to her poor boyfriend, the hideous birth story game, her fake bump, Sophie's wounded expression as the lift doors closed. Gah. If she can just block it all out, by the time Frankie gets back she won't be quite such a mess and they'll be able to have a rare evening together without one of them falling asleep.

She splashes her face with cool water and pats it dry, glancing briefly at her tear-stained reflection, her eyelids swollen and red.

She has cried most of the way home – for what? What really? A stupid baby shower hosted by a stupid person who shouts at her boyfriend and is pretending to be pregnant either to bully money out of him or get her claws into Sophie – Sophie, who will comfort her, no doubt, when she 'loses' the baby, which is the only logical outcome of this surreal affair. Jane has cried like a child in the play-ground because a mean girl has come in and stolen her best friend and now her best friend won't play with her anymore. And she has cried because now she has seen, really seen, the ugliness that girl is hiding under the mask. She longs to tell Sophie, to protect her from this evil woman. For all that Sophie has hurt her, there would be no joy, no victory to be had in revealing Lexie's deception. But she can't. How can she? Having protested twice already and not been believed, there is nothing to make her think she will be believed a third time, especially when Sophie knows Jane can't have children herself, and when she thinks Jane's been set against Lexie from the start. Loyalty has shifted like sand under the sucking tide, leaving her foothold loose, too loose to stand.

Thank God for sunglasses.

To her own reflection, she imitates her mother's screwed-up, mean-spirited face. She half closes one eye, almost alarmed at how like her mother after several too many she looks. Leaning into the mirror, she whispers: 'Never let anyone see you cry. Don't give them the satisfaction.'

She crawls into bed, now unable to stop thinking of her mother. It is weeks since she has called her; the guilt is a rock in her gut.

She will call her tomorrow. Tomorrow. Her eyes close; she feels herself drift, wells of exhaustion built up over weeks, months, years…

Her phone buzzes. She ignores it. It buzzes again and again. Not a text then but a call. She opens her eyes.

KATH flashes up on the screen, a photo of a smiling Kath clutching one of her many gold medals for best in her age category.

'Kath, hi,' Jane says.

'Wotcha,' Kath says, with immediate and obvious drunkenness. 'Everything OK?'

'Yeaaahh. Me and Hils jus' left. I jus' wanted to check you were all right. You looked a bit upset earlier. We were a bit worried aboudyer.'

Jane's eyes prick. 'I'm fine. I'm just... really tired. This stomach thing is a pain; I'm going to get it checked out.' *Lexie is a fraud. My friendship with Sophie is in tatters. I don't even know if I like her anymore, but I can't tell anyone because I can't lose my running girls, my Friday drinks, it's all that's kept me going these last few years...*

How much we want to say sometimes. How little makes it out of our mouths.

'It wasn't really our scene, to be honest,' Kath is saying, sibilant with alcohol. 'But Sophie seemed to have a good time and it was cool getting to see the inside of one of those suites, I ss'pose. Listen, d'you wannus to come over? We could swing by the offie and bring the after party to you, jus' the three of us?'

There is a pain in Jane's chest. Despite being seized by profound exhaustion, despite her despair and her confusion, the urge to say yes, to invite them over and confide in them almost overwhelms her. To tell them that she can't have kids – just get it out of her, get rid of it, tell them she doesn't want sympathy, doesn't want them censoring themselves when they chat about their children, just wants them to carry on being their funny, lovely selves. She longs to tell them what Lexie has been doing behind the scenes, her insidious campaign of hate, and, of course, the fake bump.

She wants, it occurs to her, to be believed.

'I think I'm just going to chill,' she says when Kath insists, throwing in a takeaway by way of persuasion. 'I've got work in the morning.'

'OK, babes. If you're sure. We were juss' worried about you, thassall. You know you can talk to us, don'tya? Me and Hils,

Hilary, the Hilster, the Hills Are Alivester.' She laughs. 'We're your mates, yeah? You can talk to us.'

'I know that,' Jane manages.

There is a rustle, then Hils's voice comes on the line, so loud Jane has to pull the phone away from her ear. 'I might swing by the caff tomorrow,' she says. 'Only 'cause Starbucks charge me for my coffee, mind.'

Jane laughs, her eyes filling. 'Nutter.'

'You didn't miss anything by the way,' Hils adds. 'Just more of the Lexie and Sophie show. I would've told them to get a room, but they've already got one, haven't they?' She laughs, making Jane laugh too.

The temptation to quip back something derogatory about Lexie is strong. But Hils can get away with it in a way Jane knows she can't – she would, she knows, strike the wrong tone. She just wants her friendship group back the way it was, and she will not be the one to blow it up. She will not let Lexie manipulate her into back-stabbing or creating some big scene.

'See you tomorrow,' she says. 'Thanks for checking in.'

'That's OK, matey. Shout if you need us, OK?'

She rings off, realising she is relieved that Kath and Hils are still her friends, realising then how terrible that is. Relief shouldn't come into it. Oh, how quickly this has happened, so fast it feels dreamlike, like it's not really happening at all.

'Oh, Dezzie,' she says, feeling acutely, desperately sorry for herself. 'Make it stop, will you?'

She presses her forehead to the top of his head, there, where the fur is softest.

The Lexie and Sophie show, Hils said. *I would've told them to get a room, but they've already got one, haven't they?*

Despite everything, she laughs. At least Hils and Kath are now openly taking the piss out of Lexie's love-bombing. But as the laughter dies in her throat, she feels grubby, and a bit ashamed. She doesn't want this. She doesn't want to start gossiping about a friend, even by proxy, even one who is behaving badly. And again, as so often these last weeks, her mother loops into her mind – her mother, ever the source of gossip, the shame of the entire town. The eggs splashed on the living-room window recently were an echo of what happened many years ago, except that time Jane and her mother were at home, and through the disgusting, viscous mess on the pane, Jane had caught sight of school kids running away, shrieking.

'Close the curtains,' her mother had said. 'Close the bloody curtains.'

A brick through a window: *Bitch.*

'Sticks and stones can break my bones,' her mother had said, scooping up the shards. 'But words can never hurt me.'

That word did though; Jane saw it in the line of her mother's mouth, the sheen on her eyes, the tremble of her hand as she gathered the newspaper around the glittering glass. That word is not who Jane wants to be; she doesn't want to be a woman who calls another woman that word. It is not what she wants women to be to one another, but maybe that's not why she's refusing the word and all that goes with it. Maybe right now what's really holding her back is that there seems to be no way to call this spade anything other than a digging implement without causing irreparable damage to the group as a whole, a group too dear, too precious to lose over some petty point-scoring competition, which in that moment she resolves to pull out of. She could cause a scene, tell Lexie to fuck off once and for all, or she could launch a counter charm offensive, but why should she? Why should she do anything at all? Frankly, she shouldn't have to. She has, she realises, no interest in any friendship that requires high drama or having to prove one's allegiance over and over again. Lexie has seduced Sophie with gifts and sycophancy while engaging in downright nastiness behind the scenes. Jane will walk away with her head held high. If she sees Kath and Hils, it will be at Runner Beans, just the three of them; they can catch up there, maybe go for a quick drink on the way home, find ways around this horror show.

Because while Lexie is around, it has become impossible to remain a part of this family of women and still keep hold of her dignity.

CHAPTER TWENTY-EIGHT

FRANKIE

February

In hot, thrumming panic, Frankie gathers his things. Can barely get his feet into his pants, almost falls.

'Where are you going?' she asks. Natasha. A flash – her on top of him. Moaning. Her mahogany hair. Oh God, oh God, oh God.

'I...' he says but gets no further.

'Frankie?'

Natasha. He has had sex with her. Oh God, oh God, oh God.

His phone is on the bedside table. He grabs it. It is off – he switched it off when he got out of the van, didn't want it pinging when he was in a meeting. He switches it on, waits, almost bursts into tears at the photo of him and Jane at Glastonbury last year. Jane is wearing a flower garland around her head. They both have glitter on their cheeks. There are three texts, all from Jane.

Hey, love, you OK? X

Everything OK? X

Hey again. Assuming you've been called to an emergency but please let me know you're OK. I'm getting worried xxx

He sits on the bed. Notices only then that he is still wearing his socks.

'Jane,' he whispers, eyes pricking. *I love you more than my life.*

'Hey, Frankie.' Natasha strokes his back. 'What's the matter, darling?'

He jumps up, away from her. 'I have to go. I'm sorry, I...'

'You have to *go*?'

'I'm sorry.' He pulls his T-shirt over his head. 'I've been doing such long hours, it must've just hit me. The alcohol. I didn't mean to—'

'Oh my God,' she shouts. Her hand comes up in a stop sign. 'Stop talking. Just – stop, OK? You came on to *me*, remember? You couldn't keep your hands off me, telling me all your problems, getting me to feel sorry for you. I'd had a few drinks too, but I'm not telling you now I didn't mean it, am I? Oh my God, this is outrageous.'

His hands are out, as if to hold her back. 'Please,' he says, wiping at his cheeks, his nose. 'I'm sorry. You're very... I mean, you're very pretty and sophisticated and everything, but this was – it was a mistake, OK?'

'A mistake?' She is kneeling up on the bed, her face twisted with rage. 'How dare you,' she shouts. 'Get out – get out of my house!'

He picks up his trousers and runs.

The air is cold. In the van, he struggles into his jeans, pushes his feet into his boots. His breath staggers. His heart hammers.

'Fuck,' he gasps. 'Fuck, fuck, fuck.'

Forehead against the steering wheel, he makes himself breathe, counts the seconds in, and out, in and out. Gasps leave him. Sobs break from his throat. *Breathe, Frankie. Breathe.* After perhaps ten minutes or so, he texts Jane: *OMG sorry babe, phone died.* His thumbs are clumsy; his eyes blurred. It takes him ages to spell the words. *Emergency over in Wimbledon.* Yes, that sounds OK – he can work out the details as he drives back: a flooded kitchen – no, better, a boiler, something dangerous. And he couldn't charge his phone till he got back in the van. Yes. No. Too much detail. Keep it simple, then stick to it.

Absolute nightmare, he adds: the truth, in a way. *On way back now.*

He hesitates, stares at what he's written, examines it for clues, anything he wouldn't usually write. Oh Jesus, it's two in the morning.

Love you, he adds.

And he does. Oh God, he does.

He deletes it. It's too much; he sounds guilty. He puts two kisses.

Sends.

CHAPTER TWENTY-NINE

JANE

April

She wakes an hour later to the rattle of Frankie's key in the front door. The thump of his kitbag landing in the hallway. The jangle of his keys. A sniff. A sigh. Little noises that have the power to calm her because they are his. Forget Rescue Remedy. Maybe she should make a tape of Frankie's household sounds and play it through her headphones.

She throws back the covers, gets up and makes her way downstairs.

Frankie is in the kitchen making a cup of tea. 'Hey,' he says without turning round. 'Do you want a brew?'

'Go on then. I haven't started dinner, sorry.'

'Don't apologise. It's only seven. We can make something together.'

It is only when she takes the tea from him that she notices his face. It is only on noticing that it occurs to her she has not looked at him, not properly, for ages. They have been the proverbial ships passing in the night. But now she looks closely and sees he is thinner around the cheeks, although it could be the thickening beard. Most of all, it's his eyes that trouble her. They are weary and... something else she can't quite name. Anguished, perhaps.

'Is everything OK?' she says, her heart pinching.

He clears his throat, glances at his phone. 'Yeah, fine. Just tired.'

'Can you switch your phone off? Just for tonight? I can cook pasta or something. We can grab an early night.'

He switches off his phone and tosses it onto the bar with a flourish. Another second and he glances at his tea and promptly pours it down the sink. 'Tea's not doing it for me. Let's open a bottle.'

Five minutes later, it's almost like old times: the two of them sharing a bottle of Pinot Noir and a packet of Kettle Chips, end to end on the sofa, candles flickering on the coffee table, an old The xx album playing.

'So how was Kath's birthday thing?' he asks.

'Kath's birthday?' She feels herself colour. 'Oh! Yeah, yeah, it was OK.'

'That bad?'

She half laughs. 'Am I that transparent?'

'Pane of glass. What's the matter? Did something happen?'

She shakes her head. 'No. Well, yes. It's been going on for a while actually, but I haven't seen you properly to talk about it. It's nothing really. I don't know why it's getting me so down. Playground stuff, you know?'

'In what way?'

She sighs. She'll tell him part of it, but not the fake bump bit – she doesn't want to admit she's lied to him.

'Try not to fall asleep,' she begins and takes a long slug of red. 'So. You know I mentioned Sophie's new friend Lexie? Well, Sophie invited her to Friday drinks a while ago, which I know is fine, but I dunno, it's just not something I would've done, because...' She falters. Is she at all right? Does she even have a point?

'Because you guys are tight?' Frankie fills in.

'Something like that.' She breathes, reassured. 'Only because it's something we do every week; maybe another night would have been... I dunno, anyway, maybe I'm being paranoid or over-thinking or whatever, but this Lexie woman seems to have a real problem with me. As in specifically me. Like, right from the start.'

'How come?'

'I'm not sure. At first I thought maybe it was just her way, but... but she's only rude to me when the others aren't looking. And then it's like she's trying to leave me out without it seeming like that's what she's doing. I probably sound nuts, but like today, she told everyone it was half two, but when I got there, she said she'd changed it to two and that I was late. She said she'd sent me a text but she hadn't.'

'I thought it was Kath's thing?'

Shit, shit, shit. She is a terrible liar, terrible.

'It was,' she says slowly, keeping it together while her mind races ahead. 'But... that's another thing she does, you see – she takes over. She organised it. Which is weird, because she's new to the group and she doesn't really even know Kath that well.' Lies breed lies breed...

'Any chance it was a mistake?'

'Of course. Of course there is. That's the thing, that's what she does – makes it ambiguous. She'll say something mean but make it sound... I mean, today, she kind of said I looked like a bloke, but if I'd acted offended she would've thrown up her hands and said she was only joking.'

'She said you looked like a bloke?'

'Not quite... but yes. That's the point, do you see what I mean? And the thing is, it's like she's got this crazy crush on Sophie, like she's in love with her but Sophie's not really a person but a thing – like... like a doll she wants no one else to play with. I know it sounds pathetic, but honestly it's weird and I'm just finding it really upsetting. The others don't know what she's doing to me, but they've noticed the crush thing. Hils was ripping into her earlier.

The whole thing's quite embarrassing. Like today, she gave Sophie this absolutely whopping present.'

He frowns in puzzlement. 'Even though it was Kath's birthday?'

Jane's cheeks burn. She'd be hopeless under police interrogation, would end up admitting to a murder she hadn't committed before anyone had even asked her a question. Lying to Frankie is something she never does, has never done, and it is horrible.

'Well, exactly,' she says, recovering, glad of the low light. 'The party wasn't even about Sophie. But Lexie felt the need to upstage everyone and give her this ridiculous pregnancy present. Honestly, it must've cost two hundred quid – for the baby, she said, and she was going on about how we, as in me and Hils and Kath, hadn't really spoilt Sophie enough when she had Kyle, so she was rectifying that situation.'

His eyes widen, his mouth turning down at the corners. 'Bit pass-agg.'

'Right?' Jane feels her shoulders loosen. Thank God for Frankie. 'Basically, making out like we're rubbish mates, and she's so much better. Honestly, it's like she's in love with her.'

'There's your answer then.'

'What d'you mean?'

'Why she's got it in for you. If she's got some sort of thing for Sophie, she'll know you're the closest to her, won't she? So you're a threat. She's trying to make you look bad so she can look good in front of Sophie, be her confidante, sort of thing. That's it.'

'I did think that. I mean, she takes things I've said or done and just... twists them, you know? It's like something from primary school. Do you think it is against me personally? I know I said it was, but I guess I thought I might be paranoid. I mean, look at me. I'm hardly a threat, hardly a trophy, am I? I suppose I was hoping you'd tell me I was wrong.'

He shrugs, shakes his head. On his chest, the wine glass glints pomegranate pink. 'You're not a paranoid person,' he says. 'I like to think I know you better than anyone, and you're just not. I think it's got nothing to do with who you are, more to do with who you are to Sophie. That playground stuff happens with blokes too. You'd be amazed how many toys get thrown out of the pram.'

He sips his wine, thinks for a second before continuing. 'It's like Carl and Simon are besties, right? So if they go for beers just the two of them, that's OK, but if I went for beers with Simon and I didn't ask Carl, Carl's nose would be well out of joint. But if me, Simon and Carl went for beers and we didn't ask Pete, Pete would be proper pissed off.'

Not petty when men fall out, is it? she remembers Angie saying a few weeks ago, and yes, the way Frankie has phrased it makes it simpler.

'Blimey,' she says.

'Trouble is, we're all so bloody fragile.'

'We are, aren't we? I can't believe how shaken I am. I can't stop thinking about it. I feel anxious *all the time*.'

A thought occurs to her: now that Lexie is effectively part of the group, Steve will expect to be invited to the boys' Friday drinks. There is no escape.

'It's the little things that hurt,' Frankie adds. 'And you being upset is enough. It should be enough for anyone who loves you, no matter what it is. We all drop a bollock here and there, we all hurt each other's feelings without meaning to, all the time, but this has happened a few times, so it sounds intentional. It sounds more like bullying, to be honest. And that can happen anywhere – work, sports teams, you name it. This football player was talking about it on Radio 5 Live the other day. They were doing a thing on adult bullying and this bloke was saying it had ruined his mental health. He had to stop playing and get counselling.' He sips his wine, seems to be giving it serious thought. 'I reckon, if this... what's her name?'

'Lexie.'

He nods. 'If this Lexie is being a cow to you, you'll have to call her out on it, otherwise you're basically telling her she can do it again, aren't you?'

'Right,' she says, feeling strengthened, heard, validated. 'Thank you.'

He shrugs. 'Should've been a therapist. I'm wasted as a plumber.'

'Maybe you're just good at fixing things. Including people.'

The album finishes. She picks up the remote and turns the TV on. On the armchair, Des lifts his head, as if monitoring them, before dropping it back onto his paws. As she scrolls through Netflix, she turns herself around so she can lie with her head on Frankie's chest. He has believed her, unquestioningly. That she is upset is enough for him, no matter how small the issue. That's what love is. And the thing is, Sophie believed Lexie over her right from the start. Jane has tried to bat that off, has told herself it shouldn't have hurt as badly as it did, that she is pathetic for feeling this much pain. She has told herself that perhaps she is the aggressor here, that her own unhappiness has made her mean, defensive, jealous. But did she tell herself that? Or did Sophie put the thought in her mind? And who gets to tell her what should and shouldn't hurt?

Sticks and stones, her mother used to say. She was wrong.

CHAPTER THIRTY

JANE

The following day, a little after the lunchtime rush, Sophie appears at the door of the café. She is wearing sunglasses, the line of her mouth flat. Before Lexie, Jane would have felt only joy at seeing her best friend unexpectedly like this; now she feels only the childish sense of having done something terribly wrong, a hard lump in her belly. Despite the soothing conversation with Frankie last night, she is still aware of her crime: walking out of Sophie's special day with the flimsy excuse of not feeling well. Before Lexie, Sophie would have texted later to ask if she was OK. Before Lexie, Jane would not have left in the first place. Before Lexie, they would never have got involved in such over-the-top, materialistic, high-maintenance Kardashians-on-acid living-for-Instagram bullshit.

'Coffee?' Jane offers, too brightly, far too brightly.

Sophie shakes her head. 'Just tap water thanks.' Her tone is curt.

Clearly she is not as happy to accept free coffee today, Jane thinks, bitter as a ristretto in a water shortage.

The table for two by the window that Angie likes to sit at is free. It needs clearing, so Jane gestures towards it and follows Sophie with the tray, piling the dirty plates and cups onto it and wiping the tabletop with a quick S motion. Normally this would feel natural. Today she feels like she's being passive-aggressive: *Look at me, see how hard I work.*

'Give me two minutes,' she says.

She scoops up as many empties as she can on the way back to the bar and is about to tell Jude to cover for her, but a wave of five customers all wanting takeaway iced coffees – more time-consuming than regular ones – means she can't leave Jude alone, and it is nearer fifteen minutes before she can hand over and go and sit with the woman who just a few short weeks ago was her closest friend.

'Sorry,' she says as she sits down, sliding a glass of iced water across the table.

Sophie has not taken off her sunglasses. She lifts the glass and drinks. She puts it back on the table – slowly, carefully. 'What for?'

The air freezes.

'Sorry I was longer than two minutes,' Jane says, but her dread shifts, hardens into something like resentment. 'But I'm guessing from your face that you want me to say sorry again for leaving yesterday. Well, I apologised at the time, I think, but yes, I'm sorry. I didn't feel well at all and I knew I had a double shift today. We don't all have part-time jobs.' Damn. She'd been doing so well until that last line.

Sophie's eyes widen. 'What's that supposed to mean?'

'Nothing. I'm just getting a bit sick of being in the doghouse all the time, that's all. I seem to be apologising constantly, and the funny thing is, I really don't think I've done anything wrong.'

Sophie leans forward. 'Apart from being rude to my friend and ruining my baby shower, you mean?'

Jane's scalp tingles. 'I left. I left your baby shower. I didn't ruin it. I don't have that kind of power.' But even as she says it, she knows that one person can have so much power. One person can ruin a life.

'You were forty minutes late!'

'Lexie changed the time and didn't tell me... Actually, do you know what? What's the point? It's not like you're going to believe me, is it? Why would you believe someone you've known for years over a friend you've known for all of five minutes?' Jane glances around her, worried that she's creating a scene, but no one is taking any notice.

Sophie shakes her head, her mouth pursing. 'You can't stand me having a friend who treats me well, can you? You can't stand it.'

Resentment galvanises Jane, edges her towards rage. 'Let me guess, that's a veiled attack, meaning that *I* don't treat you well, yes? Loyalty, reliability, kindness, that kind of thing not enough for you anymore, I'm guessing. You can't buy it in a shop. It's not a suite at the Ritz, is it? It's not the deluxe baby hamper. I have always, *always* been a good mate to you. I *am* a good mate. I'm kind to you *all* the time. I don't ghost you, I don't tell you off, I don't criticise you behind your back. I've helped out with Kyle and fundamentally I want everything good for you. I'm *happy* you're having another baby, I honestly am – I can be simultaneously gutted for myself and happy for someone I care about. But what I can't be is new. I can't be a *new* friend with lots of juicy layers and secrets to discover. It's normal to make a lot of effort at first – everyone does that with a new pal. But no one keeps that shit up – it would be fucking exhausting. And from where I'm standing, it doesn't so much look like she's treating you well, more like she wants to bribe you or buy you or something. The others have noticed, before you say anything. It's embarrassing.'

Sophie wipes at her cheeks with her fingers. 'Why are you being so horrible? Lexie's been an absolute angel. She texts me every morning. Every morning. Just to see how I am. So no, she's not just buying me stuff. She's really sweet and thoughtful and really, really kind.'

'I'm glad you're her first waking thought every single day, I really am. That's not weird *at all*. And if by *kind*, you mean whispering lies about your friends, turning you against them, stirring up trouble out of nothing, then yeah, sure, she's Mother bloody Teresa. She's obviously made me into an absolute monster in your eyes, which is just... just great, obviously, but once she's knocked me off, who's next? Kath? Hils? And so on until she's got you all to herself. She's a total sycophant, for God's sake. And you're so far up her arse, you can't see it. No wonder – it must be pitch-black up there.'

Jane grips the edge of the table, but it is already dawning on her that she has lost control, that she has raised her voice in her own café and has let flow a waterfall of terrible things, things that can never be taken back. Even now, temper edging back down, she can feel she hasn't quite got hold of herself, is not sure she won't push this table, hard, and knock her friend and her gaping, outraged mouth right off her chair.

'Do you know something?' In a simmering murmur, she carries on even as she tells herself not to, can't help herself. 'The Sophie I know would have hated yesterday. It was obscene. You don't measure friendship by how much someone spends on you, for Christ's sake. You don't compare one friend's gift with another and decide which one is the best and therefore which friend is best. And you don't measure friendship by how much someone does for you. It's just... there. Friends are just... there. They're—'

'I can't believe you're saying all this to me,' Sophie wails.

Jane feels a rush of mortification – it is disorientating how immediately this happens. She has upset her friend. And she has done it on purpose. What on earth has she done?

This is Lexie's fault, all of it.

'Look,' she says, conscious of lowering her voice, of holding tight, tight, tight on to a temper that is shaking the walls of her with the sheer pressure of being held in. 'The reason I left yesterday is because... because I saw something, something bad. But if I tell you what it was, if you have any affection for me left, you have to promise to believe me. I admit I've felt jealous – of the baby, but mostly of Lexie and how wonderful you seem to think she is – but I'm not talking out of jealousy now. The woman's a fraud, Sophie. An absolute con artist. I saw it with my own eyes.'

Sophie gives a derisive laugh. 'What? What did you see?'

'Take off your sunglasses,' Jane perseveres, hope still alive –

just. 'Sophie. Take off your sunglasses please. I want you to look at me.'

Sophie sniffs, takes off her sunglasses, the action grudging. Her eye make-up has run. Jane has made her cry. She still has those stupid eyebrows, and her lips look swollen and weird. She cannot look at Jane directly.

'Did you stay over at the hotel?' Jane asks, still unsure how to broach it.

Sophie frowns, nods. 'Lexie had paid for it all. I couldn't say no. And Carl said he'd babysit.'

Jane closes her eyes. Babysit. His own kid. Good for Carl. She opens her eyes. 'And did you get changed in front of one another?'

Sophie makes a moue of disgust. 'What kind of weirdo question is that?'

'Did you?'

She shakes her head. 'Lex got changed in the bathroom. Why?'

'So you never saw her in her underwear?'

'Oh my God, Jane.' She gives another cruel laugh. 'We're not lezzers.'

'I'm not. That's not...' Jane pushes her hand through her hair. Was Sophie homophobic before? She can't remember her ever saying anything like that. It sounds like Lexie talking, the kind of prejudice she might have, though Jane cannot pinpoint why she thinks this.

'Why are you being so weird?' Sophie asks.

Three tables need clearing, the floor needs a sweep and four customers have just walked in. But it's now or never.

Jane breathes in, exhales. 'You remember when I went to use the loo?'

'Yeah.'

'Well, Lexie was in the bathroom. I heard her on the phone to Steve, and she was being horrible to him, just... horrible. It sounded like she'd made him pay for the shower and it was more than he could afford. I mean, do you know how much it cost?'

Sophie shakes her head. 'No.'

'Neither do I, but I imagine it's at least a grand.'

'I don't think Lex has money worries, put it that way. I didn't really think about it.'

'Neither did I,' Jane lies, 'but when I heard how she spoke to him, it was clear he wasn't happy. But that's not the thing. The thing... the *thing* is...' Oh God, this is hard, this is so hard. 'The thing is... I saw under her blouse and she was... she was wearing a pouch.'

Sophie screws up her eyes.

Frantic, Jane mimes the pouch with her hands against her own belly. 'Like a fake bump. It was flesh-coloured and it had straps at the back, but it was a round cushion thing, like, well, like a fake pregnancy. Lexie isn't pregnant. There's no baby. I swear to God I'm telling the truth. She's faking her pregnancy and I don't know why, but I suspect it's because you've taken her in and looked after her and now she's desperate to be, you know, your best friend.'

Sophie stands so quickly she has to lean one hand on the table-top, the other flying to her head.

Jane stands too, tries to reach out. 'Are you OK?'

'Just dizzy,' she says, but as she recovers herself, she looks, more than anything, sad. 'Lexie told me you needed help and I didn't believe her. She said it's normal. She was really nice about it.'

'What? Normal to what?'

'She saw you. Spying on her. She didn't say anything because she didn't want to embarrass you. She wears a support strap for her bump because she had her appendix out when she was a teenager. And the thing is, she's so nice that even though you're trying to turn me against her and she knows you are, she still told me to go easy on you.'

'*What?*'

'I was furious at you for walking out like that, turning your nose up at the whole thing. And I know it was hard for you because of... everything... but you made it all about you and that was so selfish. It was Lexie who calmed me down, and all you can do is accuse her of something so far-fetched I can't even get my head round how you'd expect me to believe it.'

'But it's true! It wasn't a support, it was a big, round, flesh-coloured cushion!'

Sophie glances at her, but only briefly. 'Look,' she says, lowering her voice. 'You're grieving. You're still grieving for the babies you never had and never will. That's what Lexie says and I think she's right. And maybe you're jealous, maybe you're not, I don't know. But honestly, Lexie's really kind and she's really sensitive, and if she does things differently it's because she's younger than us and that's just the way it is now. She likes the high life, that's all. It's not a crime, and if it wasn't for her, I'd never have spoken to you again.'

'Hang on.' Jane's mind is racing, racing, racing... 'How would Lexie know anything about my grief?'

Sophie blushes – has the decency to do that at least. 'It just came out.'

'What did?'

'Y'know. That you can't...'

'What? When?'

Sophie has turned a deep crimson.

'It was before the shower, wasn't it?' Jane waits. When Sophie says nothing, she goes on, yet again unable to stop herself. 'Can't you see how mean that makes the whole birth story thing? You can, can't you? You couldn't look at me. You must know, somewhere you must know how monstrous she is to do that. Oh, Sophie! I don't even care about that, not really, not anymore. But not even Kath and Hils know my situation.' Tears pricking, she stares at her friend, searches her face for some shred of acknowledgement. But it is not acknowledgement she sees there. 'What?' she whispers. 'Sophie, what?' Then it dawns. 'Oh my God, they know too, don't they?'

'Lexie thought they already knew. She didn't realise. It was after you left.'

'*What?*'

The Latin-American soundtrack dies, the sudden absence of music giving the café an eavesdropping quality, as if every conversation has been paused to listen to theirs. Pulse pounding in her ears, Jane nods towards the exit.

'Outside,' she says and strides out of the café, dimly conscious of Sophie following her.

Out on the pavement, she rounds on her friend. 'So let me get this straight. As soon as the door shut behind me, you all had a good chinwag about me, did you? How cosy. How very bonding for you all. I told you not to tell *a soul*. Not a soul. You're the only person I've told apart from Frankie, and you promised me you'd never breathe a word!' Tears have spilt over, are running down her face. Out here in the street, she is crying. 'Oh God, and now everyone is going to look at me with sympathy, with fucking sympathy I don't want and never asked for and everyone is going to talk to me differently and that's going to be just... shit. It's going to be absolutely fucking rubbish.'

'Oh my God, Jane. Everyone will be fine. You're totally overreacting.'

Rage comes so swiftly it almost winds her. Her hands tighten into fists. 'What right have you to tell me what my reaction should be?'

Sophie's eyes are wet with tears. She looks confused. Afraid, perhaps. 'But it's nothing to be ashamed of.'

'I know! I know that! I'm not ashamed! I'm not ashamed of going to the loo or having sex, but there's a difference between what's shameful and what's private, and this is fucking private.' She is panting, aware that she's shouting, that she's been shouting for a while now. And that she's lying. She is lying her head off. Because she *is* ashamed. Her face is burning with the shame she's been told not to feel but at the deepest possible level cannot convince herself not to.

Sophie takes a step back, her mouth ugly, as if she's tasted something she doesn't like. 'I can't believe you're shouting at me as if *I've* done something terrible. You're the one who ruined the shower, not me. You're the one who's been unfriendly towards Lexie. And now you're making stuff up about her and you won't even admit it's because you're jealous. Maybe you don't even know you're jealous. You're not well, Jane. Get help. Go to the doctor.' She thumbs her tote over her shoulder. 'I can't do this. I'm going. Just... just get some help.'

As Sophie turns on her heel, Jane pushes her hands to her knees and makes herself breathe. In the gutter, a green crisp packet dances over the dank drain cover. A car glides past, near silent on its electric engine. In the window of the café, a little girl is kneeling on her chair, eating a blueberry muffin and staring. Staring at the madwoman snivelling in the street.

CHAPTER THIRTY-ONE

FRANKIE

February

Back at the house, there are no lights on. Hopefully Jane is in bed. There is no way, no way in hell he can face her right now.

With the stealth of a house burglar, he unlocks the door. As he steps inside, he cups his hand to his mouth, sniffs his breath. He can't tell if it smells of wine, but it might. In the fridge, he finds a bottle of the cheap Pinot Grigio Jane drinks in the week – one small glass a night; she's very good like that. He puts the neck of the bottle to his lips and swigs – almost gags – makes himself pour some into a glass. It turns his stomach – it is the last thing on earth he wants to drink, will never drink it again after this night – but if Jane smells white wine on him, she needs to think it's this.

It occurs to him that he's probably just driven home drunk and that he must smell of *her*. She was wearing that lime perfume. The lavender smell of her room in his hair.

'Shit,' he whispers.

'Frankie? Oh my God. Are you OK?' Jane is at the kitchen door, blinking with sleepiness in her White Stripes T-shirt and a pair of black pants. Her legs are bluey-white, her short hair sticks up at the back and the pillow has made a little red crease on her cheek. Her features – her long nose and wide, smiley mouth, her small brown eyes, her expressive eyebrows – they are, all of them, features he loves, loves the way they fit together in a way that is all and only hers. The Jane-ness of her.

It is all he can do not to cry.

She moves towards him.

'I stink,' he says, arm coming up to keep her from smelling that woman on him. Tells her he needs a shower.

'OK.' She stops; a fleeting confusion crosses her face. 'Did something happen?'

He downs the rest of his wine. This is every bit as hard as he thought it would be and he deserves every second of the torture. She hasn't even asked him about the job. She trusts him, blindly, as he trusts her. That's what he has ruined tonight. Because in order not to ruin them completely, he's going to have to keep on betraying her, over and over again, every day, with lies.

'Is it Sophie's news?' she asks – oh God, if only it was. 'If it is, I'm over it, don't worry.'

'That's good. That's good, babe.'

She tells him he looks terrible, that he's working too much.

He nods, tunes out, bites his lip against the tears that are welling. He doesn't deserve her. Oh God, if he had a time machine, he'd...

'... happy camping in Wales if I was doing it with you. Honestly. I hate seeing you so tired.'

He nods, self-loathing filling him.

She shivers.

He tells her he's sorry. And that he loves her.

'There's nothing to be sorry about,' she says. 'And I love you too, you idiot. Obvs.'

There is a pain in his chest. He pushes his fist to it, wonders if he's having a heart attack. Maybe that would be a good thing, if he dropped dead right now. But it passes.

'I love you so much,' he says, and she smiles, turns away and heads back up the stairs.

He closes his eyes. A flash of light, the clank of his belt buckle, Natasha pulling his jeans down his legs.

He is an idiot, an absolute idiot. And all because of a watch.

CHAPTER THIRTY-TWO

JANE

April

Two lattes and a flat white. Her friendship with Sophie is over. Three cappuccinos and a breakfast tea. She will lose all her friends. Two oat milk lattes, one soya latte to go and a vegan brownie. She has lost all her friends. One espresso macchiato, one flat white, one peppermint and a piece of carrot cake. Her friends will think she's bitter and jealous, a troublemaker. One tea, one piece of carrot cake. It's all ruined, tainted, spoilt.

At three o'clock she almost closes up. But that's not how you compete with Starbucks, and besides, the place is full.

'Ah yeah, hi,' says a bearded ginger hipster in a denim smock. 'So, can I get three skinny flat whites, a decaf oat milk cortado and a blackberry tea please?'

'Sure.' She smiles at him, gives an efficient nod – *I'm on it* – before turning to the Gaggia.

While Jude rings up the order, Jane sets four espressos to run, blasts boiling water onto the delicate mesh herbal teabag, wonders how it withstands the pressure, how it doesn't break apart, send desiccated leaves exploding everywhere. She puts the infusion on the bar, calling it as she does so: 'One blackberry tea.'

Skimmed cow's milk into one jug, oat into another. The cold milk screams against the steamer, its protest lessening as it warms. She empties three espressos into three flat-white cups. The milk begins to purr – any longer and it will growl, which means it's boiled and lost its natural sweetness and texture and she will have to chuck it and start again. She taps the bottom of the jug and pours, gently does it, her trademark fern shape unfurling in the foam.

'Three skinny flat whites,' she calls as she places them on the bar – no trace, not one trace of stress in her voice, not a flicker of angst in the smile she gives the customer she has mentally christened Hipster Prince Harry. 'Your decaf'll be two secs.'

'Cheers.'

She turns back to the machine. Realises she has made four espressos, not three plus one decaf. She sets a decaf to run, empties the caffeinated offender into the shining metal grid, where it vanishes in less than a second. In two months, her life has drained away as quickly as that espresso, she thinks. She reaches for the bar cloth and wipes off the excess coffee. If only it were that easy: pour one life away, clean up afterwards, make another.

Jane, she thinks then, hooking the jug under the frother, *you and your coffee metaphors are ridiculous.*

The day ends, thank God. Hils doesn't swing by as she said she would. Ordinarily, this would be no big deal, but by now, Jane's thoughts are running wild: her friends were all there when she feigned illness and left the baby shower; they know now or think they know why. They will be sympathetic, yes, but cross with her too for making it all about herself. Maybe last night they were going to come and talk sense into her, tell her they understand but that she has to stop acting like this: throwing tantrums, acting out. By now, Sophie might even have told them all about the fake pregnancy accusation. They will be shocked that she could make up such a thing, will have assumed, like Sophie, that she is going mad, her bitter jealousy making her mean, divisive, a trouble-causer.

That it is making her into a b...

That's why Hils has stayed away today. No one wants to be friends with someone who is constantly falling out with people. Certainly not Kath or Hils. They are like her – they don't do aggro, avoid people who do. She should have let them in – into the house last night and into her heart years ago. They are good; her gut has told her that from the start. Funnily enough, it was her gut, not her head, that threw up misgivings after she told Sophie her troubles that night in the cold van, the desire to make a friend clouding her judgement. Yes, she has always regretted that – without ever being able to pinpoint why. Now, after all this unpleasantness, she thinks perhaps that was the night Sophie claimed a kind of power over her. She took her in. She collected her: Jane, the down-to-earth girl; Jane, who drove a van and was married to a plumber not a hedge-fund manager; Jane, who was recovering from a broken heart. But now Jane's time is over; Sophie has a new piece for her collection: young, glamorous Lexie – in need of someone to take her under her wing. Once again, Sophie can play the magnanimous mother hen and bring this lost chick into the nest.

She wishes Angie would come in. She needs someone older who has perspective and who can tell her what to do. She misses her school mates, so suddenly it makes her want to cry all over again. Maybe she could call Carla and Penny – she confided in them back when she first moved schools, told them all about the awful business with her mother. She trusted them as she always trusted her mates at the school before, the mates she was wrenched away from without warning. When she thinks of all that trust, all those mates, it amazes her now that she could have ever been so open, ever have had such easy friendships. Friends have always been family for her, she realises, since actual family was never anything she could count on.

Neither Carla nor Penny told anyone that Jane had been forced to move due to a scandal with her ex-head teacher. Neither of them patronised her or started talking to her differently. Instead, they invented a nickname for her mother: the Victoriator. They helped her to laugh about her home life, which took away its power. The three of them became their own little tribe – through GCSEs all the way to the end of A levels, when Carla and Penny went off to uni and Jane, intimidated by the fees involved, instead tied up her worldly goods in a metaphorical cloth, loaded them onto a figurative pole and set off for the streets paved with figure-of-speech gold.

She pulls down the shutters and locks up for the night, double-checks the lock, tugs the base to make sure. Satisfied, she unlocks both bike locks and puts on her helmet, knee pads, elbow pads and high-vis jacket. The street is quiet, apart from some early-doors drinkers outside the Old Bear. Raucous laughter bursts from a group of well-heeled men. One of them, older than the others, is smoking a roll-up. His beard looks like it has been there since before beards were a thing. The accidental hipster.

She pulls out her phone, scrolls for Carla's number.

Hey stranger, she writes. *Was going to come up and see Victoria. You about next weekend? Xx*

She smiles – at the shorthand of this text, how quickly she is able to write it, how she sends it without hesitation or second-guessing. It occurs to her now that using her mother's Christian name, the nickname that came from it, was more than a joke. It was a way of making her mother into someone not closely related, not blood, nothing, really, to do with her. She had already started to keep her mother at arm's length. It was, she knows, survival. Perhaps that's what humour is sometimes.

She hasn't even got one leg over her bike when her phone vibrates against her thigh. A fragile sense of joy rising, she pulls it once again from her pocket. *CARLA*.

OMG! YESSSSSS! You can stay at mine! Stay as long as you like just tell me when and I'll shout Pen OMG this is gonna be epic! Whoop, whoop! Xxxxxxxxxx

She laughs, her eyes filling. In all the time they were at school, none of them would ever have even thought about mind games, point-scoring, ghosting, accusations. Maybe Carla and Penny can press the reset button – it's possible they are the only people who can.

She replies: *Let me get my ducks in a row and I'll confirm asap. Xxxxx*

Smiling, almost laughing, she begins a text to Jude:

Do you think you'd be able to duty-manage next weekend?

CHAPTER THIRTY-THREE

JANE

May

On the train she tries to calculate how long it is since she has seen her mother. Victoria. The Victoriator. More than three years, less than five. Scary how the time can go by.

An hour in, a text buzzes. *CARLA*.

Let me know when you get in. I'll come and pick you up from the station. Am so excited to see you. X

There is a GIF: two chimps running towards each other and hugging.

Cheers, Jane replies. *But will do Victoriator first then cab it over. Can't wait. Xx*

That shorthand again, something she's beginning to think is missing from her newer friendships, something she fears she might be losing with Frankie. Perhaps it is her fault.

She takes the short walk up the rise to the small terraced houses near the railway arches and knocks at number forty-six. It is a little after one o'clock. With any luck, she'll be out of here by three and on her way to Carla's. She only has one night and intends to enjoy herself. Her old mates will help her find herself

again. Hopefully she can pick herself up and take herself home
with her.

The door opens to an old lady with thinning long blonde hair
and a greyish pallor to her skin. She is wearing a green sun visor,
patterned sports leggings, which are baggy around the knees, and a
white off-the-shoulder T-shirt. It takes Jane another second to
realise that this is her mother. She is fifty-five. She looks eighty.
And quite mad.

'Mum?'

'I was just doing a workout.' Her back is a little hunched and
one of her teeth is missing on the left side, giving her a hag-like
quality. 'Come in then if you're coming.'

Jane steps inside. The house smells musty – of damp clothing
and cigarettes, closed windows and lemon-scented cleaner. She
follows her mother into the sitting room, where Davina McCall is
doing smiling sit-ups on the small screen. The sound is on high.
The overall effect is quite manic, though there is no evidence of
her mother working out, no room actually, not unless she was doing
it on the coffee table.

'Sit down if you're stopping,' her mother says. 'Cuppa?'

'Great, thanks.'

'Sit down, for God's sake – you're giving me the jitters,' she
says, muting the television with the remote. 'I won't be a sec.'

Jane sits down on the cream vinyl sofa. Apart from the three-
piece suite, a coffee table and the television, there is little furniture.
No shelves. No ornaments. No pictures on the wall. A few
minutes later, her mother returns with two mugs of tea and sits in
the armchair nearest the gas fire – synthetic sheepskin slippers,
skinny legs crossed at the ankle. She has put on a sweatshirt that
says: *DAY OFF*. Ironic. Jane cannot remember her mother ever
doing a day's work in her life.

'So,' she begins, because she can't end this without starting it,
'how's tricks?'

'Chris came back.' Victoria's eyebrows rise, though the effect is not surprised but unimpressed. The outer halves of her brows appear to have dropped off, leaving only two tufts, the brown betraying the peroxide in her hair, which, Jane now notices, is fighting not the dowdiness of what her mother would call mousy – the mousy Jane has always been fine with on her own head – but the telltale silver of middle age. She will be hating it, Jane thinks. She was always vain.

'I thought you'd gone off him?' she offers.

Her mother shrugs, shakes her head. 'Any old rag of a husband is better than no husband at all. Not that he's my husband or owt. Not yet anyway.' She cackles, the missing tooth a presence rather than an absence.

Jane opens her mouth, closes it. Brings her tea to her lips, but it is too hot to drink. She slides it back onto the stained coaster and feels the skin stretch on the back of her shoulders.

'How's Frank?' her mother asks.

'Frankie? He's well. Actually, he's been working ridiculous hours lately. He got in at midnight the other night – he was absolutely wrecked, poor sod.'

Her mother twitches. 'How long's that been going on?'

'Few months. He's trying to earn money for this world trip we're saving for. I keep telling him I'm happy camping in Wales, but he won't listen.' She smiles, but the smile won't stick. She covers her mouth with her hand.

Her mother presses her lips tight, reaches to the floor for her handbag and pulls out a packet of Benson & Hedges.

'And you're sure it's work?' She takes a cigarette, holds the pack out to Jane.

Jane shakes her head, though she is tempted. 'Of course I'm sure. What else would it be?'

The tufty eyebrows again – tiny little guinea pigs. The guinea pigs of disapproval. Focus, Jane.

'What do you mean, what else would it be?' Victoria sighs. 'Just, that's what your dad said, that's all. And Donald. Wasn't work though, was it? Never is.'

'I wouldn't know.' Jane drinks, mostly to shut herself up. *My dad is a blurry photograph, a shadow on the lens of my mind's eye, nothing more.* Too much milk – the tea is claggy against the walls of her throat. She hates who she becomes when she talks to her mother. Her mother, who is smoking as if she too is trying to stop herself from saying something she regrets. Maybe they should both sit here with corks in their mouths for an hour, say their goodbyes and have done.

'Only sayin',' Victoria says eventually, holding up her hand. 'Men. They're led by their—'

'Mum! Please! Don't talk like that about Frankie. He's my husband. He's not like that.'

Victoria gives a minuscule shake of her head, just one guinea pig of disapproval rising a fraction. 'All right. I was only sayin', that's all.'

Oh, this was never going to go well, was it? Victoria is Victoria. She doesn't change. It is foolish to hope she will. *No wonder Dad left her,* Jane thinks. *No wonder they all did. Chris won't be long.*

'Never brought biscuits, did I?' Victoria stubs out her fag, hauls herself out of the chair and leaves the room before Jane can stop her. Stale bourbon creams are the last thing she wants, frankly. Already the claggy tea and the secondary smoke have made her feel queasy. She can hear her mother banging about, swearing softly. Wonders if she's gone into the kitchen to drink. Remembers her that night, eyes half closed but still sober enough to be shocked by the smash of broken glass, the brick on the living-room floor, the note attached with an elastic band.

Bitch.

Sticks and stones. The note goes in the bin. The brick, who knows? Don't let anyone see you cry. New town, new school, new life. New dad. *Call me Donald at home.* Not that he lasted much longer than the others, though he never went back to his wife. Jane's mother was all for marching round to her house. *How dare she throw a brick through my window. I'll punch her bloody lights out. No one does that to me, no one, d'you hear?*

All talk. Fists still raised, her mother had collapsed into bed with the lightest of pushes against the chest, let herself be folded into the recovery position, covered with her yellowing quilt. Let a man move her to another town, move her daughter away from all her friends, while he continued unscathed, untouched.

'Custard creams,' Victoria says, plonking a small plate with three forlorn beige rectangles on the coffee table.

'Actually, I'd better get going,' Jane says. 'I said I'd be at Carla's by three.'

'What? You've only just got here. I've not seen you in years.'

She stays another hour, to appease her mother, but by the time she leaves, she feels like one of Des's chew toys.

From the pavement, she rings the cab number her mother gave her, then texts Carla.

On way. Open a bloody bottle. Xxx

She makes a mental note to check that the cab takes cards. They'll have to swing by a cashpoint if not; her mother has cleaned her out.

The afternoon cools, the sky clouding overhead. She pulls her leather jacket tight around her, shivering. The cab arrives, the guy cheerful, the accent of her home town a kind of music. As she begins to relax into the warmth and allow herself to look forward to seeing Carla and Penny, a sense of achievement fills her, a childish pride in herself. She's done it: she has seen her mother and managed not to scream. She did not flinch when her mother asked if she had any cash on her, handed over the fifty pounds that was in her wallet with a gracious smile, with a kindness mustered by thinking about what Frankie would do in the same circumstances. *She's a pain in the arse*, he would say. *But she can't help it.*

But the triumph soon dies, as it always does, to be replaced by a familiar creeping feeling under her skin. Victoria always says something that clings, something that burrows.

That's what your dad said. And Donald. Wasn't work though, was it? Never is.

. . .

Carla is telling Penny the story of the night she and Jane got roaring drunk on the one occasion Carla came to London – back when Jane was barely nineteen, working as a dogsbody for an advertising agency, before she met Frankie. They were on Tottenham Court Road. It was around midnight and they had staggered out of some late-night dive and decided in their alcohol-induced wisdom to order hot dogs from one of the dodgy roadside stalls.

'So, we're walking along.' Carla is giggling. 'Literally can't believe I haven't told you this one, Pen. So, Jane hasn't even touched her hot dog but I'd eaten about half mine when some guy bumps into her shoulder and next thing her hot dog goes flying up in the air and lands in the gutter, literally in the actual gutter.' She stops, laughs raucously.

Remembering, Jane begins to laugh too.

'Oh my God,' Carla goes on, wiping at her eyes. 'You should have seen her face! And so, obviously, like a true friend, I told her how sorry I was and gave her the rest of mine.'

'No you bloody didn't!' Jane is really laughing now. God, it feels good, the sheer relief of it.

'No, I didn't,' says Carla, also laughing. 'I stuffed the rest of mine into my big fat gob before she could ask me to share.'

Penny laughs hard, which makes Carla and Jane laugh even more. The laughter takes on its own life, leaves the anecdote behind, until they're laughing at nothing, can't remember what was ever so funny in the first place.

It is only the next morning, over cups of tea, the three of them sitting up in Carla's double bed in their PJs, that Jane tells them about Lexie, Sophie, the baby shower... and the mystery of the fake bump.

'Sorry,' she says. 'It's just driving me mad, you know? I feel like I'm losing my mind.'

'I'm not surprised,' says Carla. 'It would do my head in completely.'

'Me too,' says Penny. 'It's your safety net, isn't it? Your mates. I know Frankie is your number one, but you know what I mean. Mates are your rock, aren't they? I mean, not being funny, but they've treated you like shit, hon.'

They. Jane sniffs, glances from Carla to Penny. 'So you believe me?'

Penny frowns, as if she doesn't understand the question. 'Mate! Of course we believe you! Why wouldn't we?'

'Of course we believe you, you muppet,' Carla chimes in. 'This Lexie woman sounds like a total psychopath. I mean, who does that?'

Jane wipes at her eyes. 'I've been through worse.' She looks from Carla to Penny, sees that they think she means Victoria and goes with it. 'I thought I was strong... but I'm not obviously.'

'You *are* strong.' Carla pulls her into her arms. 'You're rock hard, you. You could have gone down the same road as your mum, couldn't you? Eh? God bless her, the old Victoriator. But you didn't, did you?'

'Thanks to you.'

'Not thanks to me at all, you plank. You're the one who ditched the dodgy cider habit. You're the one who did a Dick bloody Whittington, and you're the one who jacked in her job and built her own business.'

'S'pose.'

'Do you want us to come and duff her up?' Penny asks.

Jane laughs, extricating herself from Carla's bear hug. 'Nah. It's OK. I just need to grow a pair, that's all.'

'I actually think it takes balls to rise above that kind of shit,' Carla says. 'Sucks you in, doesn't it? You don't want it to but it does. You keep hold of who you are, OK? Stay classy, queen, stay classy.'

'So you don't think I'm a bad person? Like, mean and jealous and rude?'

Carla laughs. 'Now you really are being a knob.'

CHAPTER THIRTY-FOUR

FRANKIE

February–April

Frankie is shattered all the time, guilt ripping the life out of him. He works. Works hard. Works all the time, some part of him wanting to believe that if he works hard enough, he can make it right. But even when Jane's not with him, he imagines her finding out over and over and over again, sees her face crumple when she realises her husband is actually a shit. She can't find out. She just can't. He doesn't even know how it happened himself; how can he explain it to her? Other than it meant nothing, which even in his head sounds like such a cliché. Because that's what he is, a cliché, a nothing, a tiny little man. His mum and dad would be so ashamed. *He* is ashamed.

But that's not enough to make it right.

The watch he sells to a buy-now customer on eBay for a grand. Two grand down the pan is better than having to look at the stupid yellow dial.

Every time his phone beeps, he jumps out of his skin.

Every time he turns a corner, he braces himself.

Every time the post drops on the mat, he nearly has a heart attack.

But Natasha doesn't contact him. She doesn't appear on the street. She doesn't post something horrible through his door.

The weeks pass. He's still working all the hours to try and repay a debt to himself and his wife and the life he promised her. He deleted Natasha's number from his phone the moment he left her house, but that wouldn't stop her calling, would it? No, if she was a psycho, she would have hassled him by now.

He begins to calm down. He upset her, and he feels bad about that, but it's nothing compared to how terrible he feels about Jane. He should tell her, he definitely should, but what's the point? It meant nothing and it will kill her. Kill them. She didn't leave her mother behind all those years ago to end up with more mess. He can still remember the night she told him about all that – the drink, the men, having to move when her mother had an affair with the headteacher at her school, for God's sake. Using her daughter as a messenger, as a cover, telling her there was nothing going on when there was. If he ever meets Victoria, he'll have words. But Victoria isn't the problem now, is she?

He will tell no one what he's done. Not even Simon, the mate he's closest to after being there for him when he got divorced from Hils. Simon wouldn't judge. He's been there and suffered the consequences. Billy, his mate from school, wouldn't judge either. But Frankie judges. He thinks he's a useless, lying...

He will tell no one.

He works so much he makes an extra thousand, cash, on evening and weekend jobs. He keeps the notes in his bedside drawer, plans to open a secret account. He will make Jane think they're still on three K, then turn round and tell her he's done it, he's made it to ten, and they're going on that trip. Better – he'll organise the whole thing, really diamond-geezer it for her, book the flights, the accommodation, sort it all out so all she has to do is pack a suitcase and step on a plane.

God, he'd love to do that. The look on her face would make it all worthwhile – even the nightmare with Natasha. It might even make him feel a bit less terrible.

April comes. He's putting in a bathroom in New Malden. It's late afternoon. He and Rob have fitted the shower tray and cubicle and have just started tiling around the top of the bath when he gets a WhatsApp message from an unknown number: a photograph of a white plastic stick held in a woman's hand, fingernails painted red.

His stomach flips over.

'Back in a sec,' he tells Rob, pocketing his phone and heading out of the house and into the van.

As he pulls the phone from his pocket, a second photograph lands with a soft chime: black and grey and fuzzy this time. Not a photograph. A scan.

Underneath, someone has typed: *Say hello to your baby, Frankie.*

Sweat pricks on his brow. The white stick is a pregnancy test. God knows, he's seen enough of them. In the little window, two thin lines, blue and parallel. Two lines, not one, not one like all the tests he's seen in real life. And the blob, the blob is an embryo. A baby. It can't be his. It cannot be his. There is no way it is his.

But even as he thinks it, his heart is racing. For a moment he thinks he might be sick. Thank God he is alone. His breath is fast and shallow. A sharp pain in his chest – like his heart is being squeezed tight by an actual hand. He opens the van window, gasps at the air. Bends over the gutter, heaving, spitting.

He didn't use contraception. He didn't even take his own trousers off.

'Oh God,' he says. 'Oh God.'

Outside, the light is falling, the street lamps flickering on. At the end of the cul-de-sac, a woman in a cagoule is walking a brown springer spaniel. She stops, waits while it pees against the base of a spindly plum tree. For one miraculous moment, a moment so full of light his chest actually expands, it occurs to him that this might be Jane's way of telling him she's pregnant.

But Jane never paints her fingernails.

And Jane's number would have come up.

This is not from Jane.

He knows this because he has known from the second it landed who it's from.

As if in response, the phone chimes again. No picture this time, only a message:

This is Tasha, by the way. You know, in case you've forgotten. Meet me at Bar Estilo at 8 tonight. We need to talk, unless you would prefer me to come to your house?

CHAPTER THIRTY-FIVE

JANE

May

On the train home, nursing a terrible caffè latte alongside an even more terrible hangover, Jane closes her eyes and tries to catch up on some sleep. When her phone buzzes, she opens her eyes and sees a WhatsApp video call coming in from Kath and Hils.

'Hey,' she says, keeping her voice down, grinning at their lovely, silly faces.

'Surprise,' says Hils. 'We just thought we'd check you were having a great time but not so great that you're going to leave us and go back north.'

Jane laughs. 'I have such a bad hangover.'

'Did you have fun?' Kath says.

Jane nods. 'I did. It's been... really great. Looking forward to Runner Beans on Tuesday.' She means it, she realises.

'Good!'

'Did you guys do' – she braces herself – 'Friday drinks?'

'Nah,' Hils says. 'I think Lexie was taking Sophie for mocktails at some place up in Chelsea.'

In the other square on the screen, Kath is pulling a face.

'Me and Kath went to that new Lebanese small plates place,'

Hils adds. 'It's really good – they do this amazing balloon bread in this big oven thing that's right in the restaurant. It's cool – we should go. Maybe next Friday?'

'Oh, I'd love that,' Jane says, choked with emotion and blinking hard.

Kath and Hils aren't judging. They haven't taken offence. They're not asking her why she didn't tell them before. They're not accusing her of throwing a tantrum. They're not accusing her of anything at all. More than that, they seem to be acknowledging that things aren't the same anymore but that whatever's happening, they're still her mates.

And perhaps most importantly, they're not looking at her with sympathy. Just... well, just like they would normally.

'Thanks so much for calling,' she manages.

They say their goodbyes and she settles back into her seat and tries to hold on to the warmth of her time with Carla and Penny, and the joy and reassurance of the video call with Kath and Hils. But as the train passes through Crewe and heads south, her mother's words burrow deeper down, worming their way into the core of her.

Wasn't work though, was it? Never is.

She arrives home to find Frankie half asleep on the sofa with Des. Des, at least, wakes up and jumps up to greet her.

'Hey,' she says, budging the dog out of the way, sitting down.

'Hey,' Frankie says, blinking awake. 'How d'you go on?'

'Good, yeah. Great actually. My face hurts from laughing so much.'

He smiles, but the smile is flat and his eyes are ringed in black. His beard is thicker, darker, but it isn't only the shadowing that makes his face look slimmer; he has lost even more weight. Frankie never loses weight. He loves food and beer too much.

Wasn't work though, was it? Never is.

'I've picked up some bits from Markies,' she says, shaking off her crowding thoughts. 'I'm going to make us a nice quick tea, OK?'

'Can tell you've been up north.'

'How come?'

'You said tea, not dinner. And your accent has come back.' He raises his head with great effort. 'I should have had something ready.'

'Don't be daft – you've been working yourself ragged. Stay where you are. It's good to see you with your feet up for a change, and I'm feeling great. Well, hung-over, but great.'

'I feel bad,' he protests, but his head falls back onto the cushion as if he hasn't the strength to keep it raised. The whites of his eyes are bloodshot. He looks terrible – like a bloke on death row.

Trying not to let her concern show in her face, she pats him on the leg and leaves him in front of the footie.

Minutes later, she calls through: 'Frankie! It's ready.'

When there is no answer, she returns to the living room to find him fast asleep on the couch.

'Frankie?' she whispers, unsure whether to let him sleep or not. It's after eight. If he sleeps too long now, he won't sleep tonight. And he needs to eat. 'Franks?'

He opens one eye, startles. 'Oh!'

'Dinner's ready,' she says softly. 'Do you think you can get up?'

He nods, closes his eyes for a few long seconds before, with the impression of summoning all his strength, he hauls himself up.

'You look really bad,' she admits. 'Do you think we should call the doctor?'

'I'm fine.' He leans against her; slowly she walks him towards the kitchen.

'You're limping,' she says. 'Have you hurt your foot?'

'Nah. It's just gone a bit dead. I'm OK, babe. Just tired.'

He smells of sweat and the dusty work smell of his overalls.

'Have you been working today? On a Sunday? Did you work yesterday?'

'Just a repair to a cistern over in Richmond. Not a big job.'

'Oh, *Frankie*.'

They have reached the kitchen, where Jane has laid out the meal on serving dishes, poured wine into glasses and lit candles. At the sight, Frankie stops, his breath shuddering out of him.

'Frankie?' she insists.

'I can't,' he says, pressing his face into his hands. 'I'm sorry. It's too... I... I have to...'

He turns from her and climbs the stairs on leaden feet. She follows him up, lifts the duvet as he eases himself into bed, covers him, strokes his hair. His skin is clammy, greyish beneath the surface. He looks like he's been crying.

'You've made yourself ill,' she says. 'I knew this would happen. You have to stop, love. You have to. I'm going to take your phone off you at weekends and lock it in a drawer.' She says it with affection, but inside she is churned up, cross, uneasy. No world trip is worth this, if that's what this even is.

She makes her way downstairs, all the warmth and affection from the last twenty-four hours draining away. She was hoping the sight of Frankie would reassure her, remind her who he really is instead of confirming her mother's suspicions. But what she has seen is someone who isn't Frankie, someone who can't look her in the eye, someone who has lost weight, collapsed and grubby on the sofa instead of showered and changed and waiting with open arms and a Thai curry on the stove for her arrival like the Frankie of old.

Something is going on. It won't be a woman; it can't be. Her mother was insinuating he was cheating because that's all she knows, but no, it won't be that. He knows what she went through as a kid, knows it is the one thing that would finish them.

But it has to be more than work.

Downstairs, his phone is on the coffee table. She knows the password. She could check.

But no. If she does that, what is left of them? Without trust, who even are they? What becomes of the safe home they have spent the last decade building together?

Another childhood memory: a stressed-looking woman turning

up at the door of... oh, one of their addresses, asking for her mother. Jane going inside, sliding her finger along the dado rail as she walked. She must have been quite little. Victoria, younger, glamorous then, telling her to go back and tell the woman there was no one home, and if she asked about a man called... and again Jane's memory fails her – David? John? Some man's name anyway – to say that there was no one there. Except Jane, that little girl, knew that whatever his name was, he was there, upstairs.

She will not. She will not check Frankie's phone. That is not who she is; it is not who he is.

Instead, she serves herself some food, sips the Pinot Grigio, which is fresh and cold on her tongue. Preoccupied, she eats little, drinks a glass, feels her hangover abate as the alcohol kicks in. Remembering that she deposited the week's cash takings on Friday at the bank, she checks her balance on her phone. With no outgoings for repairs or maintenance this month, the business account is looking healthy, so she decides to transfer a hundred pounds to the holiday fund. Maybe that's one way of getting Frankie to slow down – show him that she too can find savings here and there, that they can do this bit by bit instead of killing themselves.

She transfers the money and checks the jar. There was about three grand in there last time she looked. Maybe Frankie's put some more in. God knows, he's done enough overtime.

She reads the figure: £158.00.

She must have the wrong account. This must be the joint current account. Because the savings account had three thousand and something in it the other week... month.

No. No, it's the Santander. The Santander is the savings account – the jar. Lloyds is the joint current account.

Leaning into the iPad, she pulls up the statement. One hundred pounds is the figure she has just transferred. So before that, the balance was, what, only £58?

'Fifty-eight pounds,' she whispers, hand rising shaking to her mouth, eyes travelling down to the last withdrawal before this evening's deposit: £3,000. Withdrawn by Frank Reece on 12 April.

Wasn't work though, was it? Never is.

Frankie has taken three grand out of their account without telling her.

That's what your dad said, that's all. And Donald.

'No,' she whispers. Frankie is not her dad, whoever he is or was. Frankie is not Donald either, or any of the others. That's not what this is. This is not another woman. This is not Frankie preparing to leave her.

But he is in trouble, financial trouble.

And he has not told her.

And it has made him ill.

His business must be failing. But how can his business be failing if he's working all the time? That makes no sense. He must have someone else; it's the only thing that adds up. Jane cannot give him a child. He has supported her and loved her and never insinuated anything other than them being in this together, but he must long to be a dad. He would be so great at it; everything about him is perfect – kind, funny, affectionate, fair, hard-working, loyal.

Is he loyal?

Why then would he take so much money without telling her?

Unless he's found a woman who can give him a family, oh God. Unless he's preparing to make that move. And he is ill because he is kind and he cannot bear to tell her.

Fat, round tears are rolling off her chin onto her plate. She picks up the paper napkin she folded so neatly when she prepared the romantic supper, now abandoned. On the table, the candles flicker, the food spread like a rejected offering. A howl of pain leaves her; she pushes her plate away, presses her hands flat to the table and lays her forehead on them. She believed she had lost her best friend, she was so wrapped up in all of that, but now she has lost her husband, a man who, she realises only now, too late, is her real best friend.

'No,' she whispers. 'No way.'

She sits up. She will not believe this of him. Not Frankie. The scales might have fallen from her eyes when it comes to Sophie, but Frankie is Frankie. Nothing he's said or done in all the years they've been together makes sense of this uneasy feeling in her gut. He would never cheat on her. Never lie to her.

It is, quite simply, impossible.

She gets up, wipes her face and heads upstairs. He is sleeping. To wake him feels like a violation, but she has to – she has to know. She shakes him, waits while he blinks, focuses.

'Frankie?' she says, her voice small. 'Where's all our savings?'

She's expecting him to tell her not to worry. He's moved the money to an ISA. He's taken advice from Simon on how to get the best interest rate. He meant to tell her but he's been so busy. But he doesn't. Instead, he shakes his head and tells her he's sorry. He's so sorry. It all started with a watch.

CHAPTER THIRTY-SIX

THE HOSPITAL

I press my ear to the cubicle door. She's gone. I ease the lock, open the door a crack. Listen. In the corridor, footsteps. I have to hope they're not hers. I wait. They pass.

I put my hands on the crutch handles and manoeuvre myself out. The padded tops push into my armpits; my hands are sore. The wheelchair is still there. I wonder about using it to get me as far as the lift.

I'm about to sit down when I hear her.

'Ah,' she says. 'You're done.'

Fuck. I smile. 'Actually, I can manage. I'll make my own way back.'

She chuckles. 'I'm sure you can, but I'll take you back anyway.'

'Have they found who they were looking for?'

'I would imagine so. It's nothing to worry about.'

Yes it is, Nursey. Maybe not for you, but it is for me.

'You must be busy,' I say, still standing, squeezing the handles of the crutch, testing my grip. 'I'd rather try on my own, you know. I'd rather walk.'

'Tomorrow,' she says, smiling kindly, gesturing to the wheelchair. 'Let's get you into the chair now.'

I bend, as if to get in. She leans forward to guide me. I drop one crutch, raise the other and bring it down – *crack* – on the back of her head before she's even aware that when I say I'd rather walk, I really would rather walk. She hits the chair seat, slides to the floor. A groan. She opens her eyes, stares at me, fear crossing her face. She grapples for the footrest, tries to pull herself up. I raise the crutch high above my head and growl at her. She stays down, whimpering, her hand up in surrender.

'Please,' she says.

'I need your uniform,' I reply.

CHAPTER THIRTY-SEVEN

FRANKIE

April

At eight o'clock, he's sitting at the back of Bar Estilo with a pint of lime and soda. He's told Jane he's working late, just has to hope none of her mates see him in here – it's not their kind of place; like most runners, they're more of a basic pub brigade, not so much tapas as pork scratchings, dry roasted peanuts at a push. Except for Sophie, who always looks like she's slumming it somehow, looks like a wine bar would be more her style. Kath and Hils wouldn't come in here. He's never seen Simon's ex in a skirt, let alone a dress, not that Jane wears anything other than jeans and T-shirts and those knackered cowboy boots most days. He was going to buy her some new ones when they went to America. He will. He's determined. He will not let this Natasha woman ruin their lives.

After his outburst in the van, he made himself get a grip. He bought a cheap shirt, soap and deodorant at Sainsbury's, used the toilets there to get cleaned up and changed. His nails are still rimmed with black. As he waits, he tries to scrape out some of the dirt with the tail of his Bic biro lid – the biro he uses to take notes for quotes; the biro he took to Natasha's thinking she wanted a bathroom, only to find out she wanted a jacuzzi, a jacuzzi, it turned out, she didn't want at all.

He gives up on his nails, takes a sip of his lime and soda. Wonders if he'll ever drink again. Ever go out. Ever go home.

No, Franks. Get a grip. There's no proof you're the father of this kid, none whatsoever. Keep it together.

She's going to ruin you.

I won't let her.

Jane will drop you like a stone.

No, she won't; I'll fight for her.

You are finished.

No, I'm not.

You're an idiot.

Fair point.

Shame on you.

Shame on me.

Shame shame shame shame shame shame shame shame.

He sees Natasha before she sees him. She is flashing her smile at the gormless, spotty teenage waiter who is holding the door open for her. In the subdued lighting of the bar, her teeth are almost neon. Hate infuses him. He wipes his eyes with the backs of his hands. He will not let her see him rattled.

Her gaze travels around the bar, lands on him like something solid.

Her head adjusts itself with a slight wobble. She's wearing a baby-pink American college sweatshirt, grey skinny jeans and pink Nikes. Her long dark hair falls to the back of her shoulders, shorter bits framing her face. When she reaches the table, he remembers the wolfish blue of her eyes, the way she looked at him when she handed him a drink. The shine of her hair as his jeans peeled away from his legs. Her breasts, swinging and strange.

Despite himself, he stands. 'Natasha.'

'Hello, Frankie.' Her head gives that weird micro-wobble again. She is not as tall as he remembers – about Jane's height, he'd say, maybe a centimetre or two taller. 'Can I sit down?'

Frankie blinks. What kind of question is that? What is she now, polite?

'Of course,' he says, gesturing to the chair opposite.

Face set in a mix of offence and determination, she scrapes the chair out and sits down, scrapes it back under the table.

The waiter from the doorway approaches and asks if she would like to order a drink. One hand flat on her stomach, she orders a sparkling mineral water with ice and a slice of lemon. She smiles a sickly-sweet smile up at the boy, whose spots glow red against his shining forehead. Frankie studies her. He doesn't find her remotely attractive. He never did. What a mess.

'So,' he says.

'I'm just going to get straight to the point, OK? Gareth's left me.' She takes a tissue from her sleeve and dabs her eye.

'Who's Gareth?'

'My husband.'

'How does he know it's not his?'

She pulls an incredulous face. 'The dates? He was away for a *month.*'

'And you're sure it's mine?'

Her eyes widen. She opens her mouth, looks like she's about to scream at him, but the waiter arrives and slides her mineral water onto the table. Hovers.

'Mate,' Frankie says kindly. 'We're not eating, cheers.'

Once the waiter has gone, Natasha leans across the table, eyes narrowing. 'Still a class act, aren't you, Frank Reece? Who else's would it be? Who do you think I am?'

A nightmare.

'I don't know. I don't know you. Look, it was a mistake. Don't get me wrong, you're a very attractive woman, but it wasn't meant to happen and I'm really sorry, all right? So if you need me to come with you to... sort it out or whatever, I—'

'*What?*' She looks at him like he's said something horrific. 'What the hell are you on about? Are you talking about an *abortion?*' She laughs – a horrible, mean laugh. 'Is that why you came, to tell me to get *rid* of it? Oh my God, you really are charming, aren't you? I'm having a baby, *mate*. Your baby. And you're going to pay me maintenance whether you like it or not – you owe me that at least.'

'What?' His head is throbbing, his vision blurs. 'Come on, that's not fair! You can't do that to me.' Already he has raised his voice, minutes after vowing he would not.

'Do what? Expect you to honour your responsibilities? You've changed your tune, I must say. You were all over me that night, couldn't get me into bed fast enough, with your sob story and your big blue eyes and your *hold me, Tasha, you're so beautiful, Tasha.'*

He can't remember a word of it, not one word. It is disorientating, being told what he said when the words are nowhere to be found in his memory, like being told you owe someone a tenner when you distinctly remember giving it back.

He throws up his hands. 'I'm sure that's true, but I'd worked a long day and the booze just went to my head. I'm surprised I even managed it, to be honest. And I just don't think you can expect me to be the father when we don't even know each other. And if you say there was only me, then fair enough. But this is my life you're... Look, it's not that I don't believe you, but I'm going to need proof. It's as simple as that.'

Her eyes narrow, almost close. She shakes her head slowly. 'You think you're so nice, don't you? Top geezer, one of the lads? But you're not nice at all.' She digs in her bag, sniffing as if upset, though her eyes are dry. 'I didn't want to do this. I really didn't. But you've forced me.'

Out of her bag she pulls an envelope. Hard copies, he imagines, of the scan. But a scan doesn't prove jack shit.

Three photographs, framed in white, land on the table between them. Polaroids, he thinks vaguely, staring at his own face reflected back at him. At her face. Her, naked, from the waist up. His bare chest, his eyes closed in what looks like ecstasy. Still, it takes him another few seconds to realise he is looking at photographs of himself and Natasha. Himself and Natasha having sex.

The flashes, the white flashes, he thinks. She took pictures? Was that what that was? While they were...

'A grand a month,' he hears her say through the humming in his ears. 'Or I'm sending these to your wife.'

CHAPTER THIRTY-EIGHT

JANE

May

They are still sitting on the bed. Frankie has told her that he has slept with another woman, that this woman claims he is the father of her child and is blackmailing him. And now, as if to go back to the beginning, as if going back to the beginning will somehow explain it, he is telling her how this came to be, how he accepted a glass of wine from this sophisticated raven-haired woman and followed her upstairs in her luxury home, how his head started to spin in her state-of-the art bathroom with its marble-clad double shower, how she held his hand as she led him to her bedroom. And Jane already knows what comes next, knows she won't believe it and that she will, that she has no choice but to believe it because of what he has already told her. And then he tells her:

'I was flat out,' he says. 'She started stroking me and I tried to push her away, but then next thing, we were... she was... she was on top of me.'

They are both crying. Somehow Jane is holding his hand. Realising this, she lets go.

'On top of you how?' She knows how. 'Naked? Do you mean naked? Is that what you mean?'

He nods, tears falling fast down his face.

'I don't understand,' she says helplessly. She feels suddenly dizzy.

'Neither do I. I swear to God, neither do I.'

'When you asked me to marry you, you said... do you remember what you said?'

'Please, babe. Please don't.'

'You got down on one knee and you said, "I'll never cheat on you and I'll never leave you." That's what you said.' Jane waits, but Frankie has dissolved into sobs. 'You know what I went through as a child. You know all of it.'

'I wish I could turn back time,' he whimpers. 'I don't know how it happened.'

'Yes you do. You do, Frankie. You know exactly how it happened and how you made another woman pregnant. Another woman is carrying your child when I can't...' A noise leaves her – a high, primal howl.

'At first she only wanted a grand,' he says, his voice far away, as if she cares, as if this has any relevance whatsoever. 'But then she wanted more, then she wanted maintenance. It wasn't just the scan she had. She had photos. Of us.'

'Us?'

'Me and her, I mean. Together.'

'Oh my God.'

Frankie shakes his head. 'I took three grand from the savings account and I had another grand in cash.'

The jar. Their world-trip fund. The withdrawal. It was not the business failing. It was not an escape plan. It was a baby, another baby in another woman's belly. She is crying too much to speak, her own belly cramped up in pain.

'I made her give me the Polaroids.'

Jane closes her eyes in disbelief, opens them. 'She'll still have them on her iPhone – please tell me you know that.'

He nods miserably. She doesn't care about the money or the

photos or maintenance or any of it. Frankie has made another woman pregnant. Another woman, not her, is having his baby.

'She says she'll put the pictures on the internet if she has to.' He shakes his head, pushes his face into his hands. 'I don't care about me. I didn't give her the money for me. I just couldn't stand her getting to you. I didn't want you to know – ever. I knew you'd be hurt.'

'*Hurt?*'

'More than hurt. Devastated. Sorry, I'm... I'm not explaining it very well... but it's the one thing, isn't it? Like you said, I promised. And I meant it. And the thing is, I can't even remember it. It's just... flashbacks. I'm not attracted to her; I wasn't ever, at any point. And I'm not going to be a dad to this kid, I'm not. I don't want that. I want you. I love you. You, babe. You're my life, you're all I want, but she... Even if I pay her, she'll ask for more, I know she will. She's never going to stop.'

Jane becomes aware that she is nodding, almost rocking. Around her the room buzzes. Her skin tingles, every cell of her alive with feelings she can't name – there are too many feelings, and they are all too awful.

She makes herself sit still.

'What do you want to do?' Frankie asks after a moment, his mouth set in anguish.

I want to kill you and then I want to kill her and then I want to stand over you until I'm sure neither of you are still breathing.

She looks down at her hands, rough from cleaning countertops and tables and coffee machines. Coffee grounds have patterned the ends of her fingers in filigrees of brown. Her jeans are worn soft with age and her old fluffy slippers embarrass her now, here, with him. She doesn't want him to see her like this. She doesn't want him to see her red-faced, snotty, broken into a thousand pieces. He has no right to see her like this, no right at all. It is private. She wants to close the door to him, fix herself up, put on her shoes, open the door only when she's got herself together. Why, she wonders then – why, when he has betrayed her and everything they are to one another, when he has inflicted the most painful blow he could ever have inflicted, does she have the impulse to change *herself*?

'Do I know her?' she asks, so quietly she doubts he has heard.

But he has. He is shaking his head. 'She's called Natasha.'

'Natasha.' Her chest swells with breath. Deflates. 'What does she look like?' It is of no consequence, not really. It is nowhere near the source of the pain. This woman is carrying Frankie's child; it is something she will never, ever get over. What she looks like is a holding question until she is able to find the strength to look directly into the abyss of what her husband has done to her.

'About your height,' Frankie says. 'Black hair. Blue eyes. Slim. Sophisticated, I suppose. Not my type at all. Like I say, I don't know how...' He falters, stops.

She is good-looking, then, the mother of Frankie's child. In shape. Groomed, polished. What her mother would call feminine, a woman who takes care of herself. *Nothing like me*, she thinks, unsure if this is worse or better. She rolls her shoulders back, sniffs. She's heard enough. Any more and she'll be physically sick.

A grim and familiar impulse flashes through her: to cut this person, this man she loves more than any other human being, out of her life, cut him out so he cannot do her any more harm. Because it is only those we love who can do us real damage.

She draws herself up as tall as she can.

'I want you to pack your things,' she says. 'I want you to leave. And I never want to see you again. Ever.'

'Jane,' he pleads. 'Please. We can get through this.'

'No, we can't. Don't you understand that? We can never get over this.'

She stands, stares down at the pathetic sight of him. And walks away. At the door of the bedroom, she stops briefly, and turns and whispers loud enough for him to hear: 'Do you know what? I just thank God we didn't have children.'

CHAPTER THIRTY-NINE

FRANKIE

Frankie is shaking so much he can hardly get the key in the door of the van. On the shabby fake-leather bench, he breaks down, bangs the steering wheel with his fists over and over until he stays like that, forehead against the steering wheel, crying thin snot onto his lap. The image of Jane's face will not leave his mind; he knows he'll see that expression of disbelief and pain over and over for the rest of his life.

After a time, he sits up. He wants his mum really, but she'll kill him, provided his dad doesn't kill him first. No, he can't face his parents. He is too ashamed. They love Jane. They will ask him what the hell he was thinking, and he won't have an answer because he wasn't. He wasn't thinking. God knows, he can barely remember it, let alone explain it.

Simon then. Simon will understand. He might even take pity on him, not that he deserves pity. To have his knob chopped off, that's what he deserves. They could take his balls too, if he had any.

He picks up the phone but lets it slide out of his hand. It's not that Simon will tell him he's a prick; it's that Simon *won't* tell him he's a prick. Simon will grin and say come on, you idiot, let's open a beer, and looking at him will be like looking into a mirror of the future, except Frankie doesn't have Simon's money. He doesn't have his car. He doesn't wear a Swatch. Simon will tell him it'll be OK, they can be the two of them together now, out on the pull. He will tell him he's better off single, his own man, because that's how Simon sees the world: for what he can take from it, what he can get, have. Trouble is, Frankie doesn't see the world like that – there is nothing in it he wants apart from Jane. To think, he bought that watch because of Simon. All this time, he looked up to him, wanted to be like him in some way. Why is it only now, now that he *has* ended up like Simon, that he realises he was happy as he was?

Jane. She is all he's ever wanted since the moment he met her, pretty much. Not watches, not cars, not stuff, just Jane. There is quite literally nothing about her he doesn't love. If he'd never met her, fine. But he did meet her and his life was better from that second on. Now, without her, his life is a piece of absolute crap. It is as bullshit as that stupid yellow-faced watch.

He lifts his head, still cringing, pulls at his shirt and sniffs his armpits. He stinks. He can feel the grime on the back of his neck, under his fingernails. But what the hell does that matter? What really? It doesn't matter if he smells like Chanel No. 5. His life is over.

He slams his fists into the steering wheel and roars: 'You fucking idiot. You fucking stupid bastard.'

He's lost her. But if he doesn't end this, he will never even have a chance of getting her back. The only way forward is to face Natasha and try not to kill her with his bare hands. Ironically, in taking everything away, she has left him with nothing to lose.

He gets to Natasha's place at half-eightish, parks behind a black Jag. Judging by the amount of lights blazing, she's in.

He rings the doorbell and waits. Nerves jangling, he tries not to think of the last time he stood here waiting like this. If she answers the door half dressed, he will not go inside. She is too dangerous.

But when the door opens, it's a bloke, not Natasha. He looks smart, even in a polo shirt, jogging bottoms and a pair of grey felt slippers that look like Birkenstocks. Some people reek of money no matter what they're wearing.

'Can I help you?'

This must be Gareth, which is awkward. Frankie wonders how to play it. Straight bat, he decides. Don't admit to anything.

'I'm looking for Natasha,' he says. 'I'm supposed to be quoting for some work for her?'

'I'm sorry,' the man says. 'I think you must have the wrong address.'

'But—'

The door is shut. Frankie saw it close, he knows he did. He heard it bang. But only now does he take in the flat refusal of it. The end of the conversation. The fuck-right-off.

Gareth must have kicked her out when she told him she was pregnant by another bloke. And now he wants nothing to do with her or anyone associated with her. Frankie doesn't blame him – it's the kind of reaction she'd provoke. He can't imagine she was gracious when she told him; probably blamed it on him for being away, earning the kind of money that kept her in a place like this, the kind that left her free to seduce losers like Frankie. Frankie wishes he could do the same – cut her out of his life. He wonders what kind of grief Natasha must have given this Gareth bloke over the years. Probably had his balls in a vice, poor bastard.

He trudges back to the van and gets in. With a pit in his stomach, he sits there for a bit, trying not to look at the sports bag full of clothes beside him on the seat, trying not to think about the fact that this bag and this van are the sum total of his life now, trying to do no more than breathe in and out into the stinking palms of his hands.

His mum and dad, no. Simon, no. Jane, no way. Natasha. She is all that's left and he has to get this sorted out...

Ten minutes or so later, he bites the bullet. And calls.

'Frankie?' Natasha answers. 'Is that you?'

'I'm outside your house. Your husband reckons you don't live here anymore. He kicked you out then?'

There is a pause. He listens, waits.

'Natasha?' he repeats. 'Has Gareth kicked you out?'

Down the line comes a sniff.

'Yes,' she says eventually. 'Can you come over? I'm... I'm really struggling.' She sounds small, like a child. 'I don't think I should be on my own.'

'I'm not stopping, all right? I just need to talk to you. Just a talk, that's all. We've got to sort this mess out.'

'OK. OK. I'll text you the address.'

CHAPTER FORTY

JANE

Jane is sitting on the floor of the hall, weeping into Des's fur.

'Oh, Dezzie,' she whispers.

Des snuffles into her neck, licks the tears from her cheeks.

She told Frankie to go, and he went. And now she is alone, consumed by the mental image of his baby curled up in the belly of another woman, fists tight, a greyish blob on a scan, a floating suspension of his genes and hers, whoever she is. Not Jane's baby, not Jane's body. The pain she feels is physical. It lodges in the very place inside her she knows is empty, will always be empty. Groaning, she lies on the floor of the hall, brings her knees up to her chest. The foetal position, she thinks, making herself sob with despair.

After a moment, Frankie's face materialises in her mind's eye, so near and real she has to blink to check he isn't there, that he hasn't come back to comfort her. She can see him so clearly: the way he was, the way he has been lately, the way when they made love it was like he was elsewhere. How thin he has become, how wretched he looked, and how, despite everything, she wanted to comfort him there on the bed they have shared for over a decade. One night versus eleven years. Can they really be over? For this? How difficult it is to untangle the threads of what you think and feel when someone you love *this much* does something *this terrible*. Love does not switch itself off; it would be so much easier if it did.

A thought comes to her like an announcement from somewhere outside herself: Frankie didn't intend to get another woman pregnant. The mistake he made has turned him into a ghost of himself. Now that he has gone, this is utterly clear. He doesn't want this woman or this child. He never did.

Holding on to these thin threads, she hauls herself up from the floor and drags her feet to the kitchen.

The kitchen is cold. It is empty, stark, nowhere she wants to be without him. He got drunk, much drunker than he meant to because he was exhausted from working far too hard for their dreams. And he ended up in a total mess. It's wrong to blame the woman, she knows that. Men have been blaming women since... well, since Eve. But even as her heart shrinks to a tight ball in her chest, even as the rage plays itself out across her skin, through her bones, her organs, her blood, she can feel the longing to forgive him like a breeze. Would forgiving him mean he would do it again? Will she end up locked into years of second-guessing and toxic outcomes like she was with her mother? Or would it simply be forgiveness, only that? Could they just start again?

Because the trouble is, while without her mother her life has been simpler, without him, her life is something she no longer wants.

After everything else she has lost, she cannot lose him too.

She picks up her phone, tracks him. He is heading towards Richmond. She grabs the keys to her Vespa and heads out. She knows there is more to his story – she feels it in her gut.

By the time she gets on the motorbike, he is through Richmond and heading towards Barnes. Weird. If he was going to Richmond, she expected him to have stopped at Simon's place. But no, he has carried on. She continues, following him.

By the time she reaches Barnes, the little dot has stopped in a circular road beyond the Wetlands Centre. She takes the left turn into the wide crescent, then switches off the app. All the houses are detached, elegant, huge. She motors slowly, head low, checking the lush, wide driveways – the turning circles, the topiary, the expensive stone flags – until, a little ahead, in a gravel driveway, she sees his van parked outside what she can only call in her mind a modern architect-type house.

She pulls up on the far side of the road, switches off the engine and takes off her helmet. Doesn't want to get too close in case he spots her from the window. She plucks at the fingers of her leather gloves and slides them off, uses them to wipe at her eyes, which have filled again with tears. Why is he here? Why is he not at Simon's or his parents' over in Sunbury? Her skin prickles; her tight heart knocks against her ribs. There is a silver orb in the front garden, a line of round lollipop bay trees, an angular hedge in front of an elegant black iron railing. She's seen this style of garden in one of the lifestyle magazines she buys for the café, imagines it must have cost a fortune. She edges nearer, but stays on the far side of the road. The front door, Scandinavian in design, she thinks, is twice the width of hers and Frankie's.

This is Natasha's place. It fits his description, and even if it didn't, she would know it instinctively. It cannot be anything else. He even mentioned the silver orb in the garden. She is rich, that much is obvious. Maybe she's a minor celebrity. Whoever she is, she is out of their league financially. They don't know anyone who lives in a house like this. Not even Sophie and Carl.

So. He has come here. To her. A woman he claimed to want nothing to do with.

She stares at the house, trying to catch shadows in the window, make sense of it. In a sense, she knows this woman better than she should, without ever having met her. She knows her from everything her husband said and didn't say. She knows that her kitchen is glossy, that her living room is the size of a theatre, but most of all she knows her the way women know other women, and knows she must have seen Frankie coming a mile away. This woman is the kind of person who would take a picture of herself and her one-night-stand lover having sex with the intention of blackmailing him. This woman probably got off on it, the power trip, her own irresistibleness. Jane suspects it was possibly her intention to get pregnant by him. It's possible she had it all worked out.

But it's not all this woman's fault, is it? She could not have done it without Frankie's consent. Her husband has been an idiot. He has been weak and foolish and unforgivably dishonest. Her mother was right after all. It is never work, never overtime, never what they say it is. It is always, always another woman. They say you're beautiful as you are, that they don't go for glamour or shiny hair or big breasts, but they do, they absolutely do – it only has to be offered and they drop to their knuckles like apes.

How depressing.

Inside, the lights are on. In the window, as if in response to her thoughts, a shadow appears, followed by another. Her breath catches in her chest. She watches, waits as the couple move closer. Embrace. Kiss.

'Bastard,' she gasps, pressing the soft leather gloves to her eyes. 'You absolute bastard.'

He has not gone crawling and wretched to Simon, or even Billy, his mate from school. He has not gone to cry on someone who would say *There, there, mate. Don't worry about Jane, she'll come round.* Instead, he's gone snivelling into the arms of his lover, the mother of his child, whom he claimed was nothing to him.

'Bastard,' she whispers again, then digs out her phone and switches it off.

If he tries to call her, he will find her unavailable. She shoves it into her jacket pocket, puts her helmet back on and roars home.

CHAPTER FORTY-ONE

THE HOSPITAL

I get out on the ground floor. Five or six hobbling steps and my leg's screaming at me to sit down. Turns out the nurse was not wrong. Too soon to walk, definitely too soon to walk while carrying the crutches as if they're for someone else. But I don't have much time. I told Nursey that if she leaves that cubicle in the next hour, I will end her. I will find out where she lives. She has no idea I won't; I'm not a psycho. All I needed was for her to believe it. And she did. Besides which, it'll take her ages to free her wrists from her lanyard and unstick the surgical tape from her mouth.

The air hurts at every step, even through the cast. My hands aren't great either. I glance at them. Jesus, I'm bleeding – the tops of the scabs all knocked off from where I hit Nursey over the back of the head.

Great. That's just great.

Seeing the Ladies, I dip in, gasp at my reflection. My eyes are black. Dried blood is crusted all over my nose; you'd think they'd have cleaned that off, wouldn't you?

I wash my face. The blood comes off but my nose is swollen and weird, making my eyes small and strange. In the uniform, I look like a completely different person – sensible, if a bit bruised. Actually, the face isn't too bad. I mean, it's bad, but the black around my eyes makes me look tired more than anything. It doesn't look like I should be in A&E, I don't think. It'll take a bit longer for the bruising to come out, then I really will look like I've gone a few rounds with Mike Tyson. My feet: one plaster cast with five fat blue toes sticking out, one white nurse's clog, a size too small. It's not perfect. But they won't be looking at my shoes.

Reception is packed. A&E, early morning – the bruised and the battered, the hung-over and the coming-down. I reach the desk, sweat pouring off me. The pain in my leg is worse with each step. My whole body is on fire. The drugs are wearing off. But I have to find her. I have to end this, and it won't end until she does. She stole my life, and if anyone can smile through pain, it's me. Smiling through pain every day, smiling through humiliation, having your mates turn against you, watching your mother struggle on for years, hearing her ask every day, why? Why though? Watching her find the answer in the bottom of a bottle.

What does she know about that?

Well, she's about to find out. I can't wait to see her face drop in shock before I smother it. I don't care how much this leg hurts – I'll run if I have to. I don't care what happens to me anymore. I don't care I don't care I don't care.

I give her name at reception, tell the guy I'm supposed to take these crutches to her but, silly me, I've forgotten which ward. He checks the system and shakes his head – sorry, they don't have her listed. Of course, she's used her other name – I should have thought of that. I fake a laugh at my own terrible memory. *What am I like? These night shifts are getting to me. I don't know what day of the week it is at the moment.* I try again with the other name, tell the guy what time she was admitted and why.

He finds her then, smiles politely and gives me the ward. *Cheers, mate. Thanks so much.*

Simples.

Back in the lift, I press 7.

Right, lady. I'm coming for you.

CHAPTER FORTY-TWO

FRANKIE

Frankie reaches Natasha's address in Hounslow about forty-five minutes later and parks up. When he stands outside the door of the small terrace, he sees the house is divided into two flats. Upstairs, one of the windows has an England flag by way of a curtain, and in next door's garden there is what looks like a television unit – against the dark chocolatey veneer, the MDF is a pale centre where it has broken apart. There are two doorbells. One has the name Joe Clegg on it. Joke Leg, he thinks; that's what he would say to Jane, if she didn't say it first. The thought makes his chest hurt with sadness. This can't be where Natasha lives. Not even temporarily. The other doorbell is blank. He pushes the blank one, and after a buzz of static, to his surprise the door clicks.

He shoulders it open to find her in the hallway, dressed in a loose, long shirt and those same Ugg boots she was wearing over two months ago. Her legs are bare just as they were that night, and black make-up coats her blue eyes. For all that her clothes are similar, she looks different, though he can't say why. Smaller, perhaps. Less sure.

'My wife's kicked me out,' he says.

'Come in,' she says softly, gesturing for him to step inside.

On the doorstep, he hesitates. But he has to talk sense into her.

He has to make her understand that he won't be blackmailed. A sense of power fills him. There is nothing more this woman can do to him now. He realises with absolutely clarity that he can tell her to put the photographs online if she wants. He will weather the storm. It doesn't matter, not at all. Nothing matters. Nothing, nothing is worse than losing Jane.

'I'm not stopping,' he says, but as he passes her to go into the flat, her perfume hits him, and instantly, hot dread fills him from head to toe. His legs tremble. He leans against the wall and closes his eyes a second while it passes. He is back in that bed, waking up, her on top of him, the white flash he now knows was her taking a photo, his trousers being hooked over his feet, himself reaching up only to collapse backwards.

'Frankie?' Natasha calls him back to the present. He comes round, sees her there, but he is still with her in the past, and for a moment he thinks there are two of her – one here, staring at him, and one writhing above him in flashbacks that are getting more and more frequent.

'I'm OK,' he says. 'Just a bit dizzy.'

The flat is tidy but the furniture is cheap and old, and again, he cannot marry the idea of her here with the house he last saw her in. The sagging sofa is covered with an ethnic-style throw and the armchair looks like a ghost with— Is that a bed sheet she's thrown over it? He has the impression she has cleaned, possibly while he was on the way over, because there's a kind of artificial fruity smell with notes of bleach. But it can't disguise an underlying whiff – something in the carpet, in the curtains maybe: stale smoke, years-old dirt, ingrained. The smell of poverty.

'I'm sorry your wife kicked you out,' Natasha says. 'I didn't mean for that to happen.' Her voice is so soft he can barely put it together with the other Natasha, the one who has blackmailed him, who is still blackmailing him horribly, the one who shouted and swore at him as he picked his clothes up from the bedroom floor, and again he has the mad idea that there are two of her.

'We've got to sort this out,' he says.

She nods. 'I know. Can I get you a drink? A beer?'

'A beer thanks.'

She leaves him, returns a moment later with two bottles of Heineken.

She opens both, hands one to him and shrugs, runs a protective hand over her belly. 'I'm not supposed to, but it's not strong and these bottles are really small.'

He thinks of Jane, who didn't drink for years, thinking it would help her conceive. He opens his mouth to speak, but nothing comes.

'Sit down,' she says.

'Was that your husband?' he asks, sinking too low into a sofa whose frame is clearly broken. 'The one who shut the door in my face?'

She settles in the armchair, brings her Ugg boots up and tucks them beneath her. Behind her, the sheet slides down, revealing tan fake-leather upholstery ripped at one corner. She puts her beer on the coffee table. Her chin lifts, her lips press tightly together.

'No,' she says, fingers spreading. 'That's not my husband. That's not my house.'

'*What?*' Frankie reels.

'It's my friend's house,' she goes on, as if he hasn't spoken. 'She was away. She told me I could house-sit for her, so that's what I was doing when we... when you came over.'

Frankie's eyes half close in disbelief. 'So... hang on, what? Let me get this straight. You called me out for a job in a house that isn't even *yours?*'

She shakes her head a fraction. When she looks at him, it is through her thick black eyelashes. She bites her bottom lip in a way he's seen some women do. With a jolt he realises he recognises the tic from the limited amount of pornography he watched many years ago now. With a sense of unease, he gets the impression she is trying to be coy. Despite everything, she seems pleased to see him.

'I never wanted you to quote for a jacuzzi,' she says with what she appears to think is harmless mischief. 'I thought you knew that. I mean, I think you did. We both did.'

He is not mistaken. She is looking at him with childlike innocence, but the effect is the exact opposite. He remembers flirting with her in the pub. Is it possible he's partly responsible for this... this mess? Straight bat, Frankie. Straight. Bat.

'I genuinely thought I was coming to quote for a new bathroom,' he says and sips his lager. He is suddenly incredibly thirsty, thinks about asking for a glass of water. He puts the beer on the coffee table, deciding in that moment not to down any alcohol while he is anywhere near this woman, who is becoming more dangerous by the second.

She is curling the end of her hair with one finger. Slowly, she untucks her legs from beneath her, plants both feet on the floor, then uncrosses and crosses her legs, all the while maintaining eye contact. What was that, some Sharon Stone reference? Is it supposed to make him wonder if she's wearing pants? Show him she isn't?

'I may have got it all wrong,' she says, still in that soft, soft voice. 'But I thought you liked me. In the pub. We chatted, I bought you a drink. We clicked, didn't we? Didn't we? When I gave you my number, I assumed you understood. I'm so sorry if I got the wrong end of the stick.' She drinks, puts the bottle down, goes back to curling her hair around her finger. 'Am I disgusting to you?'

'*What?*'

'Do I disgust you?'

'No! No, of course not. You're very attractive and all that, but I'm not... There's nothing wrong with you. I just don't like you in that way, that's all.'

She laughs. 'You don't like me in that way? I could've sworn you liked me in that way back at my friend's house.' She looks around her. 'And I know this place isn't much, but your wife's thrown you out, hasn't she? Not like you have much choice.'

'Well, yeah, but...'

'It's just that, well, I know you want kids. And you said she can't. Would it be so bad to try and make a go of it?'

It takes him a second to understand her. And then he does. 'With *you*? As in me and you?'

'Why not? I'm a nice person. I've got a good body.'

'A good... What? Hang on, where is this going? I've come here to tell you to stay away from me and Jane. And you can put the photographs where you like, by the way. I don't care. Today's scandal is tomorrow's chip papers to me.'

She frowns, apparently unable to work out what he's just said. 'But, Frankie, we could be a family. I can give you that. I'm not being funny, but she can't.'

'What the hell?' He stands up so quickly he gets a head rush. For one horrible moment he thinks he could hit her, that he's going to. His fist is curled tight, the sinews in his forearm bulge. She is looking up at him, her calm expression so at odds with the words that have come out of her mouth that he is filled with confusion.

'We don't have to live here,' she says, laughing, throwing up her hands. 'You could pay your wife off and we could buy somewhere nice for us. I know you want a family. I think we can be one, that's all.'

'No, we can't! I don't want... not like that. And I haven't got any money. You've taken it all.'

'Oh come on! You own a house in London! Have you looked in the estate agent's window recently? Victorian terraces sell for over a million in Wimbham. And your watch alone is worth thousands. No one wears a watch like that unless they're fine for money. Plus you drive an Evoque, for God's sake.'

'I don't drive a— Why would you—' He stops. That night, the night he met her, he remembers her admiring the watch, the watch he's blamed for meeting her, for getting into this bloody mess, little realising how true that was, how deep that truth went. It was the watch she saw, not him. The watch and the car. Because that night, of course, he drove the lads home in Simon's motor. She must have seen him get into the driving seat, put two and two together and got five.

'That's not my car,' he says. 'It's my mate's.'

Her face falls – for the first time her expression is genuine, he thinks. Genuine shock.

'And I only bought the watch because I won money on a scratch card.'

'*What?*'

'Look at me! Do I look wealthy to you? I can barely make ends meet.'

'But you still have the house?'

'I live in the house, yes. But we're mortgaged up to the eyeballs! We're on interest only – I don't think we'll ever pay it off.'

She blushes. Her face hardens. 'You tricked me.'

'What? Of course I didn't trick you. What're you on about?'

Her eyes narrow, her open mouth closes, becomes a grimace. 'I mean, I know you're not a CEO or anything, but you led me to believe you were pretty successful.' She speaks slowly, as if working out a puzzle. 'You *fooled* me. You said you had your own business and I obviously thought... but then you saw the house and thought *I* was loaded and so you coerced me into having sex with you – which is sexual assault, by the way – and now you won't pay up because you *can't*? And I'm left with a baby to bring up and you won't even accept your responsibility? Oh.' Her hands fly up to her face. 'Oh my God. So even if I do put those pictures online...'

'Like I said, you can do what you want with them.' His heart is battering. He has no idea who this woman is, but she scares the living shit out of him, end of. 'Do what you want. I don't care. I can't pay you money I don't have. If you want to share the photos with the entire universe, go ahead. You've already taken everything I have, everything.'

She starts to cry; to be honest, he's pretty close to crying himself.

'I never wanted to do this,' she says. 'I'm just trying to survive, that's all. You have no idea what I've come from, what I've had to do. And you seem like a nice bloke. You're different, you know? Decent. I know I said you weren't, but I didn't mean it – I was just lashing out.' She sniffs, presses the back of her hand to her nose.

'Look,' he says, panic subsiding. 'We can try and figure something out, OK? If the baby's mine like you say it is, maybe we can agree on a monthly allowance. I don't know how much, but we can work out an amount and I'll deposit it into your account, OK? I just can't be part of this. I love Jane. She's my entire life.'

To his astonishment, she nods, like a child.

'A thousand a month,' she says, through her tears.

'I can't afford that.'

She doesn't react, doesn't appear to have heard.

'And if she won't take you back,' she says, 'maybe we could try... It could work, couldn't it?'

He ignores this – it is madness. 'I have to have proof of paternity, yeah? I have to have a DNA test. No test, no money, OK?'

'OK.' She is as docile as a lamb; he almost feels sorry for her. Again he takes in her surroundings. That big architect house wasn't hers. That bloke wasn't her husband. She is skint, he thinks. Completely skint.

'Are you OK?' he asks.

She nods. 'What about you? Have you got anywhere to stay?'

He shakes his head. 'I'll sleep in the van.'

'Don't be ridiculous. You can sleep here.' She throws up her hands. 'On the couch, I mean. Don't worry, I won't try anything. You can crash here. If... you order a takeaway.' She shrugs, grins cheekily.

He shakes his head, smiles despite himself. She is a piece of work. 'All right. But just for tonight.'

She doesn't even have any spare blankets, so when she leaves him, he pulls his coat over himself and closes his eyes, only to find images of her tearing through a large stuffed-crust double pepperoni like she hadn't eaten in weeks. He can hear her upstairs, cleaning her teeth, humming to herself. More than anything, he wants, desperately, to call Jane, but knows he needs to leave her alone for now. It might be better to wait until Natasha has had the test; that way he knows what he's going back with. He's knackered, longs to sleep, but part of him doesn't dare. Natasha seemed calm enough when she said goodnight, but he has no idea what she's capable of, and now he's wondering whether, actually, he might go and sleep in the van after all.

At around 2 a.m., he is still wide awake, still debating it. He creeps upstairs to take a piss, then dares himself to open her bedroom door. She is asleep, her breathing deep and regular. He sets one foot inside the dim, silent room. She is on her back, her mouth slightly open. In the sliver of light from the street lamp, her eyelashes are thin and fair. She looks like a child, and for a moment he wonders what went so wrong with her that she would resort to blackmailing a man she barely knows. She has fed him so much bullshit that in the last few hours he has found himself arriving at solutions for the situation, only to remember the situation isn't even the situation. He thought he could go back and talk to her ex before he remembered that he's not her ex at all but her mate's husband, just some random bloke in a posh house. She said she was house-sitting – he wonders now if that's true. Did her friend know Natasha was using her house? Does Natasha even know the person who lives there? If not, how did she get in?

He returns downstairs. Finds some skimmed milk in the fridge and, after sniffing it to check it isn't off, drinks some straight from the carton. There is nothing in the cupboards, no bread in the bread bin. The only food in the house is a small hardening arc of pizza crust rattling around in the delivery box. He has not eaten, couldn't face it. But now his stomach growls with hunger. He eats the paring of crust, glad no one can see him do it, and settles back on the sofa.

Less wary now he knows she's flat out upstairs, he tries to doze. He is so exhausted that towards the early hours, sleep takes him finally like a slow-release drug, until he opens his eyes to weak daylight and a heaviness on his hips. Cool air on his chest. He opens his eyes fully.

'What the hell?'

She is on top of him. His shirt is open. She is unbuttoning his fly, her face set in concentration. Her hair is black but her eyes are smaller, the irises dark. She looks and doesn't look like herself. The effect is terrifying.

'Get off me!' He pushes her hard; she falls sideways, her head narrowly missing the coffee table.

She gives a yelp, hand flying to her head. One of her legs is still hooked over his lap. She pulls herself free, lands on the filthy carpet.

'Oh my God,' she shouts. 'You could've killed me.'

His fly is undone. She is on the floor, crying.

'I only want to be a family,' she shouts. 'Why do you have to be so mean to me?'

He clambers up and runs from the room. In the hallway, he digs frantically in his pocket for his keys, finds them. He opens the front door, panting now. Behind him he hears her shouting his name.

'You'll change your mind, Frank Reece, do you hear me? You can't do this to me. No one does this to me. I could give you everything.'

CHAPTER FORTY-THREE

JANE

She is woken by the buzzing of her phone on the bedside table. When she picks it up, the first thing she sees is *FRANKS*; the second that it is quarter to six in the morning. She's had about an hour's sleep. In normal times, she might be cross with him for waking her up. Weirdly, in this other surreal world he has booted her into, she is less cross.

She swipes to connect. 'Frankie.'

'Jane.' He is crying.

'What d'you want?'

'I'm sorry,' he snivels. 'I love you so much.'

'I'm sure you do,' she says, hating the hardness in her tone but unable to prevent it.

'Can we talk? I just want to talk to you. I'm so, so sorry. I'm in agony here.'

In agony at your lover's luxury palace, poor you.

'I'm sure you are. But if you wanted to talk to me, you should have thought about that before you stayed the night with her, shouldn't you? And do you know what? I'm sorry too, Frankie. I'm absolutely gutted.'

'It wasn't like that. I didn't go there for that. You don't underst—'

She ends the call, switches off her phone. She hates her phone. She hates her wedding ring. She hates every material thing that has ever been mistaken for love. She hates love. Hates how damn vulnerable it leaves you.

She bursts into tears. Gets up, has a shower, cycles to work.

Because work is all she has left: the hours, the caffè lattes, the cappuccinos, the babycinos, the peppermint teas, the rooibos, the black-bloody-currant infusions, the hand-carved honey-roasted ham and mature Dorset cheddar croissants, the organic vegan brownies, the French fricking patisserie, the raisin sodding Danishes. The customers. The smiling. Oh God, the constant, never-ending smiling. She is so smilingly numb that at around three, when she crosses the road to Starbucks to ask Sandra the manager if she can spare a till roll, when she walks in and sees Lexie and Sophie with their twin bumps, giggling over two lattes, she doesn't even feel the pain. She simply stops, momentarily transfixed by the sight. Sophie's hair is glossier now, ringleted at the base and highlighted in caramel tones. Her lips are plump and shining, her eyebrows thick and dark. Her cheeks blush like apples in October. Her red silk shirt rises over her neat rounded bump, and her matching red toenails peep from her tasteful wedge heels.

Hi. *Hi* is all Jane can find to say, while she stands and smiles like an idiot, even after she becomes aware of how stupefied she must look, how the two women are staring at her as if she has lost her mind, after she has shaken herself and left the café. Only then does she have the one conscious thought that penetrates her tripped-out, anaesthetised state of shock: Sophie and Lexie look completely identical.

That evening, she switches on her phone. There are eight messages from Frankie, all on the theme of how sorry he is, how much he loves her, please can they talk.

Her thumb hovers. It takes a monumental effort to ignore every last cell of her being that cries for him to come home. But no. Not yet, possibly never. She doesn't reply. Instead, she tracks him, sees he's over in Clapham. On a job then, working himself into the ground to pay his blackmail bill. At least he's not at that cow's house.

She gets up, grabs the keys to the Vespa. He wants her to talk? She can talk. She can talk for Great Britain. But not to him.

It is after seven when she arrives at Natasha's Instagram house. At the end of the drive, she falters. Confrontation. She has avoided it since the day she left home, and yet in the last few months, she has had nothing but. First Sophie, then Frankie, now this Natasha woman.

But she's ready. Her sleeves are rolled up. Bring it on.

She makes herself walk up the driveway, past the big posh black car. Wishes she'd fixed herself up. But who is she kidding? Natasha is sophisticated, Frankie said. Polished. Jane is an average-looking woman with short spiky hair, thighs of varying sizes and a stomach that sometimes resembles an oat muffin. She is a woman whose idea of dressing up is a spangly top and lipstick no one can tell she's wearing. If she wanted to compete with Natasha on looks, she'd need a lot more than water, a squirt of deodorant and a bit of hair wax.

She presses the doorbell, hears it chime from somewhere inside this ostentatious mansion of a place. Her heart quickens. She makes herself breathe in for four, out for five. In for four, hold, out for five, out, out, out.

A shadow at the frosted glass. The door opens.

'Oh,' she says.

It is a man. A good-looking man in smart trousers, a white shirt open at the neck. He is wearing black socks with a tiny hole in the big left toe, a fact that for some reason makes her blush.

'Can I help you?' he asks.

'I'm sorry,' she says, already taking a step back, cursing the tears that have come from nowhere, absolutely nowhere. 'I was looking for Natasha.' She brushes at her face, roughly, with her hands. She has not thought this through, has not imagined Natasha might also be married.

It might be her imagination, but something in the guy's face stiffens. 'There's no one here of that name, I'm afraid.'

'Right. I'm so sorry to disturb you. I'm... Sorry, I just...' The tears are falling fast now, faster than she can swipe them away. It is all too much. This man is a stranger and he isn't even wearing any shoes and she has seen the hole in his sock. She has come to his home. She is crying on his doorstep. What the hell is she doing here?

'It's quite all right.' He speaks kindly. But he has one hand on the door; Jane can tell he is desperate to close it.

'I'm so sorry for the disturbance,' she says, composing herself, pressing the palms of her hands to her cheeks. 'You must think I'm deranged. I'll get out of your way. Sorry again. Ignore the tears, it's... Well, I don't know what it is actually. Just this woman. This woman, Natasha, she's...'

The door opens a fraction more. His hand leaves it.

'Don't apologise. Can I ask why you thought someone called Natasha lived here? It's just, you're not the first person to ask.'

She exhales heavily. 'I followed... I... My husband came here last night. It's a long story, but I followed him. When I got here, he'd parked his van on the drive but he'd already gone inside.'

She's expecting him to wish her luck and send her on her way, to give her the kindest, politest *get lost*. But instead, he says: 'He didn't come inside actually. If it's the same person. A guy came by last night and was asking for Natasha. It's...' He frowns.

'She was blackmailing him,' Jane says. 'It was a one-night stand. He told me it happened here, in this house. She took pictures. Polaroids of them... y'know.'

The merest shake of his head sends a tingle like wildfire across her scalp.

He runs the flat of his hand over his hair, scratches the back briefly in what looks like a mannerism rather than an itch.

'I think,' he says slowly, 'I think I might know who Natasha is.'

'Really?' Jane sniffs, enormously. Wipes her nose with the back of her hand. It's not like she can create a worse impression than she already has.

The guy is nodding.

'I'm Gareth,' he says. 'Maybe you should come in.'

The sitting room is absolutely massive. Gareth leaves her, says he's just popping to fetch his wife.

Something about the room looks familiar. It was in *House Beautiful* maybe. Maybe that's where she recognised the front garden from. She doesn't really look at those mags, only occasionally when there are no customers and she's dreaming of doing the house up. Jesus, she thinks now, fancy having space in one room for a piano *and* a dining table *and* two corner sofas. Was Frankie in here then? With *her*? Oh my God, is Natasha Gareth's wife?

But no, she doesn't live here. Gareth said that.

Then what was Frankie doing here with her if he doesn't know this bloke and this bloke doesn't live with Natasha? And if Frankie didn't sleep here last night, then where?

A jolt lands in her chest. She saw the van on the drive. She saw lights on in the house, a couple embracing at the window. She jumped to a conclusion. Frankie had driven here but did not go inside, only spoke to this man then left. And Natasha wasn't here. Jane had stayed back, on the other side of the street. It's possible Frankie was either on the doorstep talking to Gareth or in the van while she was standing there crying.

'Take a seat.' Gareth has returned but is standing by the door.

She does as she's told. He asks her if she'd like a drink and she replies that she'll have a glass of water.

'Won't be a tick.' He leaves her in the enormous room.

Again she looks about her, fear creeping in now. There are no guarantees this Gareth is even telling the truth. And now she is in his sitting room, wondering how to get out. In the next few seconds, Natasha could walk right in. Natasha could be his accomplice, the woman Jane saw him embracing last night in silhouette.

'I only had still, I'm afraid.' Gareth has come back. He is carrying a small white tray with a lone glass of water, a separate bowl with ice, a tiny plate – smaller than a saucer – with two slices of lemon. It is a glass of water, but not as she knows it. 'Do you take ice, lemon?'

'Ice, yes please,' she says helplessly. 'No lemon thanks.'

He sets the tray on the coffee table, tongs two ice cubes into the water, tells her to help herself to more if she likes it colder. She notices he has put on some grey felt Birkenstock-style slippers, and for some reason this reassures her. Murderers don't wear tasteful slippers, do they?

No, but blackmailers might.

Oh for God's sake, Jane. Calm down.

'Hello there.' A thin, elegant woman has walked in, carrying two foggy glasses of white wine. She wears a sheer midnight-blue top, the slash neck falling perfectly around her bony, tanned clavicle. Her legs are so long and slim that skinny jeans actually suit her – they look like a different garment altogether, something sleek and sophisticated and comfortable.

'Hi.' The word catches in Jane's throat. 'Sorry for the intrusion.'

She gives a brief smile and shakes her head. 'Not at all.'

'This is my wife, Diana,' Gareth says, adding, 'She's a psychotherapist.'

'Hi,' Jane says again, impressed, intimidated, nerves still jangling. 'I'm Jane.'

'Sorry, yes,' Gareth says. 'Jane. My apologies.'

He is less composed than Jane thought. Less composed than when he first answered the door. His wife, however, is as calm as a lake on a breezeless day.

The couple sit down, almost as one, a little away from her – nothing predatory in their body language, nothing sinister, apart from, perhaps, the smooth veneer, which has something of the

Bond villain about it. With no sense of urgency and without words, they each take a sip of their wine, almost at the same moment, then, again in complete synchronicity, place their glasses carefully on the black ash coffee table.

'So, you think you might know Natasha?' Jane asks, keen to get the ball rolling and get out of there.

Gareth nods. A brief glance at his wife, who gives an almost imperceptible nod, a kind and gentle smile.

'Why don't you tell us why you're looking for her?' Gareth says, folding his hands on his lap.

Jane smooths her hands over her jeans. 'OK. So. My husband – that's Frankie, the man who came here last night – he's not been himself for quite a while, only I suppose I haven't been paying attention...'

She tells them all of it: Frankie's increasing tiredness, the weight loss, the air of misery she perceives fully only now in the telling, warm tears pricking at her eyes. She goes on, to the blackmail – thousands of pounds – an agreement no sooner made than broken. Polaroid pictures, the threat of internet exposure.

'He has his own business,' she says. 'He didn't say this, but I suppose he thought he'd lose that too, that maybe people wouldn't want to be associated with him. He said she'd hinted that he'd been all over her. It was only a hint, but I'm worried it might have been a veiled threat, where she might go with that, you know? I should've seen he was going through something, but my mind's been on... other things. I'd like to say I didn't want to burden him, but the fact is, I've hardly seen him. I thought he was working to earn money for our trip – our savings, I mean – but I think now he must've been frantically trying to replace the savings. Or avoid me maybe. He could barely look at me. Only, when he told me what had happened, I threw him out. He's cheated on me, in the cheapest, most grubby way. He promised he'd never do that, and it wasn't love or anything. It wasn't even a fling. It was just... opportunistic. Like a window cleaner, you know? Like... like some cliché of a... Sorry, I'm rambling, but... but now... I mean, I hate what he's done, but something feels off. And as much as I'm furious with him, I want to believe it's a mistake, you know? She says she's having his baby and he has to pay her or she'll put the photos online. And I can't stand the thought of him being blackmailed.' She looks from Gareth to Diana. Back to Gareth, whose head is bobbing in tiny surrenders of acknowledgement.

'Er, that's it,' she adds, throwing out her hands.

Gareth looks at his wife, as if for reassurance. Or something.

'Have you met her?' he asks. 'Natasha.'

Jane shakes her head. 'No.'

'Did your husband describe her physically?'

She shrugs. 'He did, but you know what men are like. Sorry. No offence. Frankie's not massively into the visual side of life. He said she was about my height, with dark hair and blue eyes. I think he said blue. It was all such a blur, you know? I was so angry. I still am. Oh!' She snaps her fingers. 'He said she was sophisticated. Which in Frankie-speak could mean anything from *Love Island* to *Made in Chelsea*, but I imagine she's groomed to perfection, you know? Not like...' *Not like me*, she doesn't say.

Gareth and Diana share a third meaningful glance. Diana mutters something Jane doesn't catch but which starts with 'It's possible...' and ends with the word 'hair'. The urge to tell them to share with the group comes to her, but she holds on to her manners. If they know something, she wants to hear it.

But Gareth has turned from his wife and is looking at her now.

'Thank you,' he says, his voice hoarse with an emotion Jane can't name. 'We think we might know this... Natasha. Are you sure you won't have a drink?'

CHAPTER FORTY-FOUR

JANE

'This was a few months ago,' Gareth begins – Jane by now settled with a strong cup of sweet tea, which has gone some way to stop her from shaking. 'Eight,' he says. 'Eight months or so. I had an appointment with a woman who claimed she needed an architect.' He blinks, presses his fingertips to his chest. 'I'm an architect and I was having a drink with a colleague over in Richmond and this woman knocked into me and I spilt my wine over my shirt. It was white wine thankfully. It was a good shirt.' He gives a brief, shallow laugh. 'She apologised profusely and insisted on buying me another glass. I tried to refuse, but she was very insistent. I don't know how it came up, but she must have asked what I did for a living, and then she told me her name was Katrina and that she was looking to renovate a large Georgian property over in Wimbledon, did I have a card? So of course I gave her my card, and about a week later, we made an appointment.

'Only when I got there, she was dressed in... well, not much at all. She apologised and said she hadn't been expecting me. She'd got the date wrong, she said. Thought I was coming the next day.

'I told her not to worry, I'd come back, but she insisted I come in, said it was no problem, she could easily show me what needed doing and relay the details to her husband later.' He pauses, appears to gather himself. 'So I went in. She offered me a glass of white wine, which I accepted. She was very friendly, very chatty, and seemed like she wanted a casual meeting, which sometimes happens. Sometimes clients want to find out what kind of person you are, whether they think you'll work well with them – sense of humour, taste, whether you're married, have kids, as well as professionalism, of course, but it's important to get a feel for someone. For some clients anyway.

'And so we chatted – informally. She told me her husband was a surgeon, often worked late, which was why he wasn't back. Something about that didn't chime, but I either ignored it or only thought about it later. After. She topped up my glass, and I can remember lifting it against the bottle neck so she wouldn't fill it too high. She was pouring it like water and the glasses were very large, and again, this should have struck me as... off, as you said earlier.' He has begun to speak faster, his breath coming in short gasps. 'In fact, I remember thinking they were red wine glasses, really, and I was surprised because she was very polished and the house was very tasteful and I guess she seemed like someone who would know which glasses were for white and which for red.' He is racing now, his words running together. 'Sorry, I'm not a snob, I don't care about any of that, it was just... like a wrong note in a chord or something. I didn't want to drink too much; I was intending to grab an Uber after the meeting, but even so, I wanted to stay focused, for professional reasons.'

Silently his wife lays her hand on his forearm for a second before lifting it. At her touch, he appears to collect himself, to become aware that he has started to gabble, to over-explain.

He sighs. 'I started to get the feeling something wasn't a hundred per cent right. In the moment, I mean, not in retrospect. I couldn't put my finger on it, but by then I was starting to feel incredibly drunk, like, *incredibly* for the glass and a half I'd had. I drink white wine all the time, so my tolerance for it is pretty high.

'And then...' He pauses, his head tips back a little, his eyes half closing as if to peer at the memory through a lens. 'And then she

was leading me upstairs to show me the conversion she wanted
doing. A balcony outside the master bedroom, she said.' He shakes
his head, closes his eyes fully, opens them again. 'I mean, that's up
there with asking the gardener to admire the dahlias from the
bedroom, I realise that now, but... Anyway, the window gave on to
quite a large flat-roof extension on the ground floor and she was
thinking of fitting French windows so that she could access it and
wanted my professional opinion on whether or not it would with-
stand people, and if so, how many. Sorry, you probably don't need
to know all that, but I'm just trying to get across... I guess, even
now, I'm trying to justify why I...'

Again Diana lays a soft hand on his arm, and again he pauses,
breathes, smiles shakily. A sense of foreboding gathers in Jane's
chest. Eight months ago, an understanding wife, and he still can't
really talk about it – a strong suspicion about what *it* might be is
growing by the second.

'She liked to sunbathe,' Gareth continues, 'and I think it was
when she said that that I started to really sense that something
wasn't right. I must have carried on drinking, possibly out of
nerves. I know that because I remember my glass being empty – I
remember her lifting it out of my hand. I don't think I'd put two
and two together, but yes, when she said about the sunbathing,
there was something far too... well, flirtatious about it. The way she
said it, the prolonged eye contact, and then I... I think I sat down
on the bed. I think so. I was dizzy. I was *very* tired – well, I basically felt completely inebriated. And then...'

He inhales deeply, exhales. Reaches for his wine, drinks,
replaces the glass on the coffee table. He looks towards his wife,
who reaches out her hand, this time to hold his. He continues like
that, holding hands with his wife, there in front of Jane, with a
reluctance that is palpable:

'And then she... that is, I woke up and she was... she was on top
of me. She was naked and she was...' He rolls his free hand, meets
Jane's eye for a fraction of a second before looking away, then down
to his slippers, as if ashamed. Jane wants to fill in, to help him out,

but she doesn't know him at all, so she sits perfectly still, her body heating with every word. He doesn't need to say it. They all know what he means.

'That's all I remember,' he says, unable, then, to say it aloud. 'There was a flash, maybe two or three – white flashes – I found out what they were later. And then I woke up next to her. I was naked. She was naked. It was the middle of the night. We were in her bed.' He looks up, relief at having got the words out – most of them anyway – playing across his features.

'I'm sorry,' he says. 'I didn't think I'd have to talk about it again, but if it's the same woman... The thing is, when I woke up, I was still groggy, but I got out of there as fast as I could. Funny' – he gives a brief mirthless laugh – 'I found myself apologising. I was saying sorry, over and over, picking up my clothes like something from a farce. And that's when she became abusive. She was shouting at me, swearing, throwing things. It was... sordid, like some horrible scene from... It was...' He throws up his hands.

'It's OK,' his wife says quietly, and he stops.

'I'm so sorry,' Jane says. 'I think I'm beginning to understand. I think this is what happened to Frankie too, only I... I was so angry. I didn't think it could happen to a man.'

'It can,' says Diana. 'It does.'

'If Diana didn't do the job she does,' Gareth almost interrupts, 'if she hadn't spoken to one of her colleagues, I might never have known the truth. Even now, I have trouble believing it. But Diana helped me. She's helping me with the guilt. The feeling that it was my fault. The flashbacks.' He gazes at his wife with such love, Jane has to look away.

'The miracle is that Gareth had the guts to tell me,' Diana says. 'I was like you, angry at first, but then something didn't add up. I know people whose spouses have cheated always say they never expected it, or that they feel like they don't know their husband or wife anymore, but this was different. So yes, I did speak in confidence to a trusted friend and colleague, thank God. It's not my specific area of expertise, but he'd dealt with a similar case, a guy who had got drunk, too drunk to consent. Given the amount Gareth told me he'd had to drink, we had to conclude the wine had been spiked, though we'll never be able to prove it. But he had severe PTSD. He was really quite ill, had to take time off. From what you describe, it's possible your husband has it too.'

'But how can a woman do that?' Jane asks.

'She spiked his drink,' Diana replies. 'It's as simple as that.'

Diane has answered her literally. The practicalities were not what Jane meant, but before she can press it, Gareth says: 'I should have gone to the police. But I just... I just couldn't. And then when the Polaroids arrived...'

Jane's mouth drops open. 'She sent Polaroids to you too?'

'That's why I thought it might be the same person. When you said about the photos.' He nods, his mouth a grim line. 'When I received them, I just thought: that's it. My life is over. My career, my marriage, my future. Everything. And I knew, or thought I knew – at the time anyway – that it was my fault. She wasn't my type, but she was very attractive and I... Diana helped me a lot with this... Part of me felt flattered. I must have *responded* to her. I mean, I did. And I think that's what I struggled with. I must have led her on, I thought. I mean, I *know* I was guilty of using the fact that she seemed attracted to me to my advantage – professionally, I mean. A little attraction won't do any harm, I thought. So I must have... consented, right? But I didn't. I didn't consent. Diana helped me to realise that. And then I started getting the flashbacks – the wine glass, her taking off my clothes, on top of me... like that. White flashes of light, which of course was her taking photographs.'

Jane finds that her hands are pressed to her cheeks, which are hot to the touch.

'She asked for money,' he continues, his voice strengthening, as if the worst is over. 'Said if I made her a one-off payment, she'd leave me alone. It was a lot of money. Ten grand. I paid it, but she didn't leave me alone. There was another payment, a couple of grand. She said she couldn't meet her rent because she'd been so upset by what had happened she hadn't been able to work. She said I'd used her. Coerced her, she said. She'd had to take time off. I started to worry she might sue me or bring charges or something. And... on the third demand for money, I couldn't take it anymore. I knew I wouldn't be able to make the mortgage payment for this place without dipping into the ISAs. And of course, I was lying to Diana, which was... well, it was horrible. So I told her.' He holds up a forefinger. 'Not because I'm honest or brave or anything like that, but because I knew she would take one look at our bank account and wonder what the hell was going on.' He looks at his wife, back at Jane. 'I'm pretty sure this woman, whatever her name is, has done this before, but I'm lucky beyond belief to be married to a mental health professional. It was Diana who told me I'd been abused and referred me to her colleague. I got help. If I hadn't admitted to it, I don't think I'd ever have realised. Like you, Jane, I didn't think it could happen to a man.'

He picks up his wine, sits back in his chair and gives her a weak smile. For a moment, no one speaks. They are all, Jane thinks, sitting in confetti – words drifting slowly down, settling on their shoulders: what Gareth has told her, what it means – for him, for Diana, for Frankie, for Jane, for all of them, and more – what it says about what this woman is capable of, the sheer heinousness of what she has done. Because it is not only her male victims who are violated, Jane thinks, but every woman, every single woman who has ever had consent removed and has not been believed.

'I know this kind of thing must be very rare,' she says. 'But apart from the Polaroids, what makes you think it's the same person?'

'It happened here,' Diana says. 'At least, that's what we assumed.'

'Of course,' says Jane. 'Yes, Frankie said it happened here.'

'Which is a terrible thought in itself,' Diana replies. 'It must have been while we were on holiday.' She shivers with disgust.

Jane's mind races – to empty wine glasses, to clothes discarded, to bedlinen. Did this woman clean up? she wonders. Did she put everything back in its place? How did she get in?

'We didn't know,' Diana breaks into her thoughts, 'but your husband obviously thought Natasha lived here.'

'She must have stolen my keys,' Gareth says slowly. 'When I got home that night, I couldn't find them.' He turns to his wife. 'You let me in.'

'You said you'd left them at home.' She looks at Jane. 'It was late. I was cross he'd woken me so I was rather brusque. I pretty much turned on my heel and went to bed.'

Gareth nods. 'You did. Which at the time was a relief. And then when I couldn't find the keys the next day, I did worry, but a day or two later I found them in a kitchen drawer and assumed the cleaner had put them there.' His hands rise as he begins to digest the implications. 'She must have stolen them and made copies, then let herself in and put them there. She must have done that before we went on holiday.'

'But we have an alarm,' Diana says.

'Yes, but we don't use it, do we? We've been lazy about it.'

Jane watches their private exchange, their expressions changing, skin paling almost imperceptibly as they put these new pieces together. She too is compiling information. Together the three of them are coming to understand that this woman must have entered the house while Gareth and Diana were in it, presumably asleep.

The sense of violation hangs in the air.

Diana closes her eyes. 'Oh dear God. What a bitch.'

'Shit,' Jane whispers, the words, all these words and what they mean landing heavy now, the horror of them, of this faceless, nameless woman and what she is capable of.

Why call it a digging implement if it's a spade?

A brick covered in a note: *Bitch.*

A glamorous woman with a venomous heart. A woman who would bully her boyfriend. *Anyway, it's too late, I've paid the balance...*

'Gareth,' she says. 'Do you think you could show me those Polaroids?'

He shakes his head. 'I'm sorry, I burnt them. Not even Diana saw them. I knew it was futile, knew she'd have digital copies, but I was desperate. I was half mad.'

Hope drains away. 'How would you describe her?'

'She was average height, maybe a little over. Slim. Fit-looking – worked out, you know? Polished. Expensively dressed but understated, if you know what I mean. Dark hair. Blue eyes.'

Hair colour can be changed. A wig, even. Eyes look different according to the light.

No. No matter how much she wants to put two and two together, it is not Lexie. Lexie is worked out, yes, but she's tall and absolutely not understated. And her eyes are green, hazel at a push, depending on the light. But not blue. Jane knows because they have stared directly into hers with an expression of pure hate. Gareth's description matches Frankie's of Natasha, not her own mental image of Lexie.

Thanking them, she gets up. They shake hands, an oddly formal gesture after such an intimate conversation. In the sombre light of the doorstep, she raises her hand in a wave and steps backwards onto the crunching gravel. But as the door closes, something in her shifts. Lexie's Instagram. Gareth cannot show her a photograph, but she can show him one. A long shot. But just to be sure...

'Hold on a second,' she calls out, reaching for her phone.

The door opens once again, the couple peering at her quizzically.

'I might have a photo.' She brings up Lexie's Instagram and scrolls through, finds a half-face, another, a heart-shaped backside on a wall, cocktails, a plane window, coffees, cocktails, blue skies, nouvelle cuisine, coffee, manicures, pedicures...

'Hold on,' she says, 'there's one in here somewhere.'

Cocktails, rose petals in a foot spa, the muscular forearms of a man who, it occurs to her, may or may not be Steve, coffee, coffee, cocktails...

'Hold on,' she says again, almost frantic now as her thumb flicks at the screen. There's a full face in here somewhere, she knows there is... Ah, there. 'Got it.' She turns her phone to Gareth, holds up the face of Lexie Lane. 'Is this her?'

And in his expression, she sees the answer before he even speaks.

CHAPTER FORTY-FIVE

JANE

'That's Katrina.' Beneath his year-round tan, Gareth looks almost yellow, his eye sockets blackening as if, from one moment to the next, he has become exhausted.

'Are you sure?'

He takes the phone from her, his other hand covering his mouth. He is nodding in that small, rapid way he has; she wonders if it's a mannerism he's always had or if it's come with the trauma he is so obviously still processing, the trauma she has made him relive this evening. The trauma, it seems, her own husband has been through.

From his shoulder, Diana is peering into the phone, fascinated.

'That's her,' he says, as if to convince himself. 'Natasha. Whatever she's called. Different hair colour, different colour eyes. But that's her face.'

'Contact lenses,' Diana says, shaking her head. 'Fucking hell. And that's either hair dye or a wig. Unless she has a sister?'

'I don't think so,' Jane replies. 'I know her as Lexie Lane. She's been bullying me for months and I had no idea why.'

Another thought lands, almost winding her.

She meets Gareth's shattered gaze. 'She never claimed to be pregnant, did she?'

He shakes his head. 'No. I guess I'm lucky there. Maybe that was her aim, who knows?'

The fake bump. Oh dear God.

'Frankie didn't get her pregnant either,' she says. 'Not if it's Lexie. But she claimed he had. She was going for child maintenance.'

They stare at her, confused, but she's backing away now, desperate to call him and tell him he's being blackmailed through no fault of his own and under false pretences.

'Th-Thanks,' she stutters. 'I'll... I'll let you know what I find out, OK?'

At the end of the crescent, she pulls the Vespa to the side of the road, takes out her phone and texts Frankie: *Come home. Come now. I love you. J x*

The message is much simpler than the thoughts at war in her mind. She does love him, she does, and she does want him home. She believes Gareth's story absolutely and the fact that there is, suddenly, no child has lifted something so heavy from her, she feels a physical sense of lightness. But Frankie is her husband, hers, and it is so hard to let go of the thought of him with that woman in that way, the horror of what might have been, the rage and the bitter sense of betrayal. The message will have to do. A phone call would be too complicated. This is the only way she can think of getting him home safely.

Her phone buzzes.

This is everything I love you too I love you so much I'm on my way x

She brushes at her eyes with her fingers. She can't cry now, she just can't. There's no time, and she has to drive carefully. If ever she needed to stay alive, it is now. There is, suddenly, everything to live for. She has a full life, with or without children. It is not the life she planned, but it is the life she wants with an urgency that leaves her breathless. Frankie is coming home, where he belongs. She would always have forgiven him; she thinks she's known that from the start. But now she doesn't have to. Because he has not betrayed her. He has not given another woman a child. What has happened to him is worse than anything she has imagined. And what was happening to her was linked to it somehow.

They have both been victims of Lexie Lane.

Back at home, Des mirrors her restlessness, circling the living room, barking at the odd pedestrian passing by. Every time she hears a car on the road, she checks the front window, even when the engine fizzes high, sounds nothing like Frankie's van. She's thinking about that overheard phone call at the Ritz.

I'm not being funny, but you agreed to this. And anyway, it's too late, I've paid the balance...

Gareth said something about suspecting she's done this kind of thing before. Was Steve one of her victims? Was she blackmailing several men at once? Or was Steve, as she now suspects, Frankie?

This isn't just my baby, you know. You didn't seem to have a problem making it with me.

Now she thinks about it, the wording is odd. *Didn't seem to have a problem making it with me.* Not *You said you wanted a baby too.* Not *I thought we both wanted a family.*

Steve could easily just be the name she put into her phone. Simon's lover was in his phone as Phil, Jane remembers. Hils thought he was having an affair with a bloke when she found the erotic messages. It was only when she rang from his phone and heard a woman's voice that she realised what was going on. Philippa. Just like the name Lexie, the name Steve doesn't mean anything, especially not in this context. Did Lexie actually call him Steve while Jane was listening? She can't remember.

It wasn't just Simon who used a fake name of course. Her mother's boyfriends were never stored under their real names. Donald was Booboo, as Jane remembers, a nickname that could make her physically sick even now. Steve could be anyone, anyone at all.

So... did Frankie pay for the baby shower?

Frankie said Natasha had asked for four thousand pounds before demanding more. She had already extorted what sounded like thousands from Gareth, enough to keep her alive though perhaps not enough for the high life, not in London. Yet judging by her Instagram, she is always jaunting off to foreign shores. And there was a photograph of her beside a huge shiny car, wasn't there? The garage and the manufacturer were tagged in the comments. A Jaguar, Jane thinks, or a BMW, she really can't remember. Then there are the restaurant dinners, the cocktails that would have cost fifteen quid a pop, her luxurious home... that stuff all costs a lot of money. But that's all it is: stuff. It doesn't make you happy, doesn't make you special, and you can't take it with you. Lexie's life is all stuff. To her, people are stuff. Friends are stuff. Men are stuff. Babies are stuff. It's all just stuff, stuff, stuff. Her enormous luxury house is just...

Actually, now she thinks of it, *was* it *House Beautiful* where she saw Gareth and Diana's house? Or was it...

She opens Instagram. She has not looked at it properly since she first scrolled through Lexie's feed. She has almost forgotten about the troll who posted a terrible coffee, claiming that it was from her café, but she can see more sinister-looking tags in her notifications.

But she doesn't have time for that. She brings up Lexie's Instagram once again, scrolls through until she finds the photographs: the silver orb, the topiary, the village-hall-sized living room, the corner sofa, the dining table laid for twelve – shit, she must have laid it while she was in their house – the mini grand, the picture window to the back garden, *#livinglifetothefull #cooldecor #blessed*.

'Shit,' she whispers.

She knew she recognised the place. It looked a little different in reality, in a different light, at a different angle, but yes, these are the uplighters, casting their amber glow, throwing their shadows onto the geometric shapes of the building.

She scrolls. The fake is subtle. The photographs are spaced out on the timeline, the captions detailing work done rather than *look at my house*. The tags refer to high-end suppliers: lighting by @luminescence, sphere sculptures by @orb, door by something Danish-sounding, expensive. She presses the tags, finds herself in a world of designer homes, gargantuan furniture, beachside locations... in short, the world of the super-rich. Yes, Lexie would have needed so much money to fund this...

Hang on, no. She would *not* have needed money for this. This is not her lifestyle! She would not need these funds at all, not for this, at least. This is Gareth and Diana's life – two high-flying, hard-working people with no kids. Jane suspects their lives do not feature in an Instagram account, suspects they don't have time to post.

What is Lexie's *actual* life?

What *stuff* does she actually own?

The plane window, the rose petals in the spa, the nouvelle cuisine – all super-expensive, but how much of it was real?

A suite at the Ritz...

She has never mentioned a job. Jane believed her to be supported by Steve, but maybe there's no Steve, or there's more than one Steve. Maybe Frankie is the latest in a *series* of Steves. Oh my God, is it possible to spend your life doing that to people? Is it possible that this is her career? How does she look at herself in the mirror each day?

Jane is panting, she realises. Figures swirl around in her head, wild calculations of how much things cost: holidays abroad, luxury cars, posh hotels... She has no idea about any of it. Didn't even know Sophie's bag was a fake, and even if she had, would not have known what it was a fake of. A CD is something with music on it, she had joked, back when she and Sophie made each other laugh. A chequerboard pattern is by Luncheon Voucher.

She googles the Ritz, finds the Green Park Suite. She takes the online video tour of the rooms – yes, yes, this is the one; she remembers the candy-striped sofa, those antique occasional tables, that glass coffee table and, of course, that blue-and-white master bedroom, where she stood cowering in the shadows while Lexie bullied her 'boyfriend' from the en suite.

There is no price.

There is still no sign of Frankie.

Worry heats her belly. She hopes he isn't driving too fast, desperate to see her and be reunited and forgiven. She tells herself to stay calm. No point catastrophising. The catastrophe is already here and its name is Lexie Lane.

Oh, but is it? What is her name really?

She finds the phone number for the Ritz and calls. Finds herself, ridiculously, putting on a posh voice to ask how much it is to hire the Green Park Suite for afternoon tea. Is told she must book the suite for twenty-four hours. Very well, she says, of course. Not a problem. May I ask how much it is for twenty-four hours? She waits, knows this woman must have realised she is not rich. Rich people don't ask the price. If you have to ask, you can't afford it. At least she thinks that's how it is with rich people. Frankly, she has no idea.

'Hello?' the woman from the hotel says.

'Hello, yes, still here.'

'So, for the Green Park, the price starts at four thousand pounds.'

It is all she can do not to choke.

'Thank you,' she says. 'And if I were to lay on some refreshments for my guests – afternoon tea with champagne, something like that – how much would that be?'

The receptionist sighs rather rudely. 'If you were to order our house champagne – that's the Ritz Reserve – it's one hundred pounds a bottle, and then for the afternoon tea, it's fifty pounds a head.'

'Thank you,' Jane says. 'Thank you very much – I'll pass that on to my employer.'

She closes the call, is still reflecting on her pathetic need to pretend her enquiry wasn't for her personally when she hears the low tractor-like rattle of a diesel engine.

'Frankie!'

Des startles as she leaps up and runs to the door.

CHAPTER FORTY-SIX
JANE

On the doorstep, Frankie is a bedraggled mess. Handsome too –
the thought surprises her, that she could even think something so
superficial. But it's true. Distress has given him cheekbones, melted
his pot belly. His jeans hang off him as off a fashion model.

'Oh darling,' she says and throws out her arms.

But he steps back from her, raising his hand, and she realises he
does not know what she knows. As far as he is concerned, he has
cheated on her, is now the father of a child he doesn't want with a
woman he doesn't love while longing to have a child he does want
with a woman he does love.

This is surreal.

'Franks.' Her arms are still open for him. He is still on the front
path, cowed, confused and clearly shaken.

'I don't deserve to come back,' he says, his bottom lip trembling.
'I don't deserve you.'

She drops one hand, keeps the other outstretched, as if he is a
child. 'It's OK, Franks. It's OK, I promise. There's things you don't
know but I can't tell you out here. Just come inside, eh? Come in.
This is your home. Come home, baby.'

He looks at her through his lashes, eyes still twitching with
confusion and fear. She can see how hard he is fighting not to cry.

Her heart tightens with love, with sympathy. She can believe him once he believes it himself, she thinks. Wanting to is the start.

'Franks,' she says. 'Come in, come on.'

He lowers his head and walks towards her slowly. On the doorstep, he stops and meets her eye, and again she holds out her arms, but again he shakes his head.

'I haven't showered since I left.'

'Where were you last night?'

'At hers.' He throws up his hands. 'Not like that. I kipped on her sofa. I went over there to tell her she could post what she liked, that I wasn't having it. I told her I'd need a paternity test and if it was mine I'd do right by the baby but no more.'

'Oh, Franks,' she says. 'There is no baby.'

He is staring at her as if she's grown a second head. '*What?*'

'There never was. Now come inside before I drag you in myself.'

Like strangers, they sit at opposite ends of the kitchen table. She asks if he wants a drink and he tells her yes, yes, that would be good. But when she suggests opening a bottle of white wine, he holds up his hand and says no, he can't drink white, doesn't think he'll ever drink it again. She knows why, she realises, and yet he doesn't know she knows. There is so much to tell him, and yet it is his experience, not hers.

She finds a couple of bottles of beer and holds them up. Opens them when he nods yes.

'I don't know how to do this,' he says. 'I'm sorry a thousand times. A million. How can I make it right? Just tell me what to do.'

'Here's what you do,' she says. 'You keep your mouth shut while I tell you what I know, OK? But I'll start by saying that what happened is not your fault. It isn't your fault.'

'But—'

'Shh. Drink your beer.'

She tells him how she followed him to Natasha's luxury house.

How she saw his van parked outside and assumed he was in there with her.

'I wasn't,' he says. 'She doesn't live there.'

She raises a hand. 'You have to let me talk, OK?' When he nods, she continues. 'I know that now. You must have been in the van when I got there. Maybe you were building up the courage to confront her or something.'

'I called her to ask her where the hell she was. I did that after I found out she didn't even live there. She texted me her address and I went round there.'

'OK.'

'How do you know she's not pregnant?'

'Frankie!'

'Sorry. Sorry, go on.'

And she does. This time, he settles and lets her talk. It takes a long time to tell him everything, the ins and outs of it, but what takes the longest, what she suspects will take him much, much longer to hear, is that he was raped. Because this is the word for what has happened, another word Lexie has brought into their lives, alongside *hate* and *bitch*, the two words they have strived to live without. These are the digging implements with which Lexie Lane has excavated their foundations and sunk them both.

But she hasn't told him about Lexie yet. For the moment, they are still talking about Natasha.

She was expecting him to collapse with relief, to cry *oh thank God*, but he doesn't. Instead, his face crumples in confusion and for the second time this evening he is fighting hard not to cry. Finally, he manages to speak. And as the words leave him, as he describes back to her what she has just told him, she senses he is telling himself his own story, and that this is the beginning of his understanding of what has happened to him.

'I couldn't understand how we were in bed together,' he says. 'And the flashbacks. They got more not less. And the feeling of dread, like I was going to be sick, all the time. And the shame of it, God. And the thought of what I'd done to *us*.'

'You didn't do it. You were sexually assaulted.'

'How is that even possible?' he whispers.

'I don't know. But it is. And I suspect you and Gareth aren't the only ones. I think this is how she earns her living. A con artist, a kind of sex grifter. Though I don't know that for sure.'

'So.' He has peeled the label from his bottle, which lies in a sticky mess on the table. 'How do you know she's not pregnant?'

Jane takes a deep breath. 'You know I told you about that new friend of Sophie's? Lexie? You remember Kath's birthday party? Well, it... it wasn't a birthday party. I lied, I'm sorry. Lexie was pregnant too. It was Sophie and Lexie's joint baby shower. I didn't tell you because it was all a bit much on top of Sophie getting pregnant. A double whammy, you know? You were working all the hours, and now I think about it, I should've known something was wrong. I should've known it wasn't just work.'

He shakes his head. 'You weren't to know.'

'But I would have. Normally, I would have, don't you see? I was so wrapped up in all that petty playground stuff, I didn't see what was happening to you. I stopped looking at you. Looking at you properly, I mean, and really noticing.'

When he nods, clearly unable to reply, she goes on. 'So I didn't tell you that this Lexie woman had also announced that she was pregnant, and as part of her campaign to somehow buy my best friend while rubbishing me in her eyes, she organised and paid for a huge, extravagant, over-the-top baby shower at the Ritz. And I've just checked how much that cost, and it was in the ballpark of four grand.' She watches him closely, repeats: 'Four thousand pounds.'

'Hang on,' he says, looking suddenly alert. 'So it was a baby shower, not a birthday do? And it was four grand?'

She nods. 'Four thousand pounds. You took out three grand in April, didn't you? Lexie postponed the shower a couple of times, eventually landing on the twenty-sixth. I didn't know that's how much it cost at the time, because, well, because I couldn't imagine someone spending that kind of money on a hotel room and some sandwiches. But then I overheard her shouting at her boyfriend to pay up, and it sounded like she was punishing him and I couldn't work it out. She told us his name was Steve, but I don't think she was talking to Steve, was she? That afternoon...'

His eyes are round and bloodshot. 'I called Natasha that afternoon while you were out. She'd said she wanted money to get her started, but then she texted me this bill and told me she'd decided to have a baby shower instead, because she deserved to be a bit spoilt after all I'd put her through. I called her to beg her not to spend so much, but she said it was too late, she was already in the middle of it. She said she wanted a special day, it was the least I could do. It was all our savings, every penny, and she was just blowing it...'

'And that was only the start.'

'It was.' He shakes his head a fraction. 'So this Lexie – she's your mate?'

'God, not my mate, no. Sophie's. Lexie is Natasha.'

'Lexie is Natasha? As in the same person? Oh my God.' He shakes his head, his mouth hangs open. 'And... hang on, how d'you know she's not pregnant?'

'Because I saw her fake bump. A big beige pouch thing strapped to her belly.'

'You're *joking*?'

'Nope. I've gone forwards and backwards on it thousands of times – I thought maybe I'd got it wrong. I saw her in the en suite of one of the bedrooms. I'd gone in there by accident and she was there looking in the mirror, talking to Steve – which I now know was you – and she lifted her blouse and I saw this fake pouch. I didn't think she'd seen me, but she had, and before I could tell Sophie, she'd already told her it was a support belt. She was always one step ahead. And if you can lie like that, there's nothing stopping you, is there? If you don't stop at the truth, there's no end to what you can say or do. Well, we know that now, don't we?'

His fingers bunch at his forehead. 'I can't take it in. Natasha is Lexie. You're sure it's the same person?'

She nods. 'I showed Gareth her Instagram and he recognised her.'

'Can I see it?'

She shows it to him, watches him scroll through, watches his eyes screw up as he tries to work out her real features from the teasing half-faces and profiles, the slight augmentation of the features, the heightened intensity of the colours. Until he sits back in his chair and says: 'That's her. Different hair, different eyes. But it's her. Fuck.'

'The only thing I couldn't work out was the height thing. Lexie's so tall and you said Natasha was my height. But I've been thinking about her shoes and I realised I'm always in flats and I'd never once seen her without heels. I was remembering when I got ready for that baby shower, I put my heels on and you said, "You're tall" – do you remember? Lexie always, always wore heels. Sophie never wore heels when she was pregnant – she said they made her back ache. Maybe I should have put two and two together, but then all women are different.'

'You can say that again.'

'All women are different.'

He smiles.

'We're people,' she says. 'Women, men, we're just people. I know that's obvious, but all this time, I've been fighting against calling another woman something mean because it seemed unsisterly. I'm a feminist, I thought. I don't go round slagging off or judging other women. But we call men bastards all the time, if that's what they are. If a woman is a horror show, she's a horror show. To make excuses for her is... patronising. Is it? I don't know. I just know I should've called out this woman's bullshit the moment it started. I should never have let her get her claws into Sophie.'

He shrugs. 'Sophie's a grown woman. You told her what was going on, didn't you?'

Jane nods. Much as it hurts, he's right. Sophie threw their friendship and all its history away like an old copy of *Grazia*. Jane has been collected and discarded like a thing – like stuff.

'How do you feel?' she asks her husband, who has been loyal after all, and who has believed every word she's said.

'Like I'll feel better for a bath.'

She smiles. 'Maybe I'll join you.'

Later, they are lying in bed. His arms are around her and she can feel her skin pressing against his precious skin, the unit of them both, the home they are to one another. This is the home that woman almost broke. They are both damaged – he more than her. But together, they will be all right.

Frankie has produced a packet of cigarettes, which he tells her he bought in desperation when he was facing a night sleeping in the van. They consider them briefly before agreeing they will have one each, then throw away the pack. And so they light up and smoke – like lovers from the seventies, she jokes, smoking in bed after the most intense sex they've had in years. Sex is communication – at least it used to be, for them. It was the continuation of a conversation started that day in her grotty flat with the blocked shower.

'I knew you were the one for me,' he tells her when she relays her memory.

She slaps him on the arm. 'Don't be sentimental – you know it brings me out in a rash.'

But secretly she's thrilled to hear him say it, because she'd known it too. He was everything her mother's boyfriends were not. No grand gestures, no dozen long-stemmed red roses (except for once, later, when they'd agreed to get married). His generosity has always been quiet, constant: a biscuit with her cup of coffee, a long walk, listening, hearing. He is her friend. Her best friend. And, she realises, the physical conversation that was always a continuation of their words had stalled when it became about one thing only: making a child. And perhaps because both forms of conversation looped back eventually to their unfathomable loss, communication itself quietened, faded, almost stopped.

'There's something I still can't figure out,' Frankie says, stroking her arm – they have not yet broached where, where on earth, they go from here.

'What's that?' She closes her eyes to his perfect touch.

'When I went to her flat, it was a dump, an absolute dump.'

'Well, obviously all the cash is for show, isn't it? I don't think you realise how much it costs a woman just to be a woman.'

'What do you mean, just to be a woman?'

She laughs. 'You have no idea the lengths women go to. You have a shave and a wash and you put on a nice shirt and out the door you go, thinking you're the dog's pyjamas. You're a bloke, that's what blokes do. If you get a beer belly, you pat it and say things like *all bought and paid for*, safe in the knowledge that your woman won't turn a hair. And speaking of hair, don't get me started. It grows all over the place – legs, pits, shoulders – and if it's on a bloke, wherever it is, it's fine.'

'Not for some geezers.'

'Well, admittedly, but they're still a minority, still what you'd call posers, aren't they? But you don't have to be a poser to be a woman who shaves her legs. Or a woman who has her hair cut and coloured once every six weeks. Basic grooming for women is like a tax, Franks. It's a tax.'

'You don't do all that lot.'

'Well, I shave my legs, but no, I don't dye my hair 'cause I can't be bothered, and yes, I get you to trim the back with the clippers, but some women will look at me and think, *She should make more of an effort* or *Why can't she be more feminine?* But I know Kath has her hair dyed once a month and that it costs a fortune. And Hils has acrylic nails put on once a fortnight because she bites hers, and I think she has a spray tan before her holidays because she feels too self-conscious to wear a bikini otherwise. And they're not even considered vain. They're not vain. And they're nowhere near Lexie's league. That kind of maintenance costs the equivalent of a mortgage.'

'She doesn't have to do it though. It's her choice.'

'Well, much as it pains me to say it, maybe she feels she doesn't have a choice. A lot of women do this stuff just to feel like they're enough, you know? Young women having Botox before they're thirty, boob jobs, you name it. And the biggest irony is, it's so materialistic, and yet they end up with nothing materially. Look at Lexie. Thousands on her hair, her coloured contact lenses, her eyelashes, her make-up, possibly Botox – I'm pretty convinced she's persuaded Sophie to have it too. And the year-round tan. I'm not judging, not at all – it's a choice, I mean that, and a lot of women get a lot of joy from it – but it all adds up. No wonder she's in a shitty flat.' Jane sighs. 'I mean, obviously it doesn't excuse what she's done.'

'No. But that's not what doesn't add up.'

'Oh.' She laughs. 'You could have told me before I went off on my big rant.'

He laughs too, and then of course she's in tears, because if they're laughing, it means they're still them after all – despite everything – and when she tells him this, they both get emotional.

'Stop being soppy,' she says.

'You started it.'

'Fair. Tell me what you were going to tell me. What doesn't add up?'

'It was when I told her I didn't care what she did with the photos but I'd give her what was fair if the baby turned out to be mine. It was the way she reacted. She was... sad. Like money wasn't what she wanted after all. I think she wanted me, you know? Like, if she ruined me in your eyes, I'd have nowhere else to go and I would go to her.'

'Why would she do that? I mean, no offence but if she wanted money, you're not exactly loaded.'

'Well, she only went for me 'cause she saw the watch, right? And she thought Simon's motor was mine. But then what was weird was that even when she realised I wasn't rich, she didn't chuck me out or tell me to get lost or anything. She still tried to get me to stay with her.'

Jane's hackles rise. 'In what way?'

He lifts her hand and plants a kiss on her knuckles. 'It was like, you've lost your wife now, and I'm having your baby, so you may as well make a go of it with me sort of thing.'

'Right. Do you think we should call the police?' Next to her, she feels him tense. From one moment to the next, his entire body is as rigid as a plank. 'Frankie?'

'I'm sorry, babe,' he says. 'I can't go to the police. I just... I just can't.'

She remembers Gareth talking – months had passed and he was still held together with paper and string. And Frankie, earlier, when she had to tell him what had really happened to him – the look on his face was almost unbearable.

'I get it,' she says softly. 'Pretend I didn't say it.'

He relaxes, his body sinking against hers. 'So the one big thing I still haven't told you is, she said I could kip on her couch, right? I felt weird about it, but she'd calmed down so I thought, well, I'll kip here and then I'll sort something out for tomorrow. She went upstairs and I was in the living room under my coat. I couldn't sleep, so I checked on her and she was flat out, so then I felt a bit more relaxed and I managed to drift off. But then next thing, I woke up and she was on me.'

'*On* you?' A hot flicker of doubt: horrible, horrible doubt. 'On you how?'

'She was in her nightdress – this, like, skimpy thing – and she was sitting on top of me – astride me. She was undoing my trousers – I was sleeping fully clothed, I literally just needed to crash for a few hours. I mean, I should have slept in the van, I know that now.'

The urge to interrupt him almost overwhelms her, but she says nothing, silent in the new and still raw knowledge that she should have let him tell her properly the first time.

'I told her to get off and she was like, oh, come on, you're here now. I pushed her off me and she got really lairy with me, started shouting all kinds, just like she did that night. I just legged it out of there. It was horrible. Only, it didn't make sense until now – like, why would she want to do that, especially after finding out I don't have money, you know? Why would she do that if she already had my baby inside her? But with you saying she isn't even pregnant, now I'm thinking maybe I'm not what she wanted at all. More than the money, more than me, maybe she wanted a baby. She pretended she was having my baby to somehow trick me into giving her a baby – does that make sense?'

'Wow,' Jane says. 'And all this time, I thought she was after me.'

CHAPTER FORTY-SEVEN

JANE

'Natasha,' Frankie says calmly, phone pressed to his ear. 'It's Frankie.'

Jane squeezes his hand. There is a pause. She strains to hear Lexie down the line, but there's no sound. In front of them, on the kitchen table, the remains of their cooked breakfast and two Americanos (Bolivian Java). Jane is beginning the process of making Frankie better one micro-kindness at a time.

'I know what you did to me,' Frankie says into the silence. 'I know you put something in my drink. And I know there's no baby, OK? I know you scammed Gareth, I know all of it. I'm just calling you to say I'm not going to press charges...'

From down the line, a high, angry-sounding babble.

'What? What do you mean what for?' He lets go of Jane's hand, presses his fingertips to his forehead. 'For blackmail. For false impersonation, for doing... what you did.'

Rape. He cannot say it. She wonders if he ever will. Down the line, wails of outrage continue. Jane rubs his back, a reminder to stay calm.

'Look,' he says. 'I know what you've been doing to my wife too, bullying her and trying to make her mates believe rubbish about her. I know all of it, Lexie. All I'm saying is I'm not going to do anything if you promise you'll leave us alone, OK? That's all. That's all we want. Just leave us alone.'

Jane is as still as prey, all senses trained into one. Like prey, she listens, thinks she hears sobbing now. From abuse to victimhood. How instant the transition is. She hears her husband's name, the words *don't do this to me*, before Frankie interrupts, loud and clear:

'Goodbye, Natasha. Katrina. Lexie. Or whatever your name is.'

The phone falls. He covers his face with both hands. She wants to tell him they should go to the police, but he needs more time, she can see that as plainly as his cup of coffee gone cold in front of him. Gently, she will try and persuade him. Surely other men will come forward. And at that thought, the travesty of Lexie's behaviour hits her once again.

At what point does the digging implement become the spade?

At what point do you use the word *bitch*?

Jane leaves Frankie in the kitchen, grabs her phone from her bag and sees immediately that there is a message from Lexie on the group WhatsApp, which she reads as she goes upstairs.

Hey girls. Sad news ☹ I lost the baby this morning. Still, at least I can drink now, LOL! See ya all soon!

She realises her mouth is hanging, open and slack, as if her jawbone has dissolved.

'What the hell?' she whispers, sitting down on the bed. 'What the actual hell?'

The tone, everything about it is wrong – so, so wrong. That is not how you feel when you lose a baby. That one brief positive IVF result that turned out not to be viable left Jane struggling to get out of bed for weeks; to suffer a miscarriage is even more traumatic. This message is an insult to anyone who has suffered in this way, an absolute insult. Does Lexie seriously think they will be fooled by this? What the hell is she playing at?

Fury, pure and hot, rises up in her belly, her chest, her throat.

You were never pregnant, Lexie, she writes. *Now fuck off out of our lives, you total fraud.*

She sends it. She is shaking with rage. Crying with it. But even as the seconds pass, regret stalks in, shaking its head, tutting. She shouldn't have sent that message. She has not done as Carla reminded her to do. She has not kept hold of herself. She has not stayed classy. Because this is what people like Lexie do when they reduce us to basket-item counters, to mean thinkers, to acts of aggression: they rob us of ourselves. Lexie is these people. And as the rage cools, Jane understands with shining clarity that her mother too is these people. Her mother deserved to be shouted at in the supermarket, to have eggs spattered on the window, the brick smashing through glass. And she deserved the note written on it, the word that Jane has refused to say and the feeling that comes with it: hate. She doesn't hate her mother. She cannot. She knows that her mother's mother drank, bullied and belittled her, that she kicked her out when she was sixteen after finding her with a boy, but Jane cannot take responsibility for what Victoria became, not anymore. She cannot excuse it, just as she cannot take responsibility for or excuse Lexie Lane. It isn't Jane wrecking friendships built up over years; it isn't Jane using sex to entrap men and betray all of womankind in the process. It is Lexie doing these things.

She glances at her phone, wonders if she can delete her message or if it's too late.

The phone rings in her hand, startling her. *SOPHIE RUNNING.* Too late then.

'What the hell?' Sophie is shouting, her voice thick with tears.

Jane takes a moment, waits until she's sure Sophie isn't going to say anything else.

'Sophie,' she says calmly.

'What the hell are you on, sending that message? She's just lost a baby, for God's sake. I can't even—'

'Sophie. Sophie? Sophie! Will you shut the... Will you just SHUT UP?'

At last Sophie stops. Jane can hear her breathing down the line.

'Sophie, listen to me. Lexie is not pregnant. She never was. I tried to tell you, but you didn't believe me. I tried to tell you she was bullying me, but you didn't believe me about that either. She's done nothing but shit-stir and lie and she's... She tried to seduce Frankie, tried to blackmail him. That woman has made us both ill. I'm on the verge of calling the police. I'm telling you as your friend, who you've known for years, who has never, ever been anything but kind to you, that she's a con artist. There was no baby. She was faking it to worm her way into your affections, among other things. She claimed the baby was Frankie's and... oh God, much worse things I can't even tell you about. And no, before you say it, this has absolutely nothing to do with me and my losses, so don't even try and suggest it has. It is the truth. It's just the truth, Sophie, whether you can hear it or not.' She makes herself stop, wishes she'd been more succinct, like on the films.

'Jane.' Sophie's voice is low with the kind of preternatural calm that masks utter fury. 'I want you to hear this, OK? We're not friends anymore, do you get that? I can't have you in my life. You're toxic. Stay away from me.'

'Soph?' Jane says, but the line is dead.

Heart battering now, tears rolling down her face, she pulls up the video call with Hils and Kath. Cutting people out, meeting behind closed doors – politics, that's what this is now, what that woman has reduced them to. After all Frankie has been through, she should be calling the police, but he won't let her and all she can do now is try and lobby support, save the friends she has left. She calls them both. Their faces appear, and instinctively, she smiles.

'Hi,' she says, noticing that both of them are walking swiftly – interiors shaking behind them: Hils's school, Kath's office. Shit.

'Are you OK?' Hils says, becoming still, shelves of books dimly lit behind her.

'I'm so sorry to call you both at work,' Jane says. 'Did you see the WhatsApp?'

'No,' both say.

Kath is now in a loo cubicle by the looks of things

'I'm in the store cupboard,' Hils says, almost invisible in the dark space.

'Oh God, I'm sorry. But I had to speak to you both urgently. I'll keep it brief...'

'Holy Christ,' says Hils after Jane has done her best to nutshell Lexie's behind-the-scenes campaign. 'I mean, I knew she was bad news, but I had no idea. Mostly I just thought she was, y'know, a bit young. A bit vacuous and boring, you know? And a bit scary.'

'Scary, yeah,' says Kath. 'She scared the living bejesus out of me. But poor you, Jane. I can't believe she's been doing that to you. Why didn't you tell us?'

'I didn't want to break up the gang, you know? We've all been friends for so long, and I thought if I fell out with Sophie, I'd lose you two as well. Plus it took me a while to believe it was really happening. I thought I was overthinking. No one behaves like that, I thought. I couldn't get my head around it. I kept wondering if it was my fault.'

'The woman's a lunatic,' Hils says. 'Has she replied to your big sweary WhatsApp?'

'No, but Sophie called me and basically told me she doesn't want me in her life anymore. I'm toxic apparently.'

'Oof,' Hils says. 'Nothing you can really do about it though, is there? You've tried to reason with her. You've tried not to break up the gang, but it sounds like it's cost you your health. And Frankie's.'

'It's totally not your fault,' Kath says. 'This is not on you.'

Jane breathes a long sigh. 'Listen, you guys are at work. We'll talk later, OK?'

She closes the call and looks out of the bedroom window at the bright new day. She has told Kath and Hils and they believed her without question, just as Frankie did, just as her friends from home did – the bullying behind the scenes, the manipulation, what happened with Frankie and the whole bizarre fake pregnancy. They believed all of it.

And yet she feels no sense of victory. She feels nothing actually, other than bereft. She knows Hils and Kath are still her friends, and for that she is grateful beyond words. But the rest is lost and she will never get it back. So much is written about romantic break-ups, but as far as the end of a friendship goes, there is no real frame of reference, no well-worn narrative guide for her to read and relate to, no self-help books, no how-to. It is no wonder she has struggled to find the words to describe or even identify what has been happening. There is a sense in which she didn't believe it herself.

Downstairs, Frankie is not in the kitchen. For a moment, she fears he's gone out to work, but a second later, she finds him on the sofa, fast asleep, Des a long furry strip by his side. The sight of them fills her, and she finds she is crying: for all that she's lost, and for all that she has. She texts Jude: *Do you think you could do the whole day today?*

Sure. No worries.

'Hey.'

She wakes up. Frankie is standing next to the bed.

'I brought you a tea,' he says. 'And a digestive biscuit.'

'Angel,' she says. 'Thank you. What time is it?'

'It's after five.'

'Oh my God! I've been asleep all day!'

'Me too. What a pair of slackers.'

He slides the mug onto the bedside table and walks around the bed to climb in the other side. They sit propped up against the bedhead, tea and biscuits, Jane and Frankie, just the two of...

A low woof is followed by Des, who bounds into the room and jumps onto the bed, almost spilling tea everywhere.

'Dezzie!' Jane laughs, holding up her drink until Des turns once, twice, then plonks himself down at the end of the bed. Just the three of them then.

'Let's go out to dinner,' Frankie says.

'Yes,' she says. 'Let's.'

'If we can't afford it, let's not afford it in style, eh?'

Two hours later, they are 'as ponced up as a pair of parakeets', according to Frankie, which translates into Frankie in one of his two good shirts, his best jeans and his black Caterpillar boots, Jane in a pair of black leather jeans she picked up in Oxfam, a slash-neck top with gold bits in it and a pair of tan heeled ankle boots she'd forgotten about. She adds some black eye make-up and her usual lipstick that no one can tell is there. A spray of perfume and she's ready.

'Wow,' says Frankie. 'You look sexy.'

'Yet tough.'

'Indeed. Tough as old boots.'

She laughs. 'That's not quite what I meant.'

'Sorry. Need to work on my schmoozing. Shall we go?'

They are faking it, she knows. Neither of them feels strong or tough or even, it's possible, like going out. But this is their show – for each other, for themselves and for the outside world. It is their way of sticking it to Lexie Lane, wherever she is now. Jane tells Frankie about the Instagram trolling of her café, about the eggs thrown at the house, that she suspects Lexie of these things. She wonders if Lexie will leave the WhatsApp group and slope off over the horizon, whether she will leave Sophie and find a new victim to love-bomb and take ownership of. Perhaps her campaign to win Sophie has become an actual friendship and they will now form their own pair, leaving Jane, Kath and Hils in a three. Who knows?

And it is as she is pondering this aloud to Frankie, the two of them crossing the road, that she hears the roar of a car engine, looks up to see the glare of white headlights, hears Frankie cry her name above the screaming revs, feels a hard push at her back.

Then blackness.

CHAPTER FORTY-EIGHT

THE HOSPITAL

The lift pings. Esher Wing. Level 7.

The doors scroll open. A short limp along the corridor. Two nurses appear at the far end, deep in conversation, striding fast. I stop dead, smile as them as they pass, hold up the crutches when they glance over, as if they're not for me, as if I'm here to deliver them.

They smile, nod, walk on

Canbury Ward. This is it. There – at the far end near the window. It's her. Goes by her maiden name, Preston, of course she does. I should have thought that through before I asked at reception; it's just the sort of thing she would do. The big feminist, with her ugly short haircut and her shit clothes, turning her nose up at women who bother to actually make an effort. Thing is, I know everything about her and she has no idea. She's so up herself she didn't even recognise me, not even vaguely. She thinks she's so much better than everyone else, with her coffee bar and her mates and her lovely husband and her lovely life, but I know what she left behind. I know she left her stupid slag of a mother without a backward glance. I know what her and her mother did to me and mine. So yes, I know her fucking maiden name.

I hobble over. Sweat is pouring off me. The pain is like nothing on earth.

I pull the curtain open.

Her mouth opens but nothing comes out. Her eyes are full of terror.

Good.

'Jane Preston,' I say. 'Remember me?'

CHAPTER FORTY-NINE

JANE

Jane blinks awake, knows immediately that she's in a hospital – the bright light, the smell, the strange propped-up angle of the bed. She closes her eyes against the glare. And then it comes, in pieces: last night. Her and Frankie, crossing the road, happy, oblivious, loved-up as teenagers. The car. The white glare of the headlights. Her name ringing out in the air. Frankie pushing her. The roar of the engine. The sickening thud. Oh God. Frankie. Please God, let him be alive.

Her breath quickens. She was alone when she was admitted, in a wheelchair. Blood drying on her face. She raises one hand, finds she can't. It's in plaster, a sling, fingers pressed to her chest. She raises the other hand, her right, to her head. Bandages. Last night, they asked her questions. She gave their names, she thinks, though she can't remember the details of the conversation. Frankie was unconscious. He was on a gurney. They took him somewhere; at the memory, a sob blocks her throat. The sight of him: fallen, wounded, after everything he's suffered. Oh God, where is he? Is he alive? He has to be. He cannot die, he cannot. A nurse bandaging her head, telling her she was going to be OK – does she remember that or does she only think she does because she can feel the fibrous fabric under her fingertips?

She must have lost consciousness then. Now, awake, everything hurts; she wonders what else is broken. Please God, let Frankie be OK. If anything's happened to him, if... No, don't go there. He will be OK. This cannot be worse than it already is. She has to stay positive. Think positive thoughts, Jane. Manifest. Manifest the *shit* out of Frankie being OK.

What happened was not an accident. The thought comes to her as a truth – it has the truth's round, complete weight. That car was not driving carelessly. It was driving at them. Frankie – he pushed her onto the pavement. He saved her life. Then glass smashing. Sirens. Being lifted, a tiny torch being shone in her eyes.

She opens her eyes. Her breath quickens.

Who was driving that car?

A swishing sound. The privacy curtain is being pulled open by a nurse, a nurse with a black eye, a pair of crutches in her other hand. Something about her. She seems unsteady on her feet, lumbering as she closes the curtain behind her. As she approaches the bed, she smiles, but her smile is weird; it's not kind. Her eyes are small, her nose wide, her black hair thinning to ragged points at the ends.

'Jane Preston,' she says. 'Remember me?'

Jane's throat blocks. She doesn't... but wait, yes, she does. Her hair is not caramel. It is not thick and glossy. Her eyes are smaller, less defined. She is not so tall. Her nose is fatter, swollen. But oh God, it is, it is.

'Lexie,' she whispers, fear running hot through her veins.

She tries to sit up, but Lexie is already clambering on top of her, using a crutch for leverage, bringing one leg over, her mouth set in a grimace of agony, sweat pouring down her face, darkening the collar of her blue uniform. She sits up, astride Jane now, both hands on the crutch, which lies now across Jane's waist. Jane opens her mouth to shout for help but can't make any sound beyond a breathless groan. Lexie's eyes are wild, murderous. They are pools of pure hate. Green, Jane thinks. The colour of envy. But why would a woman like Lexie possibly envy a woman like Jane?

Lexie leans towards her, her hand closing clammy and smelly and tight over Jane's mouth, her eyes widening with a kind of delight. She is mad. She is mad, mad, mad.

'Remember me, do you?' she asks.

Under the damp, stinking hand, Jane nods. Tears roll down the side of her face.

'If you stop grunting, I'll ease off,' Lexie says, quiet with menace. 'If you shout, I'll end you – you know I will.' She digs in her nurse's pocket, holds up a pair of scissors. 'Amazing what you can nick if you're quick. Lovely nurse gave me these. And her uniform, which is a bit tight, if I'm honest.' She presses the warm blade of the scissors to Jane's throat.

Jane lies perfectly still. Her heart hammers.

'Almost didn't find you,' Lexie says. 'I should've known you'd keep your maiden name – that's what women like you do, isn't it, to show everyone you're better? Meanwhile, the police are in here looking everywhere for some woman called Louise. They'll have found my purse in the car wreck, I suppose, but I don't think Louise ever checked in, did she? And there's me worried they'd see two Jane Reeces on the admissions and think, hang on a minute, something's not right, when all the time you're in here as Jane Preston.' She sniggers. 'Thing is, I know you think you remember me, but you don't, do you? I don't mean as Lexie, babes. I mean as Louise.'

Jane stares into the mad green eyes, sees nothing but fury, madness. The name means nothing to her, nothing at all.

'The Meadows Comp?' Lexie says.

Jane nods. The Meadows Comp she remembers, only too well. The knock on the headmaster's door. The smell of stale tobacco, the dog-eared stacks of paper. The eyebrows meeting over the glasses. *My mum said to give you this.*

'I was a few years below you,' Lexie says, leaning back a little, almost calm. 'I don't suppose you ever noticed me, did you? You were one of the cool girls. One of the brainy ones.'

Jane's old school, her old friends, the ones she was wrenched away from without ever being given a chance to say goodbye. Lexie is from that school. She belongs to what little life Jane had before Donald made her move to save *his* face.

'You don't remember me at all, do you?' Lexie is asking, low with menace. 'Louise Dawes? Ring a bell? A school bell?' She laughs.

Jane closes her eyes. More tears roll down into her hair. Dawes. Oh God. Donald Dawes. This is Donald's daughter. Has to be.

'You do remember, I can see it in your little face. Yeah, your mum *knew* my dad. Knew him in the biblical sense, I mean. Mr Dawes? The head teacher? I can see you've worked it out, babe. He's my dad, in case you're still catching up. Your mum couldn't leave him alone, could she? Do you know she'd already shagged two of the dads from your class by the time she got to mine? Did you know that? Did you know she sent him a note saying she'd top herself if he didn't leave my mum?'

Jane gasps. The note. The note she delivered.

But Lexie is oblivious. 'I mean, who does that? Who threatens suicide to steal someone else's husband? Someone else's *dad*?' She shifts position, winces, apparently in a great deal of discomfort.

Jane wants to scream, but she is too afraid. The wrong move and this woman will cut her throat, right here behind this curtain. Lexie is beyond the place of caring what happens to her. She has been overtaken by something deep and visceral. In her eyes, eyes that look so plain and childlike without all that black, something else glimmers.

Pain.

'I don't suppose you know my mum never got over it, do you?' Her tone is conversational, as if they are getting to know one another. 'No, you don't. You and your mum had taken my dad and fucked off to another town by then, helped along by me and my little note. Sorry I didn't use the postal service, by the way. It's just, a brick was much quicker. Do you remember the eggs? I threw some at your house the other day, actually, just to give you a little trip down memory lane. Do you remember that woman shouting at your mum in the supermarket?'

That girl in the school uniform, with her mother. She was older... well, no, she wasn't. She was just tall, tall for her age. Lexie. Louise Dawes. A little girl trying to comfort her broken mother, a woman reduced to shouting abuse in a supermarket. Jane must have recognised her somewhere too deep to reach. Why else would she have dreamt about her so recently? Why else would she have thought so much about Victoria that she ended up going to see her?

'I do remember you,' she whispers.

'Oh my God, you do?' Lexie – Louise – smiles. She looks... pleased. 'Actually made a chink in your perfect life, did we, that day? That's something, I suppose. Did you know my mum had a breakdown? Did you? She never drank more than half a lager before my dad decided he preferred your mum to mine, preferred you to me, basically chose your family over mine.' She begins to cry. 'Fuck,' she whispers, wiping at her nose with her free hand.

'He left us too,' Jane whispers.

'*What?*'

'He only stayed a couple of years. My mum... my mum drank too. Drinks. She's an alco—'

'You're lying.'

Jane shakes her head. 'Your dad's with a much younger woman now. Lives in Chester.'

Louise's mouth sets – a thin, mean line. 'You're lying. Stop lying.'

'I'm not. I promise. I know what my mum was. I know what she did. I'm sorry for what happened to you, but I'm not her. I never meant to hurt you.' If she can keep her talking, surely someone will come.

'You're a lying cow.' Louise swaps the scissors with the crutch, presses the crutch to Jane's throat. Even under the small amount of pressure, Jane feels the constriction.

'Please,' she manages. 'He left us too, I swear.'

'You don't get me to pity you,' Louise hisses at her. 'This is not my fault. None of it is. All I wanted was a good life, and you stole my dad with your big brown eyes and your grades and your nicely spoken mouth. I wasn't beautiful. I wasn't one of the cool kids. I wasn't even academic. But it's not easy being the head teacher's kid, you know. Everyone thinks you're going to be teacher's pet, so you have to prove them wrong, don't you? Act out a bit. I was only acting out, that's all I was doing. And if you think that's hard, you should try it when your dad shags one of the mums. Have you got any idea what I went through because of you? The bullying? The lads ganging up on me? The girls bitching about me? Just because I didn't get any GCSEs doesn't mean... I mean, you have to be clever to achieve what I've achieved. I've got forty thousand followers. I get gifts sent to me. Free stuff. I can get men to do whatever I want. Any man. Even yours, good old diamond geezer, top bloke Frankie. How could I do that unless they thought I was the bomb, eh? They walk right into it, believe everything they see.'

The crutch presses harder. Jane coughs, gags. But Lexie isn't even looking at her. 'My mum died five years ago,' she says. 'She was only forty-three. Not drink, by the way, so you got that wrong, Miss Smarty Pants. Painkillers, bottles and bottles of them, until she overdid it and... well, that was it.'

'I'm so sorry,' Jane croaks, half throttled, fighting now for breath. Louise is looking deeply into her eyes, as if trying to work her out. Locking on to her gaze, Jane tries to creep her fingers along to the call button.

'He didn't leave us,' Louise says sadly. 'He *abandoned* us. Abandoned.'

'He abandoned us too,' Jane whispers. She has lost Louise's eye. Louise, who has momentarily stopped pressing down on the crutch, seems to have forgotten what she came here to do. 'My mum was never the same after my dad left either.'

As the words leave her, a memory flashes: her mother, happy. Jane must have been barely three years old but she can see her mother dancing round the living room in the house they lived in before her dad left. The Stone Roses plays – 'Fools Gold'. She is laughing. Her dad is... he is just out of reach. He is a shadow. But her mother is dancing for her, and for him, and she is happy. How has Jane only remembered this now? What came after has spilt like black oil and just... covered this over, obliterated it. Her mother. Before. Before abandonment.

Returned to herself, Louise presses the crutch harder. 'Don't try and get in on the act.'

Jane feels herself choke. Her finger finds the call button and pushes it hard. 'It's him. It's not me or my mum. It's...'

The pressure lifts. Louise leans back, her face crumpling with utter grief. She looks like a child who has lost a race. But then, with a new and manic leer, she throws her hand high above her head, the scissors opened wide.

'You took everything from me. I hate you.'

With a rushing sound, the curtain scrolls back. Everything slows, quickens. Two orderlies jump forward and wrestle Louise off the bed. She cries out in pain, her leg, her leg, her fucking leg, get off me, you bastards.

The scissors clatter onto the floor, skitter. Louise too is on the floor, one of the orderlies on top of her, trying to grasp her flailing fists, the other shouting for security, for the police. She is groaning, a sad, primal sound, thudding the back of her head against the floor. She is sobbing – great hacking gasps of sheer pain. Jane finds herself crying, crying, she realises, with pity. It's like watching an animal with nothing left but rage.

'Get off me! Get the fuck off me!' The shouts stagger, quieten, stop. She is beaten, exhausted. 'I know I've lost,' she cries. 'I always do. I'm a good person. This is not my fault.'

CHAPTER FIFTY

JANE

'Ms Preston?'

A uniformed policewoman is at her bedside. She has blonde hair and a pale complexion, cheeks flushing in the heat of the ward. Outside, the sky too is pinking.

'Yes,' Jane says.

Slowly and with a kind smile, the policewoman pulls the privacy curtain across.

'Actually,' Jane says, 'can you leave it half open? Cheers.'

The woman nods. 'Of course. How're you feeling?' She approaches the bed slowly, carefully.

'A bit dazed. Shaken obviously. They told me Frankie's OK. He is, isn't he?' The nurse told her once the chaos had subsided. He has a badly broken leg, she said, but no life-threatening injuries. But until Jane sees him, she won't believe it. They took Lexie away in cuffs. No, not Lexie, Louise. Louise Dawes.

That was this morning. It feels like weeks, like a second ago.

'Your husband's out of surgery, I'm told,' the cop says. 'I think they've pinned his leg, but the doctor will fill you in shortly. My name's DC Dyer and I'm a liaison officer, OK? You can call me Nicky if you prefer.'

'OK. Hi, Nicky. Jane.'

She nods a brief acknowledgement. 'I just wanted to have a chat and bring you up to date a little bit, although we're still investigating obviously. I know you gave a statement to PC Loft earlier, is that right?'

Jane nods. 'Kate, yes, I told her what had happened. Where's Louise Dawes?'

'She's in custody.' DC Dyer – Nicky – widens her eyes and shakes her head a fraction. 'Quite a story there. Pretty hair-raising stuff.'

'I knew her. Except I didn't. I didn't recognise her. I'd never have... I knew her from school – well, knew of her. She was a few years below me. Funny, I'd remembered her as older. She was always quite tall, I think. Sorry. I'm still getting my head around it.'

'And she was blackmailing your husband.'

Jane nods. 'Yes. And she was bullying me. It had been going on for a few months, but neither me nor my husband spoke about it to the other. I thought it was for other reasons, but turns out she had her hooks into Frankie too.' She makes herself stop, aware that she is babbling. Shakes her head, feels her eyes prick, the familiar feeling of panic she knows it will take a long while to get over. Just the thought of that woman fills her instantly with cold dread, but with something else too – sadness, deep sadness. Sympathy.

'Your husband isn't her first victim.'

'I know. I spoke to Gareth. In Barnes. The architect, do you know about him?'

It's DC Dyer's turn to nod. 'We have an officer there taking a statement this evening. Ms Dawes has been surprisingly forthcoming. She's been in this game a long time, as it turns out. She's wanted in connection with a long string of fraud offences, not to mention assault, threatening behaviour, blackmail. She's given us a list of aliases, Facebook accounts, Instagram accounts, et cetera. We're hoping other people will come forward. Hopefully we can trace her victims by working backwards. There was a doctor before Gareth Hutchins – Dr Brooker. He owned the house she used to entrap Mr Hutchins under the pretence of wanting architectural work done. And before him, there was a Mr Watson, head of a sixth-form college near Widnes. I could go on.'

Jane's hand flies to her mouth as the implications of Louise Dawes' long hate campaign begin to dawn. This woman has been sexually abusing men, dozens of men, and reframing her crimes as theirs. In doing this, she has in effect been contributing to the ongoing victimhood of her sisters all over the world by making it even harder for real victims to be believed.

'My God,' she says, shaking her head.

'I know,' Nicky says. 'It's a lot to take in. She used a drug called Rohypnol – you've probably heard of it; it's pretty common. She drugged men and convinced them they'd been intimate with her, took Polaroids and blackmailed them – for cash, to let her use their houses, their cars. In fact, the car she used to try and run you and your husband over was Mr Hutchins'. She'd stolen his key. Yes, she used cars, holiday homes, all kinds of properties so she could continue the pretence of being wealthy. Actually, she claims she has been wealthy in the past, but it appears she's a compulsive spender. Likes the high life.'

'My God.'

'She describes herself as a lifestyle guru and influencer, although that's not the reality we found at her flat. Quite the opposite, to be honest.'

'I can't take it in.'

'I know, right? IT are examining her Instagram. A lot of it is completely fabricated.'

'But it was her on there, wasn't it? I mean, I know she made herself look different, but it was her?'

'Yes, well, with a lot of filters obviously. But she's admitted to posing with other people's drinks, going to bars alone and basically just getting talking to people, men particularly, getting them to buy her drinks. She's taken photographs of herself on strangers' driveways, claiming to own their car. There's air travel pictures she did with a loo seat, would you believe?'

'A *loo seat*?'

Seeing Jane's reaction, Nicky allows herself a short chuckle. 'She claims she put a loo seat in front of her window and took a photograph of half of it. She was quite proud of her initiative, I think. And I have to say, I really thought it was a plane window. She took pictures of food in magazines and tagged restaurants. These places don't have time to check, you know?'

'I guess. I wouldn't check a coffee was mine if someone tagged my café. I'm just grateful for the plug.' Unless the coffee was awful. Unless someone was trying to sabotage your business. Unless that same person drugged your husband, slept with him and tried to blackmail him to pay for a non-existent child.

'Exactly. Same with the car dealerships and the hotels and the gyms and what-have-you. She nicked roses from peoples' hedgerows and scattered the petals in the bath, on the bed, pretending to be at a spa or a hotel. Fizzy apple juice for champagne, you name it. Quite inventive really.'

'Good God.'

'Oh, and there was a collection of intimate Polaroids in a shoebox. Dozens of them.'

Jane closes her eyes, unsure whether to laugh or cry. What a way to live. There must have been so little *peace*.

'We're working on the theory that this was a long con,' Nicky says.

'Oh, it was. She systematically set about seducing my husband and poisoning my friends against me.'

'A longer con than that. We think she's been building towards this from the beginning. That's why she's coming clean about it now. She's at the end.'

'The end?'

Nicky presses her mouth closed and nods gravely. 'We think she was building her empire year on year with the sole intention of taking you down. We believe her to have become obsessed with you at an early age and to have developed a fixation. In interview, your name came up over fifty times.'

'But she had loads of victims, you said.'

'Your husband is the only one she claimed to be pregnant by. She said he told her when he was drugged that you couldn't have children, and she saw her chance. From there, she fabricated her pregnancy as Lexie and as Natasha, picking you both off independently. But her target was always you. These people are supreme opportunists. But somewhere along the line, something in her broke, we think. It can be hard to chase something for so long; hard to know what to do with it when you get it.'

A heaviness presses into Jane. Louise Dawes, a little girl rejected, her life turned upside down. Humiliated, ridiculed at school, fuelled by hate. By inadequacy. Not beautiful enough. Not clever enough. Not enough. Abandoned, she said, more than once. Jane knows how that feels. There is not so much between them, not really, but where Jane has stubbornly avoided pandering to feminine beauty standards for fear of attracting the kind of assholes her mother always dated, for Louise Dawes being sexually attractive *was* power. Where Jane's constant feeling of being unsafe as a child made her almost obsessive about safety, Louise went on what Jane realises now must have been one long and risky revenge trip – punishing men for what her father did over and over, developing her art, working her way towards Jane, to find her and make her pay for stealing her life. But even with all the glamour and the high times and the men and the legions of followers, that little girl never found a way of feeling like she was enough. She was never able to reverse the damage, because in the end, the person she damaged more than any of her victims was herself.

'My God,' Jane says. 'Poor woman.'

'Well, I suppose that's one way of looking at it.'

Into the short silence that follows, Jane says, 'You said she *convinced* men they'd had sex with her. What did you mean by that?'

Nicky raises her eyebrows along with her shoulders, brings them down with a sigh. 'Many of the men she never actually had intercourse with, as such. She and your husband never had, you know, full penetrative sex.'

'*What?*'

'He was too out of it, she said. A lot of her victims were.'

'But how did...?'

But the truth is already filtering through, as the tears run yet again down Jane's face and she apologises to this kind police-woman. There are so many lies it is hard to keep on top of what is real. For Frankie, the guilt, the photos and Louise's claim to be having his baby added up to a fake truth: his infidelity. Louise provided ninety-nine per cent of the picture, let the victim add the final one per cent. Isn't that just like her Instagram? Present just enough, let the observer infer. Poor, poor Frankie. Poor all of them.

'I'll leave you for now,' Nicky says, cocking her head. She has one hand on the curtain and has pulled it completely open.

There in a wheelchair, one leg sticking straight out in front of him, covered in Frankenstein's monster metal screws, grinning like a chimp, is Frankie.

CHAPTER FIFTY-ONE

JANE

'Frankie!'

Frankie wheels his chair around the bed. They are both crying like children, so much so that Jane only remembers the lovely policewoman after she has leant awkwardly into her husband and cried into his shoulder, repeating only *thank God* and *you're alive, you're alive, you're alive*. When she looks up, to wave in thanks, Nicky has gone.

Frankie rests his head on her legs. 'It's over,' he says, his voice small.

'It is.' She tells him what DC Dyer has just told her. As the words leave her, Frankie raises his head, his face a mask of utter incredulity.

'It was all about *you*? Not even about a baby?'

'Sophie was a thing, you were a thing. Even the baby was a thing. A thing to have, to take from me, to have something I wanted. To ruin me for what me and my mother did to her family.'

'Unbelievable.'

'And the final thing,' she adds, nodding, 'is that you and Natasha – Louise – never actually... consummated your union, let's say.'

His forehead crumples. 'We never...? How d'you get that?'

'You were too out of it. She did the same to lots of guys. The pregnancy wasn't the only fake thing. It was enough to make it look like you guys were... together in that way, then add the other fake stuff and leave you to believe her version of events. We see a cocktail in a bar, a manicured hand, and we add an entire high life. We add happiness, confidence, someone who's at ease in the world and whose life is amazing.'

'We see a loo seat and think it's a bloody plane window.' Frankie laughs, making Jane laugh too.

'Exactly.'

A silence falls. Frankie looks up at her, squeezes her hand.

'Babe,' he says. 'They said I might be left with a limp.'

'A limp what?'

He closes his eyes, the ghost of a laugh.

'Sorry,' she says, squeezing his hand. 'I knew what you meant. They told me. And I know that's tough, so tough, but we'll get through it as we've got through everything else, won't we? Together.'

A cough. Jane looks up to see Sophie standing looking sheepish at the end of the bed, her hands clenched around the top of her fake Christian Dior bag.

'Hi,' she says, gives a little wave. Her bump is bigger now. Her appearance has altered so much as to make her almost unrecognisable.

'Sophie.' Nerves flutter in Jane's belly.

Inclining her head towards Frankie, Sophie says, 'Can I have a word?'

'Anything you have to say, you can say in front of Frankie.'

She nods once, twice, three times, but looks shocked.

'OK, well, I was going to call you last night, but I bottled out and now this has happened, but I... The thing is, I know what Lexie's like now.' She pauses, almost laughs, but perhaps seeing Jane's face, her expression sobers. 'Sorry, I... After we spoke, I suppose I was a bit rattled by what you said about Frankie, so I checked Carl's phone. And I found a text from her, from a couple of nights ago. Basically she was saying her boyfriend had finished with her and she was so upset she didn't think it was safe for her to be on her own, and could he come over. Carl denies ever going, but the thing is, he'd replied that he was on his way. Like, immediately. I would have been putting Kyle to bed and I remember him saying he was popping out for milk, but Carl never pops out for milk. He never helps with anything like that. And then he came home a couple of hours later saying he'd bumped into Pete and they'd had a quick beer. But the thing is, he never even brought any milk home, but I didn't think about it till later, after we spoke, you know? So anyway, I called Lex and asked her about it and she just started laying into me, calling me stuck-up, a rich bitch, saying all kinds.' She sighs. 'So what I'm saying is, I know what she's like now. And I'm sorry.'

Jane takes this in. She looks at her former friend, who encouraged confidences, who extended the protective arm of friendship at a tough time, who collects people.

'I'm sorry that happened to you,' she says. 'But I tried to tell you. I tried to talk to you about it and you didn't believe me. It's only now it's happened to you that you believe it. I wish you well, honestly I do, and I always have, but I'm afraid we're not friends, not anymore.'

'*What?* What the *hell?*'

Jane flinches at the instant outrage, glances towards Frankie, who nods in support, then back at Sophie, whose mouth is a round pink O.

'You can't do this,' she says, beginning to wail. 'I can't believe you're doing this to me. I'm pregnant!'

'Congratulations,' Jane says. 'I'm truly happy for you. Goodbye, Sophie.'

CHAPTER FIFTY-TWO

JANE

A woman in a soft cream shirt with a white medical jacket open over the top approaches the end of the bed. A stethoscope hangs casually around her neck. She has dark auburn hair tied up in a loose bun, trendy black glasses and a spray of delicate freckles.

'I'm Dr Farnworth,' she says. 'How're you feeling?'

'Oh, you know, broken arm, sore head and totally traumatised, but apart from that...' Jane glances at Frankie, who is sitting bolt upright and trying not to look like he's been crying. It is almost an hour since Sophie left in a huge huff, and they are still picking over the last twenty-four hours and alternating between disbelief and relief. 'This is my husband, Frank,' she adds. 'He's the best man on the entire planet. He saved my life.'

Dr Farnworth turns to Frankie and gives a nod of acknowledgement. 'You certainly did. Actually, it's good that you're both here, because the blood test results have come back and it turns out you might have saved more than one life last night.' She turns back to Jane and smiles.

Jane pulls her gaze from the doctor to Frankie, who is frowning. She looks back at the doctor. 'How do you mean?'

'Have you been feeling nauseous at all? Tired? Maybe a little swollen?' She is still smiling.

'I have, but don't worry about that, it's nothing serious. I'm menopausal. I mean, I have early-onset menopause.'

'Ah.' The doctor checks her notes. 'Sorry, I didn't... but yes, you're quite right, menopausal symptoms do include nausea and tiredness, sorry, I didn't see that. But that's not what those symptoms were.' She glances at Frankie, back to Jane. 'You're actually pregnant – about five or six weeks, I'd say.'

'*What?*' Jane's scalp tingles, her breath is stuck in her chest, and even though she hasn't one hundred per cent understood what this woman, this lovely woman, this *angel* is saying, a smile is starting to form at the corners of her mouth. 'What?' she asks again, although she is beginning to hear.

She looks at Frankie, whose face is a mask of utter wonder.

'I take it this is good news,' the doctor says, beaming now. 'Congratulations to you both.'

EPILOGUE

It's a warm August evening. Not that being cold is a problem for Jane. The bump keeps her cosy as toast, though she's too hot in the sleeping bag and it's a pain having to go back and forth to the campsite toilet block twice a night. Not that she's complaining.

Over the hill, a buttery sun melts into the Pembrokeshire horizon. Sheep graze in the field beyond the fence, and the herby, meaty smell of organic sausages drifts from the barbecue, where Frankie is bent to the task of dinner. Des sniffs the air with palpable longing, sits to attention like the world's best-behaved dog, the dog who deserves a big treat like, say, a sausage. On the camping table is a huge green salad Frankie has prepared, with spinach for iron, and pomegranate seeds, which, he insists, contain antioxidants and vitamin E and are good for the baby. There is a bottle of craft beer for him, sparkling mineral water for her.

'Here you go.' He loads a sloppy dollop of caramelised onions from the frying pan onto a fat shiny sausage in a soft white finger roll. 'Ketchup?'

'Please. And mustard.'

'Both together? Gross.'

'It's not me. The baby likes spicy food, like its dad.'

'Is that right?'

Frankie hands her the posh hot dog before picking up the invisible ball and throwing it for Des. It is a good long throw, but Des stays still as a stone statue of a dog outside a stately home. He will not be running anywhere; there is too high a chance of falling crumbs. Jane wonders then whether it is Des who has been fooling them all along, whether every time she or Frankie bend to pick up thin air, he thinks: *Idiots*.

Frankie places a doggy chew into Des's mouth and, with the air of having got away with something, he trots to the end of his long lead and hunkers down in the grass to gnaw it – secretively, between his paws. And so, in companionable silence, the three – soon to be four – of them eat their dinner, watching the sky go from vanilla yellow to pink to blue. There are clouds. It will be another warm night.

'You can't buy a view like that,' Frankie says.

'Good job,' Jane replies. 'We've got no money.'

'Nothing in the jar.'

'Nuttin' in da jar. Not a darn penny.'

They share a private and tender smile. Their floors are scratched to hell, the walls scuffed, the furniture is fit for a skip. None of it ever really mattered to either of them, but now it matters even less. Louise Dawes almost stole their life from beneath them, thinking to exact a warped, misplaced revenge and gain materially in one smooth move. But their life was never made from stuff; it was made from this: this view, this dog and the deep, deep feeling of peace with another human being.

And friends. Jane still sees Kath and Hils, who come by the café every week, and on Fridays they are often at one another's houses or trying some new eatery. Kath did ask Jane to become Scarlett and Joe's legal guardian, should anything happen to her or Pete, and Jane agreed, in writing. Both women, she knows, will nag her to come back to Runner Beans after the baby is born. They have told her they will give her six months.

As she eats, she sends a WhatsApp photograph of the sunset to her mother, with the caption *Happy campers*. Victoria, a woman she now remembers, if only vaguely, as she was before her dad left. Her mother has since talked to her about the day she got home from work to find a note that said he'd gone to live in Ireland with Sandra, her best friend. Jane knew none of this. She was too young to be aware of what was happening. And by the time she was older, her mother had become the Victoriator, a cruel nickname given to her by Jane and her friends, who at fifteen knew little of what life can throw at a person and who were, looking back, so unforgiving. She and her mother will never be close, but resentment is exhausting and Jane is working towards forgiveness, for her own sake, and for her baby, for whom she will need all her strength.

As for Sophie, Jane sees her around. She smiles and says hello, but Sophie looks the other way and walks on. That is her right. It is none of Jane's concern, not anymore. She still misses the laughs they shared, the Friday nights down at the pub, the catch-up coffees, the running meets. But Jane is not the one who played fast and loose with that most precious of things: a close-knit gang of loyal mates, there for life's highs and lows, in all weathers, no matter what they looked like or owned or how much money they had, without really asking for anything much beyond that. It is a loss all of them feel, and yes, she wishes they could go back to a time before Lexie Lane walked into the Old Bear and ordered a large Sipsmith and tonic. But they can't.

What she has now is quieter. But there is so much to look forward to, so much that is real.

It is enough, more than enough.

A LETTER FROM S.E. LYNES

Thank you so much for taking the time to read *The Baby Shower*. I really hope you enjoyed it, that you found at least some of it relatable, and that it gave you food for thought. If you'd like to be the first to hear about my new releases, you can sign up to my newsletter using the link below. Your email address will never be shared and you can unsubscribe at any time.

www.bookouture.com/se-lynes

A day or two before writing this letter, I saw an advertisement for the new James Blake album: *Friends That Break Your Heart*. And I guess that's what this book is about. I wanted to provide a narrative for the heartbreak that comes with the breakdown of a close but non-romantic relationship. As Jane reflects: 'So much is written about romantic break-ups, but as far as the end of a friendship goes, there is no real frame of reference, no well-worn narrative guide for her to read and relate to, no self-help books, no how-to.'

The challenge here was to drill down into what makes petty aggression from someone you believed to be a friend so very difficult to handle. We know there are bigger things to worry about, so why does it affect us so much? There is also the challenge of staying loyal – for the sake of keeping the peace and in honour of all the good times we have shared in the past – to those who are now behaving badly towards us; the arriving at a point where this loyalty is no longer possible without the annihilation of the self. I hope readers will relate to these themes.

Jane's story is, for me, a coming of age and a coming to terms. In order to come to terms with her childhood, she needs to come of age, in a sense. She needs to wise up and find her voice. What happened with her mother when she was little made Jane a perfect victim for Lexie/Louise, and in learning to stick up for herself against Lexie, the bully, and indeed against Sophie's disloyal behaviour, she grows up. There is a loss of innocence, in a way, but she is stronger for it, because the other huge thing she must come to terms with is a life without children. Through her hideous experience of perceived betrayal, she has a kind of epiphany: her life is enough as it is, herself and Frankie and all they share. It was important to me for her to be working her way by the end towards forgiveness, particularly of her mother, because I wish her a peaceful, happy life going forward, unburdened by the darkness of resentment or hate. As for her pregnancy at the end, whilst it might appear far-fetched to some, the particulars of this aspect of her journey were taken from a real case study. Frankie's sexual assault is also inspired by real life stories from an online forum. In the fictional realm, I imagine he will be part of the investigation into Louise Dawes. Whether he is able to give evidence about what happened to him and find a way to put it behind him, I will leave for you to decide.

The Baby Shower also tries to explore the materialism that can be found at the heart of some relationships; how they can be almost transactional, how people we are supposed to love can become commodities – stuff, as Jane says. Do you have the right dress? The right car? The right house? Do you worry about having those things, whether your friends will like you less if you do not have them? If you do, as we all do sometimes, that is worth looking at. Ideally, friends should simply like or love one another without judgement, without demands. But if the world were ideal, authors would of course be out of work.

Finally, this story looks at adult bullying, which is common, comes in many forms and, as Frankie says, can take place anywhere – in sports teams, the workplace, in friendship groups. It can be difficult to recognise for what it is; that it is really happening difficult to accept. This book goes out to anyone who has been the victim of adult bullying: your feelings are valid, they are real, they matter. You matter. There is help available online on websites such as Very Well Mind (https://www.verywellmind.com/how-to-deal-with-adult-bullying-5187158). Understanding what is happening can be empowering in itself.

If you'd like to share your thoughts with me or ask me any questions, I'm always happy to chat via my Twitter account, Instagram or Facebook author page, so do get in touch. If you enjoyed *The Baby Shower*, I would be so grateful if you could spare a couple of minutes to write a review. It only needs to be a line or two, and I would really appreciate it!

My next book is well under way – it is a secret but I hope you will want to read that one too.

Best wishes,

Susie

facebook.com/susie.lynes

twitter.com/selynesauthor

instagram.com/susielynes

ACKNOWLEDGEMENTS

First thanks go to Ruth Tross, whose by now legendary 'right good Trossings' save me from embarrassment and make me appear better than I am at this writing malarkey. Thank you to my agent, Veronique Baxter, who said of *The Baby Shower*: 'It is everything I hoped it would be and so much more.' Ta!

Thanks to my mum, Catherine Ball, who is always my first reader and who helped convince me that this book was fit for public consumption.

Thank you to the continually amazing team at Bookouture, particularly Noelle Holten and Kim Nash, the magnificent marketing duo, plus all the Bookouture authors who are the best virtual colleagues a girl could wish for.

Thanks to my copy-editor, Jane Selley, and my proofreader, Laura Kincaid.

Thanks to Tracy Fenton and all the team – Helen Boyce, Claire Mawdesley, Juliet Butler, Charlie Pearson, Charlie Fenton, Kel Mason and Laurel Stewart – at Facebook's The Book Club. Thanks to Wendy Clarke and the team at Facebook's The Fiction Café, to Anne Cater at Book Connectors, Mark Fearn at Bookmark and Iain Grant at the Stay-at-Home Facebook book club. Thank you, in fact, to all the online book clubs and the people who gather there to share their love of reading. If I've missed you out, I'm sorry – if you message me, I'll make sure to give you a wave in the next book.

Huge thanks to flag-waving readers like Sharon Bairden, Teresa Nikolic, Philippa McKenna, Karen Royle-Cross, Ellen Devonport, Frances Pearson, Jodi Rilot, CeeCee, Bridget

McCann, Karen Aristocleus, Audrey Cowie, Donna Young, Mary Petit, Donna Moran, Ophelia Sings (whoever you are, your reviews make me cry), Gail Shaw, Lizzie Patience, Fiona McCormick, Alison Lysons, Dee Groocock, Sam Johnson and many more not named here. Thank you. I read every single review, good or bad. If you don't see your name here, please give me a shout.

Huge thanks as ever to the amazing bloggers, who are unpaid and who work very hard spreading the word about the books and authors they love. I would like to thank the following bloggers, using their blogging names in case you wish to check out their reviews: Chapter in my Life, By The Letter Book Reviews, Ginger Book Geek, Shalini's Books and Reviews, Fictionophile, Book Mark!, Bibliophile Book Club, Anne Cater at Random Things Through my Letterbox, B for Book Review, Nicki's Book Blog, Fireflies and Free Kicks, Bookinggoodread, My Chestnut Reading Tree, Donna's Book Blog, Emma's Biblio Treasures, Suidi's Book Reviews, Books from Dusk till Dawn, Audio Killed the Bookmark, Compulsive Readers, LoopyLouLaura, Once Upon a Time Book Blog, Literature Chick, Jan's Book Buzz and Giascribes. Again, if I have missed anyone, please let me know.

Thank you to the tremendously supportive writing community – you know who you are and are now too many to count, although Nicola Rayner and Emma Curtis, I don't think you've had a name check yet, so here it is.

Penultimately, thanks to my dad, Stephen Ball, who doesn't read but who makes an exception for me.

Finally, and as always, thanks to himself, Paul Lynes – a great dad, a great husband, a great bloke.

Made in the USA
Middletown, DE
29 June 2022